WARATAH

GHOST SHIP

is...

GHOST SHIP

When Kurt Austin is injured attempting to rescue the passengers and crew from a sinking yacht, he wakes with fragmented and conflicted memories. Did he see an old friend and her daughter drown? Or was the yacht abandoned when he came aboard?

Determined to know the truth, he soon finds himself descending into a shadowy world of state-sponsored cybercrime and uncovering a pattern of vanishing scientists, suspicious accidents, and a web of human trafficking.

With the help of Joe Zavala, he takes on the sinister organization at the heart of this web, facing off with them in locations ranging from Dubai to North Korea to the rugged coasts of Madagascar. But where he will ultimately end up even he could not begin to guess—except maybe in death . . .

KURT AUSTIN ADVENTURES BY CLIVE CUSSLER

(with Graham Brown)
Ghost Ship
Zero Hour
The Storm
Devil's Gate

(with Paul Kemprecos)

Medusa	White Death
The Navigator	Fire Ice
Polar Shift	Blue Gold
Lost City	Serpent

OREGON® FILES ADVENTURES BY CLIVE CUSSLER

(with Jack Du Brul)

Mirage	Plague Ship
The Jungle	Skeleton Coast
The Silent Sea	Dark Watch
Corsair	

(with Craig Dirgo)
Sacred Stone
Golden Buddha

NONFICTION BY CLIVE CUSSLER AND CRAIG DIRGO

Built for Adventure
The Sea Hunters II
The Sea Hunters
Clive Cussler and Dirk Pitt® Revealed

CHILDREN'S BOOKS BY CLIVE CUSSLER

The Adventures of Hotsy Totsy
The Adventures of Vin Fiz

CLIVE CUSSLER

AND GRAHAM BROWN

BERKLEY BOOKS   NEW YORK

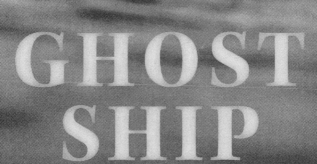

GHOST SHIP

A Novel from the NUMA® Files

BERKLEY

An imprint of Penguin Random House LLC
375 Hudson Street, New York, New York 10014

GHOST SHIP

A Berkley Book / published by arrangement with Sandecker, RLLLP

ISBN: 978-0-425-27514-6

PUBLISHING HISTORY
G. P. Putnam's Sons hardcover edition / May 2014
Berkley premium edition / June 2015

PRINTED IN THE UNITED STATES OF AMERICA

10 9 8 7 6 5 4 3 2 1

Cover illustration by Tom Hallman.

Penguin
Random
House

PROLOGUE—THE VANISHING

Durban, South Africa, July 25, 1909

They were driving into a void, or so it seemed to Chief Inspector Robert Swan of the Durban Police Department.

On a moonless night, beneath a sky as dark as India ink, Swan rode shotgun in the cab of a motortruck as it rumbled down a dusty track in the countryside north of Durban. The headlights of the big Packard cast yellow beams of light that flickered and bounced and did little to brighten the path ahead. As he stared into the gloom, Swan could see no more than forty yards of the rutted path at any one time.

"How far to this farmhouse?" he asked, turning toward a thin, wiry man named Morris, who was wedged in next to the driver.

Morris checked his watch, leaned toward the driver,

and checked the odometer of the truck. After some mental calculations, he glanced down at the map he held. "We should be there soon, Inspector. No more than ten minutes to go, I'd say."

The chief inspector nodded and grabbed the doorsill as the bumpy ride continued. The Packard was known as a Three Ton, the latest from America and one of the first motor vehicles to be owned by the Durban Police Department. It had come off the boat with the customized cab and windshield. Enterprising workmen from the newly formed motor pool had built a frame to cover the flatbed and stretched canvas over it, though no one had done anything to make it more comfortable.

As the truck bounced and lurched over the rutted buggy trail, Swan decided he would rather be on horseback. But what the big rig lost in comfort it made up for in hauling power. In addition to Swan, Morris, and the driver, eight constables rode in back.

Swan leaned on the doorsill and turned to look behind him. Four sets of headlights followed. Three cars and another Packard. All told, Swan had nearly a quarter of the Durban police force riding with him.

"Are you sure we need all these men?" Morris asked.

Perhaps it was a bit much, Swan thought. Then again, the criminals they were after—a group known in the papers as the Klaar River Gang—had numbers of their own. Rumors put them between thirty and forty, depending on whom one believed.

Though they'd begun as common highwaymen, robbing others and extorting those who tried to make an honest living doing business out in the veld, they'd grown more cunning and violent in the last six months. Farmhouses of those who refused to pay protection money were being burned to the ground. Miners and travelers were disappearing without a trace. The truth came to light when several of the gang were captured trying to rob a bank. They were brought back to Durban for interrogation only to be rescued in a brazen attack that left three policemen dead and four others wounded.

It was a line that Swan would not allow them to cross. "I'm not interested in a fair fight," he explained. "Need I remind you what happened two days ago?"

Morris shook his head, and Swan rapped his hand on the partition that separated the cab from the back of the truck. A panel slid open and the face of a burly man appeared, all but filling the window.

"Are the men ready?" Swan asked.

"We're ready, Inspector."

"Good," Swan said. "Remember, no prisoners tonight."

The man nodded his understanding, but the words caused Morris to offer a sideways glance.

"You have a problem?" Swan barked.

"No, sir," Morris said, looking back at his map. "It's just that . . . we're almost there. Just over this hill."

Swan turned his attention forward once again and took a deep breath, readying himself. Almost immediately he caught the scent of smoke. It was distinct in flavor, like a bonfire.

The Packard crested the hill moments later, and the

coal-black night was cleaved in two by a frenzied orange blaze on the field down below them. The farmhouse was burning from one side to the other, whirls of fire curling around it and reaching toward the heavens.

"Bloody hell," Swan cursed.

The vehicles raced down the hill and spread out. The men poured forth and took up positions surrounding the house.

No one hit them. No one fired.

Morris led a squad closer. They approached from upwind and darted into the last section of the barn that wasn't ablaze. Several horses were rescued, but the only gang members they found were already dead. Some of them half burned, others merely shot and left to die.

There was no hope of fighting the fire. The ancient wood and the oil-based paint crackled and burned like petrol. It put out such heat that Swan's men were soon forced to back off or be broiled alive.

"What happened?" Swan demanded of his lieutenant.

"Looks like they had it out among themselves," Morris said.

Swan considered that. Before the arrests in Durban, rumors had been swirling that suggested the gang was fraying at the seams. "How many dead?"

"We've found five. Some of the boys think they saw two more inside, but they couldn't reach 'em."

At that moment gunfire rang out.

Swan and Morris dove behind the Packard for cover. From sheltered positions, some of the officers began to shoot back, loosing stray rounds into the inferno.

The shooting continued, oddly timed and staccato, though Swan saw no sign of bullets hitting nearby.

"Hold your fire!" he shouted. "But keep your heads down."

"But they're shooting at us," one of the men shouted.

Swan shook his head even as the pop-pop of the gunfire continued. "It's just ammunition going off in the blaze."

The order was passed around, shouted from one man to the next. Despite his own directive, Swan stood up, peering over the hood of the truck.

By now the inferno had enveloped the entire farmhouse. The remaining beams looked like the bones of a giant resting on some Nordic funeral pyre. The flames curled around and through them, burning with a strange intensity, bright white and orange with occasional flashes of green and blue. It looked like hell itself had risen up and consumed the gang and their hideout from within.

As Swan watched, a massive explosion went off deep inside the structure, blowing the place into a fiery scrap. Swan was thrown back by the force of the blast, landing hard on his back, as chunks of debris rattled against the sides of the Packard.

Moments after the explosion, burning confetti began falling, as little scraps of paper fluttered down by the thousands, leaving trails of smoke and ash against the black sky. As the fragments kissed the ground, they began to set fires in the dry grass.

Seeing this, Swan's men went into action without delay,

tamping out the embers to prevent a brushfire from surrounding them.

Swan noticed several fragments landing nearby. He rolled over and stretched for one of them, patting it out with his hand. To his surprise, he saw numbers, letters, and the stern face of King George staring back at him.

"Tenners," Morris said excitedly. "Ten-pound notes. Thousands of them."

As the realization spread through the men, they redoubled their efforts, running around and gathering up the charred scraps with a giddy enthusiasm they rarely showed for collecting evidence. Some of the notes were bundled and not too badly burned. Others were like leaves in the fireplace, curled and blackened beyond recognition.

"Gives a whole new meaning to the term *blowing the loot*," Morris said.

Swan chuckled, but he wasn't really listening, his thoughts were elsewhere; studying the fire, counting the bodies, working the case as an inspector's mind should.

Something was not right, not right at all.

At first, he put it down to the anticlimactic nature of the evening. The gang he'd come to make war on had done the job for him. That he could buy. He'd seen it before. Criminals often fought over the spoils of their crimes, especially when they were loosely affiliated and all but leaderless, as this gang was rumored to be.

No, Swan thought, this was suspicious on a deeper level.

Morris seemed to notice. "What's wrong?"

"It makes no sense," Swan replied.

"What part of it?"

"The whole thing," Swan said. "The risky daylight bank job. The raid to get their men out. The gunfight in the street."

Morris stared at him blankly. "I don't follow you."

"Look around," Swan suggested. "Judging by the storm of burnt cash raining down on us, these thugs were sitting on a small fortune."

"Yes," Morris agreed. "So what?"

"So why rob a heavily defended bank in broad daylight if you're already loaded to the gills with cash? Why risk shooting up Durban to get your mates out only to gun them down back here?"

Morris stared at Swan for a long moment before nodding his agreement. "I have no idea," he said. "But you're right. It makes no sense at all."

The fire continued to burn well into the morning hours, only dying when the farmhouse was consumed. The operation ended without casualties among the police, and the Klaar River Gang was never heard from again.

Most considered it a stroke of good fortune, but Swan was never convinced. He and Morris would discuss the events of that evening for years, well into their retirement. Despite many theories and guesses as to what really went on, it was a question they would never be able to answer.

CHAPTER 1

170 miles West-Southwest of Durban, July 27, 1909

The SS *Waratah* plowed through the waves on a voyage from Durban to Cape Town, rolling noticeably with the growing swells. Dark smoke from coal-fired boilers spilled from her single funnel and was driven in the opposite direction by a contrary wind.

Sitting alone in the main lounge of the five-hundred-foot steamship, fifty-one-year-old Gavin Brèvard felt the vessel roll ponderously to starboard. He watched the cup and saucer in front of him slide toward the edge of the table, slowly at first, and then picking up speed as the angle of the ship's roll increased. At the last second, he grabbed for the cup, preventing it from sliding off the edge and clattering to the floor.

The *Waratah* remained at a sharp pitch, taking a full

two minutes to right herself, and Brèvard began to worry about the vessel he'd booked passage on.

In a prior life, he'd spent ten years at sea aboard various steamers. On those ships the recoil was quicker, the keel more adept at righting itself. This ship felt top-heavy to him. It made him wonder if something was wrong.

"More tea, sir?"

Deep in thought, Brèvard barely noticed the waiter in the uniform of the Blue Anchor Line.

He held out the cup he'd saved from destruction. *"Merci."*

The waiter topped it off and moved on. As he left, a new figure came into the room, a broad-shouldered man of perhaps thirty, with reddish hair and a ruddy face. He made a direct line for Brèvard, taking a seat in the chair opposite.

"Johannes," Brèvard said in greeting. "Glad to see you're not trapped in your cabin like the others."

Johannes looked a little green, but he seemed to be holding up. "Why have you called me here?"

Brèvard took a sip of the tea. "I've been thinking. And I've decided something important."

"And what might that be?"

"We're far from safe."

Johannes sighed and looked away. Brèvard understood. Johannes thought him to be a worrier. A fear-laden man. But Brèvard was just trying to be cautious. He'd spent years with people chasing him, years living under the threat of imprisonment or death. He had to think five steps ahead just to remain alive. It had tuned his mind to a hyperattentive state.

"Of course we're safe," Johannes replied. "We've assumed new identities. We left no trail. The others are all dead, and the barn has been burned to the ground. Only our family continues on."

Brèvard took another sip of tea. "What if we've missed something?"

"It doesn't matter," Johannes insisted. "We're beyond the reach of the authorities here. This ship has no radio. We might as well be on an island somewhere."

That was true. As long as the ship was at sea, they could rest and relax. But the journey would end soon enough.

"We're only safe until we dock in Cape Town," Brèvard pointed out. "If we haven't covered our trail as perfectly as we think, we may arrive to a greeting of angry policemen or His Majesty's troops."

Johannes did not reply right away. He was thinking, soaking the information in. "What do you suggest?" he asked finally.

"We have to make this journey last forever."

"And how do we do that?"

Brèvard was speaking metaphorically. He knew he had to be more concrete for Johannes. "How many guns do we have?"

"Four pistols and three rifles."

"What about the explosives?"

"Two of the cases are still full," Johannes said with a

scowl. "Though I'm not sure it was wise to bring them aboard."

"They'll be fine," Brèvard insisted. "Wake the others, I have a plan. It's time we took destiny into our own hands."

CAPTAIN JOSHUA ILBERY stood on the *Waratah*'s bridge despite it being time for the third watch to take over. The weather concerned him. The wind was gusting to fifty knots, and it was blowing opposite to the tide and the current. This odd combination was building the waves into sharp pyramids, unusually high and steep, like piles of sand pushed together from both directions.

"Steady on, now," Ilbery said to the helmsman. "Adjust as needed, we don't want to be broadsided."

"Aye," the helmsman said.

Ilbery lifted the binoculars. The light was fading as evening came on, and he hoped the wind would subside in the night.

Scanning the whitecaps ahead of him, Ilbery heard the bridge door open. To his surprise, a shot rang out. He dropped the binoculars and spun to see the helmsman slumping to the deck, clutching his stomach. Beyond him stood a group of passengers with weapons, one of whom walked over and took the helm.

Before Ilbery could utter a word or grab for a weapon, a ruddy-faced passenger slammed the butt of an Enfield rifle into his gut. He doubled over and fell back, landing against the bulkhead.

The man who'd attacked him aimed the barrel of the Enfield at his heart. Ilbery noticed it was held by rough hands, more fitting on a farmer or rancher than a first-class passenger. He looked into the man's eyes and saw no mercy. He couldn't be sure of course, but Ilbery had little doubt the man he was facing had shot and killed before.

"What is the meaning of this?" Ilbery growled.

One of the group stepped toward him. He was older than the others, with graying hair at the temples. He wore a finer suit and carried himself with the loose elegance of a leader. Ilbery recognized him as one of a group who'd come on board in Durban. Brèvard, was the name. Gavin Brèvard.

"I demand an explanation," Ilbery said.

Brèvard smirked at him. "I should have thought it quite obvious. We're commandeering this ship. You're going to set a new course away from the coast and then back to the east. We're not going to Cape Town."

"You can't be serious," Ilbery said. "We're in the middle of a bad stretch. The ship is barely responding as it is. To make a turn now would—"

Gavin aimed the pistol at a spot halfway between the captain's eyes. "I've worked on steamers before, Captain. Enough to know that this ship is top-heavy and performing poorly. But she's not going to go over, so stop lying to me."

"This ship will surely go to the bottom," Ilbery said.

"Give the order," Brèvard demanded, "or I'll blow a hole in your skull and pilot this ship myself."

Ilbery's eyes narrowed to slits. "Perhaps you can navigate, but what about the rest of the duties? Do you and this lot intend to man the ship yourselves?"

Brèvard smiled wryly. He'd known from the start that this was his weakness, the chink in his armor. He had eight others with him, three of them children. Even if they'd been adults, nine people couldn't even keep the fires stoked for long, let alone guard the passengers and crew, and pilot the ship at the same time.

But Brèvard was used to playing the angles. His whole life was a study in getting others to do as he wished, either against their wills or without them knowing they were doing his bidding. He'd known he needed leverage, and the explosives in the two cases enabled him to turn the odds in his favor.

"Bring in the prisoner," he said.

Ilbery watched as the bridge door was opened and an unkempt teenager appeared. This one brought in a man covered in coal dust. Blood flowed from a broken nose and a gash across his forehead.

"Chief?"

"I'm sorry, Cap'n," the chief said. "They tricked us. They used children to distract us. And then they over-powered us. Three of the lads are shot. But it's so loud down there no one heard until it was too late."

"What have they done?" the captain asked, his eyes growing wide.

"Dynamite," the chief said. "A dozen sticks attached to boilers three and four."

Ilbery turned to Brèvard. "Are you insane? You can't

put explosives in an environment like that. The heat, the embers. One spark and—"

"And we'll all be blown to kingdom come," Brèvard said, finishing the thought for him. "Yes, I'm well aware of the consequences. The thing is, a rope waits for me onshore, the kind that stretches one's neck. If I'm going to die, I'd rather it be quick and glorious than slow and painful. So don't test me. I have three of my people down there with rifles like these to make sure no one removes those explosives, at least not until I leave this ship at a port of my choosing. Now, do as I say and turn this vessel away from the coast."

"And then what?" Ilbery asked.

"When we've reached our destination, we'll take a few of your boats, a heap of supplies, and everyone's cash and jewelry, and we'll leave your ship and disappear. You and your crew will be free to sail back to Cape Town with a fantastic story to tell the world."

Using the bulkhead behind him for support, Captain Ilbery forced himself up and stood. He stared at Brèvard with contempt. The man had him and both knew it.

"Chief," he said without taking his eyes off the hijacker. "Take the helm and turn us about."

The chief staggered to the wheel and pushed the hijacker aside and did as ordered. The rudder answered the helm, and the SS *Waratah* began to turn.

"Good decision," Brèvard said.

Ilbery wondered about that, but knew he had no choice.

For his part, Brèvard was pleased. He sat down in a chair, laid the rifle across his lap, and studied the captain closely. Having spent his lifetime misleading others, from policemen to powder-wigged judges, Brèvard had learned that some men were easier to read than others. The honest ones were more obvious than the rest.

As Brèvard stared at this captain, he pegged him as one of those. A man with pride and smarts and a great sense of duty for his passengers and crew. That sense of duty compelled him to comply with Brèvard's demands in order to protect the lives of those on board. But it also made him dangerous.

Even as he acquiesced, Ilbery stood tall and ramrod straight. Though he clutched his stomach from the blow he'd taken, he kept a fire burning in his eyes that beaten men didn't have. All of which suggested the captain was not ready to relinquish his ship just yet. A countermove would come, sooner rather than later.

Brèvard didn't blame the captain. Quite frankly, he respected him. All the same, he made a mental note to be ready.

SS *Harlow*—10 miles ahead of the *Waratah*

Like the captain of the *Waratah*, the captain of the *Harlow* was on the bridge. Thirty-foot waves and fifty-knot winds required it. He and his crew were making constant corrections, working hard to keep the *Harlow* from going off course. They'd even pumped in some extra water as ballast to help reduce the roll.

As the first officer reentered the bridge following an inspection run, the captain looked his way. "How are we faring, number one?"

"Shipshape from stem to stern, sir."

"Excellent," the captain said. He stepped to the bridge wing and glanced out behind them. The lights of another vessel could be seen on the horizon. She was several miles astern, and making a great deal of smoke.

"What do you make of her?" the captain asked. "She's changed course, out away from the coast."

"Could be a turn to get more clearance from the shoals," the first officer said. "Or perhaps the wind and current are forcing her off. Any idea who it is?"

"Not sure," the captain said. "She might be the *Waratah.*"

Moments later, a pair of flashes only seconds apart lit out from the vessel's approximate position. They were bright white and then orange, but at this range there was no sound, like watching distant fireworks. When they faded, the horizon was dark.

Both the captain and first officer blinked and stared into that darkness.

"What was that?" the first officer asked. "An explosion?"

The captain wasn't sure. He grabbed for the binoculars and took a moment to train them on the spot. There was no sign of fire, but a cold chill gripped his spine as he realized the lights of the mystery ship had vanished as well.

"Could have been flares from a brushfire on the shore behind them," the first officer suggested. "Or heat lightning."

The captain didn't respond and continued to stare through the binoculars, sweeping the field of view. He hoped the first officer was right, but if the flashes of light had come from the shore or the sky, then what had happened to the ship's lights visible only moments before?

UPON DOCKING, both men would learn that the *Waratah* was overdue and missing. She'd never made port in Cape Town, nor had she returned to Durban or made landfall anywhere else.

In quick succession both the Royal Navy and the Blue Anchor Line would dispatch ships in search of the *Waratah*, but they would return empty-handed. No lifeboats were found. No wreckage. No debris. No bodies floating in the water.

Over the years, nautical groups, government organizations, and treasure seekers would search for the wreck of the missing ship. They would use sonar, magnetometers, and satellite imaging. They would dispatch divers and submarines and ROVs to scour various wrecks along the coast. But it was all in vain. More than a century after her disappearance, not a single trace of the *Waratah* had ever been found.

CHAPTER 2

Maputo Bay, Mozambique, September 1987

The sun was falling toward the horizon as an aging fifty-foot trawler sailed into the bay from the open waters of the Mozambique Channel. For Cuoto Zumbana, it had been a good day. The hold of his boat was filled with fresh fish, no nets had been torn or lost, and the old motor had survived yet another journey—though it continued to belch gray smoke.

Satisfied with life, Zumbana closed his eyes and turned toward the sun, letting it bathe the weathered folds of his face. There was little he enjoyed more than that glorious feeling. Such peace it brought him that the excited shouts of his crew did not break him from it at first.

"Mashua," one shouted.

Zumbana opened his eyes, squinting in the glare as

the sunlight blazed off the sea like liquid fire. Blocking the light with his hand, he saw what the men were pointing at, a small wooden dinghy bobbing in the chop of the late afternoon. It seemed to be adrift, and there didn't appear to be anyone on board.

"Take us to it," he ordered. To find a small boat he could sell would only make the day better. He would even share some of the money with the crew.

The trawler changed course, and the old engine chugged a little harder. Soon, they were closing the gap.

Zumbana's face wrinkled. The small boat was badly weathered and looked hastily patched. Even from fifty feet away he could see that much of it was rotted.

"Someone must have dumped it just to be rid of it," one of his crewmen said.

"There might be something of value on board," Zumbana said. "Take us alongside."

The helmsman did as ordered, and the trawler eased to a stop beside the dilapidated craft. As they bumped it, another crewman hopped aboard. Zumbana threw him a rope, and the two boats were quickly tied off and drifting together.

From his position, Zumbana saw empty cooking pots and piles of rags, certainly nothing of value, but as the crewman pulled a moth-eaten blanket aside all thoughts of money were chased from his mind.

A young woman and two boys lay beneath the old blanket. They were clearly dead. Their faces were covered with sores from the sun and their bodies stiff. Their clothing was tattered, and a bloodstained rag was tied to the woman's shoulder. A closer look revealed scabbed wrists and ankles as if the three of them had once been held in cuffs and restraints.

Zumbana crossed himself.

"We should leave it," one of the crewmen said.

"It's a bad omen," another added.

"No. We must respect the dead," Zumbana replied. "Especially those who have been taken so young."

The men looked at him suspiciously but did as they were ordered. With a rope secured for towing, they turned once again for shore with the old double-ended boat trailing out behind them.

Zumbana moved to the stern, where he could keep an eye on the small craft. His gaze went from the boat to the horizon beyond. He wondered about the occupants of the small boat. Who were they? Where had they come from? What danger had they escaped only to die on the open sea? So young, he thought, considering the three bodies. So fragile.

The boat itself was another mystery. The top plank in the boat's side seemed as if it might have once been painted with a name, but it was unreadable now. He worried if the boat would make it into port. Unlike its dead passengers, it seemed ancient. Certainly it was older than the three occupants. In fact, it looked to him like it might belong to another era altogether.

CHAPTER 3

Indian Ocean, March 2014

A flash of blue lightning forked across the horizon. For a second or two it lit up the gray darkness where sea and storm met.

Kurt Austin stared into that darkness from the rear section of a Sikorsky Jayhawk as the big helicopter shouldered its way through bands of pouring rain. Turbulence shook the craft, and thirty-foot swells rolled beneath them, their tops blown off by the howling wind.

As the lightning faded, Kurt saw his reflection on the glass. Roughly forty, with silver-gray hair, Kurt was handsome in the right kind of light. A strong jawline and piercing blue eyes saw to that. But like a truck that spent its days on the worksite instead of in the garage, his face carried the miles in plain view.

The lines around his eyes were etched a little deeper than most. A collection of faded scars from fistfights, car crashes, and other incidents marked his brow and jaw. It was the face of a man who seemed ready for anything, determined and unyielding, even as the helicopter neared the limits of its range.

He pressed the intercom switch and looked ahead to where his friend Joe Zavala sat in the copilot's seat. "Anything?"

"Nothing," Joe called back.

Kurt and Joe worked for NUMA, the National Underwater Marine Agency, a branch of the American government dedicated to the study and preservation of the sea. But, at the moment, they were part of a makeshift rescue team called on to assist a group of floundering vessels that had been caught in a debilitating storm.

As they flew on, the radio crackled with static and rapid-fire conversations between the South African Coast Guard and the small group of rescue craft.

"Sapphire Two, what's your position?"

"Sapphire Two has contact with the Endless Road. *She appears to be drifting but watertight. Four crew are visible. Maneuvering into position for basket rescue."*

"Roger that, Sapphire Two. Sapphire Three, what's your status?"

"Inbound with rescues. Two appear to have hypothermia, third is stable."

The storm had come barreling in from the southeast, gaining intensity as it approached the Cape of Good Hope. It swept up several freighters, including a thousand-foot containership, and then swung north and set its sights on a group of yachts and other pleasure craft involved in a friendly race from Durban to Australia.

The fury of the storm and its sudden arrival had taxed the South African Coast Guard to the limit. They'd called for any able assistance, enlisting the help of a Royal Navy frigate, two American supply ships, and the NUMA research vessel *Condor*.

Seventy miles east of the *Condor*, Kurt, Joe, and the pilot of the Jayhawk were nearing the GPS coordinates they'd been given. But they'd yet to spot a thing.

"We should be almost on top of her," Kurt said.

"She might have gone down," the pilot replied.

Kurt didn't want to consider that. By a strange twist of fate, he knew the family on the yacht they were attempting to assist. At least he knew one of them.

"How much fuel?"

"We're Bingo in ten minutes."

At that point, they'd have only enough fuel to make it back to the *Condor* and would have to turn around or risk splashing down short of home and needing rescue themselves.

"Stretch it," Kurt said.

"The headwinds are killing us."

"There'll be tailwinds on the way home," Kurt insisted. "Keep going."

The pilot clammed up, and Kurt turned his eyes back to the sea.

"I have something," Joe shouted, holding a hand to

his headset. "It's weak, but I think it's their emergency beacon. Turn right to zero seven zero."

The helicopter banked into the turn, and several minutes later Kurt spied the hull of a hundred-sixty-foot yacht listing to one side. She was still afloat but down at the bow, and all but awash in the waves.

"Take us in," Kurt ordered.

He yanked open the cargo door, sliding it back and locking it in place. Wind and rain whipped into the cabin.

A winch system and four hundred feet of cable would allow them to lift survivors on board, but they had no basket, so Kurt would have to go down and grab them himself. He clicked the cable to the harness he'd pulled on previously and slid himself to the edge, feet dangling over the side.

"I see no one," the pilot said.

"They could be clinging to the side," Kurt replied. "Take us around."

Kurt could feel adrenaline surging through his body, much as it had been since the details of the damaged craft came in from the South African Coast Guard station.

"Vessel Ethernet *reports heavy flooding,"* the South African controller had informed them. *"NUMA Jayhawk, please assist. You are only rescue in range."*

"Confirm vessel ID?" Kurt had asked, hardly believing what he'd heard.

"Ethernet," the controller advised. *"Out of San Francisco. Seven persons known to be aboard. Including Brian Westgate, his wife, and two children."*

Brian Westgate was an Internet billionaire. His wife, Sienna, was an old friend of Kurt's. Years earlier, she'd been the love of his life.

The message had stunned Kurt in a way few things ever did, but he was the type to recover quickly. He blocked out any thoughts of the past or fears of not reaching the yacht in time and focused on the task at hand.

"Get the spotlight on, Joe!"

As the helicopter circled the floundering vessel and dropped toward it, Kurt could see waves sweeping over the hull. The only saving grace was that the forward superstructure was being sheltered by the aft section of the ship.

Joe turned on the spotlight, and the rain became a field of slashing lines. The effect was blinding for a moment, but once Joe got the angle right, Kurt could see the hull more clearly. He caught a glimpse of orange.

"There! Near the bridge."

The pilot saw it too. He maneuvered the helicopter closer, as Joe unlatched himself and came back to operate the winch.

"This cable isn't designed to hoist people," he reminded Kurt.

"It tows a sonar array," Kurt said.

"The fish only weighs ninety pounds."

"It'll do the job," Kurt said. "Now, release the tension."

Joe hesitated, and once Kurt had looked down and gauged their position, he reached up and punched the tensioner himself. Before Joe could stop him, he'd dropped from the edge of the helicopter.

Holding a mask to his face and pointing his feet straight down, Kurt hit the water at the top of a swell and plunged through it. For a long moment, he was bathed in the strange muted silence of the sea. It was calming and peaceful.

And then he surfaced into the maelstrom.

The swells were like rolling mountains, and droplets from the torrential downpour danced on the surface in every direction.

Turning to the floundering yacht, Kurt began kicking hard toward it.

Reaching the vessel amidships, he stretched for the rail. Before he could get a firm grip, a trough rolled by, and he dropped down along the side of the hull. He fought to stay in position, until the next swell arrived. It carried him upward until he was even with the deck. This time he quickly grabbed the rail and pulled himself aboard. He clambered across the deck, scarcely avoiding being washed overboard by another wave.

He reached the bridge, where he found the windows smashed in. The orange flash he'd assumed to be a life vest was nowhere to be seen.

"Sienna!" he shouted. It was useless against the wind.

He peered inside. Several feet of water sloshed around. For a second he thought he saw a body, but the power was out, and in the darkness it could have been anything. He grabbed the hatchway door and yanked it open, forcing his way in.

The vessel groaned ominously as it wallowed in the storm. Everything around Kurt seemed to be moving. He raised his arm and switched on a waterproof flashlight that was strapped to it.

The beam played on the water and flared as it reflected off a wall of glass behind the bridge. In some corner of his mind, Kurt remembered reading about the yacht's design. Every wall in the upper deck was acrylic. It was supposed to make the inside of the vessel seem more spacious. If privacy was needed, they could be darkened with the flick of a switch.

Another wave hit the ship and she rolled a little farther. Kurt found himself sliding toward that glass wall as green seawater began pouring in through the open hatch.

Furniture, charts, life vests, and other kinds of detritus sloshed around him. Kurt stood and steadied himself. His arm came out of the water, and the light played off the glass once again. For a moment, it flared, blinding him, but as he adjusted his aim he saw a face on the other side. A woman's face framed in wet blond hair. A child floated beside her, a towheaded blond girl, no more than six or perhaps seven. Her eyes were open but unresponsive.

Kurt lunged toward them only to crash into a glass partition.

"Sienna!" he shouted.

There was no response.

The water was rising more rapidly now. It swirled up around Kurt's chest as he slammed his fist against the glass and then tried to smash it with a chair he found floating beside him. The partition held against two solid blows. And as Kurt reared back for a third swing, the ship rolled farther and the water reached his neck.

The yacht was going over. He could feel it.

Without warning, the harness snapped tight around him, and Kurt felt himself being dragged backward.

"No!" he shouted, only to swallow a mouthful of water.

He was being pulled backward against a great current flooding into the bridge. It was like being dragged upward through a waterfall. For a brief instant, he saw the faces again, and then his mask was ripped off and the world went blurry and green. The cable jerked once more, pulling him hard and slamming his head against the doorframe in the process.

Dazed and barely conscious, Kurt sensed he'd been pulled free. But his progress was slowing. Some part of him knew the reason: Joe and the pilot must have maneuvered the helicopter to drag him out of the sinking vessel. They'd managed to yank him clear, but the cable must have snapped, perhaps when he hit the bulkhead.

He tried to swim, kicking feebly, but his mind was cloudy and his muscles were mostly unresponsive. Instead of rising, he was being pulled deeper, drawn down by the suction of the sinking yacht. He saw it beneath him, a gray blur retreating from the beam of his light.

Thinking only of survival, he turned his gaze upward. Above him, Kurt saw a ring of silvery light. And then, feeling only simple fascination, he watched it close like the pupil of a vast discerning eye.

CHAPTER 4

With a jolt, Kurt bolted upright in his bed. He was drenched in sweat and gasping for air, and his heart pounded as if he'd just run up a mountain. For a moment, he held still and stared into the darkness, trying to free himself from the grasp of the nightmare and the powerful emotions that lingered in the afterlife of a dream.

The process was always the same, a quick realization of where he was and then a brief moment of uncertainty as if the mind was torn deciding which world was reality and which was illusion.

Thunder rumbled outside, accompanied by a dim flash of lightning and the sound of the rain pelting his deck.

He was at home, in his own bedroom, in the boathouse he owned on the banks of the Potomac River. Not drowning in the failed rescue attempt that had taken place months earlier and half a world away.

"Are you all right?" a soothing female voice asked.

Kurt recognized the voice. Anna Ericsson, as kind as she was pretty. A natural blonde with striking green eyes, the fairest of eyebrows, and a perfect little nose that turned up at the end. For some reason, he wished she was somewhere else at this moment.

"No," Kurt said, throwing the covers back. "I'm far from all right."

He climbed out of bed and went to the window.

"It's just a nightmare," she said. "Repressed memories working their way out."

Kurt could feel his head pounding, not just with a headache but at the back of his skull, where he'd sustained a hairline fracture as Joe had pulled him free of the sinking yacht. "They're not repressed," he said. "To be honest with you, I wish they were."

She was calm. Not one to respond to his agitation. "Did you see them?" she asked.

Thunder crashed outside, and the rain rattled against the Arcadia door with renewed vigor. Kurt wondered if the rain had triggered the nightmare. Then again, he didn't need anything to trigger them. They seemed to come almost nightly.

"Did you see them this time?" she asked again.

Kurt exhaled in frustration, waved her off, and made his way to the wet bar in the living room. Anna followed seconds later, wearing yoga pants and one of his T-shirts. He couldn't help but admire how pretty she was. Even in the middle of the night. Even without a bit of makeup.

He switched on a light. It pained his eyes for a moment

but allowed him to pluck a half-empty bottle of Jack Daniel's off the tray. He noticed that his hand was shaking. He poured himself a double.

"You know it means something," she prodded.

He gulped some of the whiskey. "Can we please keep the psychoanalyzing to office hours?"

She was supposed to be his therapist. In the aftermath of the concussion, he'd begun to have tremors and other issues. The nightmares came first, then memory problems and barely suppressed feelings of rage that those who knew him were right to consider out of character.

In response, NUMA had assigned Ms. Ericsson to act as his therapist and counselor. In a fit of spite against those who were trying to help him, Kurt had spent weeks playing the role of a curmudgeon. It hadn't been enough to ward her off, and the two had ended up seeing each other on a more-than-professional basis.

Kurt swigged some more whiskey and winced at the pain. He noticed a container of aspirin beside the liquor bottles and reached for it. How many nights this week had he repeated this same routine? Four? Five? He tried to add them up but couldn't honestly recall. It had become far too common.

"Have you been to work lately?" she said, plopping down on the edge of his couch.

Kurt shook his head. "I can't go to work until you fix me, remember?"

"You're not broken, Kurt. But you are in pain. No matter how much you want to pretend. You suffered a severe concussion, a fractured skull, and an emotional trauma all at the same time. For months, you displayed every symptom of a traumatic brain injury. And you're continuing to have some of them. Beyond that, you're a textbook case of survivor's guilt."

"I have nothing to feel guilty about," he insisted. "I did the best I could."

"I know that," she said. "Everyone involved knows that. But you don't believe it."

He didn't know what to believe. Literally.

"Even Brian Westgate knows what you tried to do was heroic."

"Brian Westgate," Kurt muttered with disdain.

She picked up on the tone in his voice, the one that signaled an uptick in his level of agitation, but she pushed anyway.

"He still wants to meet with you, you know. Shake your hand. Tell you thanks." She paused. "Have you even returned his calls?"

Of course he hadn't. "I've been a little busy."

She was studying him, nodding slightly. "That's it, isn't it?"

"What's it?"

"You were supposed to marry Sienna but you drove her away. If you hadn't done that, she wouldn't have met Westgate. No Westgate, no yacht. No yacht, no storm. No storm, no sinking. And no failed attempt to rescue her. That's what you're blaming yourself for."

Survivor's guilt was complicated. Kurt knew this. He had friends who'd come back from Iraq and Afghanistan. They'd done heroic things, more heroic than anything he'd done, and yet they blamed themselves for much of what went wrong.

He took a breath and looked away. There was too much truth in what she'd said for him to argue, but for reasons he wasn't willing to explain it didn't help him much. He turned his attention back to the aspirin, pried the top off the bottle and popped a few of the pills into his mouth. He chased them down with more whiskey.

Feeling his headache was now being properly treated, he turned back to Anna and tried to be more civil. "Why does it matter?" he asked. "Why does it matter so much to you?"

"Because it's my job," she said. "And because like an idiot I chose to care about you as more than a patient."

"No," he said, correcting her. "Why does it matter whether I see them in the dream or not? You keep asking about that. Why does *that* matter to you?"

She paused and stared up at him. The look was a mix of kindness and frustration. "It doesn't matter to me," she said. "It matters to you."

Kurt stared.

"Based on what you've told me, the dreams are all the same," she pointed out. "Except in half of them, you see this blond Caucasian woman and one of her children, while in the rest you see nothing but debris and empty life jackets. You can't even be sure the woman is Sienna. But either way, real or imagined, you couldn't reach them, the ship went down, and, unfortunately, they're gone. End of story."

She tilted her head a bit. A look of empathy settled on

her face. "To the rest of the world, it doesn't make a difference because the outcome is the same. But these alternate dreams—these alternate realities—they *must* matter to you or you wouldn't keep having them. The sooner you figure out why, the sooner you'll begin to feel better."

He could only stare. She was closer to the truth than she knew.

"I see" was all he could say.

She sighed. "I shouldn't have come over," she said, reaching for her sneakers and slipping them on. "For that matter, I shouldn't have kissed you. But I'm glad I did."

She stood up and grabbed her coat off a rack by the door. "I'm going home," she said. "Go back to work, Kurt. It might do you some good. In fact, go see Westgate. He's actually in Washington. He's making some big announcement tomorrow on the steps of the Smithsonian. He's probably not the bastard you think he is. And it might give you some closure."

She pulled her coat on, opened the door to the sound of rain on the driveway, then stepped through and shut it behind her. Seconds later, the engine of her Ford Explorer rumbled to life, followed by the sound of her backing out and up the hill onto River Road.

Kurt stared at the empty space for a minute. With a gulp, he finished the drink and wavered on whether to pour himself another. He put the tumbler down. It didn't help much anyway.

Instead of another drink, he walked through the living room and slid open the Arcadia door that led out onto the deck. The rain was relentless, beading up on the freshly stained wood like quicksilver in a lab tray. The river was covered in dancing droplets just like the sea in his dream.

Why did it matter?

He walked to the railing. As the rain soaked him, it seemed to draw some of the agony out. Far to the left he saw the red taillights of Anna's Ford as she drove off.

Why did he try harder and harder to see the truth each time the dream started?

He knew the answer to this mystery, it had come to him weeks ago, but he kept it to himself. He couldn't tell anyone, certainly not his therapist.

Soaking wet, he stepped back inside, grabbed a towel to dry his hands and face, and dropped into the chair at his desk.

Tossing the towel aside, he flicked on the computer and waited as the screen lit up. After typing in his main password, he clicked an icon that required a second password. It brought up a series of encrypted e-mails.

The latest had been sent by a former Mossad agent whom Kurt knew through a third party. Money had been wired and received, and the man agreed to investigate a rumor.

The e-mail read rather matter-of-factly.

Can neither confirm nor deny the presence of Sienna Westgate in Mashhad or surrounding area.

Mashhad was a city in northern Iran, suspected of being the headquarters of a new technical group working for the Iranian military. No one was certain just what they were up to, but the Iranians were believed to be desperately upgrading their cybersecurity and attack force. Embittered that the U.S. had somehow gotten a virus known as Stuxnet into their nuclear-processing facilities and caused a thousand high-priced centrifuges to spin out of control until they exploded, the Iranians were not only looking to protect themselves, they were planning to hit back.

Part of that effort seemed to involve foreigners who'd been spotted shuffling in and out of Mashhad, sometimes under guard.

Kurt read the rest of the e-mail.

On good authority, I've been informed that four Western persons, two male, one female, were in Mashhad for some time. They were present for at least nineteen and possibly as many as thirty days. It's unclear if these individuals were captives or paid experts. Description of the female matches Mrs. Westgate in size and approximate age but not hair color. No photographs are available. Subject did not appear to be injured or to favor either hand in daily activities.

She was seen arriving and leaving the suspected defense building in northern Mashhad under light security. No coercion was evident. No mistreatment detected.

All four individuals were spotted departing via small aircraft twenty-one days ago. No information has been uncovered to accurately suggest the destination of that aircraft or the current whereabouts or welfare of the persons on board.

Kurt closed the file.

Why did it matter what he saw in the dreams? Because, despite all evidence to the contrary, he'd become convinced that Sienna was alive. And if she was alive, he could think of only one reason she'd be doing work for the Iranians: her children, Tanner and Elise. Someone had to be holding them hostage and using them as leverage against her.

He knew it was a stretch of logic, supposition piled upon supposition. Considering the facts, it was irrational and unreasonable, and yet he felt it with every fiber of his being.

Only the dreams made him doubt.

If the empty salon and the abandoned yacht were the true memories, then he had reason to believe, to hope, and to trust his instincts.

But if he *had* witnessed Sienna and her daughter drown—and was trying subconsciously to rewrite his memories and replace what he knew with what he wanted reality to be—then he was balancing on the very edge of madness, one misstep from tumbling into the abyss.

CHAPTER 5

Western Madagascar, June 2014

The woman on horseback moved slowly, materializing like an apparition through the shimmer of the midday heat. Young and fit, in her late twenties, she held the reins of a spotted Appaloosa with quiet confidence as it trotted slowly along the sand at the edge of a muddy river.

She wore black from head to toe, stylish riding boots, and a caballero's wide-brimmed hat to keep her pale skin from the sun.

She guided the horse effortlessly, passing through a narrow section, keeping her eyes on the water's edge in case any crocodiles were lurking. As the gorge widened out, she came upon a group of zebus—Brahman cattle with sharp V-shaped horns and distinctively humped shoulders.

The cattle were part of her family's abundant wealth, a symbol of both power and plenty, though little care was given to them these days. Mostly they wandered unchecked, grazing on the vegetation that had grown during Madagascar's wet season.

She put the cattle behind her and rounded a bend in the river. It brought her to an area of natural carnage. Weeks of rain had brought on heavy flooding, the worst this part of the island had ever seen.

As the streams funneled together, the rushing torrents had grown strong enough to scour out huge sections of the banks, undercutting the land and tearing it away in parking-lot-sized chunks. Fallen trees had been swept downriver like toothpicks; those that remained lay in a tangle, their roots upturned.

Farther on, she came to a section of shoreline that had once been a peninsula sticking out into a large bend in the river. It was now an island, cut off from the land and surrounded on all sides by the arms of the rushing river.

She checked the horse with a slight movement of the reins and paused. The Mozambique Channel spread out ahead of her, its shimmering waters stretching to the horizon. Three hundred miles beyond lay the eastern shore of Africa.

She'd come to this spot often over the years. It was her favorite place on the island, though for reasons others would find odd. Alone in this desolate place, she felt something different: a certain kind of sadness that she hid from the world. It seemed to belong to her like nothing else she possessed. It was part of her, an emotion she didn't want to lose.

Unfortunately, things were changing. Events were unfolding beyond her control, and that melancholy feeling was being torn away piece by piece, like the small island eroding in the center of the raging channel.

As she watched, a section of red clay the size of a house sloughed into the water from the front of the island. It slid down at an angle, like an iceberg calving from a glacier, and began to dissolve as it contacted the churning river.

In its place she noticed something odd. Not more clay but dark, blackened metal. Flat and smooth like a wall made of iron. The churning water rushed past, relentlessly scouring the mud from it and slowly revealing more and more. A seam appeared and then another. She saw that the wall was actually great plates of riveted steel.

A chill settled on her spine, a sick feeling rising in her stomach. Fear and curiosity mixed in a cocktail of emotions. She felt drawn to what she saw and afraid of it at the same time.

An urge to cross the river and investigate came over her as if something or someone was calling to her, as if she were being asked to come to the aid of ghosts trapped beyond that metal wall.

She eased the horse to the river's edge but the animal bucked and resisted. The current was far too strong, the footing too treacherous. One step into it and she and the horse would be carried away as easily as the large trees.

The horse raised its head and neighed. Somehow, the

act brought the woman to her senses. She backed off and looked toward the small island once more.

She didn't know what lay beneath the reddish soil. And suddenly she didn't want to know. She only wanted to leave, to get out of there, before the truth was revealed.

She turned the horse sharply, pulling its head around, and kicking her heels into its sides.

"Come on," she said. "Yah!"

With a willing surge, the horse took off, galloping away, heading back inland, back to the plantation, the palacelike mansion and the life she knew.

More storm clouds were gathering above the hills in the distance. Another flood would be coming. She guessed accurately that whatever lay buried under that island would be gone before morning.

SEBASTIAN BRÈVARD waited in the main hall of his opulent plantation house. Six feet tall, trim and muscular at forty-two years of age, with smooth olive skin and dark hair that revealed his ancestral origins in the South of France, Brèvard was a handsome man in the prime of his life. His hair was thick and dark as mahogany, his eyes were lightly colored, almost hazel, and he sported a thin beard that ran along his jawline, trimmed daily by a personal barber. He carried himself with an air of confidence—some would say arrogance—that came from a privileged upbringing as master of the house.

And while he liked the finer things in life, he wore no

jewelry, save for a single gold ring given to him by his father.

The house around him was a minor palace, built in the baroque style of eighteenth-century France. The grounds, arranged in terraces on the slope of the great hill, contained stables, ornate gardens, fountains, even a hedge maze that took up several acres on the second terrace just below the main house.

The house itself was filled with splendor. As he walked the hall, he trod softly on polished Italian marble. Doric columns of granite rose on either side of the space, while extraordinary works of art lined the walls between statues and intricate tapestries.

Like his home, Sebastian was clad impeccably. He wore a three-button Savile Row suit that cost as much as a small Mercedes. His feet were covered in silk socks and two-thousand-dollar crocodile-skin shoes. Completing the ensemble was a five-hundred-dollar Eton dress shirt with French cuffs, clasped together by diamond-studded cuff links.

It was true that he had an important meeting later that afternoon, but he considered it a privilege to dress like a king. It helped those who met him know their station in life; it reassured those who worked for him that his path was a path of success.

Near the end of the hall, two men who resembled him in their features waited. They were his brothers, Egan and Laurent. They knew of the importance of today's meeting.

"Are you really going to entertain Acosta's messenger?" Laurent asked. "We should have killed him for betraying us."

Laurent, several years younger than Sebastian, was always ready for a fight, as if he knew no other way to deal with confrontation. Despite Sebastian's efforts to teach him, Laurent had never grasped that manipulation was more profitable and usually more effective than confrontation.

"Let me worry about that," Sebastian said. "You just make sure our defenses are prepared in case we have to fight."

Laurent nodded and moved away. In days past, the two had clashed, but Laurent had given way to his older brother's leadership completely now.

"What about all the explosives in the armory?" Egan asked. "Some of the munitions that Acosta left here are unstable."

"I have uses for them," Sebastian explained.

Of the three brothers, Egan was the youngest and most interested in pleasing others. Sebastian considered it a weakness, but, then, Egan had been only fourteen when their father passed. He'd not learned firsthand how to be hard.

"I'll make sure to give you an inventory," Egan said, and left by the main hall.

With the two of them gone, the sound of high-heeled boots clicking against the marble floor turned Sebastian around.

Coming down the hall toward him was the lithe form of the youngest member of the family.

Calista was fifteen years his junior and as different from the brothers as night and day. Unlike them, she dressed as a commoner. Though with only half as much style, he thought.

Today she wore black from head to toe, including a cowboy hat, which she took off and placed on the head of a priceless statue.

Her short hair was dyed the color of coal. Her nails were painted darkly, and she'd done her eyes with enough mascara that she resembled a raccoon.

"Hello, Calista," he said. "Where have you been?"

"Out riding," she said.

"And dressed for a funeral, I see."

She put an arm around him provocatively and reached up to set askew his perfectly centered tie. "Is that what's on the agenda today?"

He glared at her until she stepped back.

Restraightening his tie, he spoke bluntly. "It will be if Acosta does not return what he's taken from us."

She perked up at that. "Is Rene coming here?"

"Your personal interest in him bothers me," Sebastian scolded her. "He's beneath you."

"Sometimes a cat plays with a mouse," she replied. "Sometimes she kills it. What concern is that of yours?"

Calista was a lost child. She didn't bond well with people. Not that she avoided human relationships; on the contrary, she was always entering into or leaving one. But from their father on down, all her relationships were a mix of love and hate, anger constantly set off by a crushing devotion for all the things she could never have.

And once she possessed them, it changed. Sudden and cruel indifference was the usual response, or even a desire to cause pain and torment to that which she now controlled. How perfect, he mused, to have a beautiful little sociopath for a sister. It made her useful.

"Rene's disobedience is my concern," he told her. "He's betrayed us."

She seemed ready to defend her ex-lover. "He took the woman to Iran as you asked," she said. "She's done what we needed her to do. The Trojan horse is in place. The trapdoor link is active. I've checked it myself."

Brèvard smiled. Calista had her charms, one of which was her ability with computers and systems. At least they had that in common, for Sebastian was an accomplished programmer in his own right. But she couldn't see the big picture like he did.

"The Iranians are just one part of the plan," he reminded her. "Giving them access does us no good unless she is back here and in our possession at the appropriate time. Unless the world fears what we can do, they will not react as we need them to."

She stared at him and shrugged, hopping up on a five-hundred-year-old credenza and swinging her legs back and forth as if it were a sideboard from a secondhand store.

"That piece once graced Napoleon's summer retreat," Sebastian chided her.

She glanced at the antique wood with its perfectly curved lines and ornate finish. "I'm sure he doesn't need it anymore."

Sebastian felt his anger building but held back.

"We shouldn't have given her to Rene," she added, suddenly becoming the cold, dark version of herself again. "We should have made a deal with the Iranians ourselves."

Brèvard shook his head. "Rene is the front. His presence insulates and protects us. We set him up in business for that very reason. We need to keep that in place. But he needs to be reined in."

"Then we have to find a way to motivate him," she added. "I suggest violence. Plenty of it."

"Really?" he said. "Why am I not surprised?"

"It's all he understands."

"We are not blunt instruments like Rene," he insisted. "We must succeed with style and grace. More to the point, we are artists. When we take what we're after—"

"I know," she said, cutting him off, *"no one must know it was us."*

"No," he corrected. "No one must know it was *taken.*"

This was a point he thought he'd hammered home.

She sighed, tired of his lectures. "You will never get the woman back from Rene until he's afraid. He may be a brute, but I tell you he lives in great fear and that's why he lashes out. You want her back, you will have to tap into that fear."

Sebastian was silent for a moment. "You might be right," he said. "Come to my office. Rene's messenger should be arriving any minute now."

Twenty minutes later, a servant opened the door to Sebastian's office. "A guest has arrived, Monsieur Brèvard. He claims to speak for Mr. Acosta."

"Did he come alone?"

"He came with three men. They are undoubtedly armed."

"Show the messenger in," Sebastian said.

"And the others, sir?"

"Offer them a drink from our private stock."

"Very good, sir."

The servant bowed slightly and backtracked through the double doors.

Moments later, a stocky man in tan cargo pants and a loose-fitting polo shirt came in. "My name is Kovack," the man said. He spoke English with an Eastern European accent. He made uneasy eye contact with Sebastian and glanced nervously behind him at Calista, who stood with her back pressed flat against the wall. She didn't acknowledge him or move or even blink.

Sebastian grinned inwardly. His odd little sister had a way of unnerving even the most hardened of guests. "Where is Rene?"

"He's here and there," Kovack said flippantly. "A very busy man."

"And why has he broken our agreement? The American woman was supposed to be returned to us after the Iranian exercise was over."

Kovack took a seat in one of the chairs fronting Sebastian's ornate desk and began to explain. "We have discovered other buyers for her services."

"Who?" Sebastian asked.

"I'm not at liberty to tell you."

Sebastian guessed the Chinese were involved, and probably the Russians. Both were known to be interested in cyberwarfare and using computer hacking as a weapon. Perhaps there were others. Under different circumstances, he would have set up a bidding war and sold the woman and the others to the highest bidder just as Rene was attempting to do. But he needed her back. No one else would do.

No doubt aware of this, Kovack shifted in his seat. His new posture oozed superiority and arrogance as if he were ready to dictate terms in Brèvard's own home. His eye seemed to catch the box of Cuban cigars on Sebastian's desk.

"These are most delicious."

"You don't eat them," Sebastian pointedly explained. "But if you mean they have a wonderful flavor, then, yes, you're correct." With great calmness Brèvard picked up the box and offered it to his insolent guest. "Why don't you try one?"

Kovack reached out and plucked one of the cigars from the box. In the next instant, Calista appeared in the chair beside him. She moved quickly and startled Kovack. She didn't sit as much as perch on the armrest with her feet on the cushion.

She reached down, took the cigar cutter from Sebastian's desk, and toyed with it. "Allow me," she purred. In a swift move, she cut off the end of Kovack's cigar.

Sebastian almost laughed. How she loved that little guillotine.

Kovack seemed to enjoy the attention. He smiled and brought the cigar up to his nose, breathing in the aroma. "Do you have a light?"

Sebastian reached for a wedge-shaped block made of iridescent glass. It had sharp edges and looked vaguely volcanic. It held a butane lighter, partially recessed in one surface.

"Obsidian," Sebastian said. "From Mount Etna."

In a moment the cigar was alight. The rich flavor of the Cuban tobacco was soon wafting through the room.

Sebastian let his guest enjoy the smoke for a minute and then spoke once more.

"Back to business," he said. "What exactly does Rene want from me?"

"He wants you to bid. In *real* money."

There was a sarcastic tone to the comment.

"Real money?" Sebastian said, his eyebrows going up.

Kovack nodded. "He's arranging a new auction. Some parties have already been rejected. Their bids are too low. If you want her delivered back here, you will have to outbid the others or Mr. Acosta will have no choice but to move the merchandise to the place where it brings the highest profit."

Despite his ego and pride, Sebastian answered quickly. "Done," he said. It was foolish to quibble when billions were at stake.

"I don't think you understand," Kovack said, puffing on the cigar. "There are many bidders. I doubt you will be able to afford the going rate."

With that, Kovack exhaled a large cloud of smoke. For a brief instant it made a ring.

Sebastian found his ire growing. Mostly because Kovack was right. There was no way he could outbid the Chinese or the Russians or the Koreans, who were also rumored to want the knowledge the woman possessed. Acosta knew this. He was flaunting it in their faces.

It was obvious that Acosta had broken from them completely now. He didn't know Brèvard's plan, couldn't possibly expose it or threaten to duplicate it. But through simple greed, and stupidity, he was endangering a scheme three years in the making. A masterpiece of a long con. The longest of Sebastian Brèvard's life—and by far the most profitable, if it worked.

The time for negotiations had ended. Brèvard would not be drawn in. His will would be imposed. He smiled like a wolf baring its teeth.

"You have learned much about capitalism from Rene," he said. "I compliment you."

The tension eased a bit. Kovack offered a slight nod of the head.

"Your cigar seems to have gone out," Sebastian added. "Let me relight it for you."

Kovack leaned forward and put a hand on the desk to balance himself as Sebastian picked up the obsidian lighter once again.

Instead of relighting the cigar, Sebastian stretched out his free hand and clamped a viselike grip onto Kovack's wrist. He yanked the man forward as Calista leapt from her perch, landed behind Kovack, and shoved his chair forward.

Kovack was slammed against the desk, one of his arms pinned below the desktop, the other stretched and pulled toward Sebastian to the point where it felt as if it would be ripped from its socket. The cigar was long gone, fallen from Kovack's mouth, but Sebastian's free hand still curled around the heavy lighter.

Kovack shifted his weight, trying to get in a position to use his legs, but Calista brought a letter opener up against his throat, pricking the skin.

Kovack stopped struggling instantly.

"Make him mad," she hissed, brushing Kovack's ear with her soft lips. "I want to see what he does."

Kovack was unsure if the words were for him or for Sebastian. Needless to say, he did nothing.

"Don't listen to her," Sebastian said calmly. "She will lead you astray. You would not be the first."

"What's this all about?" Kovack shouted, panicked by what seemed like a mad game between the two of them. "We're talking business."

"This is my way of sending a message," Sebastian said. "One that will be clearly understood."

"Call for your men," Calista advised Kovack. "Perhaps the drink has not gone to their heads yet. Perhaps the poison was not as potent as intended."

"Poison?" Kovack's eyes were almost bulging out of his head. They darted back and forth until he forced himself to be still. He focused on Brèvard. The woman was insane.

"What message do you want me to deliver?" he blurted out. "I will tell him anything you ask. I will deliver it personally. You can trust me, I'm Rene's right-hand man."

Sebastian winced at the statement, an awkward look that crinkled the edges of his weathered face. "An unfortunate choice of words on your part," he said.

With that, he tensed further, raised the obsidian lighter and slammed it down on Kovack's outstretched wrist like a meat cleaver.

A bloodcurdling scream echoed through the palace, and Kovack rocked backward, released by Calista and falling to the floor. He landed on his back, cradling the stump of his wrist as blood spurted in all directions.

The double doors burst open and three of Sebastian's servants rushed in.

"See to him," Sebastian said, tossing the severed hand at the wounded man.

The servants dropped down beside Kovack and wrapped his arm quickly. A tourniquet was applied, and he was dragged out.

Sebastian glanced around, studying the blood that soaked his desk and suit. "Look at this mess," he said as if a drink had been spilled.

More servants came in and immediately began cleaning. Sebastian took off his coat and walked through a double French door out onto a balcony. Calista followed.

Thunder rumbled in the distance as the latest storm prepared to soak western Madagascar. He was thinking he'd made a mistake. Anger had caused that. "Rene will not trust you after this," he said to his sister.

"Rene has never trusted me," she corrected. "But he lusts for me, and he thinks I'm playing both sides."

"Then you will go to his auction."

"To bid on the woman?"

"To steal her back," Sebastian said unequivocally. "Rene would never accept our bid, even before all this. He's gone into business for himself. He knows if he delivered her to us, we would keep her. She's our property after all. And he would be passing up too much money. The way he spends it, he needs all he can get."

As her brother spoke, Calista nodded, though she seemed preoccupied with Kovack's blood on the back of her hand. She dipped her finger in it and drew lines up along her forearm as if it were body paint.

"Are you listening to me?"

"You know I am."

"Then tell me if you're up to it."

"Of course," she said, looking up. "But Rene is no fool. He will be watching. And if I steal what others bid for—the Russians, the Chinese—they will become a problem too."

Brèvard was not worried about enemies. When he was done with the con, he would disappear like a ghost, like smoke in the wind. And it would be as if he'd never existed in the first place.

"Figure it out," he said bluntly. "You're smarter than him. Smarter than all of them. Put that devious little mind of yours to work and get her back before everything we've planned goes up in flames."

CHAPTER 6

Kurt Austin arrived at the NUMA building in downtown Washington under an impossibly blue sky. He parked in the garage, made his way to the lobby, and took the elevator to the ninth floor. The receptionist was surprised to see him.

"Good morning," he said to her, smiling and heading down the hall.

He arrived at the bull pen near his office where several others were gathered about, sipping coffee and getting ready to put in a good day's work.

They caught sight of him and stopped.

"If even one of you claps or says, 'Welcome back,' I'll assign you to McMurdo station in Antarctica for the winter and you won't see daylight for six months."

Knowing smiles crept across their faces, and a few nods came his way, but the response was limited to his secretary squeezing his arm and someone else offering him a cup of coffee.

Joe Zavala arrived, filled with energy and smiling as he almost always did. "Hey," he called out loudly, "look who finally made it back to work."

He seemed surprised by the limited reaction from the others.

"Good luck, Joe," someone said. "Dress warm."

"Don't pack the sunblock," another coworker advised.

As they passed him, Joe turned to Kurt. "What was that all about?"

"Long story," Kurt said, surprised at how good it felt to be surrounded by friends again. "How are you on the geography of Antarctica?"

"Why do you ask?"

"Because I have to send you there now or lose all credibility with the staff."

Joe narrowed his gaze. He could guess what that meant. "Considering that you wouldn't even be here if I hadn't dove into the raging sea to pull you out after your safety cable snapped, I'd say we're even."

Kurt was the Director of Special Projects within NUMA. It meant he and his crew could be assigned to anything anytime, anywhere. Joe Zavala was the team's assistant director, a fantastic engineer and one of the most resourceful people Kurt had ever known. He was also Kurt's best friend.

"Good point," Kurt said, unlocking the door to his office and stepping inside. "But, then again, if you hadn't gotten so antsy and tried to reel me in like a prize marlin,

I wouldn't have cracked my noggin on that steel door-frame and scrambled up all my eggs. Thanks to you, I've spent the last months on a shrink's couch."

Joe followed Kurt in and closed the door behind him. "I've seen the shrink whose couch you've been sharing. You can thank me later."

Kurt nodded. There was plenty of truth to that too. He sat down at his desk. It was piled high with unopened packages and unread reports. The inbox was stacked two feet high.

"Didn't any work get done around here while I was gone?"

"Sure," Joe said. "Where do you think all those reports came from?"

Kurt began to leaf through things, most of it dull. Maybe he'd bring those files home in case he had trouble sleeping. They seemed boring enough to put him right out.

He scanned through a stack of memos and other papers requesting his presence at meetings that were long over. Into the circular file they went.

He began to look at the mail. A couple tubes held charts he'd requested months ago. He opened a box, finding a DVD inside.

"What's this?"

Joe leaned forward. "From the Jayhawk's camera," Joe said. "South African reporter turned it into a news story. It shows some of the action."

Kurt thought about watching the video but decided against it. It couldn't help him with the questions he had.

"Too bad I didn't have a camera on my shoulder," he muttered.

He put the DVD aside and went through some more interoffice mail. Finally, he got down to an envelope from the South African Coast Guard. He tore it open to find a report on the storm and the rescue. He scanned it like one might read the sports page, looking only for the highlights. His attention sharpened when he came to something he didn't know.

He sat up straight, reading the paragraph three times just to be sure.

He looked at Joe. "Brian Westgate was picked up *nineteen miles* from where the *Ethernet* went down?"

"The next day," Joe said. "After the storm passed. He was in an inflatable raft."

"I was under the impression he was found in a life jacket, bobbing up and down like a fighter pilot who bailed out."

"The story was kind of spun that way. He dove out of the raft and swam to the helicopter. When they picked him up, the only video they released was of him in the water all alone. Probably a publicity thing."

Kurt put the report down. "Doesn't it strike you odd that he was in a raft by himself while his wife and kids were drowning?"

"He said he was trying to get the raft ready while they held fast in the bridge. A surging wave crashed onto the deck and took him and the raft overboard. According to his story, he tried like crazy to paddle back, but it was impossible."

Kurt flicked on the computer and pulled up the NUMA mapping system, zooming in on the eastern coast of South Africa.

Running his finger beneath the numbers listed in the report, he memorized the latitude and longitude where the *Ethernet* foundered. He typed it into the computer and tapped the enter key. The computer marked the spot with a bright red triangle.

He did the same for the location of Westgate's recovery and a green triangle appeared.

"Nineteen miles apart," Kurt said. "No way."

"It was almost thirty hours later," Joe pointed out. "And that was a hell of a storm."

Kurt knew what Joe was thinking, but it didn't add up. "Unless he was drifting against the current and through a crosswind, he wound up in the wrong place."

Kurt turned the monitor around so Joe could see. Little gray arrows denoting the prevailing current ran opposite to the direction Westgate had drifted.

"He should have wound up southwest of the yacht, not northeast."

Joe studied it dumbfounded. "Maybe the storm caused a temporary shift in the current," he said. "Or maybe the wind changed as the storm passed."

"Not this much."

Joe looked at the map again. He exhaled. "Okay. I'll bite. What do you think happened?"

"I have no idea," Kurt said, standing up. "Why don't we go ask Mr. Billionaire himself? He's got some dog and pony show going on at the Smithsonian."

"Uhmmm . . ."

Kurt glanced at the clock and grabbed his keys. "Come on, we can catch him if we hurry."

Joe was hesitating. He stood up with all the speed of a tree sloth. "I don't know if that's such a good idea."

Kurt was beaming, almost manic. He thought it sounded like a great idea. Especially the part about it being in public.

"It's fine," he said, heading for the door. "In fact, my doctor recommended it. It's all part of my recovery."

With that, he stepped through the door, hitting the light switch on the way out. He didn't turn around to see if Joe was following. He didn't have to, he could hear Joe running to catch up with him in the hall.

CHAPTER 7

The steps of the original Smithsonian offered a grand backdrop for anyone wishing to make a big announcement. Built of red sandstone from Maryland, the "Castle," as the original building was nicknamed, had a romantic and sturdy quality to it. It looked like a fort from the Civil War era, or even the type of building that might have stood in the "rockets' red glare."

But the Smithsonian name was also renowned for its mission to teach and for its celebration of modern technology. For a man like Brian Westgate—an Internet billionaire descended from an old-money family—there was probably no more perfect spot to showcase himself or his company.

A crowd had begun to assemble under the bright blue sky, and Westgate found his nerves getting the best of him. He sat inside the building, ensconced in an office just down the hall from the main entrance. As he waited his turn to go on, two handlers primped and checked him over.

He was an easy subject to work on. Fifty-one years old, fit and trim, without the slightest hint of excess in his face, he had wavy hair, high cheekbones, and a tiny cleft in his chin. He looked more like a news anchor than the computer geek he was made out to be.

His sandy blond hair was never unruly, though a young woman named Kara made sure it was coiffed just right. "Important not to look too young or too old," she whispered.

At the same time, another handler adjusted the American flag pin on his lapel and made sure the creases in his navy blue suit were sharp enough to slice bread.

As they fussed over him, David Forrester, the CEO of Westgate's company, sat across from him.

"Feel like I'm running for office," Westgate grumbled. He waved the handlers off. He'd had enough of them.

"Maybe you should," Forrester said.

"Be kind of hard to sell Phalanx to other governments if I was the head of our own," Westgate replied.

"Good point," Forrester said. "We've already got requests from five European countries, along with Brazil and Japan. Everyone wants their data secured, and nothing comes close to Phalanx in terms of ensuring that."

"Maybe you should go out and give the speech."

"Do I look like the face of this company?"

Forrester was a lawyer who'd spent two decades with

an investment banking firm and several years working for one of the Federal Reserve banks. He was short and squat, like an old athlete gone to seed, but with great strength hidden beneath the slowly growing layer of fat. He had a jowly face, thinning hair, and wore rimless glasses, behind which were sharp eyes that did not miss a trick. Thin, almost colorless lips gave him a stern, menacing look. The disciplinarian you did not mess with.

"You're giving away a million computers to America's schools," Forrester pointed out. "And you just signed a contract with the federal government to protect American data from foreign sources. These are all good things. This is your chance to brag to a grateful nation. To tell all Americans that their data is secure."

"It feels wrong," Westgate moaned.

"Because of the sinking?"

Westgate nodded. "It's too soon."

"It's been months," Forrester said. "That's an eternity in our twenty-four-hour news cycle. Besides, the stock is up fifteen percent since the accident. Sympathy buying."

"What's wrong with you?" Westgate blurted out. "You're talking about my wife and kids. My daughter and my son."

Forrester held up a hand. "I'm sorry," he said.

"Forget it."

"Look," Forrester said. "Wasn't this Sienna's idea in the first place? Didn't she ask you what good more money would do in your bank account? She wanted you to start giving back and here you are. We all know the Phalanx design and architecture was Sienna's stroke of brilliance.

It's her legacy. As long as the system lives on, she's made a mark in the world that no one can erase."

Westgate pursed his lips, unable to either agree or disagree.

A knock at the door told them it was time to go onstage.

Both men stood up. Westgate walked out the door and onto the stage to fairly loud applause.

He began in earnest, talking almost too quickly. But as he hit his stride, he began to forget about the crowd, the contracts, and even David Forrester, and he began to talk from the heart.

He spoke about education and opportunity and the vast investment his company was making in America's schools. He spoke about how computers and training meant better jobs for single mothers and why technology and education meant a way out of poverty and off the government rolls.

He didn't mention the deals his company had just made to upgrade security for a basket of federal agencies, didn't mention the multibillion-dollar contracts with the DOD, SEC, the Fed, and Homeland Security. Nor did he mention the sinking or the loss of his family.

He didn't have to. The reporters in attendance brought up both the moment he began taking questions.

A tall woman in a red dress went first. "We understand your company has just been chosen to upgrade Internet security for most branches of the federal government. A million computers is a large gift, but it's small in comparison to a multibillion-dollar contract."

Westgate smiled. He'd been prepped with exactly the same question, phrased exactly the same way, the night before. It dawned on him that Forrester was behind it, most likely paying the woman to ask, keeping the message pure and ensuring the face of the corporation stayed on message.

Westgate held his smile just long enough for the cameras to snap a few shots.

"The computers are just the beginning," he said. "The next phase is to open secure learning centers in all the downtrodden neighborhoods. Safe places where children and adults can learn for free. We don't just want data to be secure, we want the people using it to be secure.

"As for the big contract," he added, "a billion dollars a year is small potatoes if it prevents twenty billion a year in thefts. Did you know that in the last year alone, anonymous hackers and state-sponsored groups have breached *allegedly secure* networks at the FBI, the Department of Energy, the Social Security Administration, as well as the data storage centers at NASA and the Defense Department?

"And that's just the government breaches. Every day, companies around the world are under siege from criminals, state-sponsored terrorists, and purveyors of corporate espionage. The Phalanx system my wife helped develop creates a different kind of security when it's installed. It literally thinks for itself, detects threats using logic, not just random matching of code. The Fed and the Department of Defense are thrilled. And the rest of the country will be too."

A smattering of follow-on questions were easily handled before a reporter from a local TV station asked about Sienna and the children. Westgate paused. He tried to collect himself, but when he spoke his voice genuinely cracked and he couldn't quite get the words out.

It was unplanned, and awkward for him, but from the corner of his eye he saw Forrester grinning. Some part of him wanted to apologize and deflect the question, but he pushed on, despite a sudden pain in his temple that felt like the beginnings of a stroke.

"A part of me thinks I should be in mourning," he said. "And, privately, I am. I miss my wife and children. They were the light of my life. But Sienna would be the first to say don't wallow in grief or self-pity. She was the first to stand up and help others even when she was hurting herself. This program was hers. I'd like to think it's her legacy. One that will help protect our country in what has become an undeclared war."

A hush of respect lingered over the crowd before a few easier questions came his way. When he finished, the applause was loud and heartfelt. By the time he walked off the stage, Brian Westgate was glad he'd decided to push through.

Forrester met him on the steps and the two made their way back into the Smithsonian.

"Great work," Forrester whispered.

They stepped inside and turned down the hallway toward the office they'd been allowed to use as a waiting room. As they neared the door, Westgate noticed two men approaching.

One of the men looked vaguely familiar. The square jaw, the bright blue eyes, the mane of platinum-gray hair.

"I have a question," the man said.

"No more questions," Forrester replied.

Westgate paused at the door, eyeing the man. It dawned on him suddenly. *Kurt Austin.* Before he got a chance to say anything, Austin spoke again.

"Where were you?"

"Excuse me?" Westgate said.

Forrester stepped between the two men. "I said no more questions."

Forrester made the mistake of putting his hands on Austin and soon found himself spun around, his arm bent backward and his face shoved into the wall. The impact was so abrupt it cracked the drywall.

Pinned against the wall, Forrester shouted for security. A pair of guards at the end of the hall turned slowly and then began to run down the passageway toward them.

The second intruder, a man with dark hair and deep-brown eyes, tried to keep the peace. He was flashing some kind of badge. "We're with the government," he said. "Kurt Austin, Joe Zavala. We're with NUMA."

It didn't work. Even as Austin released Forrester, the plainclothes officers pounced. Austin didn't resist, and they took him down without a fight. He seemed only focused on Westgate.

Through a tangle of bodies he shouted at Westgate. "Where were you when the *Ethernet* went down?"

"This isn't necessary," Westgate said, trying to intervene.

"The hell it isn't!" Forrester bellowed. "Arrest this son of a—"

"You were nineteen miles away," Austin shouted. "Nineteen miles!"

"Shut up," Forrester demanded.

A man appeared at the end of the hall, pulled out a camera phone, and aimed it their way. "Turn that camera off!"

A third officer entered the fray, pulling out a pair of cuffs and slapping them over Austin's wrists, which were now behind his back. Austin wasn't struggling a bit, he seemed to know better, but was still straining to see past all the men and look Westgate in the eye.

"Let him go," Westgate shouted, putting a hand to his temple. "For God's sake, there's no need for this!"

The cops yanked Kurt up, hauling him to his feet.

"We have to take him in," one of the officers explained. "Anything like this happens, we have to run them in."

"Him too," Forrester insisted, pointing to the dark-haired man.

"What did I do?" Zavala asked.

"You came with him," one of the cops said. "Now, turn around!"

"You're hiding something," Austin insisted as they began to drag him off.

Forrester had had enough. He couldn't get the police to gag this madman, but he could get his own guy out of there. He grabbed Westgate by the arm and hustled him into the office.

"Get that camera!" he yelled to an assistant. "I don't care how you do it."

Westgate was too stunned to do anything but go with Forrester. As he was pulled into the waiting room, he caught sight of Austin shouting at him one more time.

"What happened on that yacht, Westgate? What the hell happened out there?"

The door slammed, the intrusion ended, and Forrester sat Westgate on the couch. "Are you all right?"

Westgate blinked. "Of course I'm all right. Did you see someone hit me?"

"You may not feel like you were hit," Forrester growled. "But if that tape gets out, you, me, and the entire company are going to have a problem."

Westgate could hardly think. The pounding in his skull was relentless. "What are you talking about?"

Forrester didn't explain but instead moved to a makeshift bar, poured a drink, and shoved it into Westgate's hand.

"Here."

Westgate took a few sips. He felt confused and dizzy.

Forrester sat down and poured a drink for himself. He chose to do more than sip. "This could be a disaster," he mumbled.

The door opened and the assistant came in. He held the camera phone in question.

"How much?"

"Twenty K," the assistant said.

Forrester nodded. "Good, take care of it. And give the

guy a job, if he'll take it. A highly paid spot. I don't want him changing his mind."

The assistant left and Westgate looked up. His wits were returning to him, the aching in his head subsiding. "Do you know who that was?"

"Of course I do," Forrester said. "And I'm gonna have him locked away for assault, making threatening statements, and anything else I can think of."

"Are you insane?" Westgate snapped. "That man dove from a helicopter in the middle of a hurricane to try to save me and my family. You're going to prosecute him? How's that going to look?"

Forrester exhaled in frustration. Westgate could see him thinking, coming to the only logical conclusion. The calculations were easy.

"I want to meet with him," Westgate said.

"No way."

"Why not?"

"Because," Forrester said.

"Because what?"

Forrester hemmed and hawed for a second. "Because he's crazy. From what I've heard, he's been struggling. He was injured in the rescue and has been on medical leave. He's locked into some conspiracy theory about the yacht not really sinking or your wife not being on board or surviving somehow. He thinks she's working for the Iranians."

Westgate was stunned for a moment; he felt dizzy. "Working for Iran? Are you kidding me?"

"Told you he was crazy," Forrester said. "Now do you understand why you can't meet with him?"

"Why would he think that?"

Forrester looked away. "Forget it, Brian. It's nothing."

"It's not nothing," Westgate insisted. "Could he be right? Is there any possible way?"

Forrester turned and fixed his gaze on Westgate. "Don't do this to yourself. You know as well as I do that she drowned."

Westgate looked away, his mind spinning. Of course he knew that. The question was, why didn't Austin? He was the one who'd seen her. "How do you know Austin's been on leave?"

"I keep an eye on things," Forrester said. "That's my job. And when I first got the details of the incident, I started looking into it."

"And you didn't tell me?"

Forrester leaned toward Westgate, cradling the drink in both hands. His tone changed. There was venom in it. "And what would you have done if I told you?"

Westgate didn't answer.

"He's a danger to us. Whatever ax he has to grind, we need to keep him far away from you."

"Why would he have an ax to grind with me?"

"Come on, Brian," Forrester said, "don't be so naïve. He was engaged to your wife years ago. They were supposed to get married the same summer that you two met. Or didn't she tell you that?"

Westgate took the statement for what it was, a barb to

get him riled up against Austin, to prod him into green-lighting some dirty trick. And it did sting. How could it not? But it wasn't news.

"You'd be surprised what Sienna told me about Kurt Austin," he said. "The biggest thing is that he's a decent human being. As good as they come."

"Well, that decent human being could destroy this company with one wrong word."

Westgate saw fear light up in Forrester's eyes. It was something he'd never seen before. "What are you talking about?"

Forrester was blunt. "You don't know this but we're teetering on the brink of financial collapse. Working on Phalanx to the detriment of all other products has put us in a desperate spot. So far, I've managed to hide this with a few accounting tricks I learned from my Wall Street days, and some recent cash flow that's tiding us over."

Westgate could guess where the money was coming from. "The yacht belonged to the company," he said. "The fifty-four million from Lloyd's . . . that's what's tiding us over. You're worried they'll stop the payout."

Forrester waved as if he was way off. "That would be the least of our problems," he said. "Sienna's knowledge is the real threat. She designed the system. If a rumor that she's alive and hiding out somewhere got traction . . . Can you imagine? We'd be dead in the water."

Westgate looked away. "Dead in the water," he whispered. "Like my wife and kids."

"You know I didn't mean that . . ."

Westgate nodded. "What if Austin's right?"

Forrester narrowed his gaze, studying Westgate as if searching for something. He slid one hand into a pocket as if fishing for his keys and settled back on the couch. "We've talked about this before, Brian."

Westgate felt the ringing in his head once again. "Yes . . . I guess we have talked about this . . ."

"Maybe we'd better go over it again."

Westgate felt a migraine coming on. The pain was scalding, the room seemed too bright.

"What happened in the storm?" Forrester asked. "How did you end up on the raft?"

Westgate hesitated. He knew what to say. But the words stuck in his throat, and he took another swig of the gin to try and free up his vocal cords.

Strangely, Forrester began telling him the story. "The yacht was taking on water. You were prepping the raft. A huge wave hit and you got swept over the side."

Westgate remembered this. He felt the cold of the sea. "I almost drowned," he said.

"That's right, Brian. You almost drowned."

He looked over at Forrester. The pain in his head was now blurring his vision. Soon, Forrester was just a voice at the end of a tunnel. "You couldn't get back to them."

"I tried," Westgate said. He could feel the pain in his shoulders from rowing with all his might. He could taste the salt on his lips from the sea, could feel his eyes burning. "The weather was so bad . . . In twenty minutes, I couldn't even see the ship. I heard . . . I heard . . ."

"You heard the helicopter," Forrester reminded him.

"But they didn't see me."

"And before that?" Forrester asked. "Before you went out on the deck?"

Westgate remembered something. Shouting. Chaos. It seemed to make the pain in his head flare again. Even with his eyes shut, he saw a scalding light. He recalled something about the pumps. A failed hatch. He remembered Sienna and their children huddled in their life jackets. But there was something odd about the memory. It was too still. No one was moving. No one was talking.

The voice in the fog pressed, "I need an answer, Brian. What happened on that yacht before you were swept overboard? Can you tell the story without help this time?"

Westgate fumbled for the words.

"Brian?"

The truth. For once, Westgate managed to speak it. "I wish," he said. "I wish to God I knew."

As Westgate said these words, the pain spiked to unbearable levels. His vision faded, his world shrank to nothing. Nothing except the sound of David Forrester's voice.

"I'm sorry, Brian. But that's not the answer I'm looking for."

CHAPTER 8

Dirk Pitt was the Director of NUMA, a post he'd held for several years since his mentor and friend, Admiral James Sandecker, had gone on to be Vice President of the United States.

At six foot three, Pitt was lean and a little on the lanky side. His opaline eyes conveyed an intensity and a sense of mirth equally well. With thick dark hair, broad shoulders, and a square jaw, he cut a striking figure. That was especially true tonight, clad in a tuxedo, freshly shaved, and doused with a splash of musky cologne.

A charity ball for wounded military veterans was on the agenda for the evening, a cause Pitt was glad to be part of. He would give a speech, present an award, and submit a private donation anonymously. For the rest of the night, he'd mix and mingle with a crowd of interesting people. Despite all that, Pitt knew the true star of the night would be his wife, Loren Smith.

She'd chaired the ball, overseen the committees and the invitations, and even chosen the orchestra. With her striking beauty and effortless charm, she would captivate all whom she encountered. No doubt she'd look resplendent in whatever she wore, and most of the attendees might remember Pitt only as that handsome gentleman who stood beside her. Which suited him just fine.

The only drawback was dressing for the evening. They were going to be late if Loren wasn't ready soon.

Rather than badger her—which would only slow the process further—he stood calmly among a group of perfectly restored antique cars. The vehicles were part of his collection. They graced the ground floor of the aircraft hangar he lived in at Washington National Airport.

As the current Director of NUMA, and the head of the Special Projects Division prior to that, Pitt had been all around the world on various missions and expeditions. Many of the vehicles in the hangar had come back with him or were delivered shortly afterward by grateful colleagues or thankful governments.

To the victor went the spoils.

Before he could decide which of the magnificent vehicles to drive tonight, the intercom system buzzed. Pitt glanced at a monitor on the wall. He saw the face of an old friend with a neatly trimmed Vandyke beard standing at the door. Two larger men loomed behind him, no doubt members of the Secret Service.

Pitt touched a button that released the locks on the

steel door. It swung open and the Vice President of the United States walked in. The bodyguards tried to follow, but Sandecker waved them back.

"At ease, men," he said.

"Mr. Vice President," Pitt said. "I wasn't expecting to see you until later on this evening. To what do I owe the pleasure?"

"I thought you might have some time to talk before the event," Sandecker said.

Pitt glanced up the spiral staircase to the apartment above. No sign of Loren yet. "I think we're onto the third wardrobe change," he said. "You probably have at least one more before the big reveal."

Sandecker grinned. "I played the odds. You have anything in this joint to quench a weary traveler's thirst?"

Pitt walked Sandecker to the bar and filled a couple of shot glasses with Johnnie Walker Blue Label scotch.

After handing a glass to the Vice President, Pitt opened the questioning. "Why doesn't this seem like a social call?"

"Because I'm here on business," Sandecker said. "Specifically, that business Kurt pulled this morning on Brian Westgate."

Pitt nodded. "I've been fielding some blowback from that myself."

"It didn't put NUMA in a good light."

If there was anything to get Sandecker riled up, it was bad publicity for NUMA, the organization he'd built from the ground up and still protected like an avenging angel.

"True," Pitt said. "But I think Kurt's earned a free pass or two at this point."

Sandecker narrowed his gaze. "Is that what you told David Forrester? I heard he called you."

Pitt grinned mischievously and took a sip of the scotch. "What I told Forrester," he began, "shouldn't be repeated in good company. But the gist of it went like this: If he was going to go after Kurt, he was going to have to get through me first."

Sandecker grinned. "I should have guessed. Lucky for Kurt."

"Kurt screwed up," Pitt admitted, "but I'm not throwing him to the wolves. If it comes to a shoving match, I've got his record to stand on. That's good enough for me."

Sandecker nodded. There was an unmistakable sense of pride in his eyes. "I wouldn't have expected anything else. Loyalty's a two-way street and Kurt's never let us down. So you'll have my support. But there's a bigger issue. What's your take on Kurt's state of mind?"

Pitt wasn't sure how to answer. And he wasn't used to Sandecker beating around the bush. "What are you getting at?"

"Kurt's been contacting foreign sources. Wiring money to people who might work what we call the shady side of the street."

This, Pitt didn't know. "To what end?"

"Looking for any sign that Sienna Westgate might somehow be alive."

Pitt's eyebrows went up. "Are you sure?"

Sandecker nodded.

Pitt looked off into the hangar. That didn't sound healthy. Nor, honestly, did it sound like Kurt. Kurt was pragmatic, not given to flights of fancy.

"Every man has his limits," Pitt mused, considering Sandecker's original question. "Even you and I have been close to ours a time or two. I suppose it's possible Kurt's reached his."

"Possibly," Sandecker said. "But in this case, there's a twist. Trent MacDonald over at Central Intelligence handed me a file today. They've looked at the same photos Kurt received and they can't rule out the chance that Kurt might be onto something."

"'Can't rule out'? What does that mean?"

"It means they think he's tilting at windmills, but they can't prove it." From his pocket, Sandecker produced a three-by-five glossy. It showed a woman who looked somewhat like Sienna Westgate getting in a car with a burly-looking bodyguard. "This was taken in Bandar Abbas."

Dirk studied the image. It was a little grainy from being blown up. "Do they really think it's her?"

"A one-in-five chance, I'm told. Not all that high. But the possibility of a missing American being chauffeured around Iran doesn't make the government happy. Especially not when she was the guiding force behind Phalanx."

"I can see why that would make people nervous," Pitt said. "What do they plan on doing about it?"

"Well, there's the rub," Sandecker said. "Despite my efforts, the Agency is reluctant to do more than keep an eye on things. They see it as a catch-22. If that's her—and the Iranians took her—that's an act of war. And believe me, no one wants to open that can of worms. On the other hand, if it isn't her, they risk exposing precious resources in the effort."

Dirk understood the dilemma. He glanced back at the photo. The woman was made-up, her hair pulled back, her clothes conservative business style. Large sunglasses made it impossible to see her eyes or perform any type of facial recognition analysis. "She doesn't appear to be under any duress."

"That's another concern."

"Who's the jughead next to her?"

"He's a mystery," Sandecker said. "He goes by the name of Acosta. He's a minor player in the Middle East and Africa. Weapons mostly. We know he's run guns and other contraband from time to time, but he's not a big name."

Dirk handed the photo back. "So what does this have to do with Kurt?"

"It's been expressed to me that, should Kurt Austin be interested in poking around a little, no one in a position of power would be too upset about the matter. As long as he did it in the capacity of a private citizen."

Pitt raised an eyebrow. "I see."

"He already shook the tree," Sandecker noted. "If he shakes a little harder, who knows what might fall out."

Pitt wasn't sure he liked the idea. "So they want to use Kurt to sound out the edges of this dark little cave. If he finds something, we're a little wiser. And if he gets burned in the process, nothing strategic gets lost."

"That's life in the big leagues," Sandecker said.

"I don't have a problem with that," Dirk replied. "But did anyone consider Kurt's condition in all this? I'm not interested in sending a wounded man into the lion's den."

"Nor am I," the VP said. "Which brings us back to my original question. In your opinion, is Kurt Austin fit for duty?"

The conversation had come full circle, and Pitt was left to consider the question on his own.

Sandecker pulled a thin black memory stick from his pocket. A tiny green LED on the end glowed dimly. "Encrypted files. To get Kurt on his way. But only if you think he's up to it."

Pitt took the memory stick from Sandecker without comment. As he did, the door to the upstairs apartment opened and Loren Smith stepped out. She was dressed in a golden-vanilla Ralph Lauren gown that hugged her body perfectly. Her auburn hair was swept off her face and draped softly over one shoulder.

"Congresswoman," the Vice President said, "you look radiant. Beautiful enough to make up for the lunk you'll be dragging around with you all night."

"Thank you, Mr. Vice President," she said. "But one look at Dirk and I'm quite sure I'll need a club to chase away all the admiring women."

Sandecker's eyes twinkled. "Chase a few of them my way."

He leaned in and kissed her on the cheek and then turned to let himself out. "See you at the party."

As Sandecker left, Loren slid her arm around Dirk and then paused. She could instinctively sense the tension. "What's wrong?"

"I have a difficult decision to make," he said.

"You've never been one to have trouble deciding anything."

"This choice is more complicated than most," he said. "Hope you're not too hungry. We're going to have to make a detour on our way to the event."

CHAPTER 9

Kurt Austin was busy packing. He filled a duffel bag with clothes and anything he thought might come in handy. A stack of cash and various credit cards were ready, along with his passport and other forms of ID.

He'd written two notes. One for Anna, which read as a combination apology and thank-you letter. The second was for Dirk Pitt. It contained his resignation from NUMA. He hadn't expected to be handing it over in person.

"Would Loren like to come in?" Kurt asked as he met Pitt at the door.

"She'd rather we talk alone," Pitt said. "Besides, she likes nothing better than to rearrange the presets on my car radio buttons. It's one of her secret joys."

Kurt nodded and led Dirk to his office.

"Going somewhere?"

Kurt didn't try to hide it. "Iran."

"Did they open a Club Med there I haven't heard about?"

Kurt shook his head. "I have reason to believe Sienna's alive and being held in Iran. I know someone in Turkey who can get me over the border. I'll figure out the rest from there."

Pitt held steady. "Even for you that has to sound like the longest of long shots."

"It's a start," Kurt said. He opened a drawer. Inside lay his NUMA ID badge and key card. "I'm sorry about what happened today. I honestly didn't mean to fly off the handle. But I'm not myself right now."

Kurt hesitated for a second and then took the badge and card and slid them across the desk. "I know you stood up for me. It means a lot. I don't want to let you down again or do anything else to put NUMA in a bad light, but I'm not going to change my mind."

Pitt took the badge and studied it thoughtfully for a moment. "I didn't come here to talk you out of it, actually."

"Then why are you here?"

"Wondered if you were seeing pink elephants."

Kurt felt pensive and full of self-doubt. He felt like a kid running away from home, leaving a family he'd been part of for ten years. Duty to NUMA had always come first, but that was half the reason he'd lost Sienna in the first place. If she was alive and trapped somewhere, he couldn't put anything before that right now.

"So are you?" Pitt asked.

"I'm not sure," Kurt said. "I've never been less sure of anything in my life. But I can't wait around here hoping to get well. I have memories that make no sense. I have feelings that seem to be at odds with what I know to be facts. I have questions and I need to go find the answers. Until I do, I'm not going to be any good to anyone."

"Have you considered diving the wreck?"

Kurt nodded. "First thought that came to mind, but the South African Coast Guard scanned it with sonar. The yacht broke up on the way to the bottom. She's sitting in three, maybe four major pieces. Chances are anyone inside would have been swept free. So that wouldn't help."

Pitt nodded, giving Kurt the impression he knew this already. Kurt sensed Pitt studying him, evaluating. He'd had enough of that over the last three months. "You think I'm crazy?"

"I think that if someone is aware of the possibility he might be crazy," Pitt began, "then chances are he's not. And I have reason to believe there's a possibility you might be onto something."

Kurt didn't move a muscle as Pitt relayed the information Sandecker had given him. He listened intently, hanging on every word. It didn't prove Sienna was alive, or even make it sound likely, but if the CIA's analysts thought the possibility existed, it made that part of Kurt's quest seem more rational.

"Change your flight," Pitt suggested. "Start in Dubai."

"Why there?"

Pitt slid the photo out of his breast pocket and handed it and the memory stick to Kurt. "This photo was taken in Bandar Abbas, straight across the gulf from Dubai."

Kurt studied the photo. The man looked like a thug, but the woman—was it Sienna? Even he couldn't be sure. "I don't have any contacts in Dubai."

"I do," Pitt replied. "Check into the Excelsior Hotel. A man named Mohammed El Din will find you. You can trust him."

Kurt was momentarily speechless. He'd expected to be fired, or suspended, or raked over the coals. Instead, he'd found support. "Thank you" was all he could come up with.

"Since you're playing spy," Pitt added, "make sure you destroy the photo and the flash drive when you're done studying them."

Kurt nodded and then thought of one more thing. "Tell Joe not to follow me. I don't want to drag him into this. I already got him arrested by the capitol police. They've even banned him from the Air and Space Museum. You know how much he loves that place."

Pitt hesitated. "I'll find something for him to do," he said. "When do you think you'll be back?"

It was a difficult question. Kurt could only answer it by turning it around. "If Loren were out there, or if you'd known Summer was alive all those years, how long would you have looked for them?"

"Until I found them," Pitt said truthfully.

"That's when I'll be home."

Pitt grinned and slid the ID badge back across the desk

to Kurt. "Put it in a drawer," he said. "No one quits on my watch."

Kurt did as ordered, and the two friends shook hands, a rock-solid handshake between men cut from the same cloth.

Pitt turned to go but stopped in the doorway. "Be careful, Kurt. You know there is a chance you might not like what you find."

With that, Pitt slipped through the door and disappeared.

FIVE MINUTES LATER, Kurt was backing out of the driveway in his black Jeep and heading for the airport. Unknown to him, Dirk Pitt and Loren Smith were watching from their car a hundred yards up the road.

"So he's going off half-cocked after all," Loren noted.

"No," Pitt said, "he's fully loaded and gunning for bear." He started the engine and put the car in gear. "But he's not going alone. I'm going to round up Joe and the Trouts. At some point, Kurt is going to need some help. And, officially or not, we're going to be there when he does."

CHAPTER 10

Dubai, United Arab Emirates

Kurt Austin watched through binoculars as rich dark soil flew from the hooves of a chestnut Thoroughbred that was thundering down the track at Meydan Racecourse. Seven other horses trailed, but most were so far back that it seemed as if the leader was the only horse in the race.

Thousands cheered, others groaned. Kurt noted that the long shots hadn't stood a chance.

"Nothing here is what it seems," someone mentioned. The voice was an aged whisper. It carried wisdom and even a warning in its tone. "That is the first thing you must understand."

Kurt watched the horse cross the finish line. Its jockey stood up in the stirrups and slowly eased back on the reins, allowing the animal to gently run off the speed.

With the show over, Kurt lowered the binoculars and glanced at the man who was speaking.

Mohammed El Din wore a crisp white dishdasha, a shirt that went from the neck to the ankles. A white *gutra*, or headcloth, covered his hair, kept in place by a checkered band. His face looked small beneath the cloth, his shoulders were slight. Kurt guessed his age to be seventy or more.

Kurt placed the binoculars down on the edge of the table. "Are you referring to the race or something else?"

The man smiled. The corners of his eyes crinkled. "Everything," he said, and then pointed toward the track. "This race is not a race but a staged sales pitch. There are buyers down there. The lead horse is the prize. The other jockeys are paid to run slower. It makes the victory seem more impressive than what the stopwatch actually says. Even the soil beneath their hooves is artificial; it's actually a synthetic mix of sand, rubber, and wax. All of it a carefully staged deception, much like the city itself."

Kurt nodded thoughtfully. Trying to distinguish between fiction and reality seemed to be a recurring theme in his life.

"Is it a mirage, then?" Kurt asked.

"In a manner of speaking."

Kurt reached toward a teapot made of handblown glass and banded with a silver ring in a swirling Arabic motif. "Tea?"

"Please."

He poured two glasses, one for himself, one for his host.

El Din was now a wealthy businessman but had once been a purveyor of information. Rumor had it, he'd sold information to both the U.S. and Russia back during the Cold War, a fact both countries had known. But he'd never crossed lines, as far as either side could determine. And, at any rate, good information was hard to find, all of which put El Din into the category of the devil you know being better than the devil you don't.

Where El Din and Dirk Pitt met was anyone's guess, but the man had spoken admirably of Pitt and Pitt had said El Din was trustworthy. That was good enough for Kurt.

Placing the carafe down, Kurt looked back out across the racetrack. "So did we meet here to talk about the fickle nature of reality?" he asked. "Or are we here for something more concrete?"

El Din took a sip of the apple-flavored tea. "Dirk said you were eager. Look to the paddock where the winning horse is being brushed down."

Kurt picked up the binoculars again and focused on the far side of the track. He saw several men gathered around the horse. Two were dressed in Arab garb like El Din, the other three were in suits despite the heat.

"Who am I looking at?" Kurt asked.

"The one without a tie," El Din said.

"Who is he?"

"He goes by the name Rene Acosta, but he is neither Portuguese nor Spanish. He speaks passable French, but no one knows what his real name is or where he came from."

Kurt recognized the name from the electronic file Pitt had given him. He zoomed in on Acosta. It was the same man in the photo Dirk had shown him. He was broad and short, thick from front to back, with a barrel chest and a tree-stump neck. His nose was flattened like a boxer who'd taken too many punches. A buzzed head of short gray hair covered the sides and back of his skull, though the front and top were smooth and shiny in the hot Middle Eastern sun. Kurt pegged his age at forty.

"Is he a buyer or a seller?" Kurt asked, taking a quick look at the two men behind Acosta. Both were taller, more svelte, though powerfully built. By the way they stood, Kurt guessed they were bodyguards.

"Both," El Din replied. "Acosta likes the finer things in life. He trades less worthy items to get them."

"The barter system?"

"Not exactly," El Din said. "It's a triangle trade. He will deliver the items under his control to a third party if the third party purchases what he desires and delivers it to him. A very complicated, tax-free way of living."

"So he's a smuggler."

"That he is," El Din said. "And he has a new line of business that is rapidly expanding: the smuggling of human cargo, particularly experts in advanced electronics."

"Are you sure of this?"

"Unfortunately, yes."

Kurt looked back toward the paddock. "He wants the horse."

"Very badly," El Din said. "That animal will be the odds-on favorite to win the Dubai Cup and a ten-million-dollar purse. If it does that, it will be worth fifty million or more as a stud."

"That's a hefty price. Acosta must have something big to sell."

El Din nodded. "And if it's your missing friend he's offering, you can be sure there are many in the world who would pay handsomely for what she knows."

It was almost more than Kurt could have hoped for. He briefly wondered if Sienna's knowledge could be worth millions to the right person. Then he stopped doubting. Phalanx itself was worth billions to Westgate's company. If she could give the Iranians their own version, they would be secure behind an electronic wall, a goal they'd sought for years. Fifty million was nothing for that kind of security.

"Any chance you can get me into one of his meetings?"

El Din shook his head. "No," he said. "My work makes it impossible."

Kurt knew about El Din's "work" from the CIA files on the memory stick. A sad fact was that much of Dubai's glittering skyline had been built on the backs of modern slaves, foreigners brought from India and the Philippines with promises of wealth. They were not slaves in the literal sense, but they were often paid far less than what they were promised and worked twice as hard. El Din, along with a few others, had been fighting to change that. "You've made enemies trying to emancipate the workers in your country."

"And I'm afraid it makes me too well known to get you access to a man like Acosta."

Kurt admired El Din's stand. "So how do I get at him? He seems to have plenty of security."

"He has a yacht in the harbor," El Din explained. "Its name is the *Massif.* Perhaps a monument to his ego. He will be hosting a party the night after tomorrow for all his prospective buyers and sellers. A slow cruise is planned up and down the coast."

Kurt grinned. "A little sightseeing tour."

El Din nodded. "Yes, exactly. Something tells me a man like you might find a way to slip aboard."

CHAPTER 11

Kurt returned to the Excelsior by way of the harbor. He got a good look at the *Massif*, taking pictures with the zoom lens on his 20-megapixel Canon DSLR.

She was too big for any of the marina slips, so she moored offshore. Her hull was dark blue, her superstructure white. Forward, she had a sharp V-shaped bow with a large slot for a heavy anchor that was currently deployed. Amidships were the usual pen decks, a high-mounted flybridge, with a helipad on the stern, upon which a sleek helicopter with a red logo sat. Forward of the helipad, waves of heat distorted the air as exhaust from the twin stacks vented. The stacks were angled like the tail fins of some hypersonic fighter plane and painted with the same logo as the helicopter.

"Smuggling business must be pretty good," Kurt muttered to himself.

He sauntered down the waterfront, playing the tourist, taking pictures of other boats, even turning back toward Dubai and getting a few shots of the skyline. When he looked back to the *Massif*, a small launch was pulling up to her side. He took a dozen photos of the launch, catching Acosta boarding along with a blond woman. As she took off her sunglasses to clean one of the lenses, Kurt zoomed in and focused, snapping a clear shot. Even through the lens he couldn't help but notice her dark, smoky eyes.

As Kurt watched, Acosta took the mystery woman by the hand and walked toward the bow. Once they moved out of sight, Kurt turned his attention to the security team.

Armed guards were easy to see patrolling the decks fore and aft. He saw video cameras in the upper superstructure. From there, he guessed, they could see the entire length of the upper decks and anything approaching from port or starboard. A pair of spotlights and twin radar domes sprouted from the bridge, most likely one for weather, the other for traffic.

All of which meant the ship would be damn-near impossible to approach while moving at sea. That left two options: come in from above or up from below. Kurt recalled parachuting onto a moving supertanker some years back. It had been a treacherous operation even though the vessel was the size of several football fields and moving slowly. He didn't fancy the idea of trying the same thing on a yacht one-fifth the size and moving three times as fast.

His mind made up, Kurt left the harbor and continued back to the hotel, traveling on foot and fighting the strange sensation of being watched or followed the entire time. He changed course and stopped a few times, scanning the sea of faces around him, looking for anyone or anything suspicious. At one point, a male wearing a patterned dishdasha looked away and stepped into the crowd with haste.

Kurt stared, but the man didn't reappear.

"Great," he muttered.

Unhappy with the thought that his presence in Dubai might have been compromised, Kurt continued on to the hotel, occasionally checking behind him by looking in the reflections of the glass-walled stores along the boulevard. He caught glimpses of the man several times but pretended not to notice.

Finally back at the hotel, he crossed the lobby, took the elevator to the seventeenth floor, and waited around the corner.

Sure enough, the other elevator pinged moments later.

He heard the door slide open and someone walking his way. Hoping he wasn't about to mug some tourist, Kurt waited for the man to round the corner and then lunged at him. It was the same man, in the same robe.

Kurt slammed a hand over the man's mouth, shoved him against the wall, and then swung a fist toward the target's solar plexus. To his surprise, the man reacted almost instantly, arching his body and twisting to the side.

Kurt caught him with only a glancing blow, his fist hammering abs that were hardened and ready to take the shot. The man knocked Kurt's hand away and put his own hands up.

"Easy, Kurt. It's me! Joe!"

There was a moment of incoherence as Kurt's mind put two and two together, trying to reconcile his friend's voice with the clothes he saw in front of him and the fact that Joe should have been at least seven thousand miles from there.

As if reading Kurt's mind, Joe pulled off the gray-colored *gutra* that was covering half his face.

"What are you doing here?" Kurt asked.

"I came to help you."

Kurt didn't know whether to be happy or furious. He led Joe to his room and repeated the question.

"I've been following you," Joe said. "You're hard to track, you know that?"

"Not too hard, obviously. What's with the disguise?"

"I didn't want you to notice me."

"In that case, your surveillance technique needs a little work," Kurt said. "My advice: When the mark turns around and looks right at you, don't duck out of the way."

Joe smiled. "Duly noted."

"Good," Kurt said. "Now that we've got that straight, you're getting on a plane and getting out of here. I appreciate the thought, but I'm not dragging you into this. This is my problem, not yours."

"You can't send me home," Joe said.

"Why not? I'm your boss."

"You're on a leave of absence," Joe reminded him. "Technically, you're not anybody's boss at the moment."

"You're still going home."

Joe shook his head. "Sorry, amigo, no can do."

He reached into a pocket, produced an envelope, and handed it over to Kurt with a hint of glee in his eyes.

As Kurt opened it, Joe flopped down on the couch, put his feet up, and placed his hands behind his head as if he were planning on staying awhile.

Inside was a note in Dirk Pitt's handwriting. It contained no orders, only a few brief words and a quote from Rudyard Kipling.

Now this is the Law of the Jungle—as old and as true as the sky;

And the Wolf that shall keep it may prosper, but the Wolf that shall break it must die.

As the creeper that girdles the tree-trunk the Law runneth forward and back—

For the strength of the Pack is the Wolf, and the strength of the Wolf is the Pack.

We need you back in one piece, Kurt. And you need our help.

Dirk

"What's it say?" Joe asked. "I've been dying to read it."

Kurt considered what Dirk was trying to tell him. "It says I'm stuck with you. And lucky to have such good friends."

"Muy bueno," Joe said. "Anything in there about a raise and my request for hazard pay?"

"Afraid not," Kurt said, folding up the note and sliding it into his pocket. He looked over at Joe.

Despite his gruff tone, Kurt was glad to see his best friend. Joe was the kind of friend who never wavered, never hedged his bets. He was all in at all times. Always there for those he cared about. Even if the task was going to be difficult, Kurt could count on Joe to go the distance.

Just as important, Joe was a mechanical genius. He built and maintained most of NUMA's advanced submersibles, ROVs, and other exotic mechanical equipment. His work on cars was legendary: he'd made one fly and another swim. He'd even turned a golf cart into a five-hundred-horsepower drag racer.

"Maybe you can be of assistance after all," Kurt said. "I need to figure a way onto a yacht called the *Massif.* It's moored in the harbor, guarded by twenty-four-hour security and filled with armed thugs. And I almost forgot, I have to do this all without disturbing a posh gathering of people who may or may not be hardened criminals."

Joe looked at him as if he'd lost his mind. A look Kurt had gotten used to over the last months. But no more than ten seconds passed before Joe perked up.

"I suppose you can't sneak on with the catering crew."

"Not unless I learn to speak Arabic in record time," Kurt said. "Nor can I approach her on the surface. Or expect to get aboard while she's moored. I think our best bet is from below while she's moving."

"You'll need a submarine."

"My thoughts exactly."

"Kind of short notice," Joe said. "Can't exactly build one from scratch."

"What about something I can ride?"

"A diver propulsion vehicle?"

Kurt nodded. "Can you build me something that will catch a yacht?"

"Sure," Joe said. "But where do we get the parts?"

"Funny you should ask," Kurt grinned. "I have an idea."

AN HOUR LATER, while El Din was securing a fishing boat that would not draw much attention, Kurt and Joe were at the airport looking over a sprawling parking lot of dusty cars.

"I feel like I've died and gone to supercar heaven," Joe said.

"Or at least purgatory," Kurt replied.

The cars in front of them were exotics. Hundreds of them. Lamborghinis, Maseratis, Bentleys. Ferraris were as plentiful as minivans at a kids' soccer field. They were stored like one might expect to find lemons and junkers on an auction lot, parked so close the doors were touching. How long they'd been out there was anyone's guess, but most were covered in so much sand and dust that the colors were hard to make out. The tires were flat on many of them, and all of them were baking in the sun.

"Somewhere a man named Enzo is crying," Joe said.

"Not to mention five brothers from Modena."

"There are three other lots like this," the salesman who'd taken them to see the display advised.

"Why?" Joe asked.

"Foreigners in debt leave them when they run off. There is no bankruptcy in Dubai. Prison and punishment are dealt out to those who cannot satisfy their debts."

Kurt raised an eyebrow. "We'll be sure to pay in advance."

"That's wise," the man said. "What is it you need?"

"One of the rarest of the rare," Kurt said. "The new sedan from Tesla."

An hour later, their bank accounts fifty grand lighter, Kurt and Joe were taking the dusty Tesla apart in a garage provided by Mohammed El Din, who arrived that afternoon with a truckload of supplies from the nautical scrapyard. There were sections of fiberglass, a pair of wrecked Jet Skis, and the props from several high-powered outboard motors. Two of them looked hopelessly nicked up, but the third was fairly clean.

"These will do," Kurt said.

"For what?" El Din asked.

"You'll see," he said. "You'll see."

CHAPTER 12

Two days later, as dusk approached, Kurt and Joe sat on the gunwale of a small fishing boat as it rose and fell on the gentle waves of the Persian Gulf. The long-nosed boat had a small cabin at the back, twin outboards, and heaps of netting and storage containers—normally filled with ice to keep the day's catch fresh. Two rods sprouted from holders at the stern, their lines strung out into the sea.

"You sure you want to do this?" Joe asked.

"You sure you want to help a guy who might have lost a few screws recently?"

"Recently?" Joe laughed. "This may come as a shock to you, amigo, but I never thought you were playing with a full deck to begin with."

Kurt couldn't help but laugh. "You know you're the only one who hasn't asked me why I'm doing this."

"That's because it doesn't matter to me," Joe said firmly. "You need help. I'm here for you."

Kurt nodded and looked beyond the fishing poles to the glittering buildings of Dubai, lit up in shimmering gold and bronze tones as the sun began to set behind them. Ignoring the glitter, he lowered his gaze and trained a powerful spotting scope on the burly profile of Acosta's *Massif*.

"She's thick all around," Kurt said.

Mohammed El Din stepped from the small pilothouse. "Like Acosta himself, no?"

Kurt smiled and continued to study the vessel. "How fast do you think she is?"

"No idea," El Din said. "I don't design ships for a living."

"I'd guess about twenty, twenty-five knots maximum," Joe offered. "A lot faster than we'll be in this thing."

"She's making smoke," El Din said. "They must be getting ready to leave."

Kurt agreed. "Time to put this plan into action."

El Din moved to the driver's seat and turned the key. The twin outboards sputtered to life amid a cloud of bluish smoke.

Joe went to the stern and began to reel in the fishing lines as El Din nudged the throttles off idle and eased the boat forward. He brought it around in a wide semicircle that would take them toward the channel.

Kurt pulled off his dishdasha to reveal a wet suit. He dropped to the floor and slid a tarp from what looked like a small torpedo with handles.

"Do you think this contraption of yours will work?" El Din asked.

"Of course it'll work," Joe interjected. "I built most of it."

With care, Kurt and Joe had taken the batteries from the abandoned Tesla and mated them with an electrical motor from one of the car's wheels. With a little ingenuity they'd welded that motor to a propeller taken from a speedboat.

After testing the motor and confirming their ability to control it, they'd wrapped the entire design in a thick plastic lining and then constructed a watertight body around it with fiberglass sections from the ruined Jet Ski and another small craft. High-strength epoxy sealed the joints in a messy fashion, and a coat of dark gray paint had been added to make the contraption less visible.

It looked like a child's science project on steroids. Kurt would straddle it, controlling a rudder at the tail with his feet, and manipulating a pair of dive planes via handlebars would let him guide the propulsion unit.

"I admit, it's not our most aesthetically pleasing design," Kurt said. "But Joe and I were on a budget and a little pressed for time."

"At least you go on the outside," El Din said, then offered a look that suggested he might have misspoken. "You do sit on the outside, right?"

Kurt nodded. With the flick of a rubber-booted switch, he activated the power. A set of LEDs came on in the makeshift control unit. He twisted the throttle and the propeller spun with instant power. The electrical motor's whining and the displaced air were the only sounds. But the power was obvious and instant.

"If you survive this," Joe said, "I might start selling these on street corners."

"I think you'll find cash flow to be a problem," Kurt said, "considering we took all the parts from an eighty-thousand-dollar car."

As the old fishing boat chugged forward, El Din asked the next question. "How do you plan to get on board once you catch them?"

"Like Spiderman," Kurt said.

He moved to a locker, opened it, and pulled out four metallic objects. The first two were attached to a type of wrist brace. He slid them over his forearms and strapped them into place. They looked like the gauntlets worn by knights of old. The next two were attached to knee braces, like those worn by skiers who'd injured themselves. They were bulky and awkward, but they strapped on tightly, fitting over Kurt's wet suit.

Kurt smiled, proud of his ingenuity. Each brace had a lithium-ion battery of its own and a powerful electromagnet attached to it. After adjusting the braces for comfort, he powered up the one on his right arm by tapping a thumb switch and held his arm out over a metal tackle box. The box levitated from the deck and stuck to his arm with a sudden clang.

Despite pulling with his other arm, Kurt could not break the tackle box loose. He switched the unit off and the box dropped back to the deck. "If the *Massif* has a steel hull, I should be able to climb right up the side."

"What if she's made of fiberglass?" El Din asked.

"In that case," Kurt began, "I'll need you to pick me up as soon as possible and take me somewhere I can drink enough to forget all my troubles."

Joe and El Din chuckled while Kurt finished his preparations. In a minute, he was ready to go. He slid a small transmitter into a waterproof pocket designed to stash one's keys in when diving and then zipped it shut. He stashed a compact 9mm Beretta pistol in a second pocket and strapped a diving knife around his calf.

"When I get off the yacht, I'll get the transmitter wet. It will automatically activate. It has a very dim light that you should be able to see if you're within thirty feet, but farther out you'll have to use the scanner to home in on me."

Joe nodded and held up a small device that looked like a smartphone. "Checked and working," he said.

"Follow at a distance, but keep it casual. And if Acosta opens up throttles, don't try to keep up," Kurt added. "It might look suspicious if you tail her all the way down the coast at high speed."

"These waters are filled with fishing boats," El Din said.

"Yes, but most of them are engaged in fishing, not chasing yachts."

"Good point."

Kurt nodded. "If everything goes according to plan, I'll find Sienna and get her off the boat without them even knowing I'm there. In that case, wait for them to move off before you swoop in and get us."

"What if all *doesn't* go according to plan?" Joe asked.

Kurt looked at him askance.

"I only ask since it never has before."

Kurt shrugged. He couldn't deny it. "In that case, use your best judgment and adjust to the situation as needed, depending on exigencies and circumstances."

El Din looked perplexed by that response.

"He means *wing it*," Joe explained, "which I assume is what we'll be doing right from the start."

"You're wise beyond your years," Kurt said.

"I just know you too well."

By now they were nearing the end of the half-mile-long channel, the *No Wake* zone that led out of the harbor and into the open water. It would take the yacht seven or eight minutes to cover the distance if they held to the rules.

"Let me off here," Kurt said. "They'll probably start bending the speed limit before they pass the final buoy. I don't want to miss my ride."

"It's shallow here," El Din said. "Twenty feet."

"She can't draw more than eight or nine," Kurt replied. "I'll wait on the bottom and catch on as she passes by."

El Din slowed the vessel further, making a slight turn to port to shield Kurt from view.

With Joe's help, Kurt lifted the torpedo-shaped propulsion unit and balanced it on the transom. He gave the thumbs-up, pulled down his mask, and bit into the soft rubber of his regulator. With a nod from El Din, he and Joe pushed the DPV off the edge and it hit the water and submerged like a model submarine. Kurt slipped into the gulf right behind it.

With the weight of his belt, Kurt sank faster than the propulsion unit, which had only a slight negative buoyancy. He reached it quickly, guided it to a spot in the silt and then settled down on top of it, listening to the sound of the small fishing boat trundle away.

Immersed in the warm gulf water, Kurt soon heard nothing but his own breathing as the air traveled through the lines, into his lungs, and back out to the rebreather. The advantage of this system was that it left no trail of bubbles. He doubted the crew of the yacht would be looking for anything so simple—more likely, they'd be paying attention to their depth sounder and the radarscope—but he wasn't taking any chances.

CHAPTER 13

As Kurt waited on the bottom of the channel, a low-frequency thrum told him the *Massif* was approaching.

He gazed down the channel, looking for any sign of her. The first thing he spotted was the foamy V-shaped area at the yacht's bow. The leading edge of the ship's keel soon came into focus. It seemed to be grinding toward him, pulverizing the water rather than slicing through it.

Just as he'd suspected, the yacht was moving faster than the allowed three knots.

Kurt changed position, setting himself up like a motorcycle cop on the highway getting ready to chase a speeder. He goosed the throttle and the prop spun, stirring up the sediment and easing him forward. He began to move, trying to time his intercept.

It would be a tricky approach. He needed to come up beside the yacht, close enough to be hidden by the hull's overhang but not so close he would get himself run over. The best spot would be the sheltered area just behind the V of the bow wave. Any farther forward and he'd be pushed away from the ship with the displaced water; any farther back and he risked getting caught in the strongest part of the slipstream and flung backward toward the propellers.

The harmonic rumble of the yacht grew closer and Kurt increased his speed. A glance over the shoulder told him it was barreling down on him too quickly. He twisted the throttle farther, accelerated, and swung out to the side.

As he passed seven knots, Kurt realized an error in his plan. The force of the water threatening to pull him off the DPV was ten times what he'd feel riding a motorcycle. Already it was like hanging on in a seventy-mile-per-hour wind.

He pulled himself closer to the unit. The water raced past. He turned his head awkwardly. The *Massif* was still gaining, the keel moving relentlessly toward him like a great blade threatening to cut him in half. Suddenly his great idea seemed less than brilliant.

He gave the DPV full power and began keeping pace with the charging yacht. Almost immediately the propulsion unit began to flash a warning light.

That's what I get for using a repo left at the airport.

He glanced at the warning light, then back at the approaching hull. He drifted closer, feeling the pressure of the bow surge on his shoulders. The closer he got, the more violent the ride became. The sound alone was tremendous, like the noise of a waterfall and rushing freight train combined. It pounded his ears as the pressure wave hammered against his shoulders. The blinking light on the propulsion pack went from yellow to orange.

Kurt dropped back, passing under the bow wave, and was almost swung out of control. Finally behind the wave, he angled toward the hull and began inching upward. As he broke the surface, the drag on the DPV lessened and he picked up a little speed.

He accidentally banged the hull once, thrown sideways by an eddy. The impact almost sent him spinning out of control, but he reestablished his line and tried once again to move closer. The orange light was blinking now, about to turn red. The power began to fade.

In a desperate effort, Kurt swung toward the hull, stretched forward, and pushed off the DPV with his legs. He let the unit go, clicked his thumb switches, and slammed into the metal skin of the yacht's hull.

The pads on his forearms hit and locked first. The kneepads followed, snapping into place an instant later.

He was on. Just above the waterline. A stowaway of the strangest order.

He looked up. As far as he could tell, no one had seen him. Nor were they likely to. The V-shaped hull curved out over him, widening on the way up. To spot him, someone would have to lean out over the edge at least two or three feet and look straight down.

For a full minute he didn't move, gathering his strength as the powerful magnetic fields held him in place. When he felt ready, he clicked the left thumb switch and pulled his left arm away. He stretched it forward and clicked onto the boat once again. Another click and he brought his right leg up.

Left arm, right leg, right arm, left leg. He moved in this fashion, slow and steady.

By the shape and fury of the bow wave beneath him, Kurt could tell the yacht was picking up speed. He guessed they were passing fifteen knots, heading for twenty. He continued to climb. The hard part was over, he told himself.

At least the first hard part.

CHAPTER 14

The main deck of the *Massif* held a sprawling oval parlor, about twice as long as it was wide. Floor-to-ceiling windows covered the sides. Intricate repeating patterns of warm-hued inlaid wood covered the walls. Art deco furnishings wrapped in buttery-smooth Italian leather were tastefully arranged. And the entire space was lit by soft recessed lighting.

At the center of this room, like the funnel of a whirlpool, lay a circular staircase. It swirled its way into the lower levels of the yacht beneath a skylight twelve feet in diameter. The skylight allowed natural light to enter during the day, but at night it acted as a dark mirror, reflecting all that went on below.

Spread about the parlor were fifteen people, not counting the ship's staff. Some were admiring the artwork, others drank and spoke among themselves.

Calista Brèvard entered this quietly swirling landscape in a shimmering black cocktail dress. Her makeup was more restrained than usual, her dark hair hidden beneath a wig of platinum blonde that fell to her shoulders in the back and gave her graceful bangs that halted just above her eyes in the front.

She moved slowly toward a grand piano where Rene Acosta was holding court.

"The bottom line is simple," Acosta was telling a Chinese man. "You will be locked out and they will still have access to your deepest secrets."

"Can this system really be that advanced?" the man asked. "We've heard tales like this before. All systems have weaknesses. It is only a matter of time until we penetrate the Phalanx."

Acosta shook his head. "Would the United States put all its eggs in one basket if it didn't know that basket was absolutely untouchable?"

"Perhaps they're wrong."

Acosta shrugged. "Perhaps," he said. "Can you really afford to take that chance?"

The Chinese man turned and began to discuss this with two of his countrymen, and Acosta excused himself and took Calista by the arm.

"You have them right where you want them," she said. "I must admit you're far smoother than I expected."

"I've learned to be tactful," he said.

"And my brother has learned to be a brute."

"You could have stopped him," Acosta said. "Poor

Kovack. He has to learn how to shoot and stab people with his other hand now. Perhaps it would be best if you avoid him for the time being."

"I doubt he'll recognize me."

"And if he does?"

"Then he'll find that he got off lucky."

Acosta chuckled, and they moved to the bar. The bartender immediately poured him a glass of fifty-year-old port.

"And for the lady?"

"Ice water," she said.

"It runs in her veins," Acosta added.

The bartender immediately filled a lead crystal glass with ice water. He wiped the side with a napkin before handing it to her.

"You could have at least tried to limit the damage," Acosta said.

"And show my true colors? I don't think so. If I protected Kovack, my brother would have become suspicious. He may be anyhow. If you don't return the woman to us, it will be all-out war between you two."

"I only need her a little longer," Acosta said.

"Not just her, the others as well. All three of them."

"You don't understand," Acosta said. "You have no idea what these foreigners are willing to pay. Ten million for a month of work. Twenty million for six weeks. Can you imagine? She can't possibly be worth more to your brother. Hold him back. Tell him I will cut him in on the spoils."

"He has other plans," Calista said.

"What kind of plans?"

"How would I know," Calista said. "He tells me only what he wants to. But I promise, they are important to him. He sent me here to take her from you. The only way I can stop that is if you deliver her to me as planned and blame the Iranians for the delay."

Acosta hesitated and Calista narrowed her gaze. She saw something in his eyes. It said he'd already crossed the Rubicon. "What have you done, Rene?"

He didn't respond, but the tension was obvious in a tightening of the muscles in his thick neck.

"Rene?"

"She's not here," he said finally. "I delivered her to Than Rang last week. He wants the others as well."

Than Rang was a Korean industrialist. Calista's mind raced trying to figure out why he would need or want the American or the other hackers. "If that's so, you'd best retrieve her."

"I can't," he said. "Than Rang is not a man to be trifled with. I'd rather deal with your brother's wrath than his."

Calista wondered if he was lying or not. "Sebastian will not wait," she said. "The woman must be delivered into my brother's hands before the Americans finish their trial run with Phalanx or three years of effort will be ruined, that much I know. And if that occurs, Sebastian will not rest until he murders you."

As she spoke, Calista stared at her former lover with

unblinking eyes. The more nervous he appeared, the more joy it brought her. Anything to increase his agony.

"What's done is done," he said. "The only question is where your loyalties rest."

"My 'loyalties'?"

"Yes," he said. "If it comes to war, whose side will you be on?"

She tilted her head as if the question was silly. A wicked smile grew on her face. "Why, my dear Rene," she began, "I'll be on my own side of course. I thought you would have learned that by now."

She put the glass down and turned away.

He watched her walk off, headed for the spiral staircase. Despite a plan to remain calm, he found his emotions had become unbalanced, a volatile mixture of anger and lust as always where Calista was concerned.

But the facts were simple. He could not retrieve the American woman from Than Rang's clutches even if he wanted to. Nor could he forego the revenue from transactions involving the other three experts he held. To keep up his extravagant lifestyle he needed more cash and he needed it now.

He snapped his fingers and two of his men appeared. "Keep an eye on her," he said. "I don't want her causing any trouble or upsetting the other guests."

They nodded and turned to follow.

For her part, Calista expected to be followed. She walked slowly to the center of the room and took the spiral staircase down to the accommodations deck. She traveled toward the stern, where a small but warmly appointed cabin with a single berth had been reserved for her.

She opened the door and held it, pausing long enough to make sure Rene's men spotted her. They slowed their pace but kept on coming. She winked at them and then ducked inside and shut the door.

They would likely guard her until the auction. But Rene would want her there. She was a mysterious presence and a distraction. The bids would be higher because of her. That would make it easier.

She turned the radio on and started the shower. She figured that was enough. She'd already swept the room for bugs and other listening devices.

Unzipping the cocktail dress and removing the wig, she quickly changed into another outfit consisting of dark slacks and a gray silk shirt. It was fancy enough that she could pass for one of the guests but utilitarian enough to let her move freely.

Next she removed a false panel from her suitcase, pulled out a satellite phone, and slid it into her pocket. A compact Bersa .380 pistol came out next. It was a thin, nickel-plated automatic, with black polymer grips. It carried seven hollow-point rounds in a short magazine and one more in the chamber. It was a trusty weapon, accurate, with a smooth trigger pull. Calista had taken out several adversaries with it. As a final precaution she slid a four-inch knife into a thin scabbard above her ankle.

Ready for action, she made her way to the cabin's large

window. It slid open with ease. She glanced down the narrow gangway that ran around the edge of the yacht. Seeing no one, she climbed through the window and onto the deck. With smooth precision, she slid the glass shut and began walking toward the bow.

CHAPTER 15

Clinging to the side of the *Massif* like a stubborn barnacle, Kurt studied his options. The heavy yacht was now cruising at twenty knots. Light spilling from the superstructure cast a subtle glow on the waters flowing past, but other than that he was bathed in darkness.

Since he couldn't go up and over the rail without being seen, Kurt moved quickly toward the stern. He knew there were several hatches there, one of which had been wide open shortly before departure as the crew took on supplies.

He moved toward it, traveling like a crab, until he found it. Considering how close it lay to the waterline, Kurt wasn't surprised to find it battened down tight. He looked around, noticed a crack of light up higher on the hull and farther aft.

He reached it quickly, peeked around the edge, and, seeing no one inside, swung around and dropped in.

He was in a small workspace connected to the engine room. It was cramped, hot, and loud. He'd covered a few feet when a figure in white coveralls appeared. The man wore a bulky headset to protect his hearing from the whining engines and didn't notice Kurt or hear him coming.

Shock and confusion registered on the crewman's face as Kurt got his attention with the Beretta and waved a finger to dissuade him from trying anything. That done, Kurt pulled off the headset.

"You speak English?"

The man nodded.

"Are there any prisoners on board this yacht?"

The man seemed confused by the question. "Prisoners?"

"Anyone being held against their will," Kurt explained. "I'm looking for a blond American woman."

"No," the man said, shaking his head. "I just run the turbines."

It made sense. The poor guy was just a sailor. But he had to know his ship.

Kurt walked him to an electrical schematic of the ship's wiring on which the demarcations for hallways, berths, and common areas were laid out.

"Rene Acosta," Kurt said. "Which cabin is his?"

The man hesitated.

Kurt pulled back the hammer on the Beretta.

"First cabin," the man said. "Accommodations deck, forward."

Kurt studied the diagram. By the look of it, that cabin was the largest on the ship, it made sense it was Acosta's.

Kurt dragged the man to a storage room, shoved him

inside, and took out a small syringe. He jabbed it into the man's thigh and watched as his eyes rolled quickly. In a second he was out cold.

"Sleep tight," Kurt said, tossing the syringe away.

In a minute, Kurt had the crewman's coveralls on. They covered his wet suit and electromechanical gear but not his hair. He spotted a red skullcap on a peg and added that to his ensemble. With the cap pulled down snugly over his silver hair, Kurt headed down the hall toward the bow, where Acosta's cabin sat at the end of the central gangway.

Kurt found the door locked and was able to pry it open using a knife. He slipped inside and began his search. He'd been there all of five minutes when he heard a hand on the doorknob.

With surprising grace—considering the bulky equipment and the layers he was wearing—Kurt moved to the bathroom and crouched behind the curved glass block of Acosta's walk-in shower.

Clutching the Beretta again, he prepared himself for a fight. If he was lucky enough to find Acosta entering, he'd get some answers from the man himself.

The cabin door opened briefly and then latched softly. To Kurt's surprise, no lights came on. Muted footfalls on the plush carpet traveled slowly from the main door to the desk where Kurt had been rifling through Acosta's things.

The squeak of a chair told him someone had taken a seat, but the room remained dark until it was partially illuminated by a soft blue glow, easily recognizable as the light from a computer screen.

Kurt heard typing and then finally a woman's voice. "Rene," the voice said scornfully, "did you really think my own security system would stop me."

It was a rhetorical question. There was no one there to answer, and Kurt's curiosity began to get the better of him.

He moved to a new spot where he could see.

The woman behind Acosta's desk was typing furiously. "Damn you, Rene," she said, and then pulled a satellite phone from her pocket and punched in a number.

Kurt didn't hear the greeting very clearly but listened as a quick conversation took place.

"We have a problem," she said. "They're not here . . . None of them. Not the American, not the others. They're not on board."

A pause followed.

"Yes, I'm sure of it," the woman replied. "I'm reading it on Rene's computer right now. I thought he was lying, but it looks like he's already shipped the woman to Korea, and promised the other three to Than Rang as well. The auction must be a ruse. Either Rene is short of money or he's lining up buyers for the future."

Another pause, more protracted this time.

"No, I don't think that will work . . . Well, I could put a gun to his head, but that won't bring them back. We'll have to lift them from Than Rang ourselves. And that won't be easy."

Kurt strained to listen, but, try as he might, he could only make out the woman's side of the conversation.

"There's no other way," she said. "Without her, no one

will believe we can cross the air gap, breach the American Wall, and bring the system down."

Kurt had no idea what she was talking about, but he hung on every word.

"I have to go," she said finally, tapping a few keys and closing the program. "Otherwise, Rene might try to join me in the shower." She paused, and then added, "You're right, by the way. I'm too good for him."

She hung up, turned the computer off, and stepped out from behind the desk.

Kurt moved as well, making his way to the edge of the main cabin. In the low light he saw the woman put an ear up against the front door. He noticed a small pistol in her hand.

"You're forgetting something," he whispered.

She whirled around, but he had the Beretta out and ready. She saw it clearly and froze.

"That laptop was closed when you came in."

CHAPTER 16

"Toss the gun over there," Kurt said.

He pointed toward a thick rug near the bathroom door.

With a shrug she flipped the gun gently in the general direction. It landed with no more than a soft bump.

Kurt motioned toward one of the chairs across from Acosta's desk. "Have a seat."

She hesitated for just a second and then moved toward the chair, sliding onto it with effortless grace. Kurt noticed a decided lack of nervousness in her posture. She looked comfortable. She leaned back and crossed her legs as if awaiting a cocktail at sundown.

Keeping the Beretta aimed at her, Kurt moved behind the desk and tapped the computer keyboard. The screen lit up. Back to the password.

"You've already broken into this once," he said. "Care to tell me how?"

"Who are you?" she asked. There was no fear in her voice, only a subtle curiosity. Like someone who'd discovered a new plaything.

"Password," Kurt said, ignoring her.

"Are you a thief? A mole of some kind?"

"Password."

"Calista," she told him, "with a *C*. As if you could spell it any other way."

He typed the name, alternating glances between her and the keyboard.

The lock screen dissolved and a spreadsheet appeared. The white background was so bright it caused his pupils to constrict, making it difficult to see beyond the screen. He tapped the key to lower the screen's brilliance until it was as dim as he could make it.

The woman hadn't moved, though she was now leaning forward, studying him.

"You're not part of the crew," she said calmly. "And you're a little too scruffy to be one of the guests."

"My invite got lost in the mail," Kurt said. "Now, what were you looking for? And who were you talking to?"

Her eyebrows went up. "How badly do you want to know?"

"Badly enough to put a bullet in you if you don't tell me."

She laughed. "You're not going to shoot me. For one, it would make too much noise."

"I have a silencer."

"I'm no good to you dead," she said, standing up.

Kurt met her gaze. "Who said I was going to kill you? A knee shot would do the trick."

"And while I scream in pain," she said, slinking forward, "will I be able to talk clearly?"

Kurt didn't reply, and the woman climbed on the far edge of the desk, stretching out on all fours like a cat. She reached for the computer, walked her fingers onto the keyboard, and pressed F1 and F4 at the same time.

She looked up at him, licking her lips. "Do I get anything for cooperating?"

Kurt felt as if he'd landed in the Twilight Zone. If he didn't know better, he'd have guessed this woman was propositioning him. "A gold star," Kurt said.

He glanced at the screen. The spreadsheet had vanished and a darker screen opened up. It showed a pair of columns made up of boxes. Each box had a photograph of something inside, a sparkling new Learjet in one, a small cache of what appeared to be diamonds in the second box. A caption underneath it read "400 carats total, all stones VS or VVS." A third box indicated the racehorse he'd seen, Desert Rose. Numbers underneath each box indicated supplemental money contributions. Apparently, the business wasn't as cash-free as El Din suspected.

Kurt assumed these boxes contained bids for whatever it was Acosta was selling. Kurt followed the lines across the screen to the second column of images. Each of these seemed to be a work of art.

Kurt noticed a variety of artistic styles: cubist, classical, and even some old masters.

"Roll the cursor over the paintings," the woman said. "You'll get a description and a better understanding."

With one eye on his strangely helpful friend and the other on the computer, Kurt did as she said.

The descriptions were odd. Kurt quickly understood why.

"'Weapons expert, known to have worked with the Syrian government on chemical dispersants,'" Kurt read aloud.

The next "painting" was captioned "Guidance system engineer, familiar with Soviet and American designs."

The third had nothing but a group of odd words: "ZSumG," "Montresor," "Xeno9X9."

"Those are hacker names," she said. "Handles. That's what—or whom—he's selling."

Kurt thought about what she'd said on the phone. He scrolled down. There were a dozen more boxes labeled with works of art. He checked every box but found no sign of Sienna Westgate.

He looked up just in time to see the woman lunge for his gun.

She moved quickly, but Kurt had been expecting it sooner or later. He snapped his arm out of reach, grabbed her with his other hand, and threw her off the desk. She came up swinging a four-inch dagger. Kurt stepped out of range and knocked over a metallic sculpture that looked vaguely human. It crashed to the floor as the woman lunged forward again.

With his free hand, Kurt caught her by the wrist and twisted her arm until she let go of the knife. He swung her toward the wall and slammed her into it and held her there.

She struggled for a second. To make her stop squirming, he brought the silenced pistol up once again.

"I'm not interested in killing you, but I will shoot you if you put me in danger."

Her dark hair had fallen in front of her face. Her lip was gashed and bleeding. She stared at him, her eyes wide. There was something in that look, Kurt thought. It was recognition.

"I know you," she said breathlessly. "White knight . . . Fearless . . . I must say, I'm surprised to see you here. You're a bit early, I'm afraid."

Kurt kept the pressure on her. He wasn't falling for the distraction. "I don't know what you're talking about, lady. I've never seen you before in my life."

"I didn't say you had."

"Who were you speaking to on the phone?"

She didn't reply, but she ran her tongue across the bleeding lip, seeming to enjoy the taste of her own blood like some kind of vampire princess.

"I asked you a question."

"Kiss me," she whispered.

Kurt didn't reply.

"Either kiss me or shoot me," she said, "but I will scream if you don't do one or the other."

"You're not about to scream," Kurt said. "You want to be discovered here about as much as I do."

Kurt hadn't even finished his statement when she tilted her head back and shrieked at the top of her lungs.

"Damn!" Kurt shouted, clamping a hand over her mouth.

Between the screaming and the commotion, he figured it was time to shove off. He reached into her pocket, grabbed the satellite phone she'd used, and tucked it into a pocket in his coveralls.

Before he could do anything else, the door flew open and a group of Acosta's men came piling in. They tackled Kurt and knocked the gun from his hand. He managed to throw one of them off and then slammed the second guy onto the desk, but the third guy caught him in the chin with a knee.

Kurt was knocked backward for an instant, just long enough to allow the others back into the fight. Punches landed from all sides. Unable to break free, Kurt was quickly subdued.

The men lifted him to his feet and slammed him into the same wall he'd held the strange woman against.

She was behind them now with Kurt's pistol in hand. "Three against one," she said. "That's hardly fair."

Without hesitation, she began firing, drilling holes in the men who restrained Kurt. They dropped to the ground all around him. And she kept firing, making certain they were dead. With the three men lying still on the floor, she tossed the pistol to Kurt.

"Better run," she said quickly. "There's plenty more where they came from."

Kurt had no time to consider the madness. He'd landed in the middle of something strange. Damned strange.

He looked out into the hall. Men with guns were running his way. He shut the door and ducked back into the room.

"You should have kissed me," she said, raising her eyebrows.

"Maybe next time."

He turned and blasted three holes in the window and then dove through it, shattering the weakened plate glass and landing on the deck outside.

He got up quickly and sprinted for the stern as an alarm began to blare overhead. Gunshots followed, coming from above and behind, and bullets ricocheted off the deck all around him.

Taking cover, Kurt pressed himself against the superstructure, changed out the spent magazine, fired a few shots, and then scrambled beneath the steel beams supporting the helipad.

He gazed up, looking jealously at the shiny helicopter. Realizing it could be a problem for him later, he aimed for the cockpit and reeled off a half dozen shots, shattering the side window, drilling a few holes in the instrument panel and a few more in the sheet metal where the fuel tank was located. He wasn't sure if he'd hit anything vital, but any pilot would have to think twice before taking the helicopter for a spin.

Ducking back into the shadows, Kurt checked the clip in his Beretta. Four shells left. "Time to abandon ship," he muttered.

The sound of booted feet pounding the stairway from above only reinforced his decision.

He fired two shots toward the approaching crewmen and took off for the railing. At the same instant, one of Acosta's men came racing around the corner. They collided like two cars at an intersection.

Kurt hit the deck and rolled over, looking for the Beretta, turned back the other way and came face-to-face with a Colt .45 aimed at his chest. The man holding it had wispy blond hair, pale eyes, and a hollow face that looked almost skeletal in the dim light.

"Hands up," he said, inching toward Kurt until the weapon was no more than eight inches from his nose.

Kurt raised his arms slowly. The man relaxed a bit and used his free hand to depress a small radio attached to his collar. "This is Caleb," the man said. "I have the intruder. Do you want to interrogate him?"

A second of static preceded the reply. *"No,"* a man Kurt assumed was Acosta said. *"Just shoot him and bring me his body."*

As the words came from Acosta's mouth, Kurt hit the thumb switch on his left wrist guard. The powerful magnet came on instantly. It drew the heavy metal gun to the side just as Caleb pulled the trigger. Fire exploded from the barrel, and the bullet hit six inches to the left, punching a hole in the teak deck instead of Kurt's skull.

Caleb stared in disbelief as the Colt stuck to the magnet on Kurt's left arm. He never saw Kurt's right hand balled into a fist and flying toward his jaw. The blow knocked him sideways and sent him sprawling onto the deck.

Kurt sprang to his feet and dashed for the rail without looking back. At a full run, he put his hands on the rail and hurtled over it. He swung through the air—holding the rail for a split second longer than necessary—and then he vanished into the dark.

ON THE BRIDGE of the *Massif*, Rene Acosta waited to hear that the intruder was dead. To his surprise, Caleb's voice came over the radio sounding angry and somewhat panicked.

"The intruder has gone overboard," he shouted. *"I repeat, the intruder has escaped and gone over the rail."*

Acosta lifted a radio to his mouth. "I told you to shoot him!"

"I did," Caleb said.

"Then, what happened?"

"I don't know," Caleb said. *"But I'm sure I hit him!"*

Acosta burned with indignation, half at Caleb for such stupidity, half at the intruder for having the insolence to crash his party.

He glanced over at the yacht's captain and made a twirling motion with his hand. "Turn us around. We're going to have a hunting party."

At that moment Kovack came in, waving for Acosta's attention with his bandaged, handless arm. As Acosta looked his way, Kovack slung Calista onto the deck. She landed at Acosta's feet.

"She was found in your cabin."

"My cabin?"

Calista spoke up with a snarl. "The intruder broke into my cabin first," she insisted. "He put a gun to my head and dragged me out the window while your inept fools snoozed outside my door."

Acosta glared at her. Another lie. There was always another lie waiting on her lips.

"Do you really expect me to believe that?" he boomed. "You're dressed differently than you were before. Perhaps we're seeing your true colors."

"Look at me," she said. Her face was bruised, the split lip swollen and wet with blood. "Does it look like I went to your cabin of my own accord?"

Acosta turned to Kovack. "Did you or your men hit her?"

"No," Kovack insisted.

"Tell them how you found us," Calista prodded.

Kovack hesitated.

"Well?"

"Her screams alerted us to his presence," Kovack said. "If it wasn't for her, we wouldn't have known he was there."

By now Acosta could feel the ship leaning into the turn. He had bigger issues to deal with. "Lock her back in her cabin and post a guard outside her window," he ordered. "And then join me on deck with rifles and a spotlight."

"The guests are concerned," another one of Acosta's people mentioned.

"Tell them we're going to have a bit of sport," he replied. "The intruder is in the water. I'll give ten thousand dollars to whoever gets off the killing shot."

CHAPTER 17

Five miles behind the *Massif*, Joe Zavala stood at the bow of the small fishing boat, trying to keep the speeding yacht in sight. At this point he could track the warm glow from the ship's interior lights. But if she went dark, they would have a problem.

He turned to El Din, who stood at the helm. "We're still falling back. Can't you goose any more speed out of this lobster boat?"

"Patience," El Din said. "Remember, patience may be bitter, but its result is sweet."

Joe cut his eyes at El Din. "I'm not interested in learning patience. Just keeping that yacht in sight."

Without warning, the tracking scanner began to chirp. "It's the beacon. He's in the water."

"Thank Allah," El Din said. He shoved the throttles

full on to the stops, hoping for more speed than the boat possessed.

"What happened to all that 'patience'?" Joe asked.

"I was never very good at it," El Din said. "Besides, the time for patience is over. Now is the time for action."

Joe could not agree more. Kurt had been aboard the *Massif* for just under an hour, but it felt like half the night. He placed the scanner down and raised the spotter's scope up to his eye. Almost immediately he saw something he didn't like.

"Damn."

"What is it?"

"The yacht's turning broadside," Joe said. "They're coming back around."

CHAPTER 18

The *Massif* turned in a wide arc, shedding velocity as it went. By the time its rudder was back on center, the huge vessel was making no more than five knots.

Standing on the bridge, Acosta marked a spot on the GPS map where the stowaway had gone overboard.

"Hold this speed and keep the ship stable," he ordered. "I want you to make slow passes back and forth through this area until we spot and kill the intruder."

"Yes, sir," the captain said. He didn't bat an eye at the brutal order.

With that done, Acosta stepped out on the deck. Caleb waited there holding a bolt-action hunter's rifle. "Give me that," Acosta said. "You might miss again."

Caleb scowled and handed the rifle to his master.

In addition to his own hand, Acosta had stationed teams of armed men at various spots on the main deck.

Two groups stood amidships, one on each side. Two more men waited at the stern.

"Lights to full," Acosta ordered.

Around them exterior lights lit up the waters of the Persian Gulf in a swath two hundred feet wide and five hundred feet long. Two spotlights above the bridge came on and were aimed ahead and outward at forty-five-degree angles in order to cover the most water possible.

"This won't take long," Acosta promised, wrapping the rifle's strap around his forearm.

"Target off the starboard beam," someone shouted.

Acosta was on the port side. He strode back through the bridge and pushed out through the starboard door just as his men opened fire. Ribbons of water flew up where the men laced bullets into the fire zone.

Acosta raised his weapon and spotted the target quickly: a flash of white clothing. He fired once—a direct hit. The coveralls jerked as the bullet found its mark, but there was no blood or even the slightest defensive reaction.

As the target drifted closer, Acosta saw why. The stolen coveralls were empty. They floated past in a tangle, sliding gently across the waves.

More shots rang out.

"Hold your fire!" Acosta shouted. "There's no one there. He must have shed the clothing and left them behind as a decoy."

The shooting ceased, and Acosta turned his attention back toward the inscrutable waters, looking for any sign of the man who'd come aboard his yacht.

After several minutes with nothing to see, he lost his

patience. "Take us back around," he bellowed. "He has to be out here somewhere."

IN FACT, Kurt was much closer than Acosta could have guessed. He was clinging to the side of the ship, twenty feet below the main deck, about six feet from the rushing water.

As he'd hurtled over the railing, he'd held on for a split second longer than necessary, converting his outward and downward motion into a turning arc. The trajectory had slammed him into the side of the yacht just as he'd activated the magnetic pads once again.

It had been an awkward, jarring crash, but the magnets didn't care. Once again they'd done the trick, locking him to the steel hull and holding him in place.

From there, Kurt had crabbed his way forward and parked himself in a spot below the *Massif*'s four-ton anchor.

After tearing off the white coveralls and throwing them into the sea, he waited patiently as the yacht reversed course and slowed to a crawl. Aside from some strain on his arms and legs, Kurt was quite comfortable. Assuming the battery packs held out, he could hang in there for quite some time. And he intended to do just that.

Sooner or later, Acosta would give up, douse the lights, and turn back onto his original course. At that point Kurt would slip off the side and into the darkness, treading water until the yacht was far enough away for Joe and El Din to come get him.

After three runs back and forth, Kurt figured the towel was close to being thrown in. He grinned in the dark at his own tactical brilliance, all but ready to pat himself on the back, when he noticed something he hadn't expected.

Speeding toward them, just barely visible in the moonlight, was the silhouette of a long-nosed fishing boat.

"You've got to be kidding me," Kurt whispered. "What can they possibly be thinking?"

And then it dawned on him. He glanced at his right arm where the key pocket was. It had been torn open, perhaps in the scuffle with the woman or even with Acosta's thug.

With nothing to keep it secure, the transmitter had either been caught in the coveralls when Kurt pulled them off or had simply fallen into the sea as he climbed around on the side of the hull. No doubt it was now bobbing in the water somewhere, broadcasting a message to his friends and luring them unwittingly toward the monstrous yacht bristling with gun-toting thugs.

CHAPTER 19

As they raced toward the beeping transmitter, Joe divided his attention between the yacht and the section of water where he expected to find Kurt. There was no more than a quarter mile separating the two.

"They must have missed him," Joe said. "We need to hurry."

"What if they spot us?" El Din asked.

"I'd be surprised if they haven't seen us already," Joe said. "But we're not leaving Kurt out there to be run down or shot."

"They're lit up like your a proverbial Christmas tree," El Din said. "Maybe they're not able to see us out here in the dark."

"Let's hope so."

El Din kept the throttles open, and Joe dug into one of the boat's lockers.

"What are you looking for?"

"I'm thinking this is going to be one of those high-speed operations. We need something for Kurt to grab on to." He pulled out a cargo net. "This should do."

El Din nodded. "Three hundred meters," he said, glancing at the scanner.

"Slow her down a bit," Joe said.

"Two hundred."

Joe grabbed an infrared scope and scanned the water. The surface of the gulf remained dark. But the heat from Kurt's body should have stood out plainly. He saw nothing.

"Are we headed for the target?" he asked.

"Dead ahead," El Din said.

"Let's not use the word *dead*."

"One hundred meters," El Din said. "Three hundred twenty-eight feet, if you don't like the metric system."

Joe lowered the scope and squinted, looking for any sign from Kurt alerting them to his location.

"Fifty meters," El Din said, backing off the throttles.

They were soon coasting, El Din correcting their heading to port. The nose of the boat slewed around. "We should be right on top of him."

Joe felt his nerves tingling. As the fishing boat settled and its wake dissipated, the night became awfully quiet.

He glanced nervously at the yacht. It too was sitting idle, its nose pointed thirty degrees off line from them.

With their small boat in a similar condition, it felt like a stalemate between predator and prey. The yacht, a big cat crouching on its haunches; the small fishing boat, a gazelle ready to bolt at the cat's slightest twitch. For now, both held still as stone, waiting for the other to make the first move.

"They know we're looking for him," Joe said, whispering. "They're waiting for us to find him. Be ready to go."

"As soon as we have him, I'll head straight for the shore."

Joe raised the infrared scope and studied the yacht. He could clearly see the heat plume emanating from its angled stacks. The scope was working, so why wasn't it picking up Kurt's body heat?

Fearing the worst, he grabbed the scanner and stared in the exact direction of the beacon. Kurt wasn't there, but in the darkness Joe caught sight of a dim flash, too dim to be seen from more than twenty or thirty feet away.

"There," he said.

El Din nudged the throttles and then brought them back. The boat coasted forward on the impulse, closing the gap. As the dim flash came into range, Joe used a fishing net, stretching over the side. He scooped a familiar-looking cylinder out of the water.

"Is that what I think it is?" El Din asked.

Joe nodded. "Kurt's transmitter."

"So where is the man who's supposed to be attached to it?"

A sudden rumble from the yacht drowned out any reply. Joe turned to see water churning at the aft end of the big vessel and the bow of the yacht swinging around rapidly as if guided by a bow thruster. Almost simultaneously the twin spotlights on the bridge converged on the small fishing boat and the sea around it.

In quick order the behemoth was charging toward them.

"Go," Joe shouted.

El Din gunned the throttles and turned away from the yacht, setting a heading for the shore. As the chase began, Joe saw a big problem with their plan. The yacht was still accelerating and already gaining on them.

"We can't outrun it," he shouted. "Turn toward her."

"Are you sure?"

"Quickly," Joe shouted. He was amazed by the speed of the *Massif*'s acceleration. It was bearing down on them like a thundering giant, eating up the distance rapidly.

El Din spun the wheel to port. The outboard motors pivoted in their cradles and the nimble little boat curled back toward the big yacht. Joe had to hold on to keep from being tossed out.

The *Massif* tried to match their turn but was simply unable to change direction fast enough. The little boat raced by less than a hundred feet from the yacht.

Gunfire rang out and Joe dove for cover. He gazed up at the side of the yacht as it swept by.

"We have a problem," he said.

"If you mean getting shot full of holes," El Din said, "I'd have to agree with you."

"Unfortunately, that's not the problem I was talking about," Joe said. "I'm afraid we need to get closer."

"Closer? Why would we want to get closer?"

"Because Kurt is clinging to the side of their hull."

CHAPTER 20

From his position, the side of the hull, Kurt had watched the fishing boat coast to a stop. He'd felt the sudden surge of power through the hull of the *Massif* as the gas turbine engines came on full bore and her twin screws bit into the warm gulf waters.

He'd hoped the boat with his friends on board would run for the shallows, but they'd turned and raced back toward him, passing in clear view.

The two vessels were now caught in a stalemate. Like a grizzly bear being pestered by a yappy little dog, the big yacht could not turn with the small boat. But if the fishing boat tried to flee, the *Massif* would use her great speed to run the small boat down.

When gunfire rang out, Kurt knew he had to go on the offensive.

As the yacht leaned into another turn, Kurt began a

slow climb. He moved straight up, heading for the anchor and the hawsehole, where the chain came through the hull.

The higher up he went, the more angled the bow became. It was like climbing an inverted overhang. He had to be careful. If one of the magnets slipped, he might fall from his perch and hit the water in front of the ship's bulk. An image of his body getting crushed under the keel and then shredded by the propellers at the aft end flashed through his mind.

He shook it off. "I really have to learn to think positive," he told himself.

He made it to the hawsehole, squeezed through, and found himself on the foredeck just as the yacht whipped into another turn. With all eyes tracking their prey, no one saw him.

"Too bad this isn't the engine room," he muttered, thinking of all the damage he could cause back there. "But it'll have to do."

Another burst of gunfire rang out and the spotlights swung around overhead until they pointed down the starboard quarter.

Kurt scrambled to where the anchor chain was wrapped around a large capstan. A fierce-looking metal hook, known as a devil's claw, secured the chain.

A check of the control panel told him it was a standard type. He activated the power, eased the chain back, and unhooked the claw.

He considered dropping the anchor until it caught the seafloor. The average depth of the Persian Gulf was only a hundred fifty feet, and they had plenty of chain for that. But the anchor itself was a fluke type. With the yacht traveling at such a high rate of speed, it would literally fly once it hit the water like a kite on the breeze.

Even if it did reach the seafloor and catch, it would just rip out the capstan and pull free from the hull. And if it took the full length of chain—to what was known as the bitter end—it wouldn't even do that, as the last link was designed to break under such a load.

Despite the confusion it would cause, cosmetic damage wouldn't help his friends much. Kurt made some quick mental calculations and pressed the release button. The chain began to play out, the fifty-pound links chattering loudly as they went.

THE SOUND REACHED all the way to the bridge, and a warning light flashed on the control panel.

"Captain," the helmsman said. "We're losing the port anchor."

It was Acosta who replied, pushing past the captain. "What do you mean?"

"Someone's released it."

The anchor hit the water with a splash and slammed against the hull in the slipstream. The clang of the impact reverberated through the ship.

"The intruder is still aboard!" Acosta said. "That's why we couldn't find him. Get a spotlight on the foredeck!"

Acosta raced to the stubby bridge wing and watched as the spotlight changed its aim and lit up the foredeck.

"There!" he shouted, spotting a shape on the deck. "Kill him!"

Two of his men opened fire. Sparks lit out around the man on the foredeck. But with the deck pitching, it wasn't an easy shot. None of the bullets found their mark, and the intruder quickly ducked behind the bulkhead.

Acosta turned to the captain. "Can you stop the anchor from here?"

"No," the captain said. "He's switched it to manual. But . . ."

"But what?"

The captain had a perplexed look on his face. "For some reason, he's stopped it himself."

The ship began slewing to port, caused by the drag of the anchor on that side. Another tremendous clang rang out as the anchor slammed against a side of the hull farther back.

The sound was enough to send shivers down Acosta's spine. But the next impact was worse.

The anchor was now trailing out behind the vessel like a streamer out the side of a speeding car, swinging back and forth in the current. As it swung in once again, it whipped itself around the stern and caught one of the propellers.

With brutal efficiency, the four-ton anchor snapped off the spinning blades. An instant later the chain fouled the propeller shaft and was pulled tight. It snapped against the side of the hull like a plumb line, shattering windows and gouging a diagonal crease in the hull.

The sudden braking action on the propeller shaft

destroyed the transmission, and the yacht lurched and swooned to the right in response.

Acosta and the others were thrown against the control panel. The captain pulled back on both throttles immediately, and the yacht became controllable.

"What are you doing?" Acosta growled.

"Until we can slip that anchor and drop it to the bottom of the sea, we can't move at anything faster than quarter speed. Otherwise, we risk it swinging back up and destroying the other prop or punching a hole in the bottom of the hull."

Acosta's eyes bulged, the veins on his neck popped out. He turned to Caleb. "Get down there, kill him, and bring me his bullet-riddled carcass."

"I will," Caleb shouted, eager to redeem himself. He raced for the ladder with two others following him.

"If you don't succeed," Acosta warned, "don't bother to come back!"

FROM THE BACK of the fishing boat, Joe noticed the yacht losing ground. "They're slowing down," he shouted. "I think they're having some trouble."

"Can you tell what's happened?" El Din asked, craning his head around for a better look.

"No," Joe said. "But I'd bet Kurt had something to do with it."

The yacht was going off course, no longer following them. The spotlights seemed to be shining down on the foredeck.

"Now it's our turn," Joe said. "Bring us around wide and come at them from behind."

"Hold on," El Din said.

Joe grabbed the transom and held tight as the fishing boat made one more sharp turn.

ON THE FOREDECK, Kurt could tell his plan had worked. Now came the hard part: getting out alive. Each time he poked his head out from behind the bulkhead, a sniper up near the bridge took a potshot at him.

What he really needed was a way to take out the spotlights. But the Beretta was long gone, and the Colt he'd wrestled away from Caleb with the help of the magnets had been dislodged and tumbled into the sea when he'd crashed back into the side of the hull. After two more shots rang out, he saw the handle on the hatchway begin to turn. At the same moment, he noticed the fishing boat coming alongside. It was now or never.

He took off running, staying as close to the shelter of the bulkhead as possible. He raced past the hatch, slamming his shoulder into it just as it began to swing open. The heavy door closed on someone's arm with a sickening crunch.

Kurt only heard a fragment of an agonizing scream as he launched himself over the rail for a second time. This time he went headfirst, diving as far from the vessel as possible.

With perfect form, he knifed through the surface and went deep. Thin lines of bubbles probed the darkness like arrows as Acosta's men shot at him. The shots missed. Kicking hard, Kurt angled away from the yacht and down.

The yacht rumbled past, the anchor chain still fouled around the bent propeller shaft.

When the noise passed, Kurt began to swim horizontally. He kept swimming until his lungs felt as if they might burst, then surfaced in the dark and looked back.

The yacht was already turning. Out ahead of it he could see his friends coming around.

He didn't bother to yell—all that would get him was a mouthful of water—but he made every effort to kick hard, swimming at an angle that would make it easier for them to get him.

As the small boat raced in, Kurt rose up and waved. They changed course and bore down on him, slowing at the very last second.

"Grab this!" Joe shouted, throwing out a cargo net.

Kurt grasped it and began to pull himself forward. He was almost at the transom when the spotlights from the yacht swung across the water and found them.

Joe hauled him in, and El Din wasted no time in gunning the throttles.

The small craft took off again as a ribbon of shells skipped across the water, fired by Caleb and his mates from the bow of the yacht.

Splinters of wood flew in all directions. Kurt felt a bullet scrape his arm. But in seconds they'd passed out of the fire zone and were hightailing it into the dark.

The wounded yacht could not keep up. The gap widened by the moment, and after a few minutes the yacht began to turn away.

"We made it," El Din said.

Lying on the deck, exhausted and half surprised to be alive, Kurt looked around at his rescuers. "Is everyone okay?"

El Din nodded. Joe flashed a thumbs-up. "We're fine," Joe said. "What about you?"

"Never better," Kurt said.

"You're bleeding," El Din pointed out.

Kurt checked the wound. It was superficial. Another crease in the sheet metal. "Cut myself shaving," he joked. "Have to be more careful."

Joe laughed. He was glad to see Kurt's sense of humor had returned. It had been missing during his three months of recovery. "How'd it go on the yacht? Did you enjoy the party?"

"Not really my kind of people," Kurt replied. "But I can't say it was boring."

Kurt looked back. Far behind them, the lights of the *Massif* were blinking out one by one. She was resuming her original course, taking whatever secrets Kurt had failed to pry from her into the night.

Questions about the evening reverberated in his mind, beginning with the identity—not to mention the *sanity*—of the dark-haired woman he'd run into.

He wondered what she'd meant by the quips she'd thrown at him. Could she really have seen him somewhere before? Or was it just a ploy to distract him? What was she doing there in the first place? What could she possibly mean by saying he was *early*?

In some ways he owed her for shooting Acosta's thugs. On the other hand, they wouldn't have found him without her screaming. He wondered if she'd escaped the yacht during the commotion. More important, he wondered who she'd been talking to on the phone and what they were up to.

"No luck finding Sienna," Joe guessed.

"She wasn't on board, as far as I could tell."

"Any idea where she might be?" El Din asked.

"Not sure," Kurt replied. "But I overheard a phone call referencing someone they were calling 'the American woman.' Whoever she is, it sounds like she's been delivered into the hands of a guy named Than Rang."

"Who?" Joe asked.

"Korean industrialist. Probably some well-connected guy who could cause lots of trouble if he wanted to."

"When has that ever stopped us?" Joe asked, laughing.

"Never," Kurt said. "And it's not going to this time either. But something bigger is going on here. Something bigger and more complicated than a simple abduction."

"Any idea what?"

"Nope," Kurt said. "But I heard them talking about 'breaching the American Wall.' Whatever that means, we need to stop it from happening."

CHAPTER 21

"Than Rang is a stone-cold killer, not the kind of man you want to tangle with on a whim."

The words came from Dirk Pitt. They were spoken via an encrypted linkup that ended in the display screen of Joe's computer.

"Not going off on a whim," Kurt said. "If Sienna is out there, this guy Rang has her. And based on what I saw on that computer, he's gathering up a small stable of topflight hacking talent."

"I believe you," Pitt said. "The question is, why?"

"What's his background?" Kurt asked. "Maybe that will tell us something."

"He's the head of a South Korean chaebol. His corporation works in mining, waste management, and energy."

"Can you give us some details?"

"Than was born in '49, right before the Korean War.

His family fortunes were already in decline, but because the North ravaged so much of Seoul and the surrounding area when they occupied it, the decline of the family businesses intensified. At some point, his father got involved with underworld elements to keep the cash flow going. By the time Than was sixteen, the company did more smuggling and laundering than anything else. When his father died, a war broke out within the ranks. By the time it ended, Than had murdered all those who opposed him, wiped out the criminals who'd funded him, and killed every family member who disagreed with his leadership."

"A palace coup," Joe noted.

"And then some," Pitt said.

"Why didn't the government go after him?"

"Friends in high places," Pitt explained. "Most people forget that South Korea was basically a military-industrial dictatorship from 1951 to 1979. All emphasis was on growing the economy and doing so by any means necessary. They needed wealth to build a military and prepare for the next invasion by the North. Crimes had a way of being forgiven or ignored if they centralized power, brought about order, or increased industrial production."

"So Than Rang is a glorified street criminal," Kurt said. "But that doesn't tell us what he wants with computer experts."

"Could be any number of things," Pitt said. "Considering the structure of the chaebol and the intense competition in today's world, I'd lay my money on corporate espionage."

"Makes sense," Kurt said. "But the strange woman and her backers seemed to want these people for something else. She talked about breaching the American Wall. She also mentioned something called an air gap. Any idea what those terms mean?"

Pitt looked off the screen. "Hiram, you want to take this one?"

Hiram Yaeger came into view, long hair still in a ponytail, granny glasses firmly in place.

"Good morning, gentlemen," he said. "I'll get right to it. The term *American Wall* has been used in cyberspace for the last few years. It refers to an elaborate series of firewalls and defenses we've built up to protect the information infrastructure. The thing is, no one is supposed to know about them. These systems are operated exclusively by the NSA. They cover government institutions and important civilian corporations."

This took Kurt by surprise. "I keep hearing how vulnerable we are," he said. "Are you saying this isn't the case?"

"Let's put it this way," Hiram said. "We're not as weak as we pretend to be. But the fact that your friend was talking about breaching the wall and bringing the system down suggests they're contemplating something much bigger and deeper than your standard everyday hacking."

"She's not my friend," Kurt said testily, "though she did save my life."

"Odd, that," Pitt said.

"Trust me, that wasn't the only odd part," Kurt said.

Pitt laughed.

"How might Sienna and Phalanx fit into all this?" Kurt asked.

Hiram was blunt. "If Phalanx works, it will replace the existing wall. In effect, it will be the American Wall 2.0."

"What about these hackers?" Joe asked. "Any idea who they are?"

"We're working on it," Hiram said. "Aided and complicated by the fact that hackers have their own naming subculture."

"The woman called them handles," Kurt said.

"Exactly," Hiram replied. "They're more than just random call signs; they mean something. It's a way of getting in touch with the right person. For example, even though Xeno9X9 sounds like a random string of letters and numbers, it actually tells us about the hacker's skills. Xeno meaning 'foreign,' 9X9 being similar to the old radio terminology 'five by five,' meaning 'strong signal, clear signal.' My best guess is that Xeno9X9 is someone who can hack across borders with little problem."

Pitt chimed in. "Based on prodigious amounts of research, we believe he's a Ukrainian named Goshun. Interestingly enough, he went missing over a year ago. The prevailing thought was that he'd gone on the lam because his identity had become known. Now we're wondering if Acosta had something to do with it."

Kurt made a mental note of that. "What about the others?"

"We think ZSumG is short for 'zero sum game,'" Hiram said, "a term commonly used in economic and market theories. It means one side can profit *only* if the other side loses an equal amount."

"One winner, one loser," Joe said. "No way for a win-win outcome."

"Exactly," Hiram said.

"So ZSumG might be a financial hacker?" Kurt asked.

"That's our thought," Hiram said. "Based on the evidence, ZSumG is believed to have cracked the security of several major banks in the last five years, stealing millions of credit card numbers, identity profiles, and bank account pins. He then sold them to criminal groups around the world."

"Sounds like a lovely guy," Joe said.

"Or gal," Hiram said. "We're not sure. Which brings us to the last name: Montresor."

"Why does that sound familiar?" Joe asked.

Kurt had been thinking the same thing. The answer had come to him this morning. "Not keeping up on your required reading," he said to his friend.

"I wait till the end of summer break," Joe replied. "And then I cram it all in at the last minute."

Kurt laughed lightly and then spoke. "'The thousand injuries of Fortunato I had borne as best I could,'" he said. "'But when he ventured upon insult, I vowed revenge.'"

"'The Cask of Amontillado,'" Hiram explained to Joe. "The name comes from the Edgar Allan Poe classic."

"So it could be a reference to revenge," Joe suggested.

"Or to hiding things where they can't be found," Kurt guessed, "the way Montresor sealed Fortunato in the wall."

"Or he could be Italian and likes his red wine," Hiram said.

"Might want to check on Giordino," Kurt suggested.

"Don't think we haven't," Pitt said. "Turns out, he's still trying to master Space Invaders on his Commodore 64. So it's probably not him."

Kurt smiled, appreciating the moment of levity, but the fog of war had not lifted. "So we have no real answers," he said, "only more questions."

"What about the *Massif*?" Joe asked hopefully.

"We tracked her on satellite," Pitt said. "She's put into Bandar Abbas for repairs. Probably in need of a new propeller shaft. But since she's in Iranian waters, there's not much we can do to get a look at her."

"I'd guess all the big shots on board are long gone by now," Kurt said.

"Which puts us back to square one," Pitt added, taking center stage again. "We know there's some kind of hacker dream team for sale or rent out there, and at least two groups fighting over them. But we don't know why. And we're pretty certain neither group are the kind of players we'd like to be at the mercy of."

"Then we have only one choice," Kurt said. "To short-circuit both threats simultaneously."

"And how do you propose to do that?" Pitt asked.

"We go to South Korea and get this 'American woman' and the other hackers back. As long as they're in our hands, no one can use them against us."

CHAPTER 22

On the top floor of the NUMA building in Washington, Dirk Pitt and Hiram Yaeger sat on one side of the communications console. Kurt and Joe had just signed off.

Pitt decided it was time to get the temperature of the room. "Well," he said, "what do you think?"

Across from him, out of sight and silent during the call, sat Trent MacDonald of the CIA, a man named Sutton from the NSA, and two others from NUMA: Dr. Elliot Smith, who'd become NUMA's chief medical officer, and Anna Ericsson.

Pitt didn't like speaking to Kurt with these observers watching from the shadows like some kind of judging committee, but considering how the stakes were rising, it needed to be done.

Dr. Smith spoke first. "Kurt looks stable. His affect is normal and he's not reporting any symptoms."

"That's good," Pitt said.

Smith gave a noncommittal shrug. "It is, except that symptoms like Kurt's shouldn't just vanish because he got away from Washington."

"I've always found leaving this place cures a few ills," Yaeger added, clearly hoping Kurt was on the road to recovery.

"Maybe," Smith said, "but not the kind Kurt had."

Pitt jumped in. He wanted concrete statements, not vague assertions. "Meaning what?"

"I'd say we can expect his symptoms to return at some point. Most likely, under a moment of extreme duress."

"Ms. Ericsson?" Pitt asked.

"He looks well to me. Better than he did when he was cooped up back here."

"What about his story?" Sutton asked.

"What about it?" Pitt said.

"Seems a little odd, don't you think? He got on board the yacht, found something extremely vague, was attacked, and then was rescued by this strange mystery woman. He supposedly got her satellite phone but lost it. Gave us a poor description. All things we have to take on faith."

"You think he was making that up?"

"That's just it," Sutton said. "He was the only one there. So we can't prove it one way or another."

"What about the call she made?" Pitt asked.

"We've been trying to determine if that happened," Sutton admitted. "No luck yet."

"It could have been foreign service," Hiram pointed out, "someone you don't have access to."

"We have access to everyone," Sutton assured him. "Trust me."

"What about the names of those hackers?" Pitt asked. "He didn't just pluck them out of thin air."

Sutton shrugged. He had no comeback to that.

"Now for the elephant in the room," Pitt said. "We know where Sutton stands. He thinks this is all one big delusion. But what does it mean if Kurt's actually onto something?"

Trent MacDonald wrung his hands for a second. Pitt noted that the CIA rep had been awfully quiet.

"Trent?"

"If he's onto something, if Sienna Westgate is alive and in the hands of foreign nationals or persons unknown, then we may have a bigger problem than any of us know. At the very least, we should let Kurt continue and look into this Than Rang character. With a little prodding, I might be able to pledge some help. We have a lot more assets on the Korean Peninsula than we do in Iran."

Dirk nodded quietly. He couldn't recall a time he'd gotten so much cooperation from the CIA. He wondered if it had something to do with Kurt's history there or, for that matter, with Sienna's. A thought formed in his mind. "Is Sienna Westgate still working for the CIA?"

MacDonald did not reply immediately. "In a manner of speaking," he said finally. "Sienna legitimately left the Agency eight years ago. We didn't want to lose her when she went private, but we couldn't compete with a guy like Westgate and all he had to offer."

"Go on," Pitt said.

"She was brilliant," MacDonald said, nodding to Hiram. "You've seen her work."

"A savant," Yaeger said. "And I mean that as the highest compliment I can give."

"Exactly," MacDonald said. "So we made a deal with her and Westgate. We gave them the beginnings of our most advanced theoretical system and asked them to build it into an unbreakable barrier."

"Which she turned into Phalanx," Pitt said.

MacDonald nodded.

"But you never expected it to get out of the bottle," Yaeger pointed out.

"No," MacDonald said. "And that possibility is daunting for two reasons. One, we're going to lose a lot of intelligence-gathering ability if the rest of the world co-opts Phalanx and keeps us from prying into their systems. But there's a bigger worry, one we don't know how to quantify."

"Which is?"

"We all believe that Phalanx is unbreakable. We've installed it on everything from the DOD computer network to the Social Security database, but no one knows as much about it as Sienna Westgate. She was the lead designer of the project, she was the only one entrusted with the technology we gave her, and she took it ten steps beyond. That means she knows its weaknesses better than anyone. She might even have designed a back door into the system in case she ever needed to use it. We have no way of knowing."

Pitt was beginning to understand. "And Phalanx is now protecting the entire federal government."

MacDonald nodded. Sutton did likewise.

"Maybe we should pull Phalanx off active duty," Pitt suggested.

"It's being considered," Sutton said. "But it would be premature and foolish to do so based on what we know at this point. We need proof one way or the other before we act."

MacDonald summed up. "I don't know if she's out there and in the hands of our would-be enemies," he said. "But as much as I hate to say it, I'd be a lot happier knowing for certain that she'd been dragged to the bottom of the sea and drowned."

As cold as the statement was, Pitt understood the thought. "Then we'd better get a team down to what's left of Westgate's sunken yacht," he said bluntly. "It's a long shot, considering the condition of the vessel. But if we find Sienna's body, then you guys can rest easy. And I can bring Kurt home."

CHAPTER 23

The NUMA vessel *Condor* sat calmly on a glittering sea two hundred miles northeast of the South African port city of Durban. The sun was high above and there wasn't a cloud in the sky. The sea was like glass.

With no weather on the horizon and the automated station system holding the *Condor* against the current and keeping her over the proper coordinates, there was little activity on the bridge.

The aft deck was a different story. A dozen men and women were clustered around a pair of davits as twin submersibles were being readied for launch.

The subs were called Scarabs, because they resembled the beetles of Egyptian legend. Instead of narrow and tube-shaped, like most submersibles, the Scarabs were flat and wide. They had a large bulbous front, made entirely of three-inch-thick clear polymer, and a rear compartment that tapered to a point, filled with equipment, battery packs, and ballast tanks. Thruster pods housed in short tubes on either side of the body looked like stubby legs, and a pair of large mechanical arms that sprouted from beneath the nose, carrying sampling probes and grabbing appendages, were reminiscent of a beetle's pincerlike claws.

Scarab One was the older model, painted international orange, the color of life jackets. *Scarab Two* was bright yellow, the color commonly associated with experimental submersibles. It had come from the factory only a month before, equipped with more power, newer, longer-lasting batteries, and an advanced touchscreen control system.

Standing one deck above the busy crewmen, Paul Trout watched with great interest as the subs were readied for operations, though he had no intention of going down in either of them.

Paul was the size and shape of a professional basketball player, though even he would admit not as coordinated or athletically gifted. What he lacked in sporting skills Paul made up for with a brilliant mind. A gifted geologist, he and his wife, Gamay, were often called on to run NUMA's most important scientific studies. While he excelled in geology, Gamay had a Ph.D. in marine biology and had made several important discoveries of previously unknown species.

Paul realized this latest mission would not offer such a positive find.

"Hey, Paul, care to join me?"

The shout came from William "Duke" Jennings, one of NUMA's most experienced submersible pilots.

"No thanks," Paul said. "I prefer something with lots of headroom. Or even a convertible, but that's not going to work a thousand feet under."

"Good point," Duke said. His next target was one of the more shapely women on deck. "What about it, Elena? Room for two in there. Can't beat the view."

By that, everyone knew Duke was referring to himself. Duke looked like a surfer: young and muscular, with bronzed skin and a mane of blond hair. Even now, he had his shirt off. He was humorous and cocky and pretty good at everything he did to back it up.

"No thanks," Elena responded. "I'd rather be in a phone booth with an amorous octopus."

Duke feigned grave injury. "Where are you going to find a phone booth these days?"

As the crew continued working, the hatch swung open behind Paul. Gamay stepped through, headed for his side.

Five foot ten, with hair the color of red wine, and smooth pale skin, Gamay was an athlete and in fantastic shape. She had a sharp wit that was usually used in jest, though you didn't want to be on her bad side, as she didn't suffer fools lightly.

"I see we're almost ready," she said.

"Just about," Paul said. "Think we're going to find anything down there?"

"I don't know," Gamay said. "But look at this."

She handed him a printout from the multibeam sonar scan. It showed the *Ethernet* lying on the seafloor eight hundred feet below. They were lucky. The ship had landed on a shelf that stuck out like a submerged peninsula in the deeper waters of the Mozambique Channel. Ten miles in either direction and she'd be sitting under four thousand feet of water.

Paul noticed something more significant almost immediately. "She's in one piece," he said. "Kurt was told the ship had broken up into several sections on the way down. None of us ever questioned it."

"I wonder where he got his information," Gamay replied.

"Or who had sent him the incorrect information," Paul asked.

"I talked with Ms. Ericsson," she said. "If the subconscious part of his mind is running with a fantasy or delusion, it will do everything it can to keep the story alive. Knowing the ship didn't break up would mean the task of confirming the truth was easily done by searching her."

"Then it was easy for him to take the report at face value. The delusion couldn't allow that to happen," Paul guessed.

"I'm told it's fairly common."

Paul felt a knot in his stomach. It was hard to fathom one of the people he admired most could be off his game so badly. It made him all the more determined that they should find the answer.

"Let's get this show on the road," he said.

Gamay nodded and made her way to the stairs. "I'll be in *Scarab One*."

"I'll monitor you from the control room," Paul said. "Be careful."

He gave her a kiss and let her go. As Gamay made her

way down to the aft deck, Paul took a long look around. He saw nothing but the peaceful sea in all directions. Hoping it would stay that way, he stepped inside.

WITH *SCARAB ONE* ready to be hoisted, Gamay climbed in and took a seat on the right-hand side. To her left sat Elena Vasquez, the submersible's pilot. Elena was petite, with short black hair and a mocha-colored complexion. A former Navy diver, she was a recent addition to NUMA.

While Elena drove the sub, Gamay would handle the undersea communications and operate the mechanical arms, which were outfitted with cutting tools, including acetylene torches and a circular saw with a diamond-tipped carbon steel blade. It could cut through two-inch armor plate with ease. Attached to the other arm was a small hydraulic wedge, something like the Jaws of Life that paramedics used to pry open mangled cars on the highway.

The plan was simple: Cut open the side of the hull, send a remote "swimming" camera into the ship, and look for the bodies.

Gamay put on a headset and ran through her checklist. Elena did the same from her command seat.

"My board is green," Elena said.

"Mine too," Gamay replied. She spoke into the headset's microphone. "*Scarab One* ready to go. Put us in the water."

The hydraulics of the crane went into action and the

eight-ton craft was lifted from the deck and carried over the side of the *Condor*. With careful precision, it was lowered into the waiting sea.

A loud clanking sound and the feeling of the craft settling told them the submersible had been released.

"Scarab One, *you're clear of the boom. Turning you over to control.*"

With that, Paul's voice came on the radio. "*You're clear to dive.*"

Seconds later, Duke's voice came over the headset with mock indignation. "*You're cutting in line,* Scarab One. *I was supposed to go first.*"

"You snooze, you lose," Gamay replied.

Elena chuckled. "Girls rule, boys drool," she added over the radio. "Deploying communications beacon. See you on the bottom."

With a calm hand, Elena flicked through a series of switches. Air began to vent from the sub's ballast tanks, and the green seawater swirled up around the clear cockpit, soon engulfing them.

Elena engaged the thrusters. With incredible smoothness, the orange vehicle began the long dive. It would be nearly thirty minutes before the bottom would be visible.

Gamay switched the exterior lights on as they passed two hundred feet. At a depth of almost eight hundred feet, the seafloor came into view.

"*Scarab One* on the floor," Gamay said. Her radio call was transmitted up a fiber-optic cable no thicker than a monofilament fishing line to a small buoy at the surface.

The buoy had an antenna that relayed the signal to the *Condor.* "Proceeding to the wreck site."

Moments later, the wreck came into view. The *Ethernet* was sitting on its keel in the silt, almost perfectly upright. There was some crushing damage near the bow as she'd clearly hit nose-first, but little else seemed damaged.

"We have her in sight," Gamay replied. "Front end looks like an accordion, topside external structures seem fine. Radar mast and antennas are missing. But, other than that, she looks like she's on display at a boat show."

As they circled around the port side of the *Ethernet,* Gamay caught sight of lights dropping down through the black water on the starboard side. "Duke, is that you? Or are we being visited by UFOs?"

"You can all relax," he replied. *"The Duke is on the job."*

Gamay rolled her eyes. "Glad you could join us. We'll work the port side, you work the starboard. That way, we keep our comm lines from getting tangled."

"Roger that," Duke replied.

Elena turned to Gamay. "Where do you want to start?"

"Let's go in up top," Gamay said. "That's where Westgate said his wife and kids were waiting. It's also where Kurt may or may not have seen them."

Elena nodded and rotated the thrusters. The Scarab rose up along the side of the hull, moving slowly toward the shattered windows of the bridge.

"We could put the camera in through the window," Elena suggested.

"I don't like the look of all that glass," Gamay said.

"If it cuts the wire, we'll lose the swimmer. Let's pull the door off."

Elena nodded and operated the control column and thrust lever with the skill of a fighter pilot.

She focused one of the spotlights on the hatch. It was slightly ajar. When Elena brought the Scarab in close enough, Gamay was able to grasp it with one of the sub's claws. A few pulls told her it was stuck.

"We're going to have to cut it loose," she said.

The sub began drifting back.

"We're caught in a crosscurrent swirling over the superstructure," Elena explained.

"Can you compensate?"

"With ease."

As they repositioned, Duke's voice came over the radio. *"This side is in fairly good shape. No sign of damage that couldn't be attributed to hitting the bottom. Continuing inspection."*

By now Elena had repositioned the sub, and Gamay was ready with the cutting torch.

With a snap and sizzle, the acetylene torch flared to life. A stream of bubbles flowed toward the surface. They cut through the hinges and grasped the door with the gripper handle. With a light pull, Gamay drew the heavy steel door back and it toppled slowly onto the deck with a muted thump.

"Releasing camera," Gamay said.

In a moment the Scarab's little swimming camera was heading inside the sunken yacht. It had its own spotlight and power source but was tethered to the Scarab by a thin fiber-optic line through which the camera feed was relayed.

"The bridge is filled with debris," she noted. She directed the camera to pan and scan and soon they had a three-sixty swath of everything on the bridge. The glass wall—which Kurt had seen—was still in place, though it was covered with a network of cracks.

"Looks like a Pennsylvania road map," she noted.

Between the damage and the thin film of slime that had grown upon it, they could not see through it.

"Have to go around," Gamay said.

An open hatchway suggested a possible route, and Gamay sent the camera in that direction.

"Weird that all the hatches are open." This came from Paul, who was seeing the same video feed as they were. *"Considering that the ship was in distress and going down, all the watertight doors should have been shut."*

As Gamay directed the small camera toward the hatch, Duke chimed in.

"Got something over here, Condor. *Sea cocks for the engine cooling system appear to be open."*

"If the ship was taking on water, those should have been closed as well," Gamay replied.

"My thoughts exactly," Duke said. *"Heading to the stern."*

Gamay guided the camera into the main salon. She couldn't bring herself to hope they'd find a drowned woman and her children. Not even if it meant the end of the mystery.

"Scoping out the salon now," she said.

Like the bridge, the main salon was filled with debris. The heavier items remained on the floor. The buoyant items—cushions, life vests, plastic bottles, and bins—floated around the ceiling. She had to guide the camera beneath them, like flying under a cloud layer.

Fortunately, they were deep enough that little algae could grow, but there was plenty of silt in the water, courtesy of the Mozambique current and the "snow" falling from above. And despite the fact that the camera's thrusters were tiny, they stirred it up with each maneuver.

Duke came on the line again. *"Got a gaping hole at the stern end."*

"Impact or explosion?" Paul asked from above.

"I'd say neither," Duke replied. *"The edges are too sharp. It almost looks like an entire plate is missing from the hull. I'll deploy the camera and send up some pretty pics."*

Gamay listened to the chatter but concentrated on the task at hand. Having reached the far corner, she turned the camera around for another run to the front of the salon.

"Going idle for a minute," she said. "The main cabin is getting clouded by silt. I need to let it settle."

As she waited for the water to clear, Duke's voice came back over the radio. *"Something odd here. I've put the camera in through the hole on what I'm fairly certain is deck number two. Should be aft staterooms. Instead, it's like some kind of equipment bay."*

"Better check the schematics," Elena said. "Knowing Duke, he's cut into the wrong deck."

Gamay tapped the computer screen in front of her and brought up the structural drawings of the ship. NUMA had downloaded them from the manufacturer. It showed a storeroom above the keel, then cabins on deck two, then a lounge at the top.

"There's a cradle in here," Duke said. *"It's fairly strong rigging. Clearly designed to support something heavy. I see a watertight door at the far end. There's something written on the door. Trying to get close enough to read it."*

Still waiting for the silt in the main cabin to settle, Gamay switched to the video feed from Duke's camera. The lens was facing away as Duke used the thrusters to blast the slime from the watertight door he'd found.

When he spun the camera back around and pointed it toward the door, Gamay could see a gray bulkhead of heavy steel. Yellow chevrons cut across it like warning signs. Beneath the chevrons were two words.

"'Survival Pod,'" Gamay said, reading aloud. "The ship has been modified since it left the builder."

"I've heard about those," Elena said. "Just like some celebrities have panic rooms where they can hide from stalkers or the zombie apocalypse, some of these bigwigs have outfitted their ships with 'escape pods' and 'panic boats.' The owners climb in, seal the door, and eject from the sinking ship."

"That explains the smooth outline of the hole," Duke said. *"Looks like a panel was blown out with explosive bolts."*

Gamay nodded. "Once they're free, the pod can either float or submerge up to a hundred feet. Deep enough to keep them out of the reach of pirates or terrorists. Or to ride out the worst storm imaginable. Depending on how many occupants, they might have a week of supplies and at least a day or two of oxygen. They call for help with the same kind of buoy transmitter we're using and either Coast Guard or contracted security companies come in and scoop them up."

Paul broke in. *"So if the yacht had one, why didn't Westgate and his family use it?"*

"Maybe he couldn't get to it," Duke suggested. *"Maybe the lower decks were flooded."*

"Someone got to it," Gamay pointed out.

"Maybe some other crew members."

"So where are they?" Elena asked.

Gamay felt a chill on her neck. "Maybe something's going on here after all."

"Hate to be a wet blanket," Paul said, *"but any number of things could explain the missing pod, including a malfunction, or some type of auto release. Suppose the ship goes beyond a certain state, like being submerged? Let's not get ourselves all worked up just yet."*

"My husband," Gamay said. "The voice of reason. I'll make sure to repeat those words to you next time your Red Sox are blowing a lead in the bottom of the ninth."

"As long as it's not against the Yankees."

Gamay smiled and switched back to the feed from her own camera. The silt had cleared. She made a last lap in the main salon, moving slowly, trying not to miss anything.

She was about to exhale when she caught sight of a

hand floating limply beyond some roughly piled furniture. "Damn."

"What's wrong?" Paul asked.

"I think I've found someone."

"I don't see anything on the screen," Paul said.

"Hold on," she said. "Looks like everything that wasn't nailed or tied down slid forward and to one side as the yacht sank. I have to maneuver around a pile of junk."

With her heart racing more than she'd care to admit, Gamay brought the camera around the pile of furniture and focused the small floodlight until the image resolved. And she could clearly see a body, bloated by the water and trapped by the piled furniture, come into view.

"I hate to say it," Elena whispered, "but that man didn't drown."

"Nope," Gamay agreed. "By the look of things, he never got the chance."

Despite the damaging effects of the salt water, three bullet holes in his chest were clearly visible.

CHAPTER 24

Eight hundred feet above the sunken yacht, Paul stared at a computer screen that was displaying the view from Gamay's camera.

The bullet wounds were unmistakable.

Pressing a button, he froze the image and e-mailed it directly to Dirk Pitt.

He pulled the freestanding microphone closer to his mouth. "Keep searching," he said. "Be meticulous. This is no longer a recovery mission. It's now a crime scene."

Duke replied quickly. The call from Gamay was a little garbled.

"Say again, *Scarab One?*"

This time Paul heard even less. A burst of static came from the speaker and then a squeal, sharp enough to hurt his ears.

Paul clicked the transmit button. "Gamay, do you read?"

He waited.

"Gamay? Elena?"

He called across the control room to another member of the team. "Oscar, do you have their telemetry?"

Oscar was flicking through screens of his own. "Nothing," he said. "I'm getting a signal from the buoy, but no data from *Scarab One*."

Paul grabbed the microphone again. "Duke, do you read me?"

"Loud and clear."

"We've lost telemetry from Elena and Gamay. It might just be the wire, but can you get over there and check?"

"On my way" came Duke's firm reply.

Paul tried not to worry. The filament linking the buoy to the Scarab was extremely thin, and the connectors often had problems, but he didn't like losing contact with his wife when there was eight hundred feet of crushing water between them.

Paul drummed his fingers on the desk as he waited. He tapped the refresh key on the computer, hoping the data from Gamay's sub would pop up once again. It didn't.

"Come on, Duke," he whispered to himself. "Let's not dawdle."

A flutter ran through the screen, and Paul hoped the image was about to reappear. Instead, the screen froze and went black.

"What in the world . . ."

At the same time, the overhead lights went dark. All around, the little green LEDs on the computer towers and keyboards went out. And Paul could hear the sound of the ventilating system shutting down.

A group of battery-powered emergency lights came on.

"What's happening?" Oscar called from the other side of the console.

Paul looked around. Without the fans blowing, the air went still. He clicked the microphone transmit button a few times, but to no avail. "Looks like someone forgot to pay the electric bill."

With the AC units off, it got stuffy in the tiny control room very quickly.

Paul stepped over to the intercom, but it too was dead. He cracked the door. The gangway was dark. "Stay here," he said to Oscar. "I'm going to find out what's going on."

Paul slipped through the door and down the hall. Aside from the emergency lights, every compartment was dark. The engines were off. The ship was dead in the water.

He climbed a ladder amidships and entered the bridge. Only the helmsman was there.

"What's going on?"

"Power's out all over the ship."

"I can see that," Paul said. "Does anyone know why?"

"Cap'n went to check with the chief," the helmsman said. "Main electrical bus went out. Followed by the backup. All systems are dead."

Paul was about to turn and head for engineering when he felt a subtle vibration travel through the hull. The engines and auxiliary power unit were coming back on. "Thank goodness for small favors," he muttered.

He went to the intercom. It was still out. So was the radio. He flicked the light switch. Nothing.

As Paul wondered why, he noticed the *Condor* was beginning to move. Not just holding station in the current but accelerating. He stepped to the command console. There was power for the display, but as the helmsman tapped various icons on the screen nothing happened.

The ship began to turn, healing over as if the rudder had been deflected all the way to the stops.

"It's not me," the helmsman insisted. He was holding the small wheel that controlled the rudder dead center.

The ship continued to accelerate, straightening out and heading due south. They continued to pick up speed. In a moment the ship was running flat out, racing across the glassy sea and cutting a white swath away from the two submersibles and the wreck below.

A warning light on the console showed the propeller rpm's reaching maximum and going beyond. "You have to reduce speed," Paul urged.

"I'm trying," the helmsman said. "Nothing's working."

The rpm's were already three percent beyond the red line. "Why isn't the limiter cutting in?"

Another crewman joined them on the bridge and went to the circuit breaker panel.

"Hit the override," Paul shouted. "Emergency stop."

The helmsman did as Paul ordered. He slammed his palm onto the yellow-and-red emergency stop button that acted as the override. The ship continued to charge south.

It dawned on Paul that the override was just another

button to tell the computer to stop doing whatever it was doing. But if the system was faulty or had been corrupted, there was no reason to expect the override to be working correctly.

With the rpm's still climbing, a shaft failure was possible, or even bearing failure in the engines themselves.

"Keep trying," Paul said. "I'm headed to the engine room."

FROM HER SEAT in the cockpit of *Scarab One*, Gamay continued transmitting to the *Condor*. "Paul, do you read me? Come in, *Condor*?"

With no luck, she tried contacting Duke in *Scarab Two*. "Duke, how's your radio?"

There was no response. But, seconds later, *Scarab Two* appeared, rising over the far side of the wreck like the sun coming up. Gamay saw the thrusters align with the body, and the yellow submersible began to come their way. It moved slowly, its lights aimed oddly downward toward the wreck instead of forward.

"The radio must be out," Gamay said to Elena.

"I'll flash him," Elena said.

"I bet he's been dreaming about that," Gamay joked.

Elena smiled and began to toggle the lights, tapping out a quick message in Morse code: *Radio out.*

Scarab Two continued their way. It eased over the superstructure of the sunken yacht and began descending toward them. The lights finally came up and focused on them, but there was no flashed message in response.

Elena shielded her eyes. "Thanks for blinding us, Duke."

"He's coming in awfully fast," Gamay said.

"Too fast," Elena said. With a flick of her wrist, she put the thrusters in reverse and tried to back out of the way, but Duke's sub bore down on them at full speed and rammed them, cockpit to cockpit. It was a glancing blow, but they were knocked sideways just the same. Gamay felt herself thrown about in the seat.

"What is wrong with him?" Elena blurted out, struggling to get control.

Gamay looked around. There were no leaks that she could see. No cracks. The Scarabs were certified to depths of two thousand feet—their hulls were immensely strong—but the bumper car experience was one she'd rather have on dry ground in an amusement park.

She looked out through the clear dome of the cockpit. *Scarab Two* was turning around and coming back their way, moving even faster this time.

"Something's not right," she said.

"What is it?"

"I don't know," Gamay said. "Go. Just go!"

Elena slammed the throttles forward and pushed the control column down and to port. The yellow shape of Duke's craft raced overhead and turned back to the left.

"What is he doing?" Elena asked. "Has he lost his mind?"

"I have no idea," Gamay said. "Just keep us moving."

"I've got the throttles full open," Elena said. "But Duke's in a newer ride, with upgraded thrusters and newer batteries. I hate to say it but we're outclassed."

Gamay could see that plainly. This time Duke side-swiped them and tried to force them into the hull of the *Ethernet*.

Elena reversed thrust and the orange submersible slowed. Duke shot past once again.

"Now what?"

"Take us up."

"He'll catch us if we try to surface."

"Not all the way," Gamay said. "Just over to the other side of the wreck."

Elena twisted the control column upward and the thrusters pivoted into a vertical position. The sub rose up, cleared the superstructure, and sped across it. As soon as they hit the other side, Elena pushed the column forward and forced the sub down behind the yacht's stern, tucking them into a spot at the rear section of the hull.

"Douse the lights!" Gamay said, flicking a series of switches on her side.

Elena reached forward and switched off the main floods and the sub was plunged into utter darkness. Gamay sighed. "Now, hold your breath," she said. "And hope he doesn't find us."

UP ON THE SURFACE, on the racing vessel, Paul dropped onto the main deck and sprinted aft. The *Condor* was charging across the water like a three-thousand-ton speedboat, all but planing across the sea.

Halfway to the engine room, he found the captain, who was rushing forward to the bridge.

"What in the name of Poseidon are they doing up there?" the captain shouted.

"It's not the crew," Paul said. "Something's wrong with the system."

"I should have known better than to accept a ship controlled by computers," the captain said.

"We have to get back to the engine room," Paul said. "She's over-revving. We'll blow out the propulsion units if we don't shut them down."

The captain turned around and ran with Paul to the aft end of the ship. They ducked inside and took a ladder down to the engine compartment. The noise was ear-shattering and verbal communication was all but impossible.

They found the chief and another member of the crew trying desperately to slow the engines down. The captain made a cutting motion across his neck.

The chief shook his head.

"What about the fuel pumps?!" Paul shouted at the top of his lungs.

They looked at him.

He leaned closer. "Fuel pumps! There must be an emergency shutoff in case of fire!"

The chief nodded and waved for them to follow. Like many modern ships, the Condor was powered not by heavy diesel engines but by a high-tech gas turbine system. Essentially, a jet engine connected to heavy reduction gearing and then to the propeller shaft or shafts.

As they put a bulkhead between them and the turbines, the sound lessened just enough that shouted communications could be heard.

"There are two turbines," the chief said. "Two fuel pumps. Climb that half ladder and reach in behind the gauges. The red lever will shut off the fuel. I'll handle the starboard pump. You take the port."

Paul nodded and went to the ladder. The ship was shuddering and bucking with the speed. The heat from the turbines was like a blast furnace. With sweat pouring into his eyes, Paul climbed up and found the instrument cluster. He noticed the rpm indicator at one hundred thirty-nine percent. Well above the red line.

Without delay, he spied the emergency shutoff lever, grabbed it, and yanked it down hard.

The fuel cut out and the turbine instantly began a rapid deceleration. It was more than the reduction gearing could handle.

With a loud bang and the shriek of tearing metal, something major blew apart in the system. Paul found himself diving for the deck and covering his head as shrapnel flew through the compartment.

The hurtling missiles of steel cut apart several cables and a coolant line. Steam came blasting out and filled the compartment.

Paul looked up as the commotion died. He could feel the ship slowing even as the compartment filled with steam. He got to his feet, drenched in sweat, and made his way back to where the captain and the chief had been. The captain was on the ground, a nasty-looking gash on his leg bleeding badly.

"Get me up," the captain ordered, holding the wound. "I need to see if we're all right."

Paul helped the captain to his feet. The chief pushed the hatches open to help clear the room.

The ship was coasting.

"We're definitely coming to a stop," Paul said.

"What happened?" the captain asked.

"Something went wrong in the master control unit," Paul said. "It came alive on its own and wouldn't respond. We're dealing with people who know how to hack computers. And this ship is one of the newest in the fleet. It's basically one big computer."

The captain nodded weakly, getting whiter by the second. "Rip out all the computers and pull the circuit breakers. We'll row this ship, if we have to, but I'm not losing control of my vessel again."

CHAPTER 25

Down below, Gamay Trout gazed into the darkness as the superstructure of the wreck became a silhouette, back-lit by the floodlights of Duke's sub. It was an eerie sight and it sent a chill down her spine. She noticed Elena's hands on the throttle.

"Hold on," she said.

From the darkness, *Scarab Two* appeared, cruising over the *Ethernet* like some predatory fish.

"He's following our last heading," Elena noted.

Gamay watched as the glowing orb surrounding the yellow sub continued to track away from them. It was like watching a spaceship cross some void in the depths of the galaxy. There was no frame of reference. The seafloor was black, the water around them into the distance was black. Directly above was black. Though it was broad daylight at the surface with a cloudless sky, no light could penetrate this deep.

Even the lights from Duke's submersible faded as he headed into the dark. After several minutes, they too vanished, swallowed up by the depths.

"Where do you suppose he's going?" Elena asked.

"Looking for us," Gamay began. "Why? I don't know. This doesn't make any sense."

"Something big is going on here," Elena said.

"Seems that way."

"I should have known," Elena said. "When the Special Projects Division gets involved, it's usually trouble. At least that's what the scuttlebutt is."

Gamay could not disagree.

"Too much excitement for me," Elena said.

"Me too," Gamay replied. "Me too."

"Shall we surface?"

"Can you do it without the lights?"

"With ease."

Gamay took one last look into the dark. "Let's go. I want to warn Paul and the others as soon as possible."

Elena added some power and the interior display lit up to show the thruster levels. She eased them away from the yacht and was rotating the thrusters when a set of blinding lights came on, aimed right into the cockpit. The four lights surged toward them like the eyes of some undersea monster. A hideous scraping sound assaulted their ears as the grappling arms of Duke's Scarab clamped onto them like great claws.

Gamay grabbed her own controls and tried to use the arms of their submersible in defense.

But before she could do much, Duke had grasped one

of the arms and attacked it with the rotary saw. It snapped off in seconds, and Gamay was left fighting with only one arm.

"Use the torch," Elena shouted.

Gamay ignited their acetylene torch and brought it down on Duke's cockpit, planning to burn a hole in the bubblelike canopy. To her surprise, she saw Duke's face in the light and he looked terrified. He held up his hands even as his machine continued to shove the older Scarab backward.

"It's not him," Gamay shouted. "He's not in control."

Instead of torching a hole in the cockpit and killing Duke, she moved the arm to the side and tried to cut off one of his thrusters. At almost the same instant, they were pushed into the wreck and their own port thruster was bent and rendered inoperative.

Duke's sub now had at least twice their power.

"He's pinning us down," Elena shouted.

"I'm telling you, it's not him," Gamay replied.

She extended the torch and began burning off one of Duke's thrusters, but the circular saw from Duke's sub shot forward. It skipped up the cockpit glass, leaving an ugly scar, and began grinding on their back.

The hoses to their acetylene torch were sliced through and the sub was instantly surrounded by a whirlwind of bubbles that ignited. Fire engulfed both Scarabs as they battled in the deep.

In the garish illumination, Gamay saw Duke get up from his seat with a black crescent wrench in his hand. He was slamming it against the computer console, smashing the control unit. After a third or fourth hit, the lights on his sub went out and the turbulence of the battle ceased.

The subs, locked together and enveloped in bubbles and flame, fell slowly to the seafloor. They hit the silt and were still. A moment later, the acetylene tanks were fully vented and the fire burned out.

The world became utterly dark. Gamay flicked a few switches.

"He cut our power lines," Elena said. "Or his *sub* did," she added, correcting herself.

Gamay found a flashlight and switched it on. Amazingly, there were no leaks in the cabin yet. She narrowed the beam and held it to the window. It cast just enough light to see the yellow nose of *Scarab Two*.

Using the flashlight like a semaphore, she tapped out a message to Duke. *Are you all right?*

A few seconds later, a response came. *Sorry, ladies, I don't know what happened.*

Gamay realized what Paul had also discerned up on the surface. They'd been hacked. Duke's newer sub was the target. Its touchscreen control system made it vulnerable, unlike the older Scarab with its manual hydraulic systems.

It seems you've been hacked, Gamay replied with the light.

As Duke's reply came in, Gamay read it aloud. "'Nothing left to hack now. I've smashed everything in sight and ripped out all the wires . . . Don't suppose they'll take this out of my paycheck, do you?'"

Gamay smiled. And Elena shook her head as she grinned.

"Can we surface?" Gamay asked Elena.

"We have no power, but we can blow out the ballast tanks," she said. "Duke should be able to do the same."

Gamay nodded and tapped out the thought.

There was a delay in responding, and they could see Duke moving around in the cockpit, using his flashlight to check readings on the few analog gauges still present in the new Scarab. He seemed to spend a lot of time at the aft wall.

"What's he checking?"

"The emergency air valve," Elena said, pointing to a gauge and valve in the same spot on their sub.

Afraid I won't be making the trip, Duke signaled. *Seems you've cut into my compressed air tank. Not enough left to gain positive buoyancy. You gals will have to go up first and then come back and get me.*

How much air do you have?

Five hours' worth. Plus what's left in the cabin.

"Should be plenty of time," Elena said.

Gamay agreed. All they had to do was get a cable down here and they could use the *Condor*'s winch to haul Duke back to the surface.

"Good thing Paul didn't join him," Gamay said. "He'd have half as much air."

"And you'd be twice as worried."

That was true, though Gamay was worried enough for Duke as it was. She tapped out a new message.

We're going up. Hope you can stand being rescued by a couple of girls.

If it means I get to see the sunlight again, I'll wear a women's lib T-shirt for the rest of the trip.

"That, I'd like to see," Elena said, putting her hand on the release valve. "Prepare to blow tanks."

Good luck, Gamay signaled.

You too.

With that, Elena turned the valve. A turbulent hissing sound followed as high-pressure air forced its way into the ballast tanks. As the water was forced out, the submersible slowly began to rise.

There was a brief pause and some odd metallic clangs as they untangled from Duke's sub, and then they were free and ascending.

A few more flashes of light from Duke came forth. *If you spot a waiter, send me down a drink.*

Gamay laughed and turned her attention upward. For now, it remained black up above, as dark as a night without any stars or moon. She couldn't wait for the first hint of grayish green that told her the surface was not too far away.

A minute went by. And then another. Gamay began to feel a little dizzy. "I feel like I'm in a sensory deprivation tank," she said.

"My thoughts exactly," Elena said.

Gamay decided to keep her head level. Looking up was messing with her inner ear and giving her vertigo.

She glanced at her watch. "Ten minutes."

"Fifteen more to go," Elena said.

It was a smooth ride until suddenly they were jarred by an impact. Gamay was thrown forward and whiplashed back into her seat.

"What was that? Did something hit us?"

Elena was looking up as if they'd crashed into the bottom of a ledge or the hull of the *Condor* or something. Gamay didn't think so. She'd felt the impact come up through her feet and her lower back like it did when she and Paul went four-wheeling.

She pulled the flashlight from her pocket and flicked it back on. Holding it against the window, she saw clouds of silt and then the featureless gray-brown of the seafloor.

"We're back on the bottom," she said.

A light flashed on and off, perhaps thirty yards away.

Missed me that much?

Gamay released her belt and climbed halfway out of her seat. She twisted around and held the flashlight against the rear section of the canopy. Thin streams of bubbles were flowing from the ballast tanks on the Scarab's back. It looked like someone had opened a whole box of Alka-Seltzer.

"You don't even have to tell me," Elena said, "I already know. Duke holed our ballast tanks with that saw."

Gamay nodded, sat back down, and switched the light off. "So much for Duke's piña colada. And our quick ride back into the sunlight."

"It's worse than that," Elena said. "There are two of us in here. And we just vented all our spare air. By my calculations, we have less than two hours left."

CHAPTER 26

In a darkened room, very similar to the *Condor*'s control center, Sebastian Brèvard stared at the pair of flat-screen monitors in front of him. He grinned almost maniacally in the cold computer light as Calista tapped away at the keyboard.

She looked up. "I'm afraid both links are dead, dear brother."

"Yes, I can see that," he said. "We're receiving nothing from either the NUMA sub or the *Condor*."

They'd just watched in living color—via NUMA's own cameras—as a virus of Calista's design unleashed chaos in the NUMA operation. By hacking a simple navigation update, they'd downloaded viruses on both the *Condor* and the Scarab. Those programs turned control of the computerized vessels over to a remote location—in this case, the Brèvard lair.

Only *Scarab One* had been immune, because its design was older and less automated.

With the skill of a hunter, Calista had used the controls at her fingertips to turn one of the NUMA submersibles into a killer, seeking out the other and smashing it against the hull of the wreck. Last she'd seen, they were locked in a death struggle with each other. Then all had gone dark.

"Well, you've gotten what you wanted," she said. "They've discovered the missing survival pod. They'll know the truth about the *Ethernet*'s sinking before too long."

"About time," her brother said. "I was beginning to think they'd never go look for it."

"Perhaps we shouldn't have edited the sonar scan to show the vessel in ruins."

"It was necessary," Brèvard said dismissively. "Once Austin began to recover, he immediately started looking into it. He would have made a dive there months ago if we didn't trick him. And that would have thrown our whole timetable off."

Her brother and his timetables. Everything had to be so complicated. "Won't they go after Westgate now?"

"Not right away. It will only ratchet up the suspicion. They will begin to investigate from afar. Hoping not to alert him."

"And then?"

"And then we will prod them along with another clue at the appropriate time."

One step at a time, she thought. But there was a

problem. "We have to assume they know they've been hacked, at this point."

"I would hope so," he said. "We need them to understand just how vulnerable they are. It will get the gears turning in the minds of the powerful. It will begin the chemical reaction that leads to doubt and confusion, it will create a hidden sense of panic and a *need* to do something about it. Anything. That's how they work. Action. Reaction. They will not sit still."

"You're planting a seed," she said.

He nodded. "One that will lead to the flowering of our plan."

She pushed out from the console, leaned back in her chair, and put her feet up on the desk. Thigh-high boots with stiletto heels landed on the desktop, clipping the keyboard.

"I wish you would be careful," he said.

She ignored him as usual.

"Now what," she said.

"Acosta is going to trade the hackers to the Korean," he said. "You and Egan are to take a group of the men and make contact with him. If you can bargain for them, then bargain. If not, let the deal go down and swoop in. Most likely, they will lead you right to Sienna Westgate. Bring her back so we can finish this."

CHAPTER 27

Paul Trout stood on the deck and watched as the *Condor*'s captain was airlifted in the ship's helicopter. The same one that Kurt and Joe had been in when they'd discovered the *Ethernet* sinking three months before.

The captain objected to leaving, but the ship's doctor confirmed that a major artery had been nicked in his leg. He was lucky not to have bled out and he needed surgery quickly.

Having lost so much blood, the captain was too weak to argue. "Take care of my ship," he'd said to Paul as they'd loaded him on board.

As the helicopter disappeared toward the west, the *Condor*'s chief came up to Paul. "I guess you're in command now."

"Lucky me," Paul said. "What's our condition?"

"All systems are off-line," he said. "We're dead in the water."

"At least we're not going anywhere," Paul muttered.

"What do you want to do about the subs?"

Paul glanced at his watch. "It's been forty-five minutes. Standard NUMA protocol requires underwater operations to be aborted if communications with the surface vessel are lost and not reestablished within thirty."

"I've had men on watch," the chief said. "No sign of them yet."

Paul nodded, silently worried. "Can you get our systems back up and running?"

The chief took off his cap and scratched at his scalp. "Starboard engine survived the emergency shutdown. We could restart it—but only if we bring the propulsion control unit and the main computer back online."

Paul shook his head. "Find another way," he said. "No computers."

"How?"

"I don't know," Paul said. "How does Mr. Scott always get the *Enterprise* restarted when the dilithium crystals fail?"

The chief exhaled sharply and headed back to the engine room, grumbling something about the *Condor* not being a spaceship, but Paul was confident he'd figure something out.

In the meantime, Paul turned his attention to the sea. He made his way to the rail, brought a set of binoculars to his eyes, and scanned the water himself. There was no sign of the submersibles.

The Scarabs should have been on the surface by now, firing off location flares. The fact that they weren't suggested a problem. He brought up a handheld radio, the only form of electronic communication left on the ship.

"Marcus, this is Paul," he said, calling the engineer in charge of the *Condor*'s submersibles.

"Go ahead, Paul."

"The Scarabs are overdue. I want to go look for them. What else do we have on board?"

"A small ROV and the ADS."

ADS stood for "atmospheric diving suit," made of hard-plated metal and used for taking a single diver to great depths. They were often worn by divers working on pipelines and oceanic cables.

The most famous of the various ADS designs were the bulky JIM suits of the eighties and nineties. NUMA's ADS was a more modern design, still bulky and robotic-looking, but it came with its own thruster pack like a NASA suit designed for walking in space.

"Does the ADS have any kind of computer interface?" Paul asked.

"No," Marcus replied. "Why?"

"No reason," Paul said. "Get it ready. I'm going down."

Inside *Scarab One*

"Someone will come," Gamay said with determination. "Paul won't leave us down here."

Elena nodded grimly and stared into the black. "I don't want to die," she said.

"Who does?" Gamay replied.

Elena smiled at that, but it faded quickly.

What could be taking them so long? Gamay wondered. They had to know by the lack of communications that something had gone wrong. They had to have known for at least two hours.

To conserve air, they hadn't moved and had barely spoken. But the silence made it torture and the minutes felt like hours. Gamay was aware of every little creak and groan and she nearly jumped out of her skin when the hull reverberated with a bang.

Looking up, she saw a modicum of light through the frost. Excitedly, she reached forward and scraped it off with the palm of her hand.

She saw nothing at first and then recognized the *Condor*'s ADS.

She grabbed the flashlight, switched it on, and signaled to the diver that they were alive but freezing and running out of air.

In response, the diver began to tap on the hull.

Don't worry. Saving you is on my honey do list for today.

"It's Paul," she said with a sigh of relief.

He continued to tap. *Get ready to be reeled in. You first, then Duke.*

Thank you, she tapped out. *You are my knight in shining armor.*

Paul flashed his lights a few times and moved to the side. Only now did she see the ROV beside Paul, a high-strength cable gripped in one claw. Showing surprising dexterity for a man with giant metal pincers for hands, Paul hooked the cable to the Scarab's pickup bar and stepped away.

The cable went taut and the Scarab began to rise once again. This time it continued upward, hauled by the winch for thirty solid minutes, until it broke the surface at the aft end of the *Condor*. Thrilled to be on the surface, Gamay and Elena were both surprised not to be lifted aboard and instead only secured to the side of the ship.

"What's going on?" Gamay asked as she climbed out of the hatch.

"Technical difficulties," the chief replied. "Sorry it took us so long to get you but we've had our own problems."

Gamay smelled smoke and noticed that portable generators were rumbling beside the winch that had just hauled them from the seafloor. The cable was spooling out so that it could be hooked to Duke's stricken sub.

"We've had to jerry-rig everything," the chief said. "We're operating on one engine, and the men are controlling it by hand. If it gets any worse, we'll be sewing the bedsheets into a sail."

Something told Gamay it wouldn't get that far, but she wouldn't leave the deck until Paul surfaced with Duke's Scarab beside him. As he came up, smoke began pouring from the vents to the engine room, and two of the crew came stumbling out through the smoke.

"That's it, Chief," one of them said. "The bearings have gone out on the starboard gearing."

"Fire?" the chief asked.

"No," the crewman said, "just smoke."

The chief nodded. "Keep an eye on it."

Paul was lifted aboard moments later. As he was extricated from the ADS, he was given the bad news.

"Get on the radio," he said. "Call for a tow."

"Right away," the chief said.

"And, Chief," Paul added. "Tell them not to send anything fancy. We want the oldest, least automated rust bucket of a tug they can scrounge up."

CHAPTER 28

With a plan that went no further than getting themselves to Korea, Kurt and Joe had packed quickly. Their host, Mohammed El Din, gave them a lift to the airport in his armored limousine, bidding them farewell in the traditional Arab style: with a hug and a kiss on each cheek and parting gifts.

To Joe he gave a small hourglass.

"The hourglass is to help you learn patience," El Din said.

"It didn't seem to help you," Joe noted.

"Why do you think I'm getting rid of it?"

Joe laughed, and El Din's beaming smile came out again.

El Din turned to Kurt next and handed him a small case. Opening it, Kurt found an antique revolver, known as a Colt Single Action Army. It was in excellent condition, chambered for Colt's .45 caliber rounds, six of which were lined up in a neat row beneath the barrel. It was the type of weapon a gunfighter might carry—in fact, the Single Action Army was often called the Gun that Won the West. It was the standard U.S. sidearm from 1873 until 1892.

"Dirk told me you collect dueling pistols," El Din explained. "This is not exactly of that era, but I thought you would like it. It was given to my great-great-grandfather by an American who helped my family escape from Barbary pirates."

"I can't accept this," Kurt said. "I should be giving *you* a gift."

"You must take it," El Din said, "or I shall be offended."

Kurt nodded and offered a slight bow of thanks. "It's a beautiful weapon. Thank you."

A smile crinkled El Din's weathered face. "May peace be upon you," he said.

"*As-salamu alaykum,*" Kurt replied.

With El Din's influence, Kurt and Joe bypassed security and boarded their plane.

The Korean Air A380 double-decker was spacious, which would serve them well on a flight that would span nine hours gate to gate.

It was a long trip, and by the time they reached Seoul, the whole world had changed. The blinding sunlight and heat of Dubai were gone, replaced by a cold, misty rain. The nature of their mission evolved as well, though for the minute neither Kurt nor Joe were told how or why.

But instead of a rent-a-car and the next step in their privateer's underfunded journey, they were met at the airport by three men in dark suits and mackintosh overcoats.

State Department IDs were flashed. "Come with us," the leader of the group said.

With little choice in the matter, Kurt and Joe collected their luggage and climbed into the back of a van with diplomatic plates. It took them north.

As the lights of Seoul receded, Joe pointed out the obvious. "If we're going to the consulate, we must be taking the scenic route."

"We're not going to the consulate," Kurt replied. He knew who the men were. He recognized their style and their tight-lipped expressions. They were employees of the company. "We've been shanghaied," he said, "and we're not even in China."

The van continued north for another fifteen minutes until they were nearing the Demilitarized Zone. With the razor-wire fences and guard posts visible in the distance, the van turned east and drove through an unpopulated area filled with trees, huge satellite-tracking arrays, and towers bristling with strange-looking antennas. There were no buildings to be seen.

Eventually the road began to drop. Smooth concrete walls rose up on either side until the van was traveling in a channel twenty feet deep. It cruised beneath an overhang, and the channel became a tunnel lit with orange lights.

Somewhere deep beneath the rolling hills of central Korea, the underground road curved tightly and came to an end. A huge steel door opened and let them into a parking area. They were escorted from the van and led to a command center.

Inside, two men were talking. Both looked rather haggard but in different ways. The first was a Korean colonel in military dress, the second figure was an American. He reminded Kurt of a businessman staying late at the office to finish a big project. He wore a white dress shirt with rolled-up sleeves and a loosened red tie. His jacket rested on the back of the chair next to him.

"I suppose you two are wondering why you're here and not at the Ritz-Carlton," he said.

"Actually, we booked the Hilton," Kurt replied, "though it didn't quite look like this on the brochure."

A weary grin came across the table. "My name is Tim Hale," the American replied. "I'm the CIA station chief for the DMZ. This is Colonel Hyun-Min Lee, deputy director of security for the South Korean National Intelligence Service."

All four men shook hands and sat down.

"We know who you're looking for," Hale explained. "We know why. And we want to help."

"Why?" Kurt asked. "What's changed?"

"Your friends at NUMA dove on the wreck of the *Ethernet*," Hale said.

"And?"

"No sign of Sienna Westgate or her children."

"That doesn't surprise me," Kurt said, "considering the shape of the wreck. When a vessel breaks up on the way down—"

"That's the interesting part," Hale said, cutting Kurt off. "The *Ethernet* is sitting on the bottom in one solid piece."

Kurt narrowed his gaze. He suddenly felt confused. He'd seen the sonar scan. The ship had come apart.

Hale explained what they'd learned. "The report you saw was doctored. Someone tapped into the South African Coast Guard database and changed it. The SACG sent you what they thought was a legitimate file, but you saw what someone wanted you to see."

"Why?"

"So you wouldn't dive the ship and find what your friends found," Hale said. He went on to explain that three bodies were recovered from the ship: two members of Westgate's crew and his personal bodyguard.

He also told Kurt what had happened to the *Condor* and the submersibles. "To hack both of those systems and gain such control is quite a feat," he said. "Especially considering NUMA has stringent safeguards in place."

"Obviously, not enough," Kurt said.

"We're not sure what is, these days," Hale replied.

"Which leads us to your main suspect," Col. Lee said. "Mr. Than Rang, head of the DaeShan Group, and a man with many sinister connections to generals in North Korea."

Kurt sat dumbfounded. "Are you trying to tell me Than Rang is a North Korean sleeper agent?"

"No," Lee said, "the other way around. Than Rang is interested in the inevitable day when North and South finally embrace in reunification. His corporation has spent years buying up ancient deeds to land in the North. The deeds are worthless of course, but if unification ever comes about, he will have some amount of standing to claim nearly one-third of the land in North Korea. To bolster his claims, he's spent years currying favor with the generals and others who float just below the level of the Glorious Leader, Kim Jong-un. If change ever comes, these friends of his will be the first to benefit, just as the ardent defenders of communism in the old Soviet Union awarded themselves the vast majority of state-run industries as soon as the country turned to capitalism."

"What does he give them?" Joe asked.

"Cold hard cash, high-tech machinery, and advanced software," Lee said.

"And possibly well-known programmers and hackers," Hale added.

"In exchange for nearly worthless land?" Kurt asked.

"Much of it lies above proven reserves of minerals," Col. Lee said. "And Than Rang has already shown a knack for taking played-out mines and increasing their production, in many cases to record levels. He would no doubt be very successful if his scheme ever came to pass."

Joe held his phone up, bringing it close to his mouth like a pocket recorder. "Note to self: Invest retirement nest egg in DaeShan Group."

"I wouldn't go that far," Hale said. "We don't see anything happening for a long, long time."

Joe brought the phone back up. "Cancel note to self."

Kurt laughed. "I get it. You want us to do some dirty work. The question is, can you get me into North Korea?"

"No," Hale said. "You wouldn't last five minutes there if we could."

"Then what?"

"Than Rang is having an elegant reception for his business partners," Col. Lee explained. "There will be wine, women, and song, as you Americans like to say. Most important, there will be a guest arriving and delivering a very important package. I believe you know the man. Fortunately, he doesn't know you. At least not by sight."

"Acosta," Kurt said with disgust.

"He's bringing the other hackers," Joe guessed.

"Exactly," Hale said. "He will exchange them for a large sum of diamonds and a painting by one of the masters."

Kurt's mind was running now. "For such an exchange to happen, both items would need to be verified."

Hale said, "Acosta isn't interested in getting a fake, and Than Rang isn't interested in delivering a couple of dupes to his friends in the North. They'll both need experts to make sure the goods are bona fide. Than Rang will use several techs from his company to give the prospective hackers a final exam of sorts. Most likely, they'll be given a complex code and asked to break it, and then perhaps a secondary task of inserting a program through a sophisticated firewall. In the meantime, Acosta will be examining the painting and that's where we get our chance. You see, Acosta holds himself out as a big-time collector, but he knows less about art than he pretends. Far less. To make sure he's not swindled, he's arranged for a legitimate expert named Solano to go with him. For a healthy fee, Solano will verify what is no doubt a stolen work of art to begin with. It's all a very sordid business."

"What do you want us to do?" Kurt asked.

"Mr. Zavala here will pose as our friend Solano, who hails from Madrid. They're the same build, almost the same height. With a little makeup and subtle lifts in his shoes, Joe will be the spitting image of the wayward art expert."

"What if Acosta figures it out?"

"He won't," Hale insisted. "He's never met Solano. Only talked to him on the phone. And they're arriving separately. Solano comes in tomorrow, Acosta will be here the day after."

Fortunate timing, Kurt thought. But there were problems. "What about his voice? If they've talked, Joe will have to sound like Solano."

"According to his file, Joe speaks fluent Spanish."

Joe nodded.

"The only concern is that this is Catalan Spanish," Hale said. "But we're going to take Solano out of circulation before he makes it to his hotel, get him to talk, and allow Joe to practice his voice."

Kurt didn't like his friend taking the risk, but he knew they weren't likely to get another chance at this.

"Should be a piece of cake," Joe said.

"I'm going in with him," Kurt insisted.

"Of course you are," Hale said. "Because your job is to place a transmitter on one of the hackers while Joe keeps Acosta and the others busy."

Kurt nodded. That sounded fair, but then what? "I think we can all picture the outcome if we fail. But what happens if we succeed? You can't get them out of the North any more than we can."

"The thing is," Hale said, "we're not sure where they are. Any of them. North Korea has a cyberforce known as Unit 121. We've confirmed that some of them operate in China, others have been tracked to sites in Russia, and some to sites right here in Seoul. You don't have to be at home to attack a country these days. You can launch your strike from anywhere you find a computer terminal and an Internet connection. If they like, these people can wage war in their pajamas."

Kurt understood, but something was missing. He studied Hale. Both he and Col. Lee were rather inscrutable. Maybe it was the nature of their occupations or the hangdog expressions that told him they'd been working the angles long and hard on this one. Either way, something didn't quite fit. Kurt couldn't begin to guess what it was, but he had a feeling he'd find out at the worst possible time.

CHAPTER 29

NUMA Vessel *Condor*, Southwestern Indian Ocean

The *Condor* drifted with the current all afternoon, and Paul Trout began to feel like a sailor on an old galleon, caught in the horse latitudes and going nowhere.

As dusk approached, the ship was enveloped in darkness. The chief and his men rigged up an auxiliary unit that brought power back to the desalinization and ventilation systems, but because the unit was relatively small compared to the need of the ship, most of the lights were kept off and the HVAC processors were run at the lowest settings. As a result, the interior of the ship was a sweatbox and those who didn't have to be inside congregated on various parts of the deck.

Paul considered himself fortunate to be on the bridge wing with Gamay.

"What a beautiful night," she said.

"It really is," he replied. There was a soft southerly breeze, just enough to keep the humidity from being oppressive.

"Maybe there's something to be said for the old ways," she added. "No hum of machinery. No annoying computers telling us a new message has arrived."

She put an arm around his waist and pulled closer. "I wouldn't mind a candlelight dinner, if you've got nothing else planned."

Paul cocked his head at her. "Are you getting romantic on me?"

She huffed and pushed him away. "If you have to ask, I must be doing it wrong."

He pulled her back to his side. "No, you're doing fine," he said. "Now, where were we?"

"Too late," she said. "The moment has passed."

If it wasn't already gone, the appearance of a crewman sweating through his T-shirt sent it packing for good. "Sorry to interrupt but we're picking up something on radar."

"I thought the radar was out?" Gamay replied.

Paul shook his head. "Considering our predicament, I thought it would be wise to know what's going on around us. I had the chief power up the short-range unit."

"Do you want to take a look?" the crewman asked.

Paul nodded, and both he and Gamay entered the semidarkened bridge.

"Any chance it's the tug?" Gamay asked.

"No, ma'am," the crewman replied. "Target is to the

east. Tug will be coming in from the west. By our estimates, she's a good four hours away."

Paul stepped over to the radarscope. "What's the
range?"

"Forty-six miles. That's pretty much the maximum
range of the system on this power setting."

"What's her course and speed? Maybe we can hail her?"

"That's just it," the crewman said, "she has no course
and speed. The target has been intermittent, appearing and disappearing. For the last hour there was nothing
there and we thought whoever it was had moved on, but
then it came back in the same relative position."

"But we're drifting," Paul said. "Even if she was sitting
still, her bearing should be changing unless she's drifting
as well."

"Or it could be shadowing us at the very limit of our
radar coverage," the crewman noted ominously.

"Has to be a pretty big target to show up that far off,"
Gamay added. "Maybe they're keeping their distance,
hoping not to be seen."

It was all guesswork. But considering what they'd already been through, Paul was not interested in giving
anyone or anything the benefit of the doubt. "When's the
helicopter due back?"

"That's problem number two," the crewman said.
"The pilot reported a mechanical failure shortly after
leaving Durban. They've had to turn back. The last we
heard, they were trying to scrounge up a spare part. But
even if they found one right away, we won't have them
back until tomorrow morning at the earliest."

"And the tug is four hours off?"

"At least."

Paul sighed. Alone on the darkening sea and being watched was not a position he liked being in. "Contact HQ on the satellite phone," Paul said. "Tell them we might have company."

"What do you think we should do in the meantime?" Gamay asked.

Paul was pragmatic. "Either hope it's nothing and enjoy the evening or prepare to repel boarders."

Gamay folded her arms across her chest and offered a pout. "Guess I'll cancel my plans for a candlelight dinner and go scour the hold for a few rocks and a slingshot."

CHAPTER 30

As the *Condor* continued to drift, dusk gave way to darkness and the lonely feeling of isolation. The ship, normally a hub of activity, was quiet as the crew prepared to fight if necessary. But the feared boarders never materialized, and Paul began to wonder if they'd read suspicious intentions into a harmless situation.

"Any change?" he asked the radar operator as he stepped onto the bridge.

"No, sir," the crewman replied. "Whoever they are, they've drifted along with us for the past three hours."

Sensing the danger had passed, especially with the tug only an hour away, Paul had a new idea. "We have a high-speed launch on this boat, don't we?"

"An FRC," the crewman replied. "Fast rescue craft."

"Good," Paul said. "Have it readied. I'm going to take it out and investigate our mystery contact."

"Not without me, you won't," a voice insisted from behind him.

Paul turned to see Gamay in the doorway. "Wouldn't dream of it," he said. "In fact, I think we should make it a double date. Bring Duke and Elena."

Shortly thereafter, the four of them were aboard the quickest of *Condor*'s motorized launches, a sleek machine constructed by the Dutch Special Marine Group. In design, the thirty-foot boat looked like a police river cruiser on steroids, with a high bow, an open deck, and a centralized control console and navigation mast. Powered by a throaty Volvo water jet, it raced across the waves at forty knots.

Paul stood at the bow with Gamay while Duke handled the controls and Elena prepared a raft of weapons obtained from the *Condor*'s arms locker just in case they were needed.

Navigating from dead reckoning, Duke offered an update. "We should be close enough to see the target in a few minutes," he said, "assuming she has any sort of running lights on."

Peering through the darkness, Paul nodded. He saw nothing yet.

"What's our plan when we arrive?" Gamay asked.

"Plan?" Paul asked.

"Plan," Gamay repeated. "You know, that thing you come up with in advance so you can throw it out the window when everything goes haywire."

"Oh yeah," Paul said. "I figure we encircle the target and, should it be a threat, talk the captain into surrendering."

Gamay sighed. "Yep," she said, "that will go right out the window."

Paul chuckled at his wife's concern. "I don't think we're dealing with anything hostile," he said. "I think we're going to find another ship in distress like our own."

"Then why do we all have weapons?" Elena asked. She held a pistol. Two AR-15s rested on the deck. Paul and Gamay would carry the rifles.

"For the inevitable moment when my guess turns out to be wrong," Paul deadpanned.

As the FRC raced on through the darkness, the radio squawked with a barely audible signal as the chief called them.

"FRC, this is Condor. *You've gone off the scope. We're not reading your signature anymore. Based on course and speed, you should be rounding third and heading for home."*

The transmission was coded in simple terms in case anyone was listening. "Rounding third" told Paul they were about three miles from the target. He grabbed the microphone. "Are you holding us up or waving us on?"

"No sign of outfielders ready to throw home," the chief replied. *"Keep on running."*

"Wilco," Paul said. He put the radio down. "Coast is clear," he told the others.

"So thought the mouse, as she raced for the cheese," said Gamay.

Paul returned to the bow, watching and waiting.

"She must be running dark," Gamay said, "or we'd see her lights by now."

"Have to agree with that," Paul said. He looked up.

The waxing moon was three-quarters full and casting a fair amount of light on this cloudless night. Even if the target was running dark, they should have been able to see it.

"Duke, what's our heading?"

"Zero nine five," Duke replied.

"It should be right in front of us."

"Maybe it's a ghost," Elena suggested.

"A ghost?" Paul said.

Elena rolled her eyes. "On the radar. You know, a false return."

Paul had to consider that a possibility and began to wonder if they'd made the trip for nothing. He pulled on a set of night vision goggles and stared until he finally saw an outline growing on the horizon. It was low and long and just barely jutting above the calm sea.

"Dead ahead," he said. "At last."

The gray bulk of the target began to grow larger, though it was hard to calculate distance in the dark.

"Cut our speed," Paul said. "Give us ten knots."

The roar of the engine dropped down to a heavy purr, and the wind noise lessened as the FRC slowed appreciably. It didn't appear they were dealing with a threat.

Paul glanced at Gamay. "So much for a trap," he said.

"Famous last words."

They moved in closer, and the black hulk in the darkness began blocking out the horizon to either side of them. Paul estimated the target to be nearly five hundred feet from stem to stern. There were no smokestacks or antennas, no defined areas of superstructure, that he could see. And though some sections were higher than others, there was a rounded effect to them, more like a river barge piled high with coal or some other bulk commodity.

"Looks like a barge," Paul said.

"What's a barge doing all the way out here?" Elena asked.

No one ventured a guess.

"Take us around to port," Paul said.

Duke cut the wheel, and the FRC turned right and traveled down one side of the vessel. As they passed the end of the derelict, Duke took them up along the other side.

"Rounded end," Paul said. "This is the stern."

"It's not a barge," Gamay added, "it's a ship."

"A dark, dead ship," Elena said.

"A ghost ship," Gamay replied.

Even Paul had to admit there was something ominous about the vessel, something the grainy gangrene-tinted view through the night vision goggles only added to. Mist shrouding the ship, backlit by the stars and the sliver moon, gave it a spectral aura.

"Ghost ship," Gamay whispered.

Paul had seen enough. He pulled off the goggles and went to the FRC's small mast. As a rescue boat, the FRC was equipped with a row of powerful lights. Paul switched the main flood on and turned it toward the target's hull.

The garish light spread across heavy steel plate, rusted and corroded as if the ship had been drifting for years. The ship's portholes appeared to be sealed shut and were opaque with a tawny scale. A line of them ran just above the waterline.

As Paul panned the light, it revealed tangled lines running across the hull, strands of brown and green. It took a moment for any of them to realize what they were looking at.

Gamay was first. "Vines," she said.

Duke brought the throttle back to idle, and Paul angled the spotlight, tracking a tangled group of the vines that ran up the side of the hull past what should have been the sharp edge of the main deck but what was, in fact, an eroding slope of tan-colored sediment.

"What in the world . . ."

Up on top, the vines ran everywhere like ivy draping an old stone wall. Dying grasses, weeds, and tangled scrub brush grew where the superstructure should have been.

Duke shook his head at the sight. "I've found some strange things floating out at sea before, but I've never seen anything like this."

They passed the bow without sighting any markings, and Duke brought them back amidships.

"I think we should go back to the *Condor*," Gamay said abruptly.

Paul turned. "Aren't you curious about what we've found here?"

"Of course," she said, "I'm as intrigued as you are. But we came here to see if the target was a threat or a vessel in need of our help. It's obviously neither. With that established, we should get back home before anything strange occurs."

Paul studied his wife. "Not like you to be the voice of reason," he said. "Where's your sense of adventure?"

"On the nightstand back home with my car keys," she said.

He laughed. "We've come this far. Might as well go aboard."

"And how do you propose we do that?" she asked.

Paul looked at her as if it was obvious. "Tarzan style of course," he said, pointing to the vines.

CHAPTER 31

With calm precision, Duke brought the launch up against the hull where a thick group of creeper vines hung. Paul grabbed them and pulled with all his might.

"I'm going first," he said. "If these hold me, they'll certainly hold the rest of you."

Using the rim of a porthole as a foothold, he went up, climbing hand over hand, like he was going over the obstacle course wall in basic training. Eventually, he made it up onto the deck, which was covered with sediment.

Gamay came up next, and Elena followed right behind her. Duke remained on the launch.

"Feel like we've discovered a deserted island," Elena said.

"Let's hope it's deserted," Gamay added. "I'd hate to find headhunters living aboard."

Paul looked around. It really felt as if they'd made landfall. There was nothing man-made in sight. Just a foliage-covered mound in the middle of the Indian Ocean. "Looks like this ship got caught in the Sargasso Sea."

"Except that this isn't seaweed," Gamay said.

"The fact that she's still afloat tells me she's basically watertight," Elena mentioned, "though she's riding awfully low in the water."

Paul thought so as well. "I wonder if all this vegetation is weighing her down."

"Possibly," Elena said. "Considering the thickness of the vegetation and the soil, it's probably making her top-heavy. Hopefully, we don't get any big waves while we're on board. If she starts to roll, she'll almost certainly go over."

To Paul, the discovery of the ship was a bolt of adrenaline. He wanted to know what ship it was and where it had come from. He stepped to the edge and shouted down to Duke. "Throw up the paddles. I think we can use them."

Duke pulled the FRC's emergency paddles from a locker and tossed them up one at a time. Paul caught them, handing one to Gamay and keeping one for himself.

"What are we supposed to do with these," Gamay asked, "row this ship back to civilization?"

"That is not a paddle," Paul explained, "it's a shovel. And we are not going to row, we're going to dig. If this ship is watertight, that suggests all the muck is on the outside, leaving the interior intact. We're going to find a hatch and go inside."

"And I can't get you to rake the leaves at home," Gamay said.

"Not as much fun."

"I like it," Elena said.

"See?" Paul said.

"You're supposed to be on my side," Gamay told Elena. "Girl power, remember?"

"Sorry," Elena said. "This beats sitting around on the *Condor* in the dark and doing nothing."

With a smile of satisfaction, Gamay handed Elena the paddle. "Then you can help him dig."

Paul chuckled and called down to Duke once more. "Stay close. We're going on a nature walk."

"Will do," Duke replied.

With his sense of curiosity near an all-time high, Paul led the party through the foliage toward the highest point of the mounding, an area completely entombed in the thickest of vines. If he was right, the main part of the ship's superstructure was hidden beneath it.

Pushing between a pair of wild bushes, he stopped. "Look at this," he said, aiming his flashlight into a tangle of leaves.

A huge spider, the size of a child's hand, sat in the middle of an ornate web. It had a yellow color to its body and was hard-shelled, as opposed to soft and furry like a tarantula. Nearby, a second spider of similar size and color rested on an even larger web. They found three more in a ten-foot radius.

"Ewww," Elena said quietly. "They're absolutely disgusting."

"Did you have to point them out?" Gamay asked. "Now I feel like they're all over me." She was turning awkwardly, trying to see if anything was on her back.

Paul had to laugh. He'd always found spiders interesting, though even he had to admit he wouldn't want the ones they were looking at sneaking into his sleeping bag.

"Come on," Paul said. He continued forward, careful to avoid the spiders and the thicker parts of the scrub, and they soon arrived at a spot just below the peak of the mound and near the center of the ship's beam.

With Gamay providing the illumination, Paul and Elena began pulling out the vines and excavating the clumpy soil. The paddles proved to be fairly effective as shovels, and they were soon tunneling at a forty-five-degree angle, gouging a channel deep into the soil, when Gamay put a hand on Paul's shoulder.

"Stop."

He looked back at her.

"I thought I heard something."

"You mean besides my grunting at having to do all the work?"

"I'm serious."

Paul gripped the shovel. He and Elena still carried sidearms, Ruger SR9s, made in Prescott, Arizona, but no one seriously thought they'd be needed once they discovered the radar target was an abandoned ship.

Gamay used the beam of her light to scan the area. Nothing appeared out of the ordinary.

"Maybe it's a giant spider," Paul whispered. "Momma spider to all those little babies we found."

Gamay gave him a light smack on the shoulder. "I'm serious. I have a bad feeling about this."

Beside them, Elena unlatched the holster strap on her sidearm and put her hand on the grip of the pistol like a gunfighter getting ready to draw.

A light breeze rustled the leaves around them and faded away. As it did, Paul heard something too. It was low and raspy, like the sound of labored breathing. It lasted for no more than a few seconds and then ceased. He looked around in the growth but saw nothing.

"You heard it too," Gamay said. "Didn't you?"

More like their minds were playing tricks on them, Paul thought. "You two and your ghost ship," he said. "Let's not get all jumpy."

Elena nodded and took her hand off the pistol grip.

"I'm going to keep an eye out for disembodied spirits," Gamay said.

Paul nodded, returning to the work at hand. "Especially any that might be interested in digging."

With renewed vigor, he continued the excavation. Soon enough, the paddle struck something hard. Brushing the debris away, he spotted the rusted steel plate. "We've hit the wall," he said. "Literally."

They widened out the channel and came upon a hatch. Attempting to pry it open was useless, but they continued to dig and uncovered a half-shattered window. Clearing the remaining glass away, Paul looked inside.

"What do you see?"

"It's like a cave," Paul said. "The silt has filled most of the room, but farther in it seems to lessen."

"I'm surprised it isn't filled to the top," Elena said.

Paul wondered about that. "Maybe the foliage on the outside became matted at some point. After that, it might have acted like a shell. Although it seems to have let moisture in. The sediment looks smooth and wet, packed down like sand on the beach after the tide recedes."

As he panned the beam of the flashlight around, the light seemed to be swallowed up. They were certainly looking into a voluminous space.

He stepped back. "Who wants the honor?"

Elena shook her head. Gamay did the same, gesturing to the opening. "This was your idea."

Being as large as he was, Paul did not enjoy cramped spaces. It wasn't true claustrophobia, just a practical sense that tight spaces were not suited for someone his size. But Gamay was right, it was his idea.

Stepping back to the opening, he made sure there were no residual shards of glass in the sill, then climbed up and over. "Once more into the breach," he said, to groans from his audience.

Squeezing through the gap, Paul made it onto the damp sediment. The soil was compacted and damp.

"Any spiders?" Gamay called out.

"Not that I can see."

"Are you sure?"

"Positive."

With that established, Gamay crawled in after him.

To Paul's surprise, Elena came next. "You're not leaving me out there on my own," she said.

At first, they could only crawl. The sediment in the room had piled up so high that the ceiling was only three or four feet above their heads. As they moved away from the window, the space spread out and the sediment sloped downward. In one section, small ridges protruded. Paul made his way over to them and started to laugh.

"What's so funny?" Gamay asked.

"Remember that candlelight dinner you wanted?"

"The one I never got?"

"Well, here's your chance," Paul said. He worked the object out of the silt. It was a rotting chair. "I think we're in the ship's dining room."

Gamay chuckled. "Somehow, I was hoping for a little more ambience."

They moved deeper into the room, traveling down the slope of the invasive sediment until it was no more than a thin layer on the floor. As Paul stood, he found it to be packed down hard and no more than six inches deep.

Gamay stood up and wiped her palms on the front of her jeans. "Not gonna need a mud bath next time I go to the spa," she said. "What next, O fearless leader?"

Paul looked around. "Let's see if we can figure out what ship this is and where she came from."

They moved deeper into the hull, soon finding the kitchen and a storeroom.

"Look at these ovens," Gamay said. "They're ancient."

"How old?" Paul asked.

"I don't know," Gamay replied. "Old. Like the stove my grandmother had forever."

Paul took a look at the stoves and some of the other equipment. The designs belonged to another era. He began to feel as if he'd stepped back in time.

He pulled open a cabinet and it was stacked with serving plates. He picked one up and began scraping off the blackened mold. When he'd cleared enough of it, a logo became visible in the center, a stylized anchor with barbed flukes, resting sideways. It looked familiar.

He showed it to Gamay, who shrugged and shook her head.

"The storerooms are empty," Elena said, popping into the kitchen. "Not a can of beans left behind."

Paul put the serving plate back. "Let's find the bridge."

He took a step toward the door and stopped. The harsh breathing sound had returned. It was a deep sound, guttural and menacing. This time they all heard it.

Paul aimed his light for the doorway as something shot forward. A roar of some kind echoed through the dark as all three of them dove in different directions.

Paul grabbed Gamay and pulled her to safety as a shape spun toward them and what felt like a log slammed Paul in the ribs. He tumbled and sprawled in the mud. His flashlight flew from his hand, and the roaring continued.

"Run!" he shouted.

Elena clambered up onto the stoves as Gamay helped Paul up.

Something slammed against the old, cast-iron stoves, and the impact sent the serving plates Paul had discovered smashing to the ground. A burst of gunfire rang out, bathing the room in staccato flashes as Elena fired her Ruger at the attacker.

By now Paul and Gamay were scrambling out the door and into the dining room. In their haste Gamay slipped in the muck and pulled Paul down with her. They tumbled to a stop against the far wall.

Paul's light was gone, but Gamay found hers and aimed it back at the door to the kitchen. A monster emerged, charging toward them. A twelve-foot crocodile with ragged teeth and an ugly bumpy snout. It lunged just as Paul pulled his gun and fired, blasting several shots straight into the creature's gaping mouth.

Gamay screamed in Paul's ear, but the gunshots drowned her out as the shells went through the upper jaw of the animal, into the brain, and out the other side. The creature slammed into Paul, crashing onto his abdomen and knocking the wind out of him like a sack of concrete tossed from the back of a truck. But it didn't bite or thrash, it just collapsed on him, twitching and then lying there.

The long snout and what remained of the head lay right on Paul's chest. The stubby forearms and claws continued gripping Paul's legs until the muscles died. Of all things, Paul noticed how badly its breath stank.

Realizing it was dead and that they were alive, Paul kicked out from under the beast and pushed it away with his boot. Its powerful tail twitched once more before going permanently still.

It was only now that Paul realized he was leaning against Gamay. She was behind him, one arm wrapped around him tight, the other holding the flashlight and aiming it at the dead creature.

"Elena?" Paul shouted. "Are you okay?"

She came out of the kitchen, hobbling and holding her weapon up. "I'm okay. Twisted my knee, but I can walk."

Paul slid off of Gamay and moved to the side, leaning against the wall as she was. "Good work with the flashlight," he said. "Are you all right?"

She nodded. "And strangely enough, I'm no longer afraid of spiders."

Paul laughed. Among all her other wonderful attributes, Gamay's spirit and humor were two that he could never resist. "I love you," he said. He reached over and kissed her, muddy and all.

"I suppose we're having crocodile for dinner," she said.

"No," Paul replied. "But on the bright side, he's not having us either."

"He would make a nice pair of boots," Elena said. "And a matching handbag."

They all laughed at that.

"Where did he come from?" Paul wondered. "He couldn't have been in here."

Gamay pointed the flashlight back toward the entrance. Telltale claw marks and a sliding trail from the creature's body were easy to see in the muck. "It must have been living on the ship," she said. "Looks like it followed us in."

"What's a crocodile doing on a ship to begin with?" Elena asked. "Not to mention the hundred-acre woods out there."

Paul had been considering that ever since they'd found

it. "I remember Kurt and Joe telling me about a salvage job they did once. The ship had been aground for several years, beached near a protected wildlife refuge on the coast of Burma. NUMA agreed to help because it was leaking oil into the water. Kurt said the ship had become part of the land by the time they got to it. Covered in weeds and filled with plants and insects. They literally had to dig it free."

He looked around. "I'm guessing this ship had a similar fate."

"You wouldn't know it from the weather we've had lately, but there have been big storms down here over the last few months," Elena said.

"So this ship might have been beached for a while and then gotten pulled out to sea with a storm surge," Gamay proposed.

"Maybe," Paul said. "And this poor creature was probably caught on board when it was pulled out to sea."

"Why didn't he just drop back into the water and swim to shore?" Elena asked.

"Maybe the storm was too bad," Paul guessed.

Gamay looked at the dead animal. It was big in comparison to the three humans but didn't appear overly large for a crocodile. "I know saltwater crocodiles can cross large sections of ocean, but this one looks different to me. Kind of skinny. Maybe he's a different species."

Paul nodded. That made as much sense as anything.

He stood up, pulling clear of the muck and helping Gamay to her feet. It was then that he noticed the large picture frame behind them. The canvas inside was black from mold and decay, and nothing could be seen of the artwork hidden beneath, but a brass plate affixed to the lower edge of the frame seemed to offer some type of inscription.

Reaching forward, Paul began to rub the plate with his thumb, scraping years of debris away. Even as he worked, the plate remained tarnished and dark. But before too long the recessed markings of an engraving became visible. He continued scraping until he could just make out the last part of a name. Three letters: T-A-H. Despite rubbing his fingers raw, he couldn't make out anything else.

"It can't be," he whispered.

"Can't be what?" Gamay asked.

He thought about the advanced age of the kitchen appliances, the dimensions of the vessel as they'd estimated them, and the logo on the serving plate he'd found.

"You may be right," he said to Gamay. "This might be a ghost ship after all."

Gamay looked at him suspiciously. "What are you talking about?"

"Let's get to the bridge," Paul said. "I don't want to jump to any conclusions."

It would take another twenty minutes for them to find the bridge. It was eerie, standing there, with mud smashed up against the ship's windows. It was as if the ship itself had been buried in some gigantic grave.

Paul looked through every drawer and cabinet. "No charts, no logbooks, nothing of value."

"Just like the storeroom," Elena said. "Someone cleaned this ship out."

Finally, Paul found something that was too heavy to carry: a bell the size of a laundry basket, lying on its side. He rolled it over until he found another engraving. This time the carved markings were deeper, and once he'd scraped the corrosion and tarnish away, Paul could see the letters clearly. A name was engraved on the side of the bell, a name he recognized, a name that all those who'd ever studied shipwrecks knew quite well.

"The *Waratah*," Paul said out loud. "I can't believe it. This ship is the *Waratah*."

He showed the engraving to Gamay, who seemed as surprised as him.

"Why do I know that name?" Elena asked.

"Because it's famous," Paul said. "The SS *Waratah*, of the Blue Anchor Line, vanished with the crew and passengers in 1909. She was believed to have gone down in a storm somewhere between Durban and Cape Town. No wreckage was ever found. Not so much as a life jacket or a buoy with the name *Waratah* stenciled on it."

Elena narrowed her gaze at the two of them. "You're saying this ship we're on, covered in mud and wrapped in vines, is actually a hundred-year-old derelict that's supposed to be sitting on the bottom of the sea?"

Paul nodded. "Sitting on the bottom of the sea a long way from here."

"I told you those stoves were old," Gamay said.

Paul laughed and considered the irony. "Everyone who

is anyone in undersea exploration has searched for this ship at one time or another. Treasure hunters, naval historians, adventurers. NUMA even took a stab at it with the help of this famous author whose name escapes me at the moment. We thought we'd found it, but the wreck turned out to be a different ship called the *Nailsea Meadow*."

"No wonder no one could find it," Elena said. "It never actually went down."

"Which begs the question," Gamay said, "where has she been hiding out all these years? And since she seems to be empty, what happened to her passengers and crew?"

CHAPTER 32

Incheon Airport, South Korea

The passengers of Air France Flight 264 from Paris to Seoul gathered their things in the orderly but eager fashion of those who'd been cooped up in a metal tube for too long, as if the eleven hours on the aircraft were more easily endured than the five minutes it took to unload and escape into the terminal.

An announcement that the Jetway had malfunctioned was met with a universal groan. But the opening of the rear doors allowed fresh air into the cabin, and soon the passengers were streaming down the stairs at the rear of the aircraft.

This odd method of emptying the aircraft meant that the passengers in the rear went first while those in first class had to endure the interminable delay.

In the very first row, in seat 1A, Arturo Solano did little to hide his displeasure. The only solace was a few more minutes staring at the shapely American woman who sat next to him. They'd spoken all too briefly during the flight, but as the other first-class passengers filed out she turned his way.

He knew the look. A few words about art and parties and most women went weak in the knees. She was going to ask him if she might attend the party or perhaps even meet privately for dinner.

With a mischievous eye, she watched the last of the first-class passengers disappear through the curtain and then smiled.

"I know what you want," he said in his best English.

"Do you?" she replied.

"Of course," he said. "I'd be delighted to put you on the guest list."

"I'm flattered," she said, glancing forward as the front cabin door opened. "But since you won't be going, there's no need for me to attend."

Solano felt a moment of confusion. It grew deeper as three Korean men in dark suits appeared, entering through the supposedly broken Jetway. He stood up, indignant and suspicious, but the woman jabbed him with something. He felt a shock go through his body and then became rapidly drowsy. He fell into her waiting arms and began to doze even as she laid him down on the cabin floor.

Shortly before he passed out, another man entered.

This man wore a white linen suit, identical to Solano's own. His hair was coiffed in the same nouveau pompadour style and his face sported a goatee. In fact, as this new arrival stared down at him, Solano felt as if he might be looking in a mirror.

"Who . . . are . . . you?" Solano managed to whisper.

"I'm you," the man replied.

Baffled and too drowsy to form another thought, Solano closed his eyes and fell asleep.

Two of the Korean men dropped down beside him and pulled him upright. As they folded his unconscious body into a cart disguised as a catering trolley, the woman in the business suit took Joe by the arm.

"Time for us to exit," she said. "Acosta sent a driver to pick Solano up. Say as little to him as possible. We'll get Solano talking and get you some audio to listen to so you can mimic his voice."

"No problem," Joe said. He grabbed Solano's briefcase and followed the woman toward the aft end of the plane.

Minutes later, he was in the terminal, meeting with Acosta's driver, who picked up the rest of Solano's luggage and led him to a waiting limo.

"What hotel?" Joe asked, using accented English.

"Shilla Hotel," the driver insisted. "Five stars. Monsieur Acosta has spared no expense and is very excited to see you."

Joe only nodded and sat back in the plush seat until the driver shut the door. He wasn't concerned. He knew that the CIA and the South Korean security forces were listening in. They would track him and, when they were certain the coast was clear, they would contact him. Until then there was nothing to do but enjoy the ride.

MILES AWAY, Kurt Austin was less relaxed. What had begun as a personal mission in search of answers had now become an international operation that had put his best friend at the tip of the spear.

Kurt spent hours studying the schematics of Than Rang's skyscraper, where the party would be held. The fifty-two-story glass-and-steel building was a marvel of engineering. It rose like a monolith in the heart of Seoul. Eleven floors up, one side was cut away, and an ornate garden and outdoor terrace offered some of the best views in the city.

Kurt noticed that the garden was protected by a glass atrium, the rest being open to the elements. He learned that the elevators ran through a central column and that there were stairwells at all four corners. He found that access corridors ran behind certain walls and that there were many narrow spaces, designed for pipes and electrical conduits, that had entry and exit points to allow maintenance access.

Having learned all he could about Than Rang's building, he turned to other distractions: looking over the photos he'd taken of Acosta's yacht and zooming in on the faces of those who'd been caught in the snapshots.

Acosta's bulbous head was clearly visible in several

photos, as was the blond woman Acosta had spoken to out on the deck.

As Kurt studied her features, he began to think she looked familiar. Her cheekbones were high. Her eyes were a dark brown and her eyebrows darker still. She wasn't a blonde at all, he thought.

He zoomed in closer and realized who it was. "A woman in disguise," he said, recognizing the face of the mystery intruder he'd fought with in Acosta's cabin.

He plugged the camera into a computer terminal. With a few keystrokes he uploaded the shot. That done, he picked up the phone and dialed a Washington number. The phone rang a half dozen times before a grumpy voice answered.

"Hello?"

"Hiram, this is Kurt."

"I hope I'm dreaming this," Hiram Yaeger said. "Do you have any idea what time it is?"

Kurt had almost forgotten the fourteen-hour time differential from Seoul to D.C. "I've always heard time is a relative concept," he replied.

"Not in this case," Yaeger grumbled. "But I assume it's important. What do you need?"

"I'm sending you a photo of a pretty woman."

"My wife might not appreciate that."

"I think it's the mystery woman from the yacht. Only, she's wearing a blond wig. It's a clear shot through the zoom lens. Maybe you can run it through your magical machine and figure out who she is. Unless that's beyond what the system can handle."

Yaeger scoffed at the notion. "I'm hurt that you would even doubt us," he replied. "Our facial recognition technology has advanced by leaps and bounds in the last few years. If it's a clear shot and there's any record of her anywhere, we can figure it out. You throw in dinner at Citron and I'll give you her preferred drink, a list of her likes and dislikes, and where she went to school."

Kurt laughed. He figured the best way to get Hiram fired up was to challenge him. "It's a deal. I heard about the computer virus on the *Condor*," Kurt said. "Are you sure Max is secure?"

Max was the name of Hiram's own supercomputing system. Built from scratch, to Hiram's exacting specifications, Max was undoubtedly one of the most advanced and powerful computers in the world—and certainly the most unique. It had a high level of artificial intelligence and its own, distinctly female personality.

"Are you purposely trying to annoy me?" Hiram said. "Of course Max is secure. I built her from the ground up and programmed her myself. No one else in the world has even the most rudimentary understanding of her source code, and, without that, a machine can't be compromised. In fact, if everybody built their own computers instead of buying them off the shelf, the world would be a far more secure place."

"Okay, fine," Kurt said, not meaning to denigrate Hiram or his machine. "So I don't need to print this out and send it FedEx?"

"No," Hiram said. "Just use the secure line the CIA

has set up for you. I've scanned their software with ours. It's clear."

"Okay," Kurt said. "Sending now. Let me know what you find out."

"Will do."

Yaeger hung up, and Kurt had no doubt that the inquisitive computer genius was already crawling out of bed to get the research going immediately. He almost felt guilty, but he had a feeling time was not on their side.

CHAPTER 33

Joe Zavala arrived at Than Rang's building in a limo. He wore a tailored white suit and a silver tie straight from Solano's wardrobe. Kurt traveled with him, wearing a more traditional black suit and carrying a small briefcase with the tools of Solano's trade and a transmitter he and Joe hoped to secure on the hackers. As a last-minute precaution, Kurt's silver hair had been cut short and temporarily dyed black in case Acosta had any surveillance footage of him from the yacht.

Stepping from the limo, they were directed to a private elevator by Than Rang's security personnel and took a quick ride up to the eleventh floor, where they stepped out into a party that was already in full swing.

Spread out across a large ballroom and spilling out onto the rooftop garden were hundreds of South Korea's most powerful and influential people. Industrialists, politicians, and celebrities mixed with poets, artists, and philanthropists. Ambassadors from five nations were there, along with dozens of trade representatives, including a group from the United States.

To kick the festivities into high gear, Than Rang appeared on a raised stage at the end of the ballroom. He wore a traditional Korean outfit known as a *gongbok*, which was an indigo-colored robe of silk tied at the waist with a gray sash and fitted with a high collar. In the ancient dynasties of Korea the *gongbok* was the dress of a nobleman or a king. It told Kurt a lot about who Than Rang thought he was.

While there were a few others dressed similar to Than Rang, most of the guests wore Western clothing: suits and tuxedos for the men, all variety of bright formal wear for the women. It was a dizzying kaleidoscope of movement and color.

"When do you meet up with Acosta?" Kurt asked.

"His message said he'd find me when he needed me and to enjoy the party until then."

Kurt noticed Joe was speaking with a heavy accent even though he was using English. He'd been in character since they left the hotel room. The acting classes seemed to be paying off.

"Perhaps you'd like to wait in the garden, sir?" Kurt asked, speaking in the tone of an assistant.

"Yes," Joe said, "I believe I would. Let's enjoy the cool night air for a while."

They made their way outside to the ornate garden that covered half the eleventh-floor rooftop. It was lit up by thousands of tiny lights, enough to compete with the glow of the city beyond. The other half of the building rose another forty-one stories into the night behind them.

Out in the garden it didn't take long for a trio of women to catch Joe's eye. He flashed a grin, his teeth as white as the jacket he wore. The women responded with smiles of their own, and the two boldest of them began to walk his way.

"Must be the suit," Kurt whispered.

"I do make it look good," Joe replied.

"You look like Mr. Roarke," Kurt said. "They're probably hoping for a trip to Fantasy Island."

"That would make you Tattoo," Joe whispered. "Let me know if you spot *de plane*."

As the women came into range, Joe began to hold court, getting their names and their stories and discussing his position in the world of art. If they weren't already weak-kneed from Joe's looks and charm, hearing that he was an international art expert with a big hacienda on a stretch of Spanish beach made them positively melt.

As one of them sipped the last of her martini, Joe asked if she'd like another.

"I'd love one," she said.

"So would I," the second woman added.

Without a glance at Kurt, Joe sent him to the bar. "Two martinis and a Gin Rickey," he said, ordering Solano's favorite drink.

His friend was enjoying this, and Kurt could not so much as give him the evil eye. He would have to find a way to repay him later. "Yes, Mr. Solano," he said, "right away. Do you require anything else?"

"No," Joe replied with a light sigh. "I seem to have all I need right here."

Kurt handed the briefcase over to Joe and made his way toward the center of the garden, where a circular bar made of glass shimmered with electric blue color where it was lit from within.

One of the many bartenders noticed Kurt immediately. As the man went to work, Kurt studied the surroundings, looking for Acosta. So far, he hadn't seen him. But considering the number of guests, that was not a surprise.

The blue martinis arrived, made with vodka, curaçao, and an ounce of bitters. Shaken and poured, they were almost identical in color to the glowing bar. The Gin Rickey was another story: the bartender needed fresh limes.

As he went to retrieve them, Kurt's gaze settled on a couple who'd eased up to the bar directly opposite him. The man he didn't recognize, but the woman's face was unmistakable at this point. It seemed the mystery woman from Acosta's yacht had an invite to Than Rang's party.

Her hair was copper-colored now and arrow straight. It shone like a new penny beneath the lights and was coiffed in an asymmetrical style that framed her face in a way that was both striking and yet well designed to disguise her features.

Despite that, Kurt had no doubt who he was looking

at. He'd stared at the photo of her in the blond wig for hours after sending it to Hiram. He'd burned her features into his mind: the angle of her cheekbones, the narrow bridge of her nose, the arch of her eyebrows, and the little scar that ran through one of them like a part. All these things were easy to make out.

He noticed her bottom lip seemed to be swollen, almost bee-stung. Considering it had been bruised and bleeding four days prior, that did not surprise him. Nor did it surprise him that she was here. After all, they were chasing the same thing.

"Your drinks, sir."

The bartender had returned.

"Thank you," Kurt said. It was an open bar but Kurt believed in tipping. He handed over a fifty-thousand-won note. The equivalent of about forty dollars.

The bartender smiled intently. "Thank you, sir."

"You're welcome," Kurt said, lifting the small tray on which the drinks had been placed. "Us working-class guys need to stick together."

With the grace of a waiter, Kurt carried the drinks back to Joe, where the women continued to hang on his every word. As soon as the drinks were distributed, Joe handed the bag to Kurt.

Before Kurt could explain the latest complication, Acosta appeared. His arrival was enough to scatter the women like spooked doves.

The pleasantries were exchanged somewhat awkwardly. "My Spanish is not so good," Acosta managed.

"Nor my French," Joe replied. "Perhaps English is better?"

"Not better," Acosta grumbled, "but common."

Acosta laughed at his own joke and then continued the conversation in accented English. Joe did likewise, doing his best to sound like Solano.

"Are you ready?" Acosta asked.

"Whenever you are," Joe replied.

With that, Acosta and his bodyguards led Joe and Kurt to another elevator guarded by Than Rang's men. As they reached the door, one of the guards pointed at Kurt and shook his head.

"He's my assistant," Joe said.

"Do you need him?" Acosta replied.

"Of course not," Joe said. "He is simply here to carry the bags."

Joe snapped his fingers and made a *Give it to me* motion with his hand. Kurt dutifully handed the briefcase over. "Enjoy the festivities," Joe said. "I'll signal you when I return."

The elevator door opened. Acosta and Joe stepped inside. As the door shut, Kurt heard the beginnings of a conversation centered on a collection of works by the artist Degas. He hoped Joe's crash course in the world of art would hold up.

With little to do but wait, Kurt turned and went back to the bar. His main priority now was to avoid being recognized by one of Acosta's guards or the mystery woman from the yacht. He decided the best way not to accidentally run into her was to follow her and keep an eye on her from a distance.

Tracking her was fairly easy, as the shimmer of her copper locks stood out in a crowd of mostly Korean women. Avoiding her gaze was a little more difficult as her eyes seemed constantly on the move. He only hoped his surveillance technique was better than Joe's.

CHAPTER 34

On the elevator ride to the top floor of Than Rang's building, Joe continued discussing the art of Degas with Acosta, relaying facts and anecdotes with ease. By the time they reached the fifty-second floor, Acosta seemed impressed.

The elevator opened and let them out into a large foyer. A man with one hand met them there. He was Caucasian.

"Kovack," Acosta said. "This is Arturo Solano."

Joe nodded and Kovack offered him a brief glance. "Than Rang is waiting."

"Excellent."

Together, the three of them made a short trip to Than Rang's private office.

Than Rang was already there, still dressed in his indigo robe, looking out over the lights of Seoul through the floor-to-ceiling windows.

"We have arrived," Acosta announced. "It's time for the exchange."

Than Rang turned. "Assuming your experts pass their final examination."

Joe glanced around. The office was sprawling and included a conference room behind smoked glass, but the room was dark, and he saw no sign of the hackers. Wherever they were sequestered to do their final exam, it wasn't on the fifty-second floor.

"They will pass every test you can devise," Acosta insisted. "Of that I assure you."

"Then you will have your prize."

Than Rang extended a hand toward the far wall. There, guarded by two additional men, was a small easel. At the center of the easel sat a painting not much larger than a standard sheet of paper. It was surrounded by a gilded frame and bathed in a soft warm light.

"First, we'll run our own tests," Acosta said confidently.

"As you wish."

Acosta led Joe toward the easel. "I'm sure this won't take long."

Joe went to set up, but the guards didn't budge.

"Do you mind?" Joe asked. "I need some room to work."

The guards stepped back a few feet.

With some room to breathe, Joe set his case down and studied the painting in the low light. Fortunately, he recognized it. The painting was a Manet. It was known as the *Chez Tortoni*.

Joe ran through what he knew about it in his mind. Oil on canvas, painted by Manet over a period of several years and finished sometime in 1880. It depicted a French gentleman with a high top hat sitting in a café that the artist himself was known to frequent.

But there was something else . . .

"Are you surprised to see it again?" Acosta asked, all but chortling.

Of course, Joe thought. He'd almost forgotten. It had been stolen, along with a dozen other pieces from the Gardner Museum in Boston. All told, the value of the missing art was somewhere around five hundred million dollars. The bio on Solano indicated he'd been working at the Gardner when the theft happened.

Joe reacted calmly. "If it's real," he said. "I've seen half a dozen forgeries of this painting in the last ten years, some of them quite good. I'll get excited when I know it's the genuine article."

"I assure you," Than Rang said from behind them, "this is the real thing."

Joe shrugged, opened his briefcase, and removed a small device that looked like a camera.

"What are you going to do with that?" Than Rang asked.

"It's an infrared scanner," Joe said. "Set to the proper frequency, it will look beneath the paint to see if other images are present."

Than Rang looked a little nervous, and Joe wondered what would happen if an image of Mickey Mouse or Bugs Bunny appeared when he turned on the scanner. Most likely, all hell would break loose between Than Rang and Acosta and their two sets of thugs. Not a cross fire Joe wanted to be in the middle of.

He turned the scanner on and studied the painting. Fortunately, no cartoons appeared, but several stray lines were obvious. The design looked like the outline of a small building. Joe made a few notes on a pad and switched the scanner off.

"Well?"

"I'm not done," Joe said. "Lights, please."

The room was darkened, and Joe used an ultraviolet light to test the shades of white pigment.

"I see no repairs to this work," he said. "No signs that new paint has been added. In fact, the fluorescence level is right on target. The pigments match those from the 1800s."

The lights came back on, and Joe noticed Than Rang had begun to look pleased.

"What about those stray marks?"

"Few know this," Joe said, making up a story he hoped couldn't be quickly verified, "but Manet painted this work over the beginnings of another. The marks beneath are believed to be the outline of a carriage house in Toulouse."

"So this is the authentic item?"

"Or a perfect forgery," Joe said.

"What are you suggesting?" Than Rang blurted out.

"Nothing," Joe said. "But tell me, did you steal the painting?"

"Of course not."

"Then you bought it from the men or women who did," Joe pointed out. "By their very nature, that makes them criminals. Surely you didn't take it on face value when you handed them their payment."

The Korean bristled at the remark. "I would not be foolish enough to buy a fake."

"There must be some way to tell for sure," Acosta said.

"Bring the lights up to maximum," Joe said. "One thing that can't be faked is what's called craquelure. As the painting ages, the oils dry out and the paint cracks. Based on the age of the work and the type of paint used, specific patterns will appear. It's somewhat like an artistic fingerprint."

With the lights up, Joe examined the surface of the painting. From what he'd been told, French craquelure tended to form in curving, sweeping lines, while Italian paintings tended to crack in squares or little rectangular blocks, which was why the *Mona Lisa* looked the way it did up close.

To Joe's chagrin, neither pattern appeared on the Manet. There were vertical cracks, and a few horizontal ones, but nothing that looked like what he'd been taught to expect. He pulled out a magnifying glass to give himself a second look, and to buy himself some time. But the more he looked, the more convinced he became he was looking at a fake.

CHAPTER 35

While Joe played art expert, Kurt tailed the mystery woman from the yacht. The longer he followed her, the more he noticed she was moving in a deliberate pattern. Out from the bar and then back, checking a quadrant of the garden at a time, and then reporting back to her date.

"She's looking for something," he said to himself.

He moved in closer and managed to overhear part of her conversation. The man called her "Calista." So now he had a name, even if it was an alias.

She shook her head at something the man asked and then spoke. "Acosta and Than Rang are nowhere to be seen. They must be making the exchange now. Time to get in position."

The man nodded. "Very well," he said. "Let's be quick."

Kurt turned his back and eased in between two Korean businessmen who were having a spirited debate, nodding his head as if he agreed with something that was being said. The businessmen looked at him oddly, then went back to their conversation.

Calista and her date moved past Kurt and separated, heading off in different directions. Kurt followed Calista as she made her way from the terrace into the covered part of the ballroom and down a short hall. She slipped through a doorway and disappeared as it closed behind her. Squinting, Kurt noticed the sign on the door. The ladies' room.

He looked for a place to linger, but the hall was a dead end. Instead of getting too close, he actually moved back, loitering in a spot from which he could watch the hall in the reflection of a smoked glass window.

Soon enough, the door swung open again.

Kurt kept his eyes on the reflection as she made her way back toward the garden. She passed him without a glance. But Kurt noticed something different about her. Her walk had changed. It was more refined, less brisk. The dress seemed to fit a little tighter, the figure inside was a little fuller.

Kurt couldn't see her face, but he didn't have to, he knew what he knew. The woman who'd come out of the restroom was not the same one who'd gone in.

ON THE FIFTY-SECOND FLOOR, Joe stared at the painting, wondering what to do. If he pronounced it a fake, all hell would break loose. If he claimed it to be real and it was some kind of test set up by Acosta or even Than Rang, his cover would be blown.

"Well?" Than Rang said. "What is your verdict?"

Joe stroked the goatee that had been glued to his face. "It . . . it . . ." He turned to Acosta and in full character said, "It brings a tear to my eye to see such an old friend once again. Never did I think it would be recovered."

Than Rang relaxed. Acosta sighed.

Joe exhaled along with them. "Yes," he said. "I can assure you, this is the bona fide work of the master. Look at the touch. Look at the depth. You are both very lucky men."

"Very good," Acosta said. He motioned to the man with one hand and pointed to Joe. "Pay him."

A briefcase was produced that looked exactly like Solano's. "The second half of your fee. One hundred thousand euros, as we agreed."

Joe opened the case, looked over the money, and then shut it quickly. Unfortunately, even as he did so, the one-handed man was taking the case Joe had brought in with him and carrying it off with the tracking device inside.

"My pen," Joe said. "It's in the case."

Acosta laughed and slapped Joe on the back. "You can buy a whole factory of pens with what I've paid you."

Joe chuckled in an effort to cover his chagrin, but as the one-handed man was already disappearing into a conference room he decided not to draw any more attention to himself.

"Enjoy the remainder of the evening," Acosta said. "Perhaps the young women you were engaged with earlier will still be unattached for the evening."

"One can only hope," Joe said.

Than Rang gestured toward the elevator and Joe walked that way. As the bell pinged and the door opened, Joe heard Than Rang speaking to Acosta. "Your people have passed the test. Our business is complete. Get them ready to move."

Joe couldn't linger any further. He stepped into the elevator and waited for the doors to close.

As soon as the elevator began to descend, Joe activated the microtransmitter the CIA had given him, a tiny waterproof device that was clipped to one of his molars. He spoke almost silently without moving his mouth.

"Got your ears on, buddy?"

A moment of silence rang out before Kurt came back. "I'm here," Kurt's voice replied.

The tiny speaker resonated against a bone in the jaw that connected to the ear. It truly sounded as if Kurt was in his head.

"I'm on my way down," Joe whispered.

"Mission accomplished?"

"Not exactly," Joe said. "I think we'd better make a quick exit, stage left, right, center, it doesn't matter."

"What's the rush?"

"Well, for one thing," Joe said, "the painting is a fake. I'm pretty sure Than Rang knows. And if Acosta realizes it or Than Rang begins to think that I know and just didn't speak up yet . . . Well, let's just say I wouldn't want to be in Solano's shoes at that point."

"Except that you are in Solano's shoes."

"Exactly," Joe said. "Beyond that, they took the case with the transmitter in it. Gave me a matching one filled with cash. But without the tracer, we can't finish the mission anyway."

"Not necessarily," Kurt said. "I've found us a plan B."

"Plan B?"

"The one person in the world as interested in locating Sienna as we are. And if I'm right, she's just going into action."

"Your mystery woman."

"Appearing as a redhead today and going by the name of Calista."

The elevator finally hit the eleventh floor and stopped. As soon as the doors were open, Joe stepped out. "Let's make this quick. Where are you?"

"Getting ready to sneak into the ladies' room."

"I knew you were desperate," Joe said, "but that's taking it a little far, don't you think?"

"She went in a minute ago," Kurt whispered. "Someone else came out wearing her clothes. I assume that was to throw off Than Rang's cameras. But no one else has come out yet at all."

"Do you think she went out a window or something?"

"Or a back door," Kurt said. "I'm about to go in and find out."

"Makes sense," Joe said. "On my way."

By the time Joe reached the restroom, Kurt had pulled

a janitor's cart in front of the bathroom door and ducked inside. Joe found him looking for a secret panel, knocking on the walls and listening for a hollow spot. There were no windows or back doors to speak of.

"What about the air vent," Joe said, studying the louvered metal grate that covered it.

"People don't really climb through air ducts," Kurt said from inside one of the stalls. "Mostly because they are designed to carry air and people are heavier than air."

"Especially after all those hors d'oeuvres at the party."

"Look at this," Kurt said, waving Joe into the stall and pointing to the floor, where a fine layer of white dust lined the polished granite tile.

"Looks like drywall dust," Joe said.

"My thoughts exactly," Kurt said as he found a seam that had been hastily covered by a quick-drying plaster— although it wasn't dry yet.

With a little effort, Kurt was able to dig his fingers into the seam and pull the panel out. It was a three-by-three-foot square. Just big enough for someone to climb through. "Either they have very large mice or she went through here."

"Where does it lead?" Joe asked.

Kurt put his head inside. "I saw these on the building schematics. It's a crawl space between the walls. Lots of pipes and electrical wire. It's dark to the right side, but there's a sliver of light perhaps a hundred feet down on the left. It looks like the crack beneath a door."

"Can we fit?" Joe asked.

"Only one way to find out," Kurt said, climbing in.

Joe locked the bathroom stall door and followed Kurt into the crawl space. He did his best to replace the panel once he was inside and then turned, immediately banging his head on one of the pipes. The impact reverberated through the dark.

"Keep it down," Kurt whispered.

"I can't see anything," Joe said.

"Hold on."

As Joe watched, a bluish white light filled the space, courtesy of the screen on Kurt's phone. It was enough to navigate with, and Kurt began clambering forward. Joe followed until they reached the spot where the light was filtering in.

"Inspection panel," Kurt said. A small handle in a square metal door presented itself, and Kurt ducked down, twisted the handle, and eased the door open.

"What do you see?" Joe asked.

"Back office hallway and a fire escape."

Kurt wedged his broad shoulders through the narrow door and out into the hall. Joe followed, squeezing through and straightening up once he was free.

Kurt glanced back at him. "You're a mess."

Joe looked at himself. His spotless white jacket was smudged with black grease and swaths of gray dust. He took it off and removed his tie, stuffing them back into the crawl space before closing the door.

"I was getting tired of that monkey suit anyway," he said. "Which way now?"

"Good question," Kurt said. "Not much she can do

back here. If she wants to intercept the hackers, she'll have
to beat them to whatever mode of transport they're going
to be using."

"There's a helipad on the roof," Joe said.

"And a garage underneath the building," Kurt added.

"If she was going to take the elevator, she wouldn't
have come this way," Joe said.

"That means she's on the stairs."

Without delay, Kurt moved down the hall to the fire
escape and eased the door open. Like most fire escapes,
the stairs were metal, descending in a rectangular zigzag.
Even before he was fully inside, Kurt could hear rapidly
moving footfalls echoing in the space.

He moved to the edge of the rail as Joe slipped inside
and shut the door. Gazing down, he spotted a woman's
hand on the rail moving rapidly toward the basement.
But it was not alone—another hand trailed hers.

Kurt stepped back and held up two fingers. Joe nodded.
Kurt pointed to their feet. "Shoes," he whispered.

Joe pulled his shoes off as Kurt was doing the same.
"At this rate, I'm gonna be naked by the time we catch
up to her."

"That ought to scare her," Kurt replied. "Not to mention everyone else involved."

Leaving their shoes behind, they began to descend in
their socks, treading lightly but quickly, and staying away
from the inside rail, where a quick look upward from either of the targets might give them away.

They were passing the sixth floor and headed for the

fifth when the woman and her friend reached the bottom floor. The door at the base of the stairwell opened, and they could hear the unmistakable sound of a gun with a silencer on the barrel. Three dartlike shots were followed by a dull thud, and then another.

"They've taken someone out," Joe whispered.

Kurt stooped and peered over the edge. What looked like a pair of guards was being dragged into the stairwell. Calista and the man took several items from the bodies, covered them hastily with a tarp, and then went out through the door into the garage once again.

"What are they up to?" Joe wondered aloud.

Kurt had no idea. When the door banged shut, he started to move again, racing down the stairs as fast as he could. He made it to the bottom of the stairwell and pressed against the door, looking through the wire safety glass window. He saw the woman clearly now. Her hair was short and black again, and she was dressed in a uniform like one of Than Rang's guards.

"She's climbing into the cab of an eighteen-wheeler," Kurt said.

"What about her friend?"

Kurt glanced around. He couldn't see the man, but the sound of a door slamming and a slight vibration in the mirror of a second truck suggested he'd gotten in the second rig. For now, they just sat there waiting.

"What's the story on those guys?" Kurt asked, glancing back to Joe.

As Kurt watched the trucks, Joe moved back into the

recesses of the stairwell where the dead men were covered by the tarp. "Ammunition belts and empty holsters," Joe said. "Radio clips on their belts are empty. I'd guess these men are security specialists, not drivers."

"Makes sense," Kurt said. "Somebody has to ride shotgun on an operation like this. By the looks of it, our two friends have split up, taking the place of these two. They're each in a different truck."

"Guarding the cargo and waiting for the drivers to arrive," Joe suggested.

"That's my guess."

"So now what?"

"Stowaway time," Kurt said. "We get on board, they load up the other hackers and hopefully take us right to Sienna."

"What if Sienna is being held in Kim Jong-un's palace?" Joe said.

"Then we get a tour of North Korea," Kurt said.

"Not sure I like that idea," Joe said. "They don't have a lot of Mexican food up there, you know. Or much food in general, for that matter."

Kurt didn't exactly like the idea of ending up in the Hermit Kingdom himself. But he didn't think they were going there. "From what Colonel Lee said, the border is closed. Even if it were open, there's no way these guys are driving across the DMZ in a pair of big rigs with the DaeShan logo splashed all over them."

"That makes sense," Joe said. "I'd still rather call in the cavalry."

"We stop these guys on this side of the border, we'll never find Sienna," Kurt said. "I didn't come this far to show my hand before the final deal. But if you want to stay here, I understand."

Joe shook his head, and with a grunt pulled off the goatee, completing his transformation from Solano back to Zavala. "And go back to the party upstairs? I don't think so. But if we're not going into the so-called Democratic Republic of North Korea, then where are we going?"

"Hale said the cyberattacks weren't directly traceable to North Korea, even though they're fairly certain North Korea was behind them. He said this Unit 121 had people working all over the world: in China, Russia, hidden here in Seoul. If that's the case, then we might not even leave the city."

Joe broke into a grin. "I like the way you think," he said. "I'm sure you'll turn out to be wrong as usual, but there's something to be said for remaining positive until all hope is actually lost."

Kurt glanced back at the dead men, blood already oozing out from under the bodies. "That tarp won't hide them for long," he said, "which means our friends can't play impostor for any extended length of time. Whatever they're going to do, it's going to happen quick."

"Okay, let's go," Joe said. "But if we end up on the docks at Incheon or getting loaded onto a 747, I'm definitely calling in the cavalry."

"Deal," Kurt said.

As Joe covered the bodies once more, Kurt eased the door open and moved out of the stairwell. They stole into the garage as quietly as alley cats, making sure to stay out of the mirrors' lines of sight. When they reached the back of the first trailer, Kurt unlatched the door and waved Joe inside. As soon as Joe was up, Kurt climbed in and closed the door gently.

By the time Kurt turned around, Joe had his phone out, using the light from the screen as Kurt had done in the crawl space. He was examining the cargo.

"Computers," Joe said. "High-tech servers, by the look of things. I've seen racks of equipment like this in Hiram's data center."

"We're in the right place," Kurt said. "This cargo must be destined for the North Korean Cyber-Force."

They settled in, sitting down and leaning against the wall of the truck, hidden by a large stack of equipment in case anyone opened the door for a quick look.

A short time later, the sounds of activity picked up outside the vehicle. Loud voices speaking Korean were interspersed with directions in broken English. Shortly thereafter, the big rig shuddered as the engine came to life and the truck began to move. They seemed to inch their way through the garage slowly before climbing a ramp and then accelerating.

After several turns that felt like they were negotiating city blocks, the truck began to pick up speed. Kurt pulled out his phone, found he had a strong signal, and switched it to map mode. It took a moment to locate his whereabouts and calculate his direction and speed, but soon there was a little blue dot on the moving map.

"Where are we headed?" Joe asked.

"You don't want to know," he replied. To Kurt's chagrin, they were on the main highway, moving due north, heading directly toward the DMZ.

CHAPTER 36

Sebastian Brèvard sat on the veranda of his sprawling baroque palace, overlooking the Olympic-sized swimming pool where he swam most mornings, as a servant delivered his breakfast of crepes and fresh fruit.

After deeming the meal acceptable, Sebastian waved the servant away, only to have Laurent appear seconds later.

"I assume you have news," Sebastian said.

"Calista reports the infiltration plan is under way," Laurent said. "Egan is with her."

As planned, Sebastian thought. "Make sure the extraction team is ready to pull her out as soon as she signals us."

"Already done."

"What about the others?"

"Preparing to eliminate Acosta."

"Excellent," Sebastian said, grinning. "I only regret

that I won't be there to see his fat face when they dump him into the sea."

"Yes, it would have been nice to take him ourselves," Laurent said.

"Make sure there is no evidence," he said. "It will serve us well if the rest of the world thinks he's still alive."

"I've already given that order," Laurent said.

Sebastian took a sip of fresh papaya juice and gazed out over the shimmering pool to the sprawling hedge maze that covered ten acres on a lower level of the property. His grandfather had built the house and the surrounding walls. Sebastian's father had brought in the flowering plants and built the maze. *A reminder,* he often had said, *that those who don't know the path are liable to get lost.*

Brèvard knew the path he must take.

Much as his great-grandfather had done, Sebastian intended to complete the job of a lifetime and disappear. In some ways, he hated to leave the family home, but it was the only path that led to a future.

To keep the treasure he planned to take, the world would have to be fooled into thinking nothing had been stolen in the first place. To survive, if they ever figured it out, required a second trick: misdirection. He would convince the world that they'd killed him and ended the threat. And, for good measure, he'd point the finger at someone else if they needed a scapegoat to hang.

In that role, he would cast his unstable little sister and her ex-lover Acosta. They would play it perfectly.

He considered her fate for a moment, wondered if he

should feel some sense of guilt, and then dismissed the idea as if it were absurd. Much like the family home, she would soon outlive her usefulness.

Dismissing Laurent, Sebastian opened a laptop beside him and tapped a few keys. Calista had set it up to monitor activity of the NUMA crew to their south, the ones investigating the wreck of the *Ethernet*. According to the latest report, they were in the same vicinity, now getting assistance from a South African tug and setting up a salvage effort on a derelict they'd discovered.

Curious, he tapped a few keys and was able to retrieve from the NUMA database several photos of the ship. To his surprise, it was covered in foliage and tawny-colored soil. He scrolled down until he found a designation. The discovery all but sent him into shock. The salvage claim listed the derelict's name as the SS *Waratah*.

He put down the slice of orange he was chewing on and wiped his mouth with a napkin, scanning the NUMA file for more information on the ship. Her dimensions matched. The photos taken in several parts of the ship depicted old equipment and fittings. A picture of serving trays with the Blue Anchor logo in the middle were unmistakable. And an off-colored image of the ship's bell with the name and the ship's launch date engraved on it left no doubt.

"Damn," he said, tossing the napkin down.

Brèvard felt his throat constricting. It was as if unseen hands were reaching out from beyond the grave to choke him and to pay him back for his family's treachery a hundred years before.

As he scanned the remaining details on the file, he recalled his father telling him the story, a story passed down from one patriarch to the next through four generations. It was a lesson about pain and danger. A tale of escaping death and passing it on to others so the Brèvard family might be preserved.

He knew of his family's escape from South Africa with the wolves of the Durban police on their heels. He remembered hearing over and over again how it was only ruthlessness that had saved the family, how shortly after the hijacking the crew tried valiantly to take the ship back. How they'd been thwarted because his great-grandfather had expected it and had taken hostages whom he was willing to kill.

In the aftermath of the uprising, the passengers and most of the crew were put off the ship in the lifeboats, leaving only two double-enders for launches and twenty crewmen behind to run the ship itself—a far more manageable number.

As fate would have it, a storm had come up the next day, a storm so powerful the *Waratah* was almost capsized, just as the newspapers thought she had been. It seemed impossible that any of the lifeboats survived that gale, and, as it turned out, not one ever made it to shore.

The *Waratah*, on the other hand, was driven north, where, aided by the storm surge, she traveled up the narrow river farther than anyone could have expected. She ran aground in a meander that couldn't be seen from the coast in an unpopulated section of the country. It was there that the last members of the crew were killed.

Over the years, the ship seemed to burrow itself into the silt, sinking lower and lower, and soon being enveloped and completely covered.

Sebastian's father had shown him the hill beneath which the ship sat, and, years later, he'd seen part of the ship itself after a woman the Brèvard family was holding had inadvertently discovered the ship and tried to escape, along with two of her children, using one of the ship's remaining dilapidated boats.

To everyone's surprise, the wooden launch actually stayed afloat long enough to reach the African coast, but the woman and her children had died from exposure long before they reached safety.

Sebastian had always considered it poetic. They were, in some ways, the last victims of a doomed ship. But the superstitious part of him now wondered if this ancient ship could somehow be in the process of evening the score.

"How is this possible?" Sebastian whispered to no one.

He could only conclude that the torrential rains of the month prior had somehow unearthed the ship and pushed her out into the channel, and from there the current had taken her south, right into the path of the NUMA team. But how had she remained afloat? How had she not broken apart and sunk to the watery grave long rumored to be her home after a hundred years of rotting away?

Whatever the reason, it seemed karma, the random nature of the universe, had dealt him a terrible card at the very moment he was getting ready to play his hand. He didn't know what evidence of his great-grandfather's actions might remain on the *Waratah*, but it was possible that clues left on that ship would reveal the family's treachery or even lead the world to his door before he was ready to entertain them.

He called for Laurent and waited. He had to speak carefully. No one else knew the secret of the lost ship. Not even the other family members.

"What do you need, brother?" Laurent asked upon returning to the veranda.

"Gather up your pilots and get the helicopters ready," he said. "It's time to attack our friends at NUMA once again before they become too complacent."

"You want us to attack them from the air?" Laurent asked. "I thought you and Calista had already sabotaged them with the computers."

"We did," Brèvard said. "But instead of being towed into port, they've remained on station and even found themselves a derelict to salvage. They're proving more resourceful and persistent than I care to allow. I need them distracted further. At this moment, with their salvage operation under way, they seem to have made themselves vulnerable."

"We have a few torpedoes in the armory," Laurent said. "Acosta was going to sell them to the Somalis before he betrayed us."

"Perfect," Brèvard said. "Arm the helicopters with those torpedoes. I want that derelict sent to the bottom. And while you're at it, make a few strafing runs over the other ships in their little fleet."

"You want us to attack the derelict?" Laurent said, sounding confused.

Sebastian stared. He could understand why the order sounded odd. "Don't question me," he growled, "just do as I order. Trust me, I have my reasons."

Laurent held up his hands in an act of contrition. "I'm sorry," he said. "I just wanted to make sure I understood."

"How soon can you launch?" Sebastian asked.

"Within a few hours."

"Excellent," Sebastian said.

As Laurent disappeared, Brèvard turned back to his breakfast but found he'd lost his appetite. The last thing he needed was to be exposed before he was ready to move.

CHAPTER 37

Kurt and Joe rode in the back of Than Rang's tractor trailer as it cruised along South Korean highway Route 3. Through the wonders of modern technology, Kurt could track their progress on his phone.

"Still heading for the DMZ?" Joe asked.

"Like a homing pigeon," Kurt said.

Forty-five miles from Seoul, and no more than a mile from the edge of the DMZ, they felt the truck gear down. A series of twists and turns made it feel as if they'd gone off the highway. At the same time, Kurt's reception went out and didn't come back. Wherever they were, it was beyond the range of the cell phone towers.

He put the phone away and glanced over at Joe. "You can forget about calling the cavalry, we've lost our signal."

"Great," Joe muttered.

Kurt eased from his spot and crawled to the far wall

where a pinprick of light was coming through a hole in the truck's metal skin. He cozied up to it and stared through.

"Any signs saying 'Welcome to North Korea'?" Joe asked.

"Not yet," Kurt said. "Mostly bright lights, and a rather funky smell."

Joe smelled it too. "It smells like . . ."

"Garbage," Kurt said. "We're driving into a giant land-fill. I see overhead lights and dump trucks and bulldozers mashing everything down. Looks like half of Seoul's trash is out there."

"One of Than Rang's companies," Joe said, remember-ing the briefing.

Kurt nodded. "You know what they say: Where there's muck, there's brass."

"Brass?"

"Coins," Kurt explained. "*Dinero*, big bucks."

"Right," Joe replied. "Let's hope that where there's muck, there's computer experts."

"Better here than across the border," Kurt added, agreeing with his friend.

The truck rumbled along, moving slower with each passing moment, eventually lurching to a stop with a hiss of the brakes. From Joe's perspective, the glare from the arc lights illuminating the landfill was suddenly cut off. "We've pulled inside a shed of some kind. Maybe a loading bay."

Kurt stretched, and made sure he was ready for action, as the truck rumbled to a stop for a second time. He got in position behind a stack of computer parts and made sure he couldn't be seen from the rear door of the trailer. Joe did the same.

They waited in the darkness, listening to voices speaking Korean, until the sound of a heavy mechanical gearing drowned them out. Almost immediately Kurt felt the truck moving. Not forward or backward but descending.

"Why am I getting a sinking feeling?" Joe whispered.

"Because we are," Kurt said.

The rate of descent picked up and then seemed to ease, but Kurt knew that was an illusion, like the feeling of being motionless in an airplane when one is actually moving at six hundred miles per hour. They were still dropping, but at a constant rate. Their bodies had just grown used to it.

He glanced at his watch and noted the second hand moving past twelve. It made it all the way around once and had almost reached the six o'clock position when the descent finally slowed and stopped.

"Ninety seconds," he whispered. "How fast do you think we were moving?"

"Not all that fast," Joe said, "maybe two or three feet per second."

Kurt made a quick calculation. "That puts us somewhere around two hundred feet below the surface."

After the smooth ride down, the next move was a jolt as a large crane grabbed the shipping container and lifted it off the back of the truck.

Kurt looked out through the pinhole and gave Joe the play-by-play. "A big overhead crane has us, by the look of things. Appears to be moving us to some kind of platform."

They began to pivot as the crane operator manipulated them into a proper alignment.

"I can see the other truck," Kurt said. "And Calista. She's headed for what I'd guess is the control room."

Kurt watched her rap on the door of the control room and wait for the door to be opened. "Don't do it . . ." he whispered.

No one heard his psychic warning. The lock was released and the door pushed open. She handed the first guard some type of manifest and, as he looked at it, she calmly drew her gun and opened fire. The shots were accurate, fired in rapid succession, but unhurried and without a sense of panic. She was cold and efficient.

At almost the same instant, Calista's friend grabbed the other driver and broke his neck with a quick twist and a sickening crack. Two men came running from beside the crane to intervene but were quickly gunned down. The room went still.

"What about the other driver?" Joe whispered.

"He's probably dead," Kurt suggested, figuring Calista would have killed him before she got out of the truck.

"This girl of yours is cold as ice," Joe said.

"She's not my girl," he said.

"Are they coming this way?"

"No," Kurt said. "They're going into the control room."

*   *   *

UNAWARE THAT SHE was being watched, Calista strode into the control room and immediately began working one of the computers. It took only thirty seconds for her to break into the system.

Egan, her third brother, ducked in. "The loading platform is secured," he said. "Does anyone know we're here?"

"I got them before they could sound the alarm," Calista said. She ran through the security protocols and checked for any sign of trouble. "We're fine. Get the hackers out of the second van. We'll escort them through."

"How many men on the other side?" Egan asked.

"A full million in the North Korean Army," she said with a smile.

"You know what I mean."

"According to the duty roster I was able to pull up on the computer, the North Korean station is manned by a hundred twenty. Most of them are restricted to the surface level and the topside loading zone. Only forty are cleared to enter the lower levels and they comprise two shifts, so we'll be dealing with no more than twenty at a time."

"There are only two of us," he pointed out.

"Makes it interesting, doesn't it?"

He stared.

"Relax," she said, opening a pack with three silver canisters that had odd numeric markings on them. "This will even the odds."

"Nerve gas?"

"Nothing so dangerous," she explained. "It's an RPA, a rapid paralytic agent. Freezes the central nervous system for ten minutes or so. It won't knock them out or kill them, but it will make them easy to hit. We take the main control room by surprise, then pump this through the station, and the rest will be easy."

"Do we have gas masks?"

Calista produced two small filters that looked like bulkier versions of the masks surgeons wore. They fit over the nose and mouth. "Won't need them for long," she said. "The gas goes inert after sixty seconds."

"We still have to get through the tunnel first."

At that moment a message appeared on the screen. It was in Korean. Calista scanned it with a handheld device that translated it to English.

"Our invitation," she said. "They're awaiting transfer of the hackers. Get them out of the truck and into the tram."

"What happens to them when we fire off the gas?"

"They get frozen in place," Calista replied, "which will keep them from getting in the way."

Done asking questions, Egan left the control room as Calista made one last check of the system and patched command of the system to a remote unit she'd brought for just this purpose.

From there, she made her way to a tram that sat at the entrance to a long tunnel. With an open top, it looked more like an ore car than the passenger tram so familiar to most airport travelers.

She climbed in as Egan dragged the hackers from the rear of the second truck.

Xeno9X9, ZSumG, and Montresor were powerful men

in the underworld of computing but were less than magnificent to behold in real life. Three scrawny, scruffy-looking specimens. Their faces were pale, their eyes sunken, and their arms and legs thin and spindly. There seemed little about them to suggest danger or the ability to bring down nations all around the world. Not one of them had offered any resistance since their capture, though that probably had more to do with the sisters, wives, and children being held at the Brèvard compound than any sort of docile natures.

"Get in," she growled.

They climbed onto a tram that rested just in front of the platform on which the first trailer had been deposited.

With Egan in front, Calista took the rear seat, keeping the hackers between them. By typing a code into the remote, she activated the equipment, and the sound of a powerful generator spooling up reached everyone's ears. When a light flashed green on the remote, she pressed the go switch and the tram began to accelerate down the long lighted tunnel.

CHAPTER 38

"They're gone," Kurt said. "They took off down some tunnel. Now's our chance."

He made his way to the door and unlatched the panel on the back of the trailer. Hopping out, he took a quick look around. There were only dead men left in the control room. Dead men and blinking computers that Calista had tampered with. If he guessed right, anyone watching the room from a remote location would get nothing but a report that said *Situation normal*.

"We'd better arm ourselves," he suggested, grabbing a pistol from one of the dead men. Joe crouched by one of the other bodies and did the same. Then they left the control room to take a quick look around.

The space was huge, the size of an aircraft hangar. On one side, the big rig that had hauled them sat alone on an octagonal platform. Stripped of the container that had once been on its back, it looked small, out of place.

"Reminds me of a turntable in the railroad yard," Joe said.

Kurt agreed. He looked up. An empty shaft, matching the dimensions and shape of the platform, ran upward into the darkness. The walls of the shaft were notched, and huge wheeled gears that must have intersected these notches sprouted from four of the platform's eight sides.

"I'd guess those gears move it up and down," Joe said. "Like an incline railway, only vertical."

Kurt had to agree. "That explains how we got down here, but it doesn't explain why."

Looking for the answer to that question, he moved to the horizontal tunnel, the one Calista and her friend had vanished down on a silent tram. It seemed to run on to infinity, colored in bands of white and gray where the overhead lights and the shadows between them alternated.

"What do you make of all this?" Joe asked.

"I'm not sure," Kurt admitted, "but I'm getting the idea that Than Rang isn't quite as neutral as Colonel Lee and the CIA seem to believe."

"You think this tunnel goes under the DMZ?"

"It's the only conclusion that makes any sense," Kurt said. "For one thing, we're right up against the border. For another, the North has been digging tunnels under the DMZ for years. I can't remember how many have been found, but there are at least three or four major ones. Most were smaller and designed for infiltration, but supposedly the largest of them was capable of handling a division of men and light equipment in an hour or so. From the pictures I've seen, even that has nothing on this place."

Joe nodded. "I thought the South was always listening for signs of more tunneling. Shouldn't they have heard this thing being excavated?"

"We're directly under a landfill," Kurt pointed out. "With all those bulldozers moving around, not to mention the cranes, the dump trucks, and the compacting equipment, this place is a constant source of noise. I'm guessing that any stray sounds detected from this area could easily be written off as coming from the landfill. Beyond that, we're down here pretty deep. That has a tendency to muffle noise as well."

"Gotta hand it to them, the landfill's a perfect cover. Even gives them a place to hide all the dirt and rock they had to excavate."

Kurt nodded but didn't reply. He was gazing down the long tunnel and had caught sight of movement. There was no sound like a subway train screeching down the rails, but something was definitely headed their way.

"Take cover," Kurt said.

He and Joe crouched down and readied their guns as the approaching target continued to race toward them. It had no wheels or cables. It simply seemed to be flying.

"Maglev," Joe said, using the short term for "magnetic levitation." "That explains the high-voltage generators."

"Another way to keep the operation quiet," Kurt said. "It's almost silent."

The car slowed rapidly the last hundred yards and was

almost motionless as it exited the tunnel and slid onto a platform similar to the one their shipping container now rested on. As the sound of the humming generator waned, the new arrival dropped several inches, settling onto the platform with a surprisingly dull thud.

Kurt waited but no one came out.

"Empty car?" Joe guessed.

Suspicious of the whole scenario, Kurt crept up to the square cart and looked over the edge. "No passengers," he said. "But it's not empty."

He reached inside and scooped up a handful of the cargo. "Pellets," he said. "Extremely light."

Joe took a quick look, rubbing one of the pellets between his fingers. "Titanium," he said. "Not fully processed yet but halfway there."

"I think I get it now," Kurt said.

"Get what?"

"Than Rang's played-out mines that are producing three times what they did a decade before . . . His alliance with the shadowy figures in the North . . . He's salting his own mines," Kurt said. "The generals send him half-processed titanium that he ships to a processor as if they came from his own mine and he sends them computer hackers, high-tech supplies, and probably a steady diet of cold hard cash in return. The North Koreans get technology and access to markets the UN sanctions prevent them from touching, and Than Rang gets cheap ore at fire-sale prices."

As if in response to the arrival of the ore-bearing car,

a series of yellow lights began to flash around the base of the platform on which the shipping container had been placed—the one Kurt and Joe had been riding in with the high-tech servers.

"Last train to Clarksville," Kurt said. "Let's make sure we're on it."

He and Joe dashed for the open door of the shipping container, jumping inside just as the platform levitated upward. Kurt pulled the door shut and the container began to accelerate rapidly and smoothly. In seconds, they were moving fifty miles an hour, all without the slightest sound of machinery or even the grind of wheels on the road.

"Since we seem to be on the express train here," Joe began, "I should probably ask what we're going to do when we get to the other side."

"My guess, we'll either be entering a dead zone or an all-out firefight," Kurt said.

"We could have waited for them to come back."

"What if they plan to take another way out?"

"You got me there," Joe said.

It wasn't long before the big container began to slow. As it settled onto the receiving platform at the far end, it became clear there was no firefight in progress. A minute of silence rang in their ears before Kurt dared crack the rear door open.

A quick look revealed several dead soldiers in North Korean uniforms and no sign of fighting or alarms in sight.

Kurt and Joe hopped out of the container and did a quick survey. Nine men down. No sign of reinforcements. Ruthless and precise.

Oddly enough, the three hackers lay on their sides in the tram they'd come over in. They were not moving but didn't appear to have been shot.

Joe shook one of them but got no response. "They look drugged to me," he said. "They're still breathing."

"We can figure that out later."

They followed the trail of bodies to a corridor, where they found an elevator. Joe was about to press the button when Kurt blocked his hand. "Let's not announce our arrival."

They pried the doors open and found a narrow elevator shaft. On the far side, a maintenance ladder traveled up a shallow, recessed channel that was carved into the wall.

Kurt counted five floors between them and the underside of the parked elevator car.

"What do you bet that's where our friends are?" Kurt asked.

"Sounds like a place to start. We can't search this whole complex."

They moved into the elevator shaft and began climbing the ladder. Kurt went first. Joe braced the door to keep it open. It gave them a little light to work with and would make for a quicker getaway if they had to come down the ladder as well.

Climbing quickly, they passed the first two floors. As they cleared the third, Kurt heard a clink beneath him and then a dull metallic clatter as something fell down the shaft to the concrete below.

He looked down and saw Joe, holding on for dear life with one hand and clinging to a broken part of the ladder with another.

"What are you doing?"

Joe hooked the broken section of the ladder onto one of the rungs and climbed past it. "We're in a lot of danger here, Kurt."

"I don't think anyone heard that."

"I'm not worried about the guards," Joe said, "I'm worried about North Korean construction practices. Have you looked at this concrete? It's flaking away like a day-old croissant. I'm thinking they used way too much sand. And this rebar . . . It's all rusted and loose." As if to emphasize the point, Joe pulled on one of the bars and it came right out. "I say we make this quick before the whole place caves in on us."

Kurt smiled. His friend was an engineer and a perfectionist. He would never allow such shoddy work on his watch.

"I'll be sure to send a strongly worded letter to Kim Jong-un when we get home," Kurt said. "'Please construct your secret bases with better materials so we don't get injured when infiltrating them. Otherwise, you'll be hearing from our lawyers.'"

"I'm sure that'll spur him to action," Joe said.

By now they'd reached the elevator car. Kurt squeezed by it and climbed on top. He pried open the emergency escape panel and dropped in as quietly as possible. Joe followed. The door was already open. The equivalent of a hold switch was in the locked position.

Two more bodies lay in the hall, and for a moment the silence held. But as Kurt stepped forward, a commotion rang out at the far end. Multiple gunshots. A stun grenade going off. And then return fire from the silenced pistols of Calista and her partner.

Whatever trick had gotten them this far without resistance had apparently failed at the last moment. Alarms were now sounding throughout the complex.

"So much for the peace and quiet," Joe said.

"Come on," Kurt urged, running forward, headed straight for the sounds of the battle.

CHAPTER 39

Pressing himself up against the wall beside an open door, Kurt heard another volley of gunfire, a shout of pain, and then a second explosion from a stun grenade.

Glancing inside the room, he saw Calista lying on her side, blood streaming from her ear. Her friend was firing into a smoke-filled room when a bullet knocked him backward and a second shell hit him dead in the center of the chest.

On the ground beside them lay Sienna Westgate.

A spike of adrenaline surged through Kurt. He could hardly believe his eyes. She *was* alive. Or at least she had been. But now . . .

A trio of North Korean soldiers rushed through the smoke, and Kurt instinctively opened fire, dropping the first two quickly and winging the third, who dove back through the smoke to a position of relative safety.

"Cover me," Kurt shouted to Joe.

Joe swung into position and unleashed a hail of bullets as Kurt crawled into the room, grabbed Sienna, and dragged her out. She groaned as he pulled her into the hallway. At least she was alive.

As he pulled her around the corner, a new volley of return fire came from the depths of the room, peppering the doorframe and the wall.

Joe snapped off a few more shots, and the last soldier dashed through the smoke toward the rear of the room and out into a stairwell.

"Something tells me he'll be back with the posse," Joe yelled.

"Let's not wait around to meet them," Kurt said. "Get the elevator."

As Joe ran off, Kurt began to pick Sienna up.

"Kurt?" Her voice was husky like someone whose throat was dry.

"Are you okay?" Kurt asked.

"How? What? What are you doing here?"

She was clearly disoriented. "Long story," he said. "Can you walk?"

She tried to stand but fell. "My legs," she said. "I can't feel them."

"Put your arm around me," he said. "We have to get out of here."

Sienna did as Kurt asked, and he helped her down the hall to the waiting elevator. There, he leaned her against the wall and pointed to Joe. "Stay with him."

"Why?" she asked. "Where are you going?"

"To return a favor."

Joe shot him a look. "Kurt, this place is going to be crawling with North Korean troops very shortly."

"All the more reason," he said.

Kurt let Sienna go and stepped out of the elevator.

Joe flipped the hold switch back to operate and pressed the button. "I'll send the car back up once we're out."

Kurt nodded and took off back down the hall. Sienna didn't take her eyes off him until the doors closed between them.

The smoke from the firefight and the stun grenades had filled most of the hallway by now. The flashing lights of the fire and smoke alarm systems pulsed through the haze.

Kurt found the room where the fight had taken place and discovered Calista beginning to wake up from what he guessed was a stun grenade that landed too close.

He dropped down beside her and shook her. "Remember me?"

Like Sienna, it took Calista a second to recognize him. When she did, she reached for her gun, which Kurt knocked out of her hand and across the floor.

"You wouldn't kill your rescuer, would you?"

She looked around. "Egan . . ."

"If you mean your date," Kurt said, "he's dead."

The news brought little reaction from her. Kurt began to help her up.

"Wait," she said. She pulled out a small silver canister. "Throw it in the stairwell, it'll give us a few minutes."

* * *

HE DRAGGED HER over to the door and cracked it open. The sound of feet pounding down the metal stairs told him the North Koreans were on the way.

"Twist the top," she said, now standing on her own. "And don't breathe."

He did as she directed and tossed the canister onto the landing. It skittered to the wall and began hissing as two high-pressure jets of gas burst forth. Kurt slammed the door and heard the sound of men falling in their tracks and tumbling down the stairs.

"Don't worry, they're not dead," she said.

"I'm more worried about us," he said. "Go."

She began to move, lurching forward unsteadily, but Kurt wasn't about to get too close.

"Down the hall," he ordered.

With a wall to lean against, she made better progress, slamming her hand onto the elevator call button as soon as she reached it.

The doors opened and she fell inside. Kurt followed and stood on the opposite side of the car, the pistol in his hand. He punched the bottom button and the elevator began a slow creaky descent.

She laughed. "You really are a white knight," she said. "Can't resist a damsel in distress. Even one like me."

"Don't flatter yourself," he said. "You have answers, that's all I want from you. Who are you? Who are you working for? What do you want with Sienna and the others?"

An exaggerated pout appeared on her lips. "I was hoping for something more than boring conversation."

The elevator reached the bottom floor and the doors opened.

Joe and Sienna stood at what appeared to be the control panel for the maglev train. To Kurt's surprise, the three hackers from the tram were awake and helping.

"Can you work it?"

Joe looked at Kurt and shook his head. "It's all Greek to us," he said. "And by that I mean Korean."

Calista made her way over. "Maybe I can help."

Kurt didn't trust her but even she couldn't possibly want to stay where they were.

She studied the panel and flicked through a couple of screens. "They've cut the main power from up above. I can probably override their command."

As she fiddled with the controls, Kurt looked over a battery of closed-circuit TV feeds. One showed the hallway where the firefight had been. Another camera showed the stairwell. There seemed to be one on each floor. He checked through all of them. Men were piled like cordwood on each of the upper landings, but at the top level a new group of soldiers were rushing in. They wore gas masks.

"Better hurry."

"I think I've got it," she said. "Get in the tram."

At her command, the three hackers began to move. Joe helped Sienna while Kurt stood by Calista, waiting for the inevitable trick.

"Relax," she said. "I'd rather spend time in a Western prison than a North Korean one."

She flipped a switch and the power pack came to life.

The hum of electricity and the whine of high-voltage generators were a welcome sound to everyone.

"Get on board," Kurt said.

"We need to transfer control to the remote," she said, reaching into her pocket and grabbing for something.

The act brought about a quick jab from Kurt's pistol. "It's just a remote control," she said, pulling out a small device with a glowing screen. "We're going to need it, unless you want to stay behind and press go."

He snatched the device from her and pushed her toward the tram. As soon as they were all in it, he pressed the flashing green button. But instead of the tram accelerating, a lightning bolt flashed in Kurt's eyes and across the synapses of his brain. A wave of pain shot through his body combined with the sensation of dropping from a great height.

Aided by a push from Calista, he fell backward, tumbled over the side of the car, and was unconscious by the time he hit the ground.

"I told you I'd be ready next time I saw you," Calista whispered.

Dumbfounded, Joe watched Kurt fall. There was no sound, no indication anything had happened, Kurt just dropping as if someone had turned off a switch in his brain.

Sienna screamed, and Joe instinctively jumped out of the car and began to pull Kurt up. Kurt was deadweight, a two-hundred-pound rag doll.

Behind him there was a commotion.

"Sienna," Calista said. It wasn't a shout but a scolding, the way one might address an inattentive child.

Joe turned around. Sienna was aiming a weapon at Calista. Good work, he thought.

Calista obviously felt otherwise. "If you ever want to see your children again, you'll point that somewhere else."

Slowly, as if in a trance, Sienna turned the weapon on Joe. Not so good, Joe decided.

Confident she was now in control, Calista addressed Joe directly. "Pick up the remote and toss it to me," she said.

Joe shook his head.

"Please," Sienna managed, tears pouring down her face. "She has my children. She has *all* our children. If we don't go back, they'll be killed."

"We can rescue them," Joe insisted. "She knows where they are. Just give us twenty-four hours."

Sienna wavered, but Calista pressed her. "If I don't bring you back home alive," she began, "none of your relatives will live to see the morning."

Sienna retargeted Joe, more firmly this time. "I'm sorry," she said, "tomorrow will be too late. Please, give me the transmitter."

Joe held still, but one of the hackers intervened, climbing awkwardly out of the tram car and grabbing the remote from the floor of the tunnel. As soon as he had it in his hand, the man climbed back in the car and gave it to Calista, who tapped the screen a few times and offered Joe a satisfied grin.

"Au revoir," she said as the tram began to accelerate away. "Give your friend my love when he wakes up."

Joe watched the tram pick up speed and vanish into the gloom of the tunnel. "I knew we should have called the cavalry."

Hoping to wake Kurt, Joe shook him twice but got nothing. Kurt was catatonic, exactly the way he'd been when Joe pulled him from the water three months earlier. The parallel was eerie. And Joe began to think perhaps it was not entirely coincidental.

"This is bad," he said.

It may have been the understatement of Joe's life. He was trapped in a secret base on the wrong side of the DMZ, with an unconscious friend, a 9mm pistol carrying perhaps five shells in the clip, and an angry battalion of North Korean soldiers barreling down on them.

"Bad" did not begin to cover it.

CHAPTER 40

With little time to waste, Joe eased Kurt to the ground and began to look around for options.

First, he raced over to the panel and checked the security video once more. The feed showed more North Korean soldiers picking their way through the piles of unconscious men who'd made the initial descent. Counting up from where he was, Joe could see that the new troops in their gas masks had reached the seventh floor and would soon reach the sixth, where the battle had occurred. He guessed they would clear that floor and the ones beneath it first before making their way to the bottom, but time was not on his side.

He studied the control panel, but it was an incomprehensible mess of Korean and flashing icons. No way he was going to be able to decipher that in time. He looked around, desperately seeking a mode of transportation that didn't require a physicist to operate. In the dark corner to his left he saw something that might fit the bill.

"Of course," he said. "The ore had to get down here somehow."

There, sitting on a platform like the one in Than Rang's underground base, was a big North Korean tractor trailer. It was a bulk hauler with an open top, more like a dump truck than the modern intermodal shipping containers Than Rang was using.

Joe ran to the cab, climbed in, and was ecstatic to find the keys in the ignition. "Thank God for the internal combustion engine," he said, twisting the key and listening to the sweet sound of the rumbling diesel coming to life. Forcing it into the lowest gear, Joe managed to get the truck moving and eased it over to where Kurt lay on the floor.

Stopping the truck and jumping out, Joe picked up his friend, carried him to the passenger's side, and hauled him onto the tattered vinyl of the old bench seat in the cab of the truck. As he settled, Kurt began to thrash around a bit, almost as if he was trying to swim, but then he slumped against the seat and went quiet once again.

Joe climbed back into the cab on the driver's side and slammed the door.

"Don't worry, amigo," he said, putting the truck in gear. "You just enjoy your power nap. I'll get us out of here. And when you wake up, we're going to have a long talk about the kind of women you rescue and the kind you leave behind. Because clearly no one has explained the difference to you yet."

As Joe spoke, he maneuvered the steering wheel and managed to get the behemoth of a truck pointing down the maglev tunnel toward freedom. Pressing the accelerator brought a roar from the engine and began filling the tunnel with thick black exhaust. The truck moved forward and was soon picking up speed.

He hadn't gone too far when gunshots rang out from behind. From the cab of the rig, all Joe heard was the ping of ricochets bouncing off the thick walls of the truck bed and the boom of a tire exploding.

Trying not to think about the danger, Joe kept his foot on the throttle and continued to gain speed. Between the unmuffled exhaust, the noise of the big engine reverberating off the walls, and the old chassis bouncing and shaking on its leaf springs, the ride back to the south could not have been more opposite from the smooth, quiet ride in on the maglev tram.

Joe cycled through the gears, grinding every one of them. He began to laugh, enjoying the sound and the fury. It had to be a hundred twenty decibels or more. For the hell of it, he reached up and pulled the big rig's horn, which echoed down the tunnel as it blared.

Soon enough, they were passing forty and then fifty miles per hour. Ahead Joe saw a problem. Every half mile or so in the tunnel was a choke point, where a reenforced concrete ring constricted the diameter of the tunnel. As he closed in on the first one, Joe was pretty confident the truck would fit. As it turned out, he was wrong. At fifty miles an hour, the metal top of the trailer clipped the roof, blasting chunks of concrete loose. It sounded like a bomb had gone off.

The second choke point was even narrower, but Joe didn't slow down. More concrete was blasted free. This time a large section of the trailer's side was torn off, clanking to the floor and tumbling loudly across it.

In the mirror, Joe saw the remnants of the twisted bed sticking out two feet to the side. It gave him an idea. Without slowing down, he eased over to the wall until the bent section of the truck bed was grinding against it, gouging a line in the wall, shedding sparks, and adding to the din. Eventually, the metal tore further until the whole side was ripped off and dragging behind the truck.

Joe glanced at Kurt. "You must really be out cold if this isn't waking you up."

Joe pulled on the horn lever once again and held it, letting it blare until his ears were hurting. Even then he kept sounding it. He wanted the world, and particularly the South Korean military, to know he was coming. The way Joe saw it, that was their only hope.

SEVEN MILES AWAY, in a listening post manned by the South Korean military, a young private named Jeong studied her monitors. The South Koreans had placed sound detection equipment all along the DMZ to listen for any possible underground incursion by the North.

From time to time they detected odd signals. Small

earthquakes had been a problem, and the North Korean atomic bomb and other underground disturbances had sometimes triggered false readings, but nothing like what she was getting now. She called her supervisor over.

"Listen to this."

He moved slowly, appearing unconcerned. "Something must be wrong with the system."

Private Jeong shook her head. "I checked, sir. Plus, we're detecting the sound at several stations. That is not a sign of malfunction."

"Let me hear it."

He plugged a headset into her console and listened as she turned up the sound. "Trucks," he said. "Heavy trucks." There was also a grinding noise that sounded like metal tank trucks.

The computer agreed, assessing the vibration as multiple heavy vehicles moving at high speed.

Suddenly alarmed, the supervisor picked up the phone and checked with a major in the post's operations bunker. He told the major what he was hearing and then received more disturbing news. "We are witnessing sudden, frantic activity among North Korean units just on the other side of the DMZ."

"Where?"

The coordinates relayed to him were alarming. North Korean units were on the move, near the very spot where the subterranean noise had originated.

"Calculate its direction and speed," the supervisor ordered.

"Already done," Private Jeong said.

"Show me."

She tapped a button and the signal's path appeared on the computer screen. It led straight from a suspected base in the North to a commercial site on the southern side of the DMZ.

"What is that place?" the supervisor asked.

Private Jeong was checking. "Landfill," she replied. "DaeShan Landfill Number Four."

The supervisor put two and two together. He could not believe what he was seeing. He called the major back and gave his assessment. "Confirmed large-scale subterranean incursion under way. Entry point must be in or around the DaeShan landfill. Recommend defense condition one. Immediate alert!"

RACING BENEATH THE DMZ, Joe had no idea what forces he'd set in motion, but he hoped it would mean a warm welcome instead of a firefight through a group of armed thugs loyal to Than Rang.

As he entered the last third of the passageway, the grade ramped up just a bit and the truck began to slow. Instead of the light at the end of the tunnel, he saw the darkness of Than Rang's underground transportation center. There was no sign of any resistance awaiting him, nor were there South Korean soldiers, which for the moment was probably a good thing.

It was a different story behind him. Vehicles were heading their way, catching up quickly. Based on the silence, he guessed they were running on the maglev system.

As one of the trams raced up beside him, Joe spun the wheel to the right and knocked the tram off the centerline of its magnetic track. Deprived of its support, the tram crashed to the ground amid a shower of sparks.

Gunshots rang out from the second vehicle that was also closing in from directly behind. Once again the bulk of the big truck protected them.

This time Joe simply stomped on the brakes. The big rig skidded to a stop amid a shriek of squealing tires and a cloud of blue smoke. Unable to adjust its speed as quickly, the second tram rear-ended the truck with jarring impact.

Their pursuers now successfully dealt with, Joe put the truck back in gear and began to accelerate, working through the gears and heading into the homestretch. The truck labored on the slight upward grade and chugged into the loading bay at the end of the tunnel, bumping the ore car filled with the titanium pellets, which dumped out and spread all across the floor.

As the sound of a thousand marbles rolling in all directions ceased, Joe peeked out of the truck. There was no one there to greet them. No angry brutes with drawn weapons. No sign of Calista and the hackers. And still no soldiers.

Joe looked back down the tunnel. The North Koreans had given up the chase. He could see them running the other way. He guessed they were not interested in getting caught on the wrong side of the border.

Joe looked over at Kurt. "We made it," he said. "And just like the last time, you missed the whole thing."

Joe considered looking for a stairwell but was not interested in lugging Kurt up twenty flights. Instead, he drove over and parked next to the octagonal platform they'd originally descended on.

He got out of the truck, pulled Kurt from the passenger's side, and found the controls. With the flick of a switch, he engaged the power system and moved the control lever upward from the neutral position. The incline gearing came to life and began to turn, and the platform began to rise slowly.

As they went up, Joe pulled out his phone, hoping he would get a signal before they reached the top. No such luck. In fact, the phone was acting weird as if it was being jammed. When the slowly rising platform finally reached the surface, Joe found out why.

Thirty Korean soldiers were waiting for him with weapons drawn. Humvees with .50 caliber machine guns were arranged in a semicircle around them. A spotlight snapped on, blinding Joe. Shouts that needed no translation told Joe to put up his hands, which he had already done.

A pair of soldiers rushed over and forced him to his knees.

"I'm an American," Joe said.

To Joe's right, another soldier had a rifle aimed at Kurt.

"He's injured!" Joe shouted. "He needs a doctor."

More shouts came his way.

"We're American," Joe replied. "We're on your side. We're operating undercover. For Colonel Lee of the National Intelligence Service."

No response.

"CIA," Joe shouted, hoping they knew the acronym.

With the spotlight on his face, they could clearly see that he was not Korean. A quick discussion was held, and Joe and Kurt were cuffed, thrown in the back of one of the Humvees, and driven off.

As they pulled out of the warehouse, Joe got a first-hand look at the effectiveness of his plan. South Korean helicopters, armed with missiles and spotlights, were circling the landfill. Several others were patrolling down the line of the DMZ, looking for invading troops or infiltration units of the North Korean Army.

In addition to the helicopters, soldiers were everywhere. And as they took the road out, Joe saw Abrams tanks moving into position, while a flight of F-16s flashed overhead in full afterburner.

Joe looked for the lights of Seoul, but the city had gone dark in response to the expected invasion.

"Hmm," Joe whispered to himself. "Maybe that plan of mine worked a little *too* well."

They were taken to a military base and quickly separated, Kurt whisked off to the infirmary, Joe to an interrogation room. For two hours, Joe was subject to continuous interrogation by officers of the South Korean military. He told them all the same thing, and he asked repeatedly about Kurt. He got nowhere until Col. Lee and Tim Hale arrived.

They were livid.

"You two must be insane," Hale said, "following them into North Korea."

"We were following the lead," Joe said. "What did you want us to do? Just let them go?"

"Maybe you should have," Hale said.

"You know this will calm down," Joe said. "It's a minor incursion. And let's not forget who built the damned tunnel."

"I wasn't talking about the political situation," Hale said, "I was referring to Kurt."

"Why? What's happened?" Joe said, concerned.

"He's in a coma," Hale explained. "The doctors can't say when—or if—he's going to come out of it."

CHAPTER 41

Indian Ocean, 1230 hours local time

Seven thousand miles and six time zones from Korea, a small flotilla of ships was in the process of linking themselves together with heavy steel cables.

Over the course of a day, two oceangoing tugs had arrived from South Africa. The *Drakensberg* had reached the *Condor* and towed it to where the *Waratah* lay drifting in the current, while a second tug, known as the *Sedgewick*, had arrived six hours later and was preparing to run lines to the foliage-encrusted hulk of the old ship.

But before she could be put under tow, an inspection had to be made. At Paul's direction, a salvage crew had gone aboard, splitting into three groups. The main contingent began clearing the accumulated growth and sediment from the ship's hull, hoping to make her lighter in the water and less top-heavy. As they excavated up above, the *Condor*'s chief engineer went down into the lower recesses of the ship to check the integrity of the hull and internal bulkheads. As they worked on the inside, Duke and another diver were finishing up a survey of the hull's exterior below the waterline.

The radio cackled at Paul's side. *"Paul, this is the chief."*

Paul put the radio to his mouth. "What's the word?"

"The engineering spaces are pretty gunked up. At least two feet of sludge down here. And in some places several feet of water."

That didn't sound promising. "Can you find the leak?"

"No leaks," the chief reported happily. *"It's freshwater. Rainwater, if you want me to guess, must be leaking in somewhere. But if you ask me, the hull itself is sound."*

"That's good news," Paul said. "What about corrosion?"

"I think we're fine," the chief said. *"To be honest, the old gal is in great condition for a ship that's passed the century mark."*

"Any idea why?" Paul asked. "She should have rusted to pieces years ago."

"I think it's the sediment," the chief said. *"It's very dense, more like clay. It seals so tightly it blocks out most of the oxygen. Less oxygen means less rust, less rust means a strong hull."*

"Sounds good," Paul said. He wondered how the exterior looked. "Duke, are you finished with your survey?"

Duke's voice came back after a slight delay. *"Affirmative,"* he said.

"How's she looking below the waterline?"

"The plating is in great shape," Duke replied. *"If the chief is right, then I'd guess the exterior was sealed up with mud almost from the moment she went aground."*

Paul was glad to hear that. "Good news all around."

"Okay if we head back to Condor *for some lunch and dry clothes?"*

Duke had been in the water for three hours already. "You've earned it," Paul said.

"Roger that. Duke out."

Paul turned his attention back to the interior. "What do you think, Chief? Are we going to make it in?"

NUMA had plans to bring the *Waratah* into Durban two days hence. She wouldn't make Cape Town—her official destination when she'd vanished—but if she reached Durban, it would be a triumphant homecoming.

"We have a good chance," the chief replied. *"The only real danger is that she was obviously sitting aground somewhere for a long time. A ship isn't supposed to be out of the water and resting all its weight on the bottom like that. We can already see some deformity in the plating underneath."*

"Is that going to be a problem?"

"I wouldn't want to ride out a storm on her," the chief said. *"But if the weather stays nice, I think we'll be okay."*

"Good work," Paul said. "Check in with me when you get topside."

"Wilco," the chief said. *"Going to recheck the stern and make sure we're not taking on water through the propeller shaft tube."*

Paul clipped the radio back on his belt, grabbed a shovel, and joined the crew in clearing the deck.

Meanwhile, Gamay and Elena explored the interior of the ship, hoping to shed some light on the mystery. A dedicated search of the bridge, captain's quarters, and other official spaces gave little away. The logbooks were gone, along with the vast majority of personal possessions.

"Let's check the passenger cabins," Gamay suggested.

Elena nodded and followed Gamay deeper into the ship. They descended the main stairway, encrusted with black mold and layers of gunk, arrived at the main passenger level and entered a hall as dark as any mine shaft. With only their flashlights for illumination, the two women moved slowly.

Down here, the musty odor was almost overpowering, as the floor, ceiling, and walls were covered in the same gunk as the stairwell. The sound of water dripping added to the cavelike atmosphere.

"Kind of creepy down here," Elena said.

"On that we agree," Gamay said.

From above they heard occasional clanging and the disembodied echo of the deck crew's voices as they shouted to one another, but they were muted and distant like voices from the past.

"Do you believe in ghosts?" Elena asked.

"No," Gamay said. "And neither do you."

Elena chuckled. "Well, if I did, this is where I'd expect to find one. All those people lost and never found. I've heard that angry spirits cling to the last place they were alive. Haunting it. Waiting for someone to find them and set them free."

With Elena going on about ghosts, Gamay felt the

prickle of goose bumps on her skin. "I'll take a ghost over another crocodile any day," she said.

It took a while but they'd soon checked through every one of the first-class cabins.

"Notice something?" Gamay asked.

"No clothing. No luggage," Elena said.

"And no jewelry," Gamay said. They'd been working on the theory that the ship ran aground somewhere and the passengers and crew died waiting for rescue. But the fact that they'd found only one of the ship's lifeboats suggested something else.

"If they abandoned ship," Gamay said, "they'd have had to leave their steamer trunks behind. But strands of pearls and diamond-studded bracelets are easier to carry."

"I'd bring mine," Elena agreed. "But why leave a ship that was obviously not sinking?"

"No idea," Gamay admitted as they made their way back to the main stairwell.

"Should we go down one more level?" Elena asked.

Gamay nodded. "At the risk of sounding like my husband, let's keep going until we get to the bottom of this."

Down they went, checking the smaller cabins that lay on the next deck.

"Crew stations," Elena noted, studying the cramped cabin arrangements.

"Or steerage," Gamay said. "The *Waratah* was designed to carry a lot of immigrant passengers. Fortunately, she wasn't loaded to the gills when she left Durban."

They searched persistently. But beyond the everyday items from another century that would generate great historical interest, there was little to explain what might have happened.

That began to change when Gamay forced open the next door.

The space was larger but no less cramped. Gamay offered a guess, based on the look of the beds and storage cabinets. "Ship's infirmary."

She stepped into the compartment and went right. Elena fanned out to the left. They'd gone several paces when Elena let out a gasp.

Gamay spun around and found Elena aiming her light at a skull with desiccated skin stretched across it, a tangle of wispy gray hair on top and the bristles of what had once been a thick handlebar mustache on the upper lip. Another body rested beside it.

Gamay crouched beside them for a closer look. The man wore a uniform. "He's a crewman," she said. "Or at least he was."

A small badge seemed to indicate he might have been a foreman in the engine room, perhaps in charge of keeping the boilers stoked. A hole in his shirt led to a hole in the torn and dried skin. Gamay began to get a sick feeling. The same feeling she'd had upon discovering the body on the *Ethernet*.

She checked the other body. It was shirtless and the skin was more decayed. She couldn't tell what had happened to this man, but as she stepped away her foot hit a stainless steel tin resting beside him. Something clinked.

Gamay picked up the tin, pried off the top, and dumped the objects out onto the palm of her hand. The first was flattened and mushroomed out at one end. The second was in relatively good shape.

"Bullets," Elena said.

Gamay nodded. "Taken from these men, I'd bet, either to try and save them or after they died."

Without speaking another word, they finished their survey of the infirmary, discovering three additional bodies in the rear section, one of which was strapped to a bed. A clipboard with ancient yellowed paper still attached to it had fallen from the peg on the footboard. Gamay picked it up. She couldn't make out anything on the top sheet. The second page was in better shape. And as the light hit the paper at just the right angle, one small notation became readable.

"'Time of death,'" she said. The hour was obscured, but the date next to it was legible. "'August 1, 1909.'"

The significance dawned on Elena quickly. "Five days after the *Waratah* went missing."

Gamay nodded. They'd found their first real clue. "We need to go tell Paul."

Paul was busy with the deck crew when Gamay and Elena came up to him.

"We've found something," Gamay told him breathlessly.

Paul put his shovel aside as she began to explain, handing the lead slugs to Paul as she finished.

"No passengers, no lifeboats, no logbooks," Paul whispered, going over the facts, "but several crewmen dead in the sick bay and at least one recovering from bullet wounds several days after the ship vanished."

"Could there have possibly been a mutiny?" Elena asked.

"This isn't the HMS *Bounty*," Gamay said. "It was a cruise ship. No one here had been press-ganged into work. The sailors were professionals. Working on her was a fairly coveted job."

That left only one answer. "Then it had to be piracy," Paul said.

"Which would explain a great deal," Gamay replied, "including our present location."

Paul nodded. They were over three hundred miles northeast of the *Waratah*'s last reported position. Given that the current in Mozambique Channel flowed north to south and then around the Cape, she couldn't have drifted to their current location unless her resting place had been even farther up the coast, even farther from where she should have been.

"To be honest," Paul said, "I've been thinking it might have been piracy for a while. I can't come up with any other reason for her to wind up this far from where she should have been."

Gamay nodded. "But if you were a pirate and you'd just taken a large ship for a prize, the first thing you'd do is sail it in the opposite direction, out of the shipping lanes, away from where anyone would look."

"Explains why the search and rescue vessels from the Royal Navy and the Blue Anchor Line never found her either," Paul said. "They were looking in the wrong place."

Elena chimed in with a summation. "So a group of pirates board the ship, take control of her, and turn her north, knowing it will be days before a search even begins. By that time the culprits can be hundreds of miles from the danger zone."

"Must have been easy to disappear back then," Gamay noted. "Radios weren't in use on ships yet. And the airplane had only been invented six years prior, which meant they were few and far between and of relatively short range. Certainly not suited for long missions out to sea looking for missing ships."

"It was a different time," Paul said, "even compared to ten years later."

Paul found himself intrigued by the mystery, which seemed to grow deeper and more complex by the moment. "So where *did* she end up?" he wondered aloud.

"Considering the current in this section of the world, it could be anywhere from here to Somalia," Elena said.

"That's true," Gamay said. "But I've come up with an idea how we might narrow it down. Strangely enough, it begins with taking a closer look at those spiders."

Paul raised an eyebrow. "You really are cured."

"Only temporarily," she said. "You still have to kill them for me at home."

"I set them free out the back door," Paul said.

Gamay shook her head. "Of course you do."

"So what's the plan?" he asked.

"Before we toss all the foliage, insects, and debris over the side, we should take samples of everything. The seeds, the bugs, the spiders. We should even have someone examine what's left of our crocodilian friend before Elena turns him into a handbag.

"If we can determine what kind of plants and bugs we're dealing with, we might be able to use that information to narrow down where the ship has been all these years."

It sounded like a great idea to Paul. "You're the expert and the gardener of the family," he said.

"I'll help," Elena said. "Especially if it means I don't have to go down below again."

Paul laughed. "I'll tell the crew to stop excavating until you two have collected your samples. I'm sure they'll enjoy the break."

Paul walked over to the deck crew and gave them the good news. He was getting ready to radio their findings to the *Condor* when the sound of a helicopter approaching became audible.

Paul looked west, expecting to see the *Condor*'s Jayhawk finally returning from Durban, but instead the sound came from the north, where two black dots were descending from a higher altitude and coming directly toward them. They were staggered, with the first one perhaps a mile in front of its partner.

Suspicious, Paul took out a pair of compact binoculars and focused on the nearest of the two craft. It was dark green in color, clearly military, and carrying ordnance in pods on either side.

Flashes caught Paul's eye, like sunlight reflecting off the canopy, but it wasn't the sun. Ribbons of water flew up on a track toward the bow of the ship. The heavy thunking sound of .50 caliber shells tearing through metal followed.

"Hit the deck," Paul shouted, stepping away from the rail and diving behind the piles of dirt as if they were sandbags.

The other crewmen dove to the ground around him, and Paul caught sight of Gamay and Elena racing his way.

"What's happening?" Gamay shouted.

The first helicopter thundered overhead, heading to the south and banking into a right-hand turn.

"Not sure," Paul said. "But I'm beginning to think someone doesn't like us very much."

He looked up and trained the binoculars on the second helicopter, coming in low and slow. It was over a mile away and less than a hundred feet above the water when it released its payload.

Paul had been on heightened alert since the incidents during the dive on the *Ethernet*, but even he needed a moment to process what he was seeing. The payloads were long and thin. They hit the water with tiny splashes and then vanished, leaving only thin trails of bubbles stretching out behind them to mark their course. It was clear to see that they were tracking straight for the *Waratah*.

"Torpedoes," he said.

"Torpedoes?" Gamay sounded as shocked as he was.

"Coming right at us," he added and then turned to the crew. "Everyone off! Abandon ship!"

CHAPTER 42

Paul's urgent warning reverberated across the deck. The crewmen, who had recently scrambled for cover, got back on their feet and charged toward the rope ladders that led to the launches below.

"Go," Paul said, helping people over the edge. "Quickly."

As they scampered down the ladders, Paul glanced around. The helicopters were swinging around, strafing the tugs first and then the *Condor*. At the same time, the torpedoes they'd dropped were tracking slowly inbound.

The torpedoes were running toward the *Waratah* at just over thirty knots, and with a mile between them, it gave the crew nearly two full minutes to abandon ship and move out of harm's way. It was just slow enough that something extraordinary began to happen.

In the distance, the red hull of the FRC flashed into the picture, racing at full speed and dropping in behind the charging torpedoes.

Paul grabbed the radio. "Duke, what on earth are you doing?"

"Intercepting the torpedoes," Duke replied. *"Seems like an awful shame to let that old rust bucket go down now. Especially when she's just recently returned from beyond like this."*

Paul watched as Elena went over the side and down the ladder. Gamay was next. But the chief was still down below.

"You're damn right it is," Paul said into the radio. "Do what you can."

DUKE HAD BEEN halfway back to the *Condor* when the helicopters appeared and launched their attack. He saw the strafing run and watched the torpedoes drop, realizing quickly that the *Waratah*, for whatever reason, was the target.

Instead of continuing on toward the *Condor*, Duke had slammed the throttles forward and spun the FRC's wheel until it was tracking back toward the old derelict. His first thought was that he might be needed to help get the crew off the ship, either before or after it was struck. But as the speedy little boat raced toward the hulk of the old liner, it quickly came across the trail of bubbles from one of the torpedoes and, in that moment, Duke came up with a different plan.

"Pull the guns out of the weapons locker," he shouted to the other divers.

Ahead of them the broad flank of the *Waratah* loomed, growing larger in his sight with each passing second, but they were gaining rapidly on the second torpedo.

"Don't hit the warhead," Duke shouted to his gunners. "We'll be blown to pieces. Hit the prop or the motor or the fins. We just need to get it off course."

The men nodded and switched off the safeties on their weapons. They had only handguns to work with. But if Duke got them in close, it would be enough.

Skipping across the surface at full speed, they came up alongside the torpedo. It was a light gray color beneath the water, running at a depth of five feet.

"Take it out," Duke shouted, matching the torpedo's speed.

The divers began firing, drilling holes in the water with the Ruger pistols. Duke would have given a year's pay for a rifle, but two of the rifles were on the *Waratah* with Paul and the rest were back on the *Condor.*

Despite both weapons being emptied at the target, the torpedo continued on undeterred. It was no more than thirty seconds from impact.

"It's too deep," one of the gunners said.

"Reload," Duke shouted. "I'm going to try something."

He gunned the throttle and crossed in front of the torpedo and then back over it again. By the third pass he could see the torpedo bucking up and down like a Jet

Ski crossing the bow wave of a passing cabin cruiser. It nosed down and then came up, breaching the surface momentarily. At that moment the divers opened fire, plunking the rear casing with several direct shots. Whatever they'd hit, the torpedo dove out of control, twisting to the right and spiraling down.

Duke cut the wheel to the left and had covered a hundred yards when there was a flash beneath the water. A concussion wave hit next and a ball of white water erupted, blasting up into the air and raining down in a wide circle.

"One down, one to go," Duke shouted, turning back to the right, looking for the other torpedo trail.

"It's too far ahead," one of the divers shouted.

"I'm not giving up," Duke insisted. But even as he got the FRC back on track, he could see it was too late. They were racing headlong toward the *Waratah*'s stern. The space between them would be used up faster than they could hope to catch the fleeing torpedo.

"Duke, peel off!" came a shout over the radio. *"That's an order."*

Duke followed the command and cut to the left as two streams of gunfire came from the deck of the old ship.

Paul and Gamay were standing at the rail, firing down at the incoming torpedo with the two AR-15 rifles. At a range of a hundred feet, one of them hit the warhead just right. A new shock wave erupted and a column of water exploded upward from the surface of the sea like a geyser. Heat and flame chased the water, burning some of it to steam in midair.

Up on *Waratah*'s deck, Paul and Gamay were thrown backward by the shock wave. They landed together amid a pile of weeds that the deck crew had yet to clear.

Paul opened his eyes as mist from the torpedo's explosion drifted down on them. His ears were ringing. He glanced over at Gamay, saw that she was all right, and sighed with relief. "Pretty good shooting, if I do say so myself."

Gamay propped herself up on one elbow and stared at him. "How do you know it wasn't my shot that did the trick?"

"You were wide left," he said. "I could tell from the start. Wind correction."

"Those were your bullets going left," she insisted.

Paul laughed and got to his feet. He looked around for the attacking helicopters, hoping they wouldn't make another run. Thankfully, they were heading back to the north.

They left behind two patches of churning water, a smoking tug, and a bewildered group of people who wondered what could be so important about a derelict ship that someone would want to sink it.

Paul found the radio that had been knocked from his belt. He picked it up and made sure it was working. "Thanks for the help, Duke. You must be half crazy, but it's much appreciated."

"You're welcome, Paul, sorry I couldn't get them both. Nice shooting, by the way."

"Thanks," Paul and Gamay said in unison and then glanced at each other.

Duke signaled that he was heading back to the *Condor* and Paul acknowledged the message before reaching out to the *Condor*.

"*Condor*, this is Paul," he said. "I need a damage and casualty report."

"*Mostly cosmetic,*" the voice replied. "*Two crew were injured by shrapnel. Another seems to have a nasty bump from diving into a bulkhead. But no major injuries or fatalities.*"

"Sounds like we got off lucky," Paul replied. "Contact the tugs and get me a report. I see a lot of smoke coming from the *Drakensberg*."

"*Roger that,*" the crewman said.

"And get in touch with HQ," Paul added. "We need some protection out here. I haven't the foggiest idea why someone would try to sink an old derelict like this, but there's no denying that's what they wanted to do. Until we figure out who they are and what they want, we can't put it past them to try again."

As the *Condor* signed off, the chief called in from down below. "*What the heck is going on up there?*"

"Believe it or not, we almost got torpedoed," Paul explained.

"*Torpedoed?*"

"I realize it makes no sense," Paul said. "Just trust me. It was close but we seem to have survived intact."

There was a long pause before the chief radioed back. "*Maybe not,*" he said grimly. "*The shock wave must have buckled the old plating. We've got water coming in down here.*"

CHAPTER 43

The chief's message was grim news to Paul.

"We may have won the battle but lost the war," Gamay said, giving words to Paul's thoughts.

"I'm going down below," Paul said, handing the radio to Gamay. "Get in touch with *Condor* and the tugs. We need pumps. We need divers with salvage gear. If there's a buckled plate, they can weld a patch over it."

"Are you crazy?" she said. "It's a miracle this ship is still afloat as it is."

"I can't explain," Paul said, "but I've grown attached to this ship and I'm not giving up on the old gal yet. Not after all she's been through."

"Who are you?" Gamay asked. "And what have you done with my sensible New England husband?"

Paul gave her a quick kiss, took her flashlight, and ran

for the stairs. He heard her calling over to the *Condor* as he raced down into the dark.

Four flights down, he could already hear the sound of water coming in. It was a powerful rushing noise as if a fire hydrant had been busted wide open.

As he reached the bottom landing, Paul's feet plunged calf-deep into water.

"Chief, where are you?" he shouted.

"Aft bulkhead!" a voice shouted from down the hall. "Hurry!"

Paul charged toward the stern, past the boilers and coal bunkers, to the old engine room. He saw light coming from a ladder well that descended into the aft bilge, which was the lowest section of the ship where all the bilgewater collected. Beneath it lay only the cold sea.

As Paul played his light around, he spotted water blasting in through a ruptured seam in the hull plating. It coursed through the compartment in an angry, foaming stream, before swirling down the ladder like it was a gigantic drain. The water level was rising with alarming speed.

"We can't stop this," Paul said, suddenly shocked back to reality. "We have to get out of here."

"I can't," the chief said. "I'm trapped."

Paul saw nothing holding the chief in place. "What are you talking about?"

"My legs are stuck in the sediment," the chief shouted. "The shock wave from the explosion liquefied the muck. When I dropped down here to take a look, I sunk knee-deep into it. It might as well be quicksand."

Paul stepped onto the ladder, grabbed the chief's hand, and pulled with all his might. The chief remained stuck right where he was. Paul aimed the flashlight down into the water. The chief was indeed sunk up to his knees.

Paul stepped down another rung as the water swirled around him and pounded his shoulders. Hanging on tight, he got into a position where he could use more leverage, grabbed under the chief's arm, and pulled again. It was no use.

"Wiggle your feet."

"I can't," the chief said. "It's like they're stuck in concrete."

By now the water was up to the chief's waist and rising fast. Paul stepped back. He needed something to dig the chief out with. Shining the light around, he caught sight of a metal pipe with a barbed end. It might have been a picker bar used by the firemen on the old ship to rake the coals with. It would have to do.

He grabbed the picker bar, came back to the well, handed the chief his flashlight, and jabbed the bar into the sediment near the chief's legs. Shoveling at first and then stirring, he began to dislodge the muck.

"It's working," the chief said. "Keep going."

Paul could hardly see. He worked vigorously as the water reached the chief's chest and then his neck. The chief tilted his head to keep his nose and mouth above the water.

Paul kept digging and the chief began to come free, pulling on the rungs of the ladder and drawing himself up.

One leg came free and then the other, minus a boot. The chief went up the ladder and Paul followed. The last six inches of the bilge filled rapidly, and soon the main engine room began flooding.

Exhausted from the struggle, the two men stumbled for the bulkhead. By the time they reached it, water was pouring over the sill like a miniature version of Niagara Falls.

"Think it'll hold?" Paul asked, looking at the hundred-year-old version of a watertight door.

"Only one way to find out."

Paul grabbed the door and tried to force it shut, but a century of corrosion prevented it from moving much. Putting his shoulder into it, Paul managed to move it halfway to a closed position before it seized once again.

Stepping back, he took the iron picker bar and banged on the hinges, trying to knock the corrosion off. A few flakes were all he managed to clear. Putting the bar down again, he and the chief got behind the door and leaned into it. It closed three-quarters and then almost flush, but the weight of the water pouring through was too much and it pushed them back.

"It's no use," the chief said.

"One more try," Paul said. From the corner of his eye he saw a figure come running down the stairs behind them. Some assistance at last. "Help us!"

With the water surging through waist-high at this point, Paul leaned into the door one more time. He felt the chief pushing with all his might and then felt a powerful shove from behind as the crewman who'd come to help reached them.

Between the three of them they overcame the force of the rushing water. The door clanged shut, and Paul wrenched the wheel over to lock it tight.

The seal was less than perfect, after all these years, and water sprayed through around the edges in several places, but it could be measured in gallons per minute. Pumps could handle that, at least as long as the door held.

Paul collapsed onto the floor and looked at the chief, who was smiling from ear to ear. "Just another day at the office," the chief said.

"Think I'm ready for a day off," Paul replied. He turned to thank the crewman for coming to their aid but there was no one there. He looked around in all directions, but even after grabbing the flashlight from the chief he saw nothing but the dark hall. They were alone.

"Did you bring anyone else down here?" Paul asked.

The chief shook his head. "Everyone else went topside before the attack. Why?"

Paul gazed down the hall to the stairwell. He now realized that in the dark it would have been impossible for him to see someone standing there. But he distinctly remembered a broad-shouldered man with a mustache.

He decided his mind was playing tricks on him. "No reason," he said finally. "Just making sure. Let's get up top in case this door gives way."

Paul grabbed the picker bar, climbed to his feet, and helped the chief up off the deck. Wearily, they slogged their way toward the stairwell and climbed up into the daylight.

In the hour that followed, pumps from the *Condor*

and one of the tugs were brought in. The watertight doors were braced and reinforced inside the ship, while the salvage divers quickly found the ruptured seam and welded a patch job over it.

The ship was still leaking, and it was anyone's guess if the hull would hold out, but as the tow got under way and the ships began to move they did so under the watchful eye of the South African Air Force, which sent fighter aircraft and armed helicopters overhead in a series of revolving sweeps.

As evening came on, the small flotilla met the first ship in what would prove to be a substantial honor guard. Within the hour, two additional warships joined it, followed by a dedicated repair vessel ready to lend a hand.

It seemed that having endured the *Waratah*'s loss once already, the South African government was determined not to let anything happen to her again.

With a protective force around them, Paul began to feel more at ease. He found Gamay on deck, placing samples of many different things into plastic baggies, labeling them, and zipping them shut.

She had her hair tied back, a pencil behind one ear, and her most studious look firmly in place.

Paul sat down beside her. "Almost done?"

"With the collection part," she said, placing the samples into a plastic cooler. "I'm flying back to Durban to meet with a biologist regarding these samples. Want to come?"

"I'd love to," Paul said, "but I want to make sure this ship reaches port."

"I'd say you've done enough," Gamay replied, "but I've seen that look before."

"The job is not done until it's done," he said.

"I'll be there to see you arrive," she said, placing the lid on the container and locking it down.

He smiled, thinking back to all the times one of them had waited onshore for the other to come home. It was always an enjoyable reunion.

She stood and picked up the cooler. Paul grabbed a second cooler and they began walking to the stern, where a launch waited to whisk her over to the *Condor* and the military helicopter waiting to fly her to Durban.

"Do you believe in ghosts?" he asked.

She laughed at the question. "Not really. Why?"

"No reason," he said. "Just checking."

They'd reached the ladder, where a crewman helped lower down the containers.

"I'll be ready for that candlelight dinner by the time I make port," Paul said.

"I'll make us a reservation," she said.

Paul hugged and kissed her and then stood back as she climbed down the rope ladder to a waiting boat.

As the launch peeled off and made for the *Condor*, Paul decided he was a man with a lot to look forward to over the next few days—dinner with Gamay, bringing the *Waratah* into port after a hundred and five years, and, if Gamay was right, some new insight into where the ship had been hiding all these years.

CHAPTER 44

At the Brèvard lair, the family mourned the passing of Egan with a somber ceremony, counterbalanced by the fact that Acosta the traitor had been killed and the hackers returned to their rightful owners.

Without delay, Sebastian put them to work. Using their own skills and the offensive capabilities of Phalanx, they were soon hacking into the American Department of Defense, the European air traffic control system, and various other entities, with the intention of wreaking havoc.

"Is all this really necessary?" Calista asked.

"We need a smoke screen for our true plans," he said. "A little carnage will do nicely."

Calista nodded and walked to the front of the control room, where the floor-to-ceiling windows looked out over the Olympic-sized swimming pool. A pool where she'd learned to dive. Where she and the others had trained for the mission to attack the *Ethernet*.

Thinking about that moment, her mind wandered to Kurt Austin. Since encountering him there, she'd hacked into the medical files NUMA was keeping on him and learned of his relationship with Sienna.

She wondered what would possess a man to risk life and limb for a woman he could never have. A woman whose rescue would only result in him losing her again, as he delivered her back to another man's arms.

Either Sienna was the type of woman who inspired such love or she was fortunate enough to have encountered a man whose sense of duty was more important than his own self-preservation. In either case, Calista found herself jealous. She had never known such a man and probably never would.

"Get Laurent up here," Sebastian said, breaking her train of thought. "We need to make sure all his men are brought back to the compound and ready to fight. Even the ones we've simply hired for local jobs."

"Expecting company?"

"Not right away," Sebastian said, "but soon enough. When they do come, we must be certain that they bleed. They must find it as difficult as possible to overcome our defenses or they won't truly believe they've won."

She understood. It was all part of the game.

CHAPTER 45

Durban, South Africa

Gamay arrived in Durban and found herself something of a local attraction. The discovery of the *Waratah* was being kept secret until the ship was brought safely into South African waters. But the rumor had begun to spread. And hearing that a member of the NUMA team had been flown in with samples of something that she needed examined, she was met with an excited response.

Several experts flew in on their own dime and convened with her at the University of Durban-Westville campus. They quickly set up shop, examining the samples of the insects, dead rodents, and various seeds and plants discovered on the *Waratah*.

While they worked, Gamay took the opportunity to visit the library and found a microfilm machine, where she could peruse the old newspapers printed at the time of the *Waratah*'s disappearance.

"Are you sure you don't want to use a computer?" one of the librarians asked. "All of this is online."

"Thank you but no," Gamay said. "I've had quite enough of computers for a while."

Left alone, she read article after article. It was an education into a different time. She'd grown so used to today's world, where plane crashes and mishaps of any kind were covered live and the information distributed and verified almost instantly, that it was odd reading about the disappearance. Initially, the ship was just thought to be overdue, a common occurrence. Even days and weeks later, there were articles suggesting that the *Waratah* might yet arrive or that the search vessels would encounter her and tow her in. Estimates of how long her food supplies would hold out were offered as reason not to panic.

But then hope faded and the reality set in. Speculation and rumor began to run rampant. The storm of July 27th was considered the likely culprit. The statements of a man named Claude Sawyer became a focal point. He was the sole passenger bound for Cape Town who decided to disembark the ship in Durban. He sent a telegram to his wife that read, in part, "Thought *Waratah* top-heavy. Landed Durban."

Mr. Sawyer also claimed to have had a dream shortly before the ship reached Durban in which a knight crying the ship's name came charging through the waves with a sword raised high. After getting off in Durban, he claimed to have had another dream in which the *Waratah* was swamped by a massive wave, capsized, and vanished from sight.

A different theory was espoused by Captain Firth of the steamer *Marere*. He believed the *Waratah* too big and strong to be taken by a rogue wave and thought it more likely that she'd lost a propeller or rudder and was adrift in the current, being slowly hauled past the Cape of Good Hope and out into the Atlantic Ocean.

Firth was certain the *Waratah* would be found, much like a similar vessel, the SS *Waikato*, which broke a propeller shaft on the way to Auckland and drifted for six full weeks before eventually being discovered. Some speculated she would drift all the way to South America.

As Gamay read the newspapers over, she found her attention turning to other stories of the day: news of the storm, political arguments, and ads for products, including one that touted smoking as a cure for the common cold.

Most striking, she read a long dispatch about the Durban police battling a group of criminals known as the Klaar River Gang. After an explosion and a conflagration that burned up a fortune in paper currency, it was finally determined that the notes were actually near-perfect forgeries. While most of the Klaar River Gang had indeed perished, Robert Swan, chief inspector of the Durban police, feared the leaders had escaped and would resurface.

"May you live in interesting times," Gamay whispered to herself.

"Excuse me," a voice said from behind her. "Are you Gamay Trout?"

She turned to see a man wearing a navy blue suit and an open-necked, button-down white shirt. He offered his hand. "My name is Jacob Fredricks. I've heard a rumor that you might have discovered the SS *Waratah*. Is that true?"

Gamay hesitated.

"I worked with NUMA on an expedition looking for the ship years ago," the man explained. "Unfortunately, we came up empty."

She recalled the name. And though she wasn't sure if this man was who he said he was, she doubted there was much danger to her or the ship anymore. As the truth was obviously leaking out from several sources, she decided to tell him what she knew.

They spent the next two hours discussing the ship's vanishing and the time Fredricks thought he'd found it, only to learn he'd discovered a World War Two cargo ship torpedoed by the Germans.

"I'm almost relieved to know the ship has been beached somewhere all this time," he told her. "Makes not finding her on the bottom a little easier to take."

Gamay smiled and told him about the incidents that had occurred since the discovery. Fredricks seemed surprised by what he heard but mentioned that odd theories and occurrences had always surrounded the ship.

"A psychic once held that they'd made land and started a new civilization," he explained.

"Closer to the truth than we might have guessed,"

Gamay said, though it was pretty clear that the passengers never made land.

"One of the strangest stories took place in 1987," he said.

"When you thought you'd found the wreck?" she asked.

"No, that was years later," he said. "Back in '87 an old, double-end lifeboat was found adrift off the coast of Maputo Bay, Mozambique. By some fisherman, if I recall. There were three people in it. A woman and two boys. The woman had a slight bullet wound, but it was not fatal. Unfortunately, dehydration was . . . for all three of them. They were identified as part of a family that had been abducted years before. Authorities thought they'd escaped from somewhere up the coast. Somalia was the prime suspect. It was a pretty lawless place even back then."

"Sounds terrible," she said. "But what does that have to do with the *Waratah*?"

"The old lifeboat they were in was rotted half to the core. It had been hastily patched and sealed with household items and wouldn't have lasted much longer, had it not been found. Several experts insisted it was a design used and built from 1904 to 1939. Years later, someone did a computer analysis of the photos taken then and claimed to discover the remnants of lettering still visible on the highest plank, basically because the layers of paint had limited the erosion. I truly can't remember how they did it, but in the photo the writing could have been interpreted to spell *Waratah*."

Gamay sat back, stunned. "You're joking."

He shook his head. "At the time, everyone assumed it was a hoax. Like that alien autopsy video. But now, after what you've found, there is a possibility it might be true.

"And then there was the Klaar River Gang," he said, moving on to a new subject.

"I was just reading about them," she said.

"Some think they bribed their way aboard the ship," he told her.

"Really?"

"Yes. And then drowned when it went down."

"Except that it didn't go down," Gamay noted. "Could this gang have hijacked the ship?"

"From what I've read, they were ruthless," he told her. "If the ship was taken over, they would have been just the kind of people to do it."

Gamay found her mind swirling. She wanted to investigate everything this man had told her. But before she could do anything, her phone buzzed. A text message requested that she return to the laboratory, where the samples were being analyzed.

"I have to go," she said. "I would love to talk more when I have some time."

"Anything for NUMA," he said, handing her a business card and shaking her hand.

Gamay left the library and returned quickly to the lab. The biologist who'd led the team summarized the results.

"Have you been able to give us some idea of where the ship might have been?" she asked.

"You're in luck, Ms. Trout," the biologist told her.

"You've found several species that exist in only one place on Earth."

He showed her the skeleton of a small animal that one of Paul's deckhands had dug up during the excavation. She thought it looked unique when she was putting the remains in the plastic case.

"What is it?" she asked.

"A fossa," he said, showing her a picture of the animal.

"It looks like a cross between a cat and a kangaroo," she said, looking at the picture.

"It's actually a type of mongoose," he replied. Next he showed her a large moth—it had been just emerging from a cocoon when Elena had spotted it. Neither of them could believe how large it was.

"This is a moon moth," the biologist said, before moving over to the spiders they'd found on the first night. "Golden orb-weaver spider," he explained. "While there are many species like this around the world, what we found in its web is unique." He pointed to an insect, one that had been wrapped up in spider silk. "Giraffe weevil," he explained, handing her a magnifying glass.

She focused her vision. The little bug looked fairly normal except for a long, skinny neck and head that stuck out from its body like an extension attachment on a vacuum cleaner.

She couldn't believe they'd gotten so lucky. She figured the bad news was coming next. "Let me guess. Somalia?"

"No," he said. "Much closer. The west coast of Madagascar."

"Madagascar?" she repeated.

He nodded. "You see, the island of Madagascar broke off from Africa a hundred sixty million years ago," he explained. "India was still attached to it at the time. But, eighty million years ago, India itself was torn loose by plate tectonics.

"As the three landmasses were pulled farther and farther apart, animals and plants left on Madagascar evolved differently from those in the rest of the world. As with Australia, there are hundreds of species that call only Madagascar home. You've discovered three of them on your floating wreck. Which tells us it was parked there for quite a while before it floated back out to sea."

"And the crocodile?" she asked.

"Plenty of them in Madagascar," he said.

Gamay nodded. The evidence was clear. The *Waratah* had spent her time aground on the western shores of Madagascar. The only questions now were where, and why someone was interested in sinking her.

CHAPTER 46

Kurt Austin felt himself falling, dropping weightless, into the darkness, his nerves tingling at the sensation. He plunged into the water and the cold sting opened his eyes. Suddenly he could see. Murky blue surrounded him, but there was light up above and the strange sight of waves toppling from beneath as they rolled over him.

He kicked for the surface and came out into a storm. Wind-driven rain lashed the sea, and swells the size of railroad cars buoyed him up and then dropped him down once again. The yacht, the *Ethernet*, was ahead of him. Sienna and her family were on it.

He kicked toward it and pulled himself aboard as a wave brought him up on the deck that was nearly awash in the storm. Struggling toward the bridge, shouting for Sienna, he found himself pushing through the main hatch only to be clubbed in the back of the head and slammed to the floor.

The impact at the back of his skull nearly knocked him unconscious; he was woozy and dazed. The next thing he knew, someone was slamming him against the bulkhead and trying to choke him.

"Where the hell did he come from?" a voice shouted from the other side of the bridge.

"There's a rescue copter outside," the man holding him called back.

Kurt knocked the man's hand from his throat, but the man flung him down and put him in a headlock.

Not one to lose many fights, Kurt was aware of weakness in his limbs that must have come from the initial blow to the back of his head. Having been concussed several times in his life, Kurt recognized the symptoms. The ringing in the ears, tunnel vision, dizziness. The blow should have put him out, might have even killed him. But, then again, Kurt had always been a hard head.

He looked up, trying to assess the situation. The man at the far end had a woman by the arm.

"Sienna?" Kurt said weakly.

She looked over at him. "Kurt?" she said.

She tried to pull free and reach for him, but the man yanked her back and handed her off to a subordinate. "Get her to the escape pod. Her husband and the children are already there."

Sienna struggled against them but could not break free. As she was dragged into the ship, Kurt could hear her shouting his name. He tried to stand, but his assailant was too heavy for Kurt to overcome in his current state.

"What about the rest of us?"

"We'll be joining her as soon as we get rid of this one." The man dropped down beside Kurt, flipped open a knife, and went for the cable that attached Kurt to the harness.

Kurt heard the helicopter through the storm and saw the spotlight probing around. It spurred the dim realization that he wouldn't survive if these men cut the cable connecting him to it.

He snapped free, kicked the man with the knife, and lunged for the door only to be tackled again.

"Kill him."

The man cocked the hammer on the pistol, but Kurt spun and kicked the man's knee. The weapon discharged, hitting the clear ceramic wall. The wall didn't shatter, but cracks spread across it like veins. Before Kurt could make a second move a boot caught him in the chin, and the man holding him pressed him down into the water, trying to drown him.

Despite every effort, Kurt could not push hard enough to rise up.

"Wait!"

The order came from a female voice. The man pulled Kurt from the water and held him there.

"We can use him," the woman said.

As he was allowed to breathe, Kurt stared at the woman. He recognized her. The short dark hair, wet and matted to her head. The high cheekbones. He knew her somehow. Her name was . . . Calista.

"He'll tell the world about us," the man said, objecting.

"Someone has to," she said cryptically. "You idiots have killed the captain and the crew. We planned on using them for that purpose."

"We didn't expect them to fight."

She dropped down beside Kurt and opened a small case.

Kurt could feel the yacht rolling in the swells. It was in danger of going over. Almost unconscious, Kurt fought to stay awake. His strength was gone. His mind clouding over.

The woman produced a syringe and jabbed it in his neck. Kurt's mind drifted further.

She moved close to his face and held it in both hands. "You came aboard the yacht," she said, her voice a distant echo. "You saw Sienna beyond this wall."

She turned his head toward it. The cracks caught his eye. "She was floating facedown. Her hair was wet, waving like sea grass."

Kurt stared at the glass wall. The glare of a flashlight reflected off it, blinding him. When it was gone, he could see through the glass. The room was half filled with water. The cushions and papers floated in muck.

Sienna was there, he saw her. He lunged toward her only to bang into the glass.

"She drowned," the voice told him. "Along with her daughter. Such a pretty child. Such a shame."

Kurt could see it happening. The little girl in her dress,

a towheaded blonde. Her small fingers were still curled around her mother's hand. He remembered hearing that her name was Elise.

"Her eyes are open," the woman said.

Kurt winced at the image. He tried again to get to them but was thrown back to the deck.

"The yacht is sinking," the voice told him. "Filling with water. Break the glass! It's your only hope."

Kurt slammed his fist into the glass wall but it was no use. He couldn't break through.

"You tried to smash it with the chair but the glass would not fall. Instead, you did."

He was pushed onto his back.

"The yacht is rolling over. You've run out of time."

"No!"

"They're pulling you out!"

"No," Kurt shouted. He felt himself being drawn backward. His mask was ripped off. And then the back of his head slammed against something once again.

But instead of finding himself out in the sea, he realized, through the haze in his mind, that he was still on the bridge.

He saw the woman and the others walking away. He heard her speaking to someone by radio. "Open the sea cocks. Sink this ship. And let's get out of here."

"What happens when he starts to remember?" another of them said.

"He won't," she insisted. "Not until we let him."

Kurt lost track of them and tried to move. He had to get out of there, he had to escape. He tried to stand, but his arms felt as if they were made of lead. His legs were useless.

The water began rushing away from him. The ship was rolling. Suddenly the harness pulled taut around him, dragging him toward the door. It pulled him free and then snapped with a loud twang.

He dropped back into the sea.

Dazed and barely conscious, he tried to kick for the surface but knew he was going deeper, pulled down by suction from the sinking yacht. The flashlight on his arm pointed downward, and Kurt saw the blurry outline of the yacht disappearing into the darkness below.

He turned his gaze upward, caught a glimpse of the silvery light, and then watched the darkness close around it. Everything went black. Until a hand grabbed him and pulled him above the waves.

CHAPTER 47

Kurt woke up quietly. Unlike all the other nights he'd woken from the memory/nightmare, this time he returned to consciousness in a state of peace. He could hear a soft beeping and the sound of a ventilating duct. He opened his eyes slowly and found himself bathed in blazing light.

He was not at home but in a hospital, with a white ceiling, walls, and floor. His pupils, dilated by some medication, were letting in vast amounts of light that turned the dimly lit room into a blazing solarium.

He raised a hand to block the glare, but the IV line taped to the crook of his arm made it awkward. He let his arm fall and noticed a pulse meter attached to his finger, which was in turn connected to the monitor emitting the soft beeping sound.

He guessed that meant he was alive.

Looking through the glare, he saw a figure across the way. It was Joe, sitting in a chair, on the far side of the small room.

Joe looked like he'd been up forever. Three days of stubble covered his face, dark circles rested beneath his eyes. He had a cup of coffee in one hand and a comic book across his knee.

"Didn't know you were a Manga guy," Kurt said.

Joe looked up, a warm smile cutting through the haggard look. "I just look at the pictures," he said. "Especially when the words are in a foreign language. As far as I can tell, this one's about an orphan robot who befriends a boy and girl with mutant powers who have a penchant for samurai swords and cupcakes . . . Though I could be wrong about that."

As Joe held the comic up, Kurt could see the surreal drawings and the Korean lettering in bright red. "Sometimes pictures don't tell the whole story," he said, thinking about his own experience. "What am I doing in a hospital?"

"Don't you remember? Your girlfriend tricked you into zapping yourself."

"'Zapping myself'?"

"In the tunnel under the DMZ."

It took Kurt a minute to recall the extracurricular activities beneath the DMZ, but thankfully he did. He even remembered falling after pressing the button on the screen of the woman's remote. "Considering the quality of care," he said, "I'm going to assume we're in the South. How'd we get back here?"

"We made a run for the border, Zavala style," Joe said. "Basically, I saved you . . . once again. And you missed the whole thing . . . once again."

"I'll take your word for it," Kurt said. His eyesight was returning to normal. "How long have I been out?"

"Three days," Joe said.

"Three days?"

Joe nodded. "They did some minor brain surgery on you," he explained. "I pointed out to them that any brain surgery on you would *have* to be minor, but they didn't get the joke. Lost in translation, I guess."

Kurt chuckled. "You've been waiting for me to wake up just so you could say that, haven't you?"

"Pretty much," Joe said. He put down the comic book and slid his chair over to Kurt, presenting him with a clear plastic vial. Inside was a tiny metal fragment half the size of a Tic Tac. A microchip.

"What is it?"

"Simple device," Joe said. "It emits an electronic signal that short circuits your brain every time they expose it to a certain frequency. The doctors say they've tried similar systems on patients with Parkinson's to control tremors. Or on people who've experienced emotional trauma, in an effort to rewire the recollection and reduce the emotional pain."

Kurt looked at the chip. He wondered if its removal had allowed his memory to clear or if the jolt Calista had given him was so powerful that it had somehow overridden the false memory.

"According to the docs, the little thing has to be

triggered by a transmitter," Joe added. "Hearing that, Dirk sent a team to sweep your house. They found a transmitter hidden in your garage."

Kurt considered all the trouble the tiny chip had caused him. "That's why the nightmares stopped once I left D.C. And, I'm assuming, why I can remember being on the yacht now. I even remember you pulling me out of the water."

"That alone has to be worth all the trouble," Joe said.

Kurt nodded and told Joe the memories he'd finally recalled. "Some of it's still fuzzy," he added, "but Calista was definitely there. They had Sienna. They had her husband and her children, which makes me wonder what he's doing back in the States."

"You mean . . ."

"I mean if they're forcing her to do something by holding the children hostage, what are they forcing him to do?"

"You didn't hear it from me," Joe said, "but I'm told the CIA is already wondering the same thing. Supposedly Westgate's about to get the chance to explain himself in person."

Kurt considered that progress. He sat up and pulled the pulse meter off of his finger, causing the monitor to flatline. An alarm sounded, bringing a nurse. She shut off the chirping, checked Kurt's vitals, and called a report into the nursing station.

As she left, new visitors arrived: Hale from the CIA with his ever-present partner, Col. Lee.

"You're lucky to be in a hospital," Hale said, "and not in a North Korean prison camp."

"Or one of ours, for that matter," Col. Lee added. "You two almost caused a second Korean War."

"Technically," Joe said, "the first one never actually ended. There was no peace treaty, only a cease-fire. So it would really be a continuation of the first war."

"You think this is funny?" Col. Lee asked.

"No," Joe said. "But I think the fact that Kurt and I discovered a threat to South Korean security in the form of a secret tunnel from the North has to count for something."

Hale gave Col. Lee a look that said *He has a point*.

"You're both very lucky," Col. Lee said. "Lucky you didn't end up dead or in a North Korean gulag. Lucky that Kim Jong-un is denying any such tunnel exists and claiming these are all imperialist lies rather than admitting two dozen of his men were killed in the skirmish. Lucky that calmer heads prevailed. It's taken three days for the sides to calm down. But tensions are almost back to normal."

Kurt was glad to hear that. "Maybe we went too far," he said. "We'll definitely be more careful next time."

"Sorry, Kurt, but there's not going to be a next time," Hale said. The words were delivered with a tinge of regret, even sadness.

"What are you talking about?" Kurt said. "We've proved Sienna is alive. We know these people have her and the other hackers on that list. We have to go after them before they do something terrible."

"The trail's gone cold," Hale explained. "There are no leads left to follow. Than Rang is locked up in a maximum security prison, surrounded by guards and lawyers, and he's not talking to anyone. Your mystery woman and the hackers have vanished without a trace."

"What about Acosta?" Kurt said. "He took our tracking device. You should be able to activate it and find him."

"We tried that," Hale said. "No luck."

"This country is a peninsula," Kurt pointed out. "Considering the roadblock to the north, it might as well be an island. They can't just drive off into the sunset, especially when they're supposed to be under surveillance."

"We're watching the airports and all the major harbors," Hale said, "but we've seen nothing so far."

Acosta wouldn't be fool enough to book a commercial flight. There were too many other ways to get out. Hundreds of merchant vessels steaming in and out of Korean ports every day. Beyond that, there were thousands of small watercraft or privately owned jets.

"And even if something does turn up," Hale added, "it won't be your job to follow up."

Kurt narrowed his gaze, all but burning holes in Hale with his eyes.

"I've been on the phone with your boss back in D.C.," Hale said. "He agrees with me that NUMA's involvement in this situation has run its course and is now at an end. If any other leads do surface, they'll be followed up on by Central Intelligence or Special Forces personnel under the direction of the NSA."

Kurt knew the sound of a dismissal when he heard it. It sucked the air right out of him. He glanced over at Joe.

"I spoke with Dirk too," Joe said. "He wanted you to know, 'It's time to let this go.'"

Kurt leaned back against the bed. If there was an emptier feeling on Earth, Kurt hadn't felt it. They'd been so close. He'd finally found Sienna. He'd actually had her in his arms. Now she was gone . . . again.

"The doctors insist you're ready to be discharged," Hale said. "We're going to move you immediately, since we have reason to believe that Than Rang or even Acosta may have agents hanging around who'd like to kill you both. You'll be flown out of here at dusk on a military C-17 headed for Guam. From there, it's on to Hawaii and some R & R. Enjoy it, if you can."

Kurt didn't respond, and Hale straightened up and made his way toward the door. He stopped to offer one more comment before he left. "I'll give you this, Kurt. You put on one hell of a show."

AS DUSK FELL, Kurt and Joe were driven to an American air base and a battleship-gray C-17 that sat on the tarmac, illuminated by a series of floodlights.

They entered from the tail ramp, cleared by a loading officer, who was busy strapping down a Humvee and some other tarp-covered equipment, and were offered seats near the front.

Kurt dropped into his seat, dejected and exhausted. Joe offered a few jokes to cheer him up, but Kurt didn't have it in him. He sat in silence and stared straight ahead as the huge four-engine transport taxied and then took off into the dark sky.

As they climbed to altitude, Joe fell asleep, but Kurt found he couldn't close his eyes. He racked his brain for one more avenue to explore, one tiny thing they might have missed that could lead them to Sienna, the other hackers, and whoever was behind a plot that Kurt was certain hadn't truly begun to unfold yet.

Try as he might, he came up empty. And as the drone of the engines and the chill of the cabin numbed him, he stood and walked toward the front, stopping to stare through the small window in the aircraft door.

The sky was dark up ahead, but with a line of light on the horizon. Silver lining, Kurt thought, how ironic. As drained as he was, it took Kurt a minute to realize that there should not be a silver lining up ahead. If they were headed to Guam, they would be flying into the teeth of the night. They'd only been airborne a few hours and, despite the time zone change, it couldn't be anywhere near dawn yet.

He looked backward. The sky behind them was pitch-black. "We're going the wrong way," he said to himself.

Before he could hazard a guess as to why, the cockpit door opened and a familiar figure stepped out.

"Hiram?" Kurt said.

Seeing Hiram Yaeger outside of the NUMA building was like running into the high school principal out on the town somewhere. It was off-key somehow. Adding to that effect was Hiram's clothing: instead of his trademark

T-shirt and jeans, Yaeger was zipped up in an olive drab military flight suit, with his ponytail tucked up into an Air Force ball cap pulled down tight over the top of his head.

"Are you undercover?" Kurt asked, half joking.

"In a way, I am," Yaeger replied. "Dirk wanted me to brief you in person."

"Brief me about what?"

"The mission."

Kurt paused. "I thought there was no mission," he said. "In fact, Tim Hale gave me the distinct impression that if I pushed it any further, I might end up in a stockade somewhere."

Hiram laughed. "Hale is actually rather fond of you, from what I hear. He was very impressed with everything you two accomplished in such a short time."

"So why the cold shoulder?"

"It was for Colonel Lee's benefit," Yaeger said. "And anyone else who might have been listening, for that matter. We think the Korean Security database has been hacked. And we're not too sure about our own or the DOD's. So we figured we'd lay out a story for Colonel Lee to enter into his system while I came here with handwritten notes to get you up to date."

"Handwritten? That must have been hard for you," Kurt joked.

"You have no idea," Yaeger replied. "Might as well be using a slide rule or an abacus."

Kurt laughed, happy to see a friendly face in an unexpected place for the second time in as many weeks. "So what tidings do you bring, O messenger of the realm?"

Yaeger waved at a pair of seats that faced each other. Kurt took one seat as Hiram sat across from him and zipped the flight suit down far enough to pull out a manila folder he had tucked inside. "An awful lot has happened while you were napping in that Korean hospital."

"Good or bad?"

"A little of both," Hiram said. "As soon as Joe positively identified Sienna Westgate among the group of people that had been smuggled out of North Korea, the administration went into overdrive. Brian Westgate was called in to explain himself. In the middle of a tirade about how Phalanx was unbreakable—even if someone had Sienna in their clutches—he suffered a mental breakdown of some kind and what we thought was a stroke. Turns out he'd been given the same treatment as you. They pulled a chip from his occipital lobe. A team from the FBI found prescription drugs in his house that had been tampered with and laced with memory-inhibiting compounds. He's recovering and under guard for his own protection."

"Does he remember anything?" Kurt asked.

"Not much. Seems they worked his mind over worse than yours."

Kurt sat back. He'd harbored a natural dislike of the Internet billionaire ever since he'd learned of Sienna's engagement to him. And from the beginning of this mystery, he'd been certain Westgate had some part in it. Finding out that Westgate had been given the same rough treatment and had been used as a pawn in some bigger scheme put Kurt in the odd place of feeling he'd misjudged the man. He could only imagine what was going through Westgate's mind at this point.

"They pulled him from the yacht," Kurt said, remembering what he'd heard. "After they escaped in that pod and the storm had passed, they put him in that raft and waited for someone to find him."

Yaeger nodded. "Seems likely," he said. "The thing is, with both Brian Westgate and Sienna compromised, it's become obvious to everyone that Phalanx cannot be relied upon to protect the computer systems and networks it's been tasked with guarding."

"What's being done about it?"

Yaeger sighed. "Everything that can be," he said. "A crash effort is under way to pull Phalanx and replace it with alternate systems. In addition, other security measures are being strengthened and reviewed. Some systems are being disconnected from the grid entirely."

"A step in the right direction," Kurt said. "But when the people behind this mess realize that Sienna is no longer useful to them, neither she nor her children are going to last very long."

"No," Yaeger agreed. "The most likely outcome has them being killed. The group behind all this will simply start over. Whatever their ultimate goal is, they've spent considerable time and energy trying to bring it to life. Nothing we've seen suggests they would give up."

"Any idea what they're up to?"

"We've detected a massive increase in hacking attempts

but no clear pattern," Yaeger said. "We think they're try-ing to disguise their true objective."

"Which means we have to find them," Kurt urged. "The only way this ends is if we stop it at the source."

Yaeger nodded. "And that brings me to why you're here and flying west with the night instead of east to Guam. We have a new lead. And, strangely enough, you're the one who gave it to us."

As he spoke, Yaeger pulled another photograph from the file folder. Kurt had seen it before. It was the picture he'd taken of Calista on the deck of Acosta's yacht.

"Max has finished the facial recognition analysis on your mystery woman."

"Any hits?"

"Not at first," Yaeger replied. "We checked through the civilized world's DMV bureaus, passport-issuing organiza-tions, and court archives. Even Interpol. No matching photographic record of this woman exists. So I asked Max to scan all publicly available images and see if we could find a counterpart."

"There must be billions of photos out there," Kurt said.

"Trillions," Hiram said. "Many trillions when you include video images. Even for Max it was a big task. Took three full days. And when she finally came up with an answer, I almost asked her if she was joking."

"I didn't know computers could joke," Kurt said.

"Max has been known to pull a prank or two. But this time she was serious."

Hiram produced another photo, this one copied from

an old three-by-five glossy. It showed a handsome couple in their thirties. Gathered around them were three children, two boys and a girl, who looked to be the youngest child. Judging by the clothes, the photo had probably been taken in the mid-eighties.

"Nice-looking family," Kurt said. "Who are they?"

"The woman's name is Abigail Banister," Hiram said. "She was a telecommunications expert."

Kurt studied her. Aside from the clothes, the woman could have been Calista's twin.

"The man is her husband," Hiram continued, "Stewart Banister. He was a satellite guidance specialist. They're English. They disappeared while on safari in Zimbabwe twenty-eight years ago. At the time, there was some suspicion that they'd defected to the Eastern bloc. It seems British Intelligence had a low-level alert on them because of certain political beliefs and some old friends they'd made back in their college years. Though, for reasons that will become clear to you shortly, the world soon learned that such was not the case."

Kurt had an idea where this was going. "The woman looks just like Calista. And the little girl . . ."

"According to Max, her facial structure shows an eighty-nine percent correlation with those of the woman you know as Calista. Once we did a computerized age progression, using her own features and those of her siblings and parents, we end up with a ninety-six percent correlation. For all intents and purposes, it might as well be a fingerprint match."

"You're saying the little girl is Calista?"

Yaeger nodded.

Kurt had great respect for what Hiram and Max could do—certainly they'd pulled off near miracles before—but this seemed like a shot in the dark. "Is there any way we can prove what you're suggesting?"

"We already have," Yaeger said.

"How?"

"DNA analysis."

Kurt raised an eyebrow. "Where'd we get her DNA from?"

"From you," Yaeger said. "You had Calista's blood all over you, not to mention a few strands of black hair caught in the buttons of your coat. Joe pointed it out to one of the CIA techs when he got to the hospital. They were smart enough to save the samples. We've since matched Calista's DNA with surviving relatives of the Banister family."

"So the girl in this picture *is* Calista," Kurt said.

"Her real name is Olivia," Yaeger said.

They looked so normal. "Are you telling me these middle-class suburbanites left England, faked their disappearance, and started some kind of international crime family?"

"No," Hiram said. "The real story is much sadder than that. As I told you, they disappeared while on vacation. The father resurfaced six months later when he was shot to death in Bangkok. His hands were bound, his face was bruised, and he was clearly trying to escape from someone when he was gunned down. The responsible party was never found. A year after that, the bodies of the mother and the two boys were discovered."

"Where?"

"In a dilapidated lifeboat drifting off the coast of Mozambique."

Hiram passed another photo over, this one of the lifeboat as it was discovered. The three bodies were covered, but there were several containers at their sides. Here and there, Kurt saw patches to the rotting wooden boat and a pair of makeshift oars. In one corner was a broken splint of wood and a tattered bolt of cloth that might have been used as a mast and sail.

"They died of dehydration," Hiram explained.

"No water in those containers?" Kurt asked.

"Perhaps at first," Yaeger said. "But if that's what they held, it wasn't enough. Based on the condition of the bodies, the coroner guessed they'd been in the boat for at least two weeks, maybe three. Not enough water for three people for that much time. Not even if those containers were filled to the brim."

Kurt looked back at the photo of the smiling family and guessed at the sequence. "Somehow, Calista got left behind. Maybe they knew there wasn't enough water for four and were hoping three could make it."

"Who knows," Hiram said. "The only thing we're sure of is that the smiling little girl in that picture has been with whoever took her for almost three decades."

"She doesn't know, does she?"

"She may remember some of it," Hiram cautioned.

"She would have been four when they were abducted, five going on six when her mother and brothers made what we can only assume was a desperate attempt to escape. But considering what we've learned about people in captivity, it's highly probable that whatever memories she had of the situation have been suppressed. Between Stockholm syndrome and the human desire to survive, the mind can be bent into accepting even the strangest of things. In her case, as a young child, it would probably have been as simple as just making her part of a new family."

Kurt considered the irony. "She's gone from abductee to abductor."

"She wouldn't be the first."

Kurt nodded. Looking at the photo, he felt sorry for the little girl who'd become Calista. But his main concern was the madness she and her partners were now spreading over the world.

"So this is a break for us," he said. "If we find the people who took her, we find the mastermind behind all this."

"Exactly our thinking," Hiram said. "Which leads us to a leap of faith. Take a look at the old lifeboat in the picture. Can you make out the name stenciled on the upper plank?"

Kurt squinted. He could see a discoloration, but that was it. He shook his head.

"Here's an enhanced photo."

Kurt took the new printout. Computer augmentation had made the name more legible. Kurt read it twice to be sure, and then a third time. "I know you wouldn't be joking at a time like this, but are you certain?"

Hiram nodded.

"The *Waratah*?" Kurt said. "The Blue Anchor Line's *Waratah* that vanished in 1909?"

"One and the same," Hiram said. "Between St. Julian Perlmutter's vast number of records on the subject and a South African who spent years looking for the *Waratah*, we've confirmed that she had two double-enders of exactly this type among her complement of auxiliary craft and lifeboats."

Kurt stared at the name on the photo. It certainly looked correct. But it seemed impossible. "It's got to be a mistake," he said.

"Logic would tell you that," Hiram agreed, "except that I know something you don't. The *Waratah* never went down."

With that, Hiram pulled out another photograph. On it Kurt saw a derelict vessel covered in sediment, corrosion, and what Kurt guessed to be vegetation. She didn't have much shape to her.

"I present the SS *Waratah*," Hiram said. "Discovered by Paul and Gamay Trout, three days ago, adrift in the southern reaches of the Indian Ocean."

Kurt looked at the photo. He realized that Hiram wouldn't be joking about such a thing, not at this point, but it boggled his mind and he had to make sure. "You're serious?"

Yaeger nodded.

"How is it possible?"

Hiram explained their theory about how the sediment she was buried in stunted the corrosion on her hull, and what Gamay and Elena found in her sick bay.

"We're operating on a theory that a violent group took over the ship," he continued, "and sailed her north."

"Any idea where she ended up?"

Hiram nodded. "The west coast of Madagascar," he said, then followed up by explaining how Gamay had led them to that answer, passing yet another photo from the file to Kurt.

Two satellite images were printed on the photo side by side. They showed a muddy river snaking and turning.

"Before and after," Yaeger explained. "The picture on the left is two months old. The picture on the right was taken last week."

Kurt's eyes went right to a highlighted section where the channel bent ninety degrees and then ran out to the sea. In the older photograph there was a large obstruction, like a hill or sandbar, that seemed to force the bend. In the newer photo the hill was gone, the river had carved out a new course, and the channel had widened and straightened substantially.

"Torrential rains last month scoured a new route to the sea," Hiram said. "They took everything in their path along with them, including the hull of the SS *Waratah*. The hill in question matches her dimensions almost perfectly."

Kurt rubbed the stubble on his chin. "So the *Waratah* was hijacked and stashed in this river, not lost at sea like everyone thought. Eighty years pass, and the Banisters, being held captive, discovered her, patched up one of her lifeboats, and tried to sail to safety, leaving five-year-old Olivia behind. They don't make it. The hijackers keep the young girl and slowly indoctrinate her. All these years later, we have Calista to deal with."

Hiram nodded. "You'd have made a good detective," he said. And, with that, he presented one last piece of the puzzle. This time the image depicted a large plantation-style estate, complete with hedges shaped into a complex maze, terraced gardens, a large pool, and various other structures. A row of satellite dishes sprouted along one side of the main building, while a helipad with a moderate-sized hangar lay on the other. Kurt could see the tails of two military-looking helicopters sticking out of the hangar.

The property was sprawling, and the grounds beyond the walls looked like pastureland. Kurt could see livestock roaming free. At the very top of the property was a jagged bluff of weathered gray stone. It ran the entire width of the photo.

"This compound is five miles upriver from the spot where the *Waratah* was hidden. It's owned by a mysterious but powerful man named Sebastian Brèvard. For four generations the Brèvard name has been connected with various types of criminal activity. Money laundering, bank fraud, trafficking in weapons and stolen goods. But strangely, there is no record of their existence before 1910, when they purchased this large tract of land."

"I'm guessing documents were fairly scarce back then," Kurt said. "Especially in Madagascar."

"You'd be surprised," Hiram said. "The fact is, from 1897 to 1960, the island was part of the French empire. In the land purchase records filed with the colonial governor's office, the Brèvard family claim emigration from France. And a distant level of nobility. However, the coat of arms they lay claim to is made up. It has no true heraldic provenance in the annals of French society. Nor is there any record of a wealthy French family bearing the Brèvard name leaving France for warmer pastures during that time."

Kurt saw what Hiram was getting at. "So this false band of nobles appear out of nowhere six months after the *Waratah* goes missing and they buy the land on which the ship is hidden, presumably to keep it that way."

"Not just the land where the ship was hidden," Hiram corrected, "but a mile-wide swath all the way from the water's edge up to this impassable outcropping of granite."

"I think I can guess where the money came from," Kurt said. "Jewels, gold, and cash stolen from the passengers and crew of the *Waratah*."

"Our thoughts exactly," Hiram said. "Supplemented, we now think, by a stack of counterfeit notes that were considered among the best ever produced during that era."

Kurt sat back and considered the implications. It seemed likely that Sienna's kidnappers were the same group of thugs who'd abducted and destroyed the Banister family thirty years before. Beyond that, the evidence suggested they were descended from a group that pirated the *Waratah* back in 1909.

Instead of anger, Kurt felt only a cold determination

to put an end to their destruction. "I guess the apple really doesn't fall far from the tree," he said. "Any idea who they really are? Where they came from?"

"It's all speculation," Yaeger said, "but a band of criminals known as the Klaar River Gang had been terrorizing Durban through the winter of 1908 and into the summer of 1909. Records show that the gang fractured in a power struggle and turned on itself just as Durban police were about to round them up. Most of the members were killed, but several high-ranking associates were never accounted for. Despite initially thinking the gang had been wiped out, the chief inspector of the Durban police soon came to the conclusion that the leaders of the gang had escaped and had killed the others to cover their tracks. He stated publicly that he expected them to surface again, but they never did. Later in his life he became enamored with the idea that they'd made their way aboard the *Waratah* and perished when it went down."

"What made him think that?"

"Timing, for one," Yaeger said. "They'd vanished two days before the *Waratah* sailed. But there was another reason as well. Counterfeit ten-pound notes eventually surfaced in the Blue Anchor Line's payroll, very hard to distinguish from the real thing. It was assumed that some tickets had been purchased with the notes and that's how they got into the office's cashbox. Similar notes, and burned fragments, were found at the gang's hideout."

Kurt thought he saw the line of reasoning clearly at last. "So the leaders fake their deaths and slip aboard the *Waratah*, paying for passage with forged notes, only to vanish with the ship. Even those who guess where they might have gone think that's the end of it, karma catching up with the gang or some grand cosmic rebalancing of the scales of justice. No one realizes they've hijacked the ship, taken it to Madagascar, and hidden it on this river. They use the wealth stolen from the passengers and their own forged banknotes to buy a new life. But instead of going straight, they slowly turn back to what they know: crime. And every generation since has followed the pattern."

"That's about the size of it," Hiram said.

"If we're even half right, I think it's time we put an end to it," Kurt said. "Any chance we have the Delta Force or a team of Navy SEALs standing by?"

"Afraid not," Hiram said. "A strike force *is* being readied. Believe me, no one back home is happy with what's going on or with the possibility that such a prominent American is being used and held by a group as unsavory as this bunch. But there are logistical problems."

"Such as?"

"For one, we have no proof," Hiram said. "Beyond that, even if our theory is correct, we can't be sure that the cyberattacks are emanating from this compound or that Sienna and the others are there. If we tip our hand and ask for help from the government of Madagascar, we'll lose the only advantage we have going: the element of surprise."

"You need boots on the ground to get you proof," Kurt said.

Hiram nodded solemnly. "That's where you and Joe

come in. It's strictly volunteer at this point, but we'll be crossing over Madagascar in a few hours. That puts you and Joe four hours closer than the next-best option."

"You know I'm game," Kurt said. "And I'm sure Sleeping Beauty back there won't want to miss out on all the fun. But what happens once we get proof? Assuming we can find it."

"Call it in and sit tight," Hiram said. "Special Forces will do the rest."

Kurt liked that idea. But there was one concern. "What if the Brèvards know that Special Forces is being readied? They've been one step ahead of us all along."

"Not this time," Hiram said. "Like my trip out here to see you, all orders and logistics connected to this operation are being drafted up on old-fashioned typewriters and hand-carried to the commanders in question. The Brèvards can tap all the computers they want, but they won't find what isn't there. And if they do look, what they'll discover is misinformation.

"Right now, the NUMA database, the Air Force database, and even the international air traffic control system, show this plane winging its way to Guam. Orders putting you back on medical leave have already been set in motion, while Joe's being reassigned to a whale-watching mission off the coast of Venezuela. In the meantime, a CIA threat assessment has labeled Acosta as the prime suspect, putting him in league with the Iranian cyberforce and North Korea's Unit 121."

Kurt grinned. "That's not bad. If this Brèvard guy is

taking a peek into our systems, he's probably feeling awfully good about himself right now. We might even catch him flat-footed."

"We might at that," Hiram said.

Kurt stood up, stretched, and glanced back toward Joe. "I'll go wake Joe. I think we'll need some coffee."

CHAPTER 48

Sebastian Brèvard, his brother Laurent, and his "sister" Calista stood in the control room surrounded by computers, discussing the situation.

"I've brought all the men in," Laurent said. "We have a total of fifty at this point. But they're sitting around with nothing to do. When do you expect this attack to occur?"

"Sooner or later," Sebastian explained. "I'm monitoring their most important channels. We have nothing to worry about at the moment."

"In the meantime, we're spending a fortune on these hired guns," Laurent said. "I'm sure our regulars would have done just fine."

Sebastian dismissed his brother's whining. "It doesn't matter," he said. "A pittance, compared to what we'll control."

"I don't see why we have to draw them in," Calista said.

Sebastian glanced toward her as he sat at his own workstation. "How many times have I told you, dear sister, a con is never about convincing your mark to do any particular thing. They must convince themselves to take action, firm in their belief that it was their idea all along."

"That, I understand," she said. "But why bring them here?"

"To make this work they must attack with vengeance and retribution in their eyes. The carnage and annihilation it brings will make the world think we're dead. It will make them think this sordid chapter in their pitiful lives is over and the threat effectively neutralized. Only then will we be truly hidden and able to act with impunity. I told you I would give us a new life, one where no one is looking for us, and I shall."

For the first time she could remember, he moved closer to her. Instead of the stern older brother, there was something more in his eyes. It made her uncomfortable in a way she was used to making others uncomfortable.

"What about the hostages?" she asked, pulling back.

He looked at her with disappointment. "For the second time in as many weeks you seem concerned with something other than our family. Are you feeling all right?"

"I just need to know," she snapped.

"They can identify us," Sebastian explained. "To prevent that, they will be destroyed in the conflagration. Their quarters are lined with napalm, much like the explosives that line our home. When the attack comes and the fire-fight begins, I will detonate the charges and the whole place will go up in flames. Make sure you're on the helicopter with me when it does."

She smiled, the slightly sadistic smile he was more used to. "Of course, dear brother. Where else would I be?"

"Good," he said. "Now, bring Sienna Westgate to me. I have at least one last job for her."

Calista nodded and left. With the door shut tight, Laurent reengaged Sebastian.

"She's getting soft," he said.

"Well," Sebastian said, "it's to be expected. She's not really one of us, is she?"

Laurent smiled. Both he and Sebastian had enjoyed taunting her when she was a child; it had been a game. They both knew who and what she was. They were surprised by what she became, how strongly she bought into the family. In many ways she'd always seemed intent on proving herself as if she knew deep down inside that she didn't belong.

"You know her purpose as well as I do," Sebastian continued. "They will find her body and that of two others in the downed helicopter. Burned perhaps, but considering the jewels and treasures they'll discover on board, there will be no choice but to assume it is the three of us. You and I will escape in the tunnel and destroy it behind us. I have rigged the explosives to go off in an acceptable progression. The outer buildings first, then the wings of the mansion. And finally the control room and the tunnel. It will give us extra time to escape."

*   *   *

SIENNA WESTGATE sat with her children in a one-story windowless lodge that was the communal prison of the hostages and their family members.

In an effort to shield her children from any more pain, Sienna's trip to Iran and then Korea had been called a vacation. She'd promised them she would come back quickly, though she obviously had no control over when or if she would return. And the feeling of her children's tears had remained with her all during her absence.

Her arrival back at the compound was met with smiles and kisses, and she wrapped her arms around them so tightly that she almost squeezed the air out of them. But after a brief moment of euphoria, Sienna began to fall into a pit of despair. She could see that constant fear and stress had already taken its toll on them.

Elise had become withdrawn and quiet, the opposite of her outgoing nature. Her face looked pale and gaunt as if she weren't being fed or was unwilling to eat. Tanner was worse. He had a fever and insect bites all over his legs. He quickly became demanding and angry. He wanted his father. He wanted to go home. He *hated* it there.

Sienna hated it too, but there was nothing she could do about it. She'd given in to her captors and done everything they'd asked—everything any of them had asked— all to keep the children safe and buy them some time. But now her spirit was beginning to weaken.

Video she'd seen of her husband talking to the press as if she and the kids had drowned was confusing and disheartening to her. He knew she'd been abducted. He was there. He'd seen it with his own eyes. She only hoped it was a ruse and that rescue would eventually come, but she now doubted it. Especially after what she allowed to happen to Kurt and his friend in Korea.

Seeing them appear out of nowhere had been like a dream. But when Calista had gained the upper hand, Sienna had no choice but to obey her.

Her only solace was that, given another chance, she would make the same choice. She couldn't face life knowing she'd chosen freedom and left her children behind. If they were going to die, she wasn't going to let them face it alone.

The door to the room opened. Everyone looked up. Two of Brèvard's men stood there. Calista was with them. "Sienna," she said.

Sienna stood, but her children refused to let go, clinging to her hands, gripping her fingers.

"Don't go," Elise cried.

"It's okay," she said, "I'll be right back."

"Mommy!" Tanner was screaming.

Sienna dropped down to their level and squeezed them together. Tanner broke out in tears; Elise looked almost numb at this point. "I'll be right back," she told them. "Take care of each other."

As Sienna stood, another woman, who was married to the hacker named Montresor, came to her assistance. "I watch them for you," she said.

If there was one positive to this communal prison, it was that they weren't alone. "Thank you."

Sienna left with the guards and followed as they led her along the pathway from what had once been the servants' quarters and up to the main house.

Sienna glared at Calista. "You must have a heart of stone."

"If I have a heart at all," Calista replied proudly.

Sienna dutifully climbed the steps that led to the main compound and from there was led through the security doors to the control room. She began to feel sick as she approached, knowing that Sebastian Brèvard would be waiting on the other side, ready to order her to use her skills and the offensive capabilities of Phalanx against a new target, as he'd done each night since her return.

A day would come when he asked her to do something truly evil and she would have to decide between her children's lives and the lives of countless others. She almost prayed he would shoot her before then.

"Tonight's targets are the power plants in California," Sebastian said. "We'll start with the regular ones. I just want a large rolling blackout. Think of all the coal and natural gas that will be saved."

Sienna sat at the console as ordered and began to work. She'd long contemplated hiding a message in the code she was supposed to send. Someone smart enough on the other side might find it, even if it slipped under the noses of Sebastian and Calista. But the only message of any value would be to tell the world where she was and that was something she didn't know.

Considering the climate, the strange birdcalls she

heard at night, and some odd trees she'd seen in the distance, she figured they were somewhere in Africa. But that didn't exactly narrow it down.

She settled in and did as she was told. For now, that was all she could do.

AT THAT VERY MOMENT, five hundred miles north of Madagascar, the USS *Bataan*, an amphibious assault ship sometimes referred to as a helicopter carrier, was steaming at flank speed to the south. She was rigged for battle, blacked out and operating under strict radio silence. But while she could not transmit, she was capable of receiving messages.

Late on the second watch, a member of the communications crew overheard several puzzling messages and reported them to the officer in charge.

The officer looked at the messages and then at the radioman. "What's the problem, Charlie?"

"It's these intercepts, sir. Someone is using our call sign. They're transmitting and receiving uncoded messages and giving out our old location."

The communications supervisor studied the transmission sheet. "Yep," he said. "Looks that way."

Without another word, he handed the sheet back to the radioman and turned his attention to other matters. The radioman stared at him dumbfounded.

"You have a post to man, sailor."

"Yes, sir," the radioman said, turning and heading back

to his console. Something was obviously going on, but having seen the look on his superior's face, Charlie knew better than to ask.

Meanwhile, down on the hangar deck of the ship, a swarm of mechanics and technicians worked on a group of UH-60 Black Hawk helicopters, making sure all five were in perfect shape for the mission.

In a nearby ready room, forty-six Marines, comprising two Force Recon platoons, were getting briefed on the island compound they were about to attack.

"We go in under cover of darkness," Lieutenant Brooks told the men. "Secure the perimeter and then search the grounds and buildings with the following objectives. First, to rescue Ms. Westgate and her children. Second, to rescue any other civilians found on the site. Third, to capture the individuals responsible. Fourth, to gather any intelligence regarding their activities or associates."

"Are we going in as friendlies?" someone asked.

"Negative," Brooks replied. "We have not been invited and we *will not* be overstaying our welcome. From wheels down to departure, we have no more than forty minutes. So don't get lost in the hedges."

A wave of laughter went around the room.

"How many defenders are we likely to encounter?"

"Based on the two bunkhouses and the size of the main structure, it could be anywhere from thirty to fifty. But not all of those will be armed combatants. Honestly, it should be a walk in the park. Just be ready in case it isn't."

Thirty minutes later, the Force Recon Marines were

up on the flight deck and boarding the Black Hawks. A long, grueling stretch awaited them, four hours of flight time that included refueling the helicopters from a tanker aircraft approximately one hundred miles from the target.

Assuming they went in and got out in forty minutes, the total trip would be eight hours. At least the journey home would be shorter as the ship would be nearly two hundred miles closer by the time they reached it.

With the pilots going through their preflight checks and the Marines boarding the helicopters and stowing their weapons, the company commander made his way over. He spoke briefly with Lt. Brooks.

"We have the green light to launch, but you won't get attack authorization until we have confirmation that Ms. Westgate and her children are on-site."

"Understood," Brooks said. "Any idea how or when we're going to get that?"

The commander checked his watch. "A two-man team will be making a LAPES insertion several miles from the compound. They should be on the ground anytime now. They'll have a ways to go before they're on-site, but I would expect a go or no-go decision shortly after you refuel."

Brooks nodded. "LAPES insertion? Who'd they sucker into pulling that duty?"

"A couple of guys from NUMA."

Brooks stared at the commander blankly for a moment. "NUMA? Aren't they a bunch of marine biologists or something?"

"They're something, all right," the commander said

with a strange look on his face. "Anyway, I'm told these guys are good."

"Right, sir," Brooks said with disdain in his voice. "I'll expect our cover to be blown and to be looking for more hostages or dead bodies when we land."

The commander didn't respond, but he shared the assessment. "Crack open the operations file once you get airborne. There are photos of the NUMA personnel inside. Make sure you're familiar. Don't want to shoot them if they happen to survive. Good luck."

Brooks offered a salute, received one back from the commander, and then climbed aboard the lead Black Hawk.

As the rotors above him began to turn, he wondered what kind of oceanographer or marine biologist would be up for such a stunt or how such a person would even have the skills to perform what they were being asked to do. With a shrug of his shoulders, Brooks decided they had to be half crazy, whoever they were. At least they had guts, he'd give them that.

CHAPTER 49

Had they overheard Lt. Brooks's candid assessment of their mental health, Kurt and Joe might have agreed with him. Considering the odds alone, they were at least "half crazy."

Fortunately, the military had brought along a few items that would even the odds a bit.

Kurt and Joe were changing into combat gear that was far more exotic than anything Kurt had ever heard of. The clothing looked more like a two-piece wet suit than standard fatigues. It fit snugly and had some compression to it, bulging only where armored Kevlar pads covered the chest, thighs, and forearms.

"Feel like I'm suiting up for some futuristic sport," Joe said as he pulled the garment tight.

Kurt laughed as he pulled his own suit on and ran

his hands over the outer layer. "Odd texture," he said. "It feels like sandpaper."

An Air Force staff sergeant named Connors explained the clothing. "These are what we call infiltration suits," he said. "The guys call them Chameleon Camo, because of the way they work. There are twenty-nine thousand microsensors sewn into the exterior. They detect ambient light in all directions and change the color of the suit to match what is behind and around you. Try them out."

Kurt found a small switch and clicked it to the on position. Then went over and stood by the wall of the aircraft. The suit changed almost instantly from a dark navy blue to battleship gray. Where his right leg crossed in front of a black seat, the suit turned black. And where a yellow cable crossed behind him, a matching yellow strip crossed from his shoulder.

He wasn't exactly invisible, but it looked like he'd been painted over to match the wall. Only his face and hands were obvious and they would be covered by gloves and a hood once he was on-site.

"That's incredible," Joe muttered.

"If you think they work well inside a brightly lit aircraft," the sergeant said, "wait till you get on the ground. If you two aren't careful, you'll lose track of each other from ten feet away."

"What about infrared?" Kurt said.

"The suit has a cooling unit," Connors said. "It will counteract your body heat for about thirty minutes once you switch it on. After that, the exterior of the suit will start to warm up and you'll lose both your thermal protection and your chameleon-like powers. From that point on you're just wearing expensive body armor. And I mean *real* expensive. Each of these suits costs more than you guys make in a year."

Kurt switched his suit off and watched it return to a dark blue color in the time it takes a lightbulb to dim. From there the sergeant led them over to an equipment table that had been folded down from the wall of the cavernous aircraft.

"You'll breathe through these," he said, picking up two devices that looked much like divers' regulators.

"What's wrong with the air on the ground?" Joe asked.

"We can't have your breath giving you away."

Kurt chuckled. "I told you go easy on the onions."

"What can I say?" Joe replied. "I like a little flavor."

"It's not the odor," Connors explained, "it's the heat. Breathing out vents a lot of hot air into the world, easy to spot on a thermal scope. No sense covering the rest of you in a cool suit if you're going to walk around with a plume of ninety-eight-point-six-degree vapor coming from your nose or mouth."

He pointed to a lever on the front of the regulators. "Twist this when you're ready to go dark. From then on the regulator will mix cold air with every outgoing breath, effectively cooling it to the ambient air temperature and neutralizing the danger."

"How long will it last?"

"As long as your compressed air holds out. Depends

on your level of exertion. The tank is small so you're looking at fifteen, maybe twenty minutes tops. Make sure
you're through the outer layer of security by then."

Both Kurt and Joe nodded.

Next came the weapons and guidance equipment. First
off, the sergeant strapped a gauntlet to Kurt's arm. It had
a curved, low-light screen on it. "Standard GPS, moving
map display," he said. "It will illuminate with less than
one candlepower. You'll be able to read it with your night
vision goggles on, but no one else will. Remember, this
is military GPS, so it's good to within three feet."

From there they moved to a rifle rack.

Connors handed them matching weapons. Once again
they were like nothing Kurt had ever fired. Considering
how much he knew about guns, that was surprising.

"Are these phasers?" Joe asked. "I've always wanted one."

Connors chuckled. "Electromagnetic railguns," he
said. "Completely silent. Accurate up to a thousand yards.
They fire ferrous projectiles—in other words, the bullets
are made of iron, not lead, so they're more lethal in terms
of penetrating anything they encounter. Also, since they
don't require gunpowder, your standard-sized magazine
carries fifty projectiles. You have a second magazine in
your packs."

Kurt held the weapon up, testing the weight and feel.
It had a long barrel and was definitely nose-heavy.

"How does it work?" Joe asked.

"Superconducting magnets along the barrel and a
high-potency battery pack. Pull the trigger and they ac-

celerate the projectiles to a thousand feet per second in the blink of an eye."

Joe nodded approvingly.

"Why are there two triggers?" Kurt asked.

"Since they are already equipped with a substantial power source, someone got the great idea to add a long-range Taser to the bottom rail. The lower trigger fires it. You can hit someone accurately up to fifty feet or simply hold the tip of the barrel against them and give a half pull to zap them manually."

"So we don't have to kill everything we see," Joe mentioned.

The sergeant nodded.

A red light went on at the far end of the aircraft and they could feel the plane begin a rather steep descent.

"We're approaching the drop zone," the sergeant said. "Any questions?"

Joe raised a hand. "You said 'drop zone,' but we don't seem to have parachutes."

"You won't need them," Connors said. "You'll be going out in the Hummer."

"Does it fly?"

"Nope. But it can be put on a pallet and tossed out the back from an altitude of no more than twenty feet."

Joe turned to Kurt. "You said we'd be using parachutes."

"LAPES," Kurt said. "Low altitude parachute extraction system. It's all right there in the acronym."

Joe shrugged, secured his weapon, and made his way

toward the Humvee. "Why not? I'm open to new things, different experiences, novel ways of risking my neck in the name of science, why not try driving an SUV off an airplane moving at a hundred fifty knots? Somebody's got to do it."

Both Kurt and the sergeant laughed.

"Good luck," Connors said.

Kurt nodded. "You want us to bring you anything back? T-shirt? Postcard? Puka shell necklace?"

The sergeant grinned. "I prefer a shot glass that says 'We came, we saw, we conquered.'"

Kurt returned the smile. "I'll see what I can do."

THIRTY MINUTES LATER, Kurt and Joe sat belted into a Humvee that was secured to a sturdy wooden pallet and a harness that would deploy two large drogue chutes. Joe was harnessed in at the wheel, though he wouldn't actually do any driving during the insertion, as the danger of the wheels turning sideways and getting ripped off was far too great. Instead, the Humvee would use the pallet beneath it as a sled while the parachutes trailing out behind them would both slow the vehicle down and keep them from nosing over.

Kurt made one last check of his equipment. Out of an abundance of caution and a certain sense of nostalgia, he had added an additional weapon to his arsenal. Hidden in his pack was the Colt revolver that Mohammed El Din had given him. He doubted he'd need it. But if the recent past had taught them anything, it was that modern technology was vulnerable to tampering or failing at precisely the wrong moment. That being the case, having a backup weapon from a bygone era didn't sound all that bad. He kept it zipped up in a front pocket that ran diagonally across the vest.

For less logical reasons he'd brought the pictures of Calista's family and the lifeboat they attempted to escape in. After searching for the truth so painfully himself, some part of him thought she deserved to know hers.

The light on the wall turned yellow and Sergeant Connors pressed a switch that opened the ramp at the tail end of the C-17.

They were descending through two thousand feet into utter darkness. The sea was below them for a moment and then sand as they flew over the beach.

As they flew lower and slower, the howl of the airstream whipping past the open door took on a different tone. With full flaps and its gear down, the C-17 could move incredibly slowly for such a huge machine. But the wake turbulence caused by flying at a high angle of attack in such a "dirty" condition created a buffeting and whining sound that seemed to trail behind the plane as if banshees were chasing it.

On the map, the drop zone was labeled Antsalova Airport. Joe seemed concerned about that. "You think the people at this airport are going to be surprised when we drop out of the sky and drive off without stopping at customs?"

"It's not much of an airport," Kurt said, "more of a dirt strip with a grass hut at the far end. We're only coming here because we need a flat surface to slide on. But there are no planes. No rental-car desks. No white courtesy telephone."

"No Admirals Club?" Joe said, looking perturbed.

Kurt shook his head. "Sorry, buddy."

Joe sighed. "I really have to talk to my travel agent. This trip is getting worse all the time."

As Kurt and Joe waited for the light to go green, the pilots up front were easing the huge aircraft down over the trees. A crosswind coming down off the slope of the island was making it difficult and they were actually flying sideways, a tactic pilots call crabbing. The problem was that they couldn't drop the Humvee in that alignment or it would land sideways and flip, killing the occupants instantly.

The copilot was on the instruments while the pilot flew with night vision goggles on.

"Ninety feet AGL," the copilot said.

"Can't get any lower until the trees clear," the pilot replied.

"We should be over the site in ten . . . nine . . . eight . . ."

The trees finally dropped away from under them and the pilot saw the dirt strip stretching out before him in a long thin line. He corrected to the left and brought the C-17 almost to the surface, stomping on the rudder to straighten the huge bird out.

The C-17 was now thirty feet off the dirt strip, screaming at full power and headed for the trees five thousand feet ahead.

In a chair behind them the loadmaster hit a switch, changing the jump light in the rear of the aircraft from yellow to green. "Release the payload," he said into the intercom.

For what seemed like an interminable length of time but was, in fact, only a few seconds, nothing happened except the trees ahead looming larger. Then the pilot felt the plane rise as the five-thousand-pound payload was pulled out the back.

At almost the same instant, Sgt. Connors's voice came over the intercom. "They're away. Payload clear. I repeat, payload clear."

In a synchronized move, the pilot jammed the throttles to full as the copilot retracted the gear to reduce the plane's drag coefficient.

"Positive rate," the copilot called out, seeing the altimeter begin to move.

The pilot heard but did not reply. The dirt strip was only a mile long. The trees at the far end were no more than a few hundred yards away. It was a very tight window.

"Climb, baby, climb," he whispered to the plane.

With its engines screaming and its nose pointed skyward, the gargantuan aircraft clawed for altitude. It crossed the end of the dirt strip and pulled just clear of the trees, close enough that the mechanics who inspected her later would find streaks of green chlorophyll all across the underside of the fuselage.

Clear of the danger, the pilot leveled off, picked up airspeed, and then turned to the southwest. In short order, they were out over the Mozambique Channel. Only now did the pilot consider the fate of the men they'd just dropped, wondering if they would live out the night.

FOR THEIR PART, Kurt and Joe had wondered if they would survive the drop itself. It felt as if the plane was maneuvering desperately the last thirty seconds or so. As the light went green, Connors had pressed a red deploy button and shouted "Go," or something along those lines.

Neither Kurt nor Joe truly heard him as the sound of the drogue chutes deploying and the sudden whiplash of being pulled backward out of the aircraft snapped their heads forward and commanded all their attention.

The Humvee was yanked out of the aircraft and in free fall for all of two seconds. Kurt distinctly remembered the sight of the aircraft pulling up and banking to the right as the vehicle skidded across the dirt on the pallet like a toboggan out of control on an icy slope. The first sensation was like skipping like a stone on a lake. And then they decelerated as the pallet maintained contact with the packed dirt of the runway. The last forty or fifty feet seemed smoother. And then suddenly they lurched to a stop.

Up ahead the C-17 just barely cleared the trees, and Kurt was certain he saw brief fires in the treetops where the heat of the engines singed them.

At that moment just being alive was a thrill. Kurt looked over at Joe and saw him grinning from ear to ear. "Okay, I'd do that again," he said giddily. "I'd even pay for another ride."

Kurt had to agree, but duty called. He opened the door and released the lock that connected them to the parachute and another lock that held them to the pallet. Joe performed the same task on the driver's side and then climbed back inside, turned the key, and brought the Humvee's 6.2-liter fuel-injected diesel to life.

In a moment they were speeding across the last hundred yards of the runway and onto a dirt road that led them south.

"Hope you've got the map ready," Joe said, "'cause I'm not from around here."

"Just stay on this road," Kurt said. "We've got seven miles to go."

CHAPTER 50

With their infiltration suits switched off and well-worn robes covering them, Kurt and Joe raced along the dirt road in the Humvee. The landscape flying past in the dark was hard to see, but this section of Madagascar was made up of wide grassy fields, occasional copses of small trees, and plenty of sky.

So far, they hadn't passed a single hut or another vehicle.

Joe let off the gas to negotiate a bend in the dirt road and they began to drift sideways as the rutted ground gave way beneath them. But with a slight punch of the throttle, the knobby tires bit a little deeper into the soil and the four-wheel-drive Humvee snapped back into a straight line and continued forward.

Kurt was in the passenger's seat, holding on to the roll

bar with one hand and checking the GPS with his other. "You always drive like this?"

"You should see me at rush hour."

"Something tells me I'd rather not."

"First time I've ever been late for a meeting and not ended up in traffic," Joe said.

"This section of Madagascar is pretty sparsely populated," Kurt said. "According to the map, the biggest town in a fifty-mile radius is a place called Masoarivo and it's only eight thousand people."

"Lucky for us," Joe said. "Doubt we'll see another car out here."

Kurt agreed, but livestock was another story. In sections where the rainwater had pooled, they'd passed grazing cattle and sheep. "Watch out for cows," he said. "As I recall, you hit one in the Azores and had to fight for the town's honor as part of your community service."

"I was exonerated," Joe insisted. "A court inquiry ruled the cow to be at fault and fined her for grazing without a license."

"We don't have time to go to court," Kurt replied, laughing at the memory, "nor do we have a replacement front end handy. So just be careful."

Joe promised he would do just that as they raced onto a straightaway and he stomped the gas pedal to the floor once again.

A mile and a half from the Brèvard property they slowed. In place of blazing headlights, Joe and Kurt pulled on their night vision goggles. The Humvee became a growling beast of the night, hidden in the darkness.

"I can see the fence up ahead," Kurt said. "Pull off the road here. We can hide the vehicle behind those trees."

Joe allowed the Hummer to slow on its own, he man-handled the wheel and took them off the dirt road and onto the soft ground with its waist-high grasses.

They came to a stop behind some low-lying brush and the wide trunk of a strange-looking tree that grew straight up like a concrete pillar. The only branches on the tree sprouted seventy feet above at the very top. It looked more like a giant stalk of broccoli than a tree. Several more of the odd trees grew close by.

"I feel like I'm in a Dr. Seuss book," Joe said.

"Baobab trees," Kurt said.

"Trees like this won't give us a lot of cover."

"We shouldn't need it with the suits," Kurt replied as he pulled off the oversize cotton tunic and rolled it into a ball.

As Joe did the same, Kurt removed the night vision goggles and clipped the breathing regulator onto a notch at the shoulder. The small tank of compressed air that would be used to cool his breath was strapped to his side.

He scanned the fence. It was rusted old barbwire, al-ready broken in places. There was no sign of anything more modern protecting the land at this point, but Kurt didn't want to chance it.

"According to the GPS, it's about half a mile from here to the compound, over this low dirge and then up a long slope," Kurt said. "We need to cover that ground in no more than ten minutes. That'll give us fifteen minutes of thermal invisibility once we reach the compound walls."

Joe nodded and slipped the satphone into a zippered pocket of the infiltration suit. Into another pocket he slid the extra clip for the railgun. "I figure we travel as light as possible and leave the rest of this stuff behind."

"Couldn't agree more," Kurt said. "Let's go."

They switched on their suits, pulled the hoods over their heads, and readjusted the night vision goggles. Kurt took point crossing the road, heading into the tall grass on the other side and moving quickly to a break in the fence.

Joe followed, staying close. "I'll give them this, these suits work as advertised," he said. "I'm ten feet behind you and really have to work just to see you. Even through these goggles you're more of a shadow than anything else."

"I'm going to head straight for the point on this ridge," Kurt said. "Stick close. If you get lost, give me a birdcall or something."

"The only birdcalls I know are Woody Woodpecker and Daffy Duck."

"That's de*spic*able," Kurt said, lisping the words in his best imitation of the cartoon duck. "Let's go."

With that, Kurt was off. Joe followed, finding he could track Kurt more easily by the sound of his feet scuffing through the brush and grass and over the dusty soil of the higher ridge. They came down the other side of the ridge and onto a sloping field that ran all the way up to the granite formations behind the compound. At the base of those rocks the lights of the plantation house were clearly visible.

Kurt checked his watch. "We have thirty minutes to confirm that the hostages are there and radio in. Any later and the Marines will be turning around."

Joe nodded and Kurt began to move again. They couldn't run full out, but a brisk jog would do the trick. Halfway up they encountered a small heard of zebu, the horned cattle seeming skittish at the approach of something they could smell but not see.

They pricked up their ears, grunting and making strange gurgling noises deep in their throats. A few of them shuffled off, unnerved by the intrusion, but Kurt and Joe were long past them by that point, just shadows moving through the dark.

As he continued up the slope, Kurt felt the ache in his shoulder from the bullet wound and the weight of the heavy railgun. He ignored it and continued on.

Three-quarters of the way up the slope they came within sight of the compound walls. A quiet whistle got Joe's attention. They huddled together.

"What do you think?" Kurt asked.

"The wall looks rough, unfinished."

"Probably hard to get stonemasons out here."

"Front gate has cameras," Joe said, studying the layout. "Can't see any others."

Kurt glanced along the dirt road that led up to the gate. "If a pizza delivery guy came by right about now, that would be ideal. But considering that isn't likely to happen, I say we climb the wall."

"I can see a spot over there where a tree is growing up beside the wall," Joe said.

"Too inviting," Kurt replied. "Let's just use our hands and feet."

Joe nodded again and Kurt began to move, heading farther upslope. Joe followed, and the two met up again at the base of the stone wall. In a moment they were over the top and inside, and the first thing they came to was the maze of manicured hedges.

Unlike the gentle slope of the hill outside the walls, the grounds inside had been excavated and flattened. The entire compound was built on a series of terraces, with the lowest by the front gate, then two intermediate levels containing the hedge maze and the other small buildings, and finally the main house in all its grandeur sitting up on the highest of the four terraces.

Unlike the rest of the grounds, the house was well lit. Kurt studied what he could from where he was. A pair of guards milled around the main entrance. At least one other man stood near the far side.

"Not exactly girded for battle," Kurt said.

"You say that like it's a bad thing."

"Just not used to so much going our way."

Kurt ducked down behind the hedge and opened the flap that covered the GPS tracking unit strapped to his right arm. In dull gray and black tones, it displayed the grounds around them. There were three buildings on the lowest terrace that were considered possibilities. According to Hiram Yaeger, men who appeared to be armed had been seen going in and out of all three.

"We have to get to the other side of this maze," Kurt said.

"Do we risk going through it?" Joe asked. "The hedges are at least six feet high. They'll help keep us hidden."

Kurt was about to say yes, considering that he had an overhead diagram of the maze displayed on his arm, but as he navigated the labyrinth in his mind he discovered one salient feature: there was only one way in and one way out.

"Better go around," Kurt said. "The maze has no other way out. It's a big circle that doubles back around and only takes you back to where you started. Considering how this undertaking has felt from day one, I'd say I've had about enough of that."

Joe laughed. "We still have eight minutes of chameleon time."

Kurt motioned to the right. "Around that side. Stay close to the hedge. We should come across a building that looks kind of like a shed."

This time Joe led the way and it was Kurt's turn to marvel at how rapidly he vanished, like a ghost in the fog. Kurt moved quickly to keep up, and on the far side of the hedge he came upon Joe.

The shedlike building was right in front of them. Kurt was just about to step forward when a door opened and spilled some light onto the grounds. Kurt froze as two men came out, allowing the door to bang shut behind them.

Leaning against the building, one of them lit a ciga-

rette. The tip brightened to an orange-red hue as he in-
haled. After releasing a puff of smoke, he turned to the
other man. "I'm telling you, Laurent is on the rampage.
Don't get him angry right now or question him. I asked
him about Acosta and he told me to back off."

"Acosta is a gutless traitor," the other man said. "He
sold us out on one of Sebastian's deals. Mark my word,
we're going to be at war with him soon. Next time you
make a delivery, you watch your back."

"It's more than that," the smoking man said between
drags on the cigarette. "Sebastian is edgy. I think he's
losing it. Been spending too much time with Calista."

Both of them laughed at that. "Who cares?" the other
man said. "We just got paid. Now, finish that smoke and
get back in the game so I can take your money."

The man with the cigarette laughed. "Sure," he said.
"Set me up a drink, I'll be there in a minute."

The first guy went back inside while the second man
smoked for a moment longer before tossing the cigarette
to the ground and crushing it out with his boot. As he
finished grinding it into the dirt he looked up, staring
almost directly at Kurt. He lingered in that pose for a
moment the way a hunting dog might freeze as it pointed
toward a sound its master couldn't hear.

Kurt held perfectly still. Hidden in the shadows at a
distance of forty feet, he doubted the man could see him.
All the same, he firmed his grip on the railgun and slid
his gloved finger onto the trigger.

The smoker held his place for another second and then

he turned, grabbed the door handle, and stepped back inside.

"Cover me," Kurt whispered. He moved quickly toward the door and placed his ear beside it. He heard the sound of a radio and voices. Too many voices. They were loud and boisterous and, as near as he could tell, all male. It sounded like a locker room inside.

Convinced the prisoners were not present, he moved back to where Joe waited.

"Do we have the right address?" Joe asked.

"Not unless you're looking for a frat party. I think this is a bunkhouse of some kind. Brèvard's men are blowing off some steam."

Joe looked around. "So where to next?"

Kurt glanced down at the screen on his arm. The next building was a hundred yards off. Closer to the wall of the third terrace. "Just up the road," Kurt said. "Follow me, if you can."

"Better be quick," Joe said. "We turn back into pumpkins in less than five minutes."

Moving past the building that housed Brèvard's men, Kurt and Joe snuck onto another path. The next building was much like the first, low-lying and rather plain, without any windows, but it was guarded. Two men at the door, one sitting in a chair with his feet propped up on a bucket, the other standing with a rifle over his shoulder.

The main problem was a pair of exposed bulbs on a black wire above the entrance. The suits would not keep them hidden in that kind of glare.

"This has got to be it," Kurt said. "I'm going to work my way around back and find the power line. Get in position. When I cut it, take the closest guy out with your Taser. By the time the second guy figures out what's happened, I'll be on him."

"Sounds like a plan."

As Joe moved to a new position, Kurt doubled back and went around the far side of the building. Moving quickly and quietly, he arrived on the far side of the structure and began looking for the power cable. He found a spot where a buried line came out of the ground and ran up the wall, held in place by rusted clamps. Pulling out his rubber-handled knife, Kurt sawed through the insulation and then with a quick cut severed the cable.

As the light spilling from the front of the building flickered and died, Kurt raced for the corner. He came around it just as Joe hit the standing guard with his Taser. The man went stiff as a board but made no sound, and all Kurt heard was the rapid clicking and snapping sound that the Taser made as it electrified the man's body and triggered his muscles into a rigid state.

Realizing that something was wrong, the guard in the chair grabbed for his rifle, but Kurt was on him before he could bring it to bear. He clamped one hand over the man's mouth and yanked him backward, bringing the black carbon steel blade of the knife up against the man's throat.

"You make a sound, it'll be your last," he warned the man.

The guard went still and then nodded, his sense of shock growing as Joe appeared under the overhang like a specter materializing from another dimension. As Joe dropped down on the ground to truss up the other guard, his movements were a blur as the armor continuously changed both its color and texture. Kurt noticed the man he'd captured scrunching his eyes shut and then looking away as if he were hallucinating.

"You people are holding some friends of ours," he whispered to his captive. "Are they here? In this building?"

The guard nodded.

Kurt glanced at Joe. "Check the door."

Joe was already in the process. "Locked tight."

"Keys," Kurt demanded.

The guard reached a shaking hand into his breast pocket and pulled out a ring with two keys on it.

Joe took the ring and went to work, finding two bolts, one for each key. Having unlocked the door, he cracked it open. "It's dark, I don't see anyone."

"I must have cut the power to the entire building," Kurt said, pulling the guard to his feet.

As Joe pulled the door open, Kurt pushed the guard through first in case someone attacked. Fortunately, that didn't happen.

Looking around, Kurt saw a dozen people huddled in the far corner of the darkened room. They were hiding behind a pile of mattresses, a small table, and several chairs. He counted three men, three women, and seven children of various ages. They seemed as frightened of him and Joe as the guards had been. After what they'd been through, Kurt didn't blame them.

"It's all right," he said, "we're here to help you. We're getting you out of here."

They seemed too afraid to respond, so Kurt flipped up his goggles and pulled out a flashlight, shining it on them. He didn't recognize most of the group, but two of the grimy-faced children looked like Sienna's son and daughter.

"You're Tanner, right?"

The boy nodded.

"And you're Elise?"

The girl was too afraid to say anything. She just stood there, gripping the hem of her shirt.

"It's okay," Kurt said, brushing her hair back. "We're taking you home. Where's your mom?"

Elise just stared at him, but Tanner pointed at the guards. "They took her."

Kurt looked at the guard on his knees.

"Where's Sienna Westgate?"

"I don't know," the guy said. "They took her up to the main house, but I don't know where."

One of the other adults came forward. He looked familiar. "I saw you in the tunnel in Korea," the man said.

His English was vaguely European. Kurt guessed that Spanish, Portuguese, or even Italian was his first language.

"You're Montresor," Kurt said, using his hacker name.

The man nodded again. "My real name is Diego. I

know where they took her. The man who runs things, Sebastian, he has a control room on the top floor. He watches everything from there, I think. Directly below him is a networked series of high-end processors and computers. When they took me up to the house to work, that is where they kept me."

"What did they have you do?" Kurt asked.

"I hack into a system and edit programs. I create hidden doorways and what we call hides or blinds."

"Those are hunting terms," Kurt said. "What do they mean in the programming world?"

The man paused as if thinking of a way to explain it. "They're like black holes into which we can hide a virus. Even the most advanced antivirus software will not find it. And then at a later date, we activate the code."

"And what does the code do?" Kurt asked.

"I just create the blind," Montresor said. "Others build the virus."

"And what does the virus usually do?"

"Takes control of the system," he said. "Forces it to do something it is not supposed to do."

Montresor, Kurt thought to himself. How perfect a handle for someone who hides things in a labyrinth where they will never be found.

"What kind of systems did you hack? Pentagon? CIA?"

Montresor shook his head. "Banking systems mostly. Accounting programs. Transfer protocols."

Kurt's mind raced. Banks and a gang descended from bank robbers and counterfeiters. He wondered if there could be a connection and then decided this was not the time to find out. All that mattered was stopping the Brèvard family, whatever they were doing.

He turned to Joe. "Call it in," he said. "I'm going to find Sienna."

"I should go with you," Joe said.

"No," Kurt said, "stay with them. They're going to need you to lead them out when the Marines come over the wall."

CHAPTER 51

Aboard the lead Black Hawk, code-named Dragon One, Lt. Brooks studied his men as the strike team continued inbound. Some of the men talked and joked, some checked their weapons and gear repeatedly in some kind of ritual, and others had faces of stone. Different personalities got ready for battle in different ways, but one look told Brooks they were ready.

So far, they'd come three hundred miles south, met up with the tanker aircraft, and completed the tricky nighttime refueling operation without incident. From that point they'd turned southeast and were now tracking for the coast, traveling in formation, at a hundred thirty knots a mere fifty feet above the surface of the Mozambique Channel.

"We'll be crossing into Madagascar airspace in seven minutes," the pilot informed him.

"Any word from the *Bataan*?"

"Nothing yet," the pilot said. "If we don't get final authorization by the time we hit that limit, I'll have no choice but to abort."

Brooks understood. He was in charge of the mission, but those were the standing orders. "Throttle back a bit," he suggested. "And take us parallel to the line for a while."

"Sir?"

"It'll save us some fuel," Brooks said, "and it'll give those marine biologists a little more time to make contact."

"You really think they're going to pull this off?" the pilot asked skeptically.

"I'm not sure," Brooks said, "but I'd hate to be headed home if they call for help."

The pilot nodded his agreement, made a quick radio call to the other helicopters, and then banked to the right and began reducing speed. The other Black Hawks matched him, and the headlong race toward the coast became a more leisurely flight parallel to it. There was little danger of them being picked up on radar—Madagascar had only a primitive network. Fuel and time were bigger concerns.

"Okay, Lieutenant," the pilot said, "we've dialed it down to the economy setting. But we can't do this for too long."

As it turned out, they didn't have to. Fifteen minutes later, a signal came over the satellite downlink.

"Dragon leader, this is Courthouse. Do you copy?"

Courthouse was the *Bataan*'s code name. Brooks pressed the transmit switch. "Courthouse, this is Dragon leader, go ahead."

"You are cleared to the objective. Current target status is green. Friendlies have been identified. Total of fifteen, possibly sixteen. Their location will be marked by a green flare and smoke. Other buildings are believed to hold up to twenty hostiles. Light weapons are indicated."

A surge of adrenaline pumped through Brooks and he glanced at the pilot and toward the coast like a referee signaling first down. The pilot took the hint, turned inbound once again, and brought the Black Hawk back up to full speed.

"Roger that, Courthouse. We are two minutes from continental divide and inbound to the target. Will contact you on our way home."

As the mission director from the *Bataan* signed off, Brooks considered the state of things. In a world that had grown used to watching their military operations play out in real time, this one was being blacked out. There was no feed being broadcast to the Situation Room in the White House, no group of generals and politicians watching the play-by-play as if it were a movie or a big game. With the whole government unsure which systems were still secure and which had been hacked, no one was taking a chance. The powers that be would wait in silence. Eventually, they'd receive a simple phone call from the *Bataan*'s commander telling them if the mission had succeeded or failed.

AS THE MARINE STRIKE FORCE turned inbound, Kurt made his way around the side of the Brèvard palace. Lights aimed up at the structure meant the last ten feet or so would expose him no matter how the infiltration suit attempted to compensate. Instead of crossing through them, he swung wide, passed an Olympic-sized swimming pool, and made his way around the back. There he found an overhanging veranda.

Using a chair to boost himself up, he clambered onto the deck and sprinted forward. He managed to force the door and slip inside.

Thankful that he'd set off no alarm system in the process, he moved into the hall and found himself surrounded by framed works of art, intricate tapestries, and statues that looked as if they might belong in a museum.

He needed to find a stairwell that led upward and began to move down the hall, stopping at the sound of footfalls coming his way from an adjacent corridor.

He backtracked and took cover behind a statue of some Greek hero with a laurel leaf on his head and pressed himself as far into the shadows as possible until the figure passed by.

It was Calista. She was speaking into a radio, giving orders about something. She never saw Kurt or even looked in his direction. As she reached the far end of the hall, she disappeared into a room.

In a house of many rooms, Kurt knew he'd be hard-pressed to find the right one in time. But seeing Calista pass by brought a new idea to mind. Checking the hall in both directions and seeing no one else coming, he moved from behind the statue and backtracked, heading toward the room Calista had just entered.

CHAPTER 52

Calista was ready to leave. Over the years she'd begun to feel claustrophobic in the family home, a sensation that had only gotten worse over the past few months. Grabbing a small backpack from a shelf in her closet, she began to pack.

Ever the pragmatist, she didn't care for the clothes or the jewels. Her items of importance were those that would be useful: passports in several names, bundles of cash in a few different currencies, a knife, a pistol, and three spare magazines. The one item of sentimental value she had was a necklace with a diamond ring hanging from it that had belonged to their mother. Sebastian had given it to her.

She eyed the necklace for a moment and then placed it into a side pocket and zipped the pocket shut. Nothing else in the opulent mansion mattered to her. It was all fake. The artwork, tapestries, and the antique furniture were nothing but good forgeries. That's what their family did. They gave life to lies.

About the only thing she would miss were the horses.

As she thought about her favorite, a horse named Tana, which meant "sunshine" in Malagasy, it dawned on her that Sebastian might have rigged the stables to explode like everything else in the compound.

This struck her as cruel. Humankind was fairly worthless in her eyes, but animals, in their innocence, were something else. They had no schemes or desires other than to please their masters and receive their rewards in the form of food and shelter and attention.

She zipped the bag shut and decided to hike down to the stable and turn the animals out. There was no reason for them to burn to death.

Throwing the pack over one shoulder, she left the bedroom, entered her sitting room, and tracked straight for the door. As she approached the door, she noticed it was closed but not shut. That was more than odd, she never left the door unlatched.

She put her hand in the bag, grabbing for her pistol.

"Sorry, Calista," a voice said from behind her. "I'm afraid it's game over."

She froze in her tracks. The timbre of the voice was easily recognizable, as was the calm and certain delivery of the words. She had no doubt that Kurt Austin was standing behind her.

"Toss the bag on the floor and turn around slowly," he said.

She let her shoulders sag and flipped the backpack into a corner. Pivoting slowly, she found Kurt sitting in a high-backed Victorian chair, aiming a lethal-looking rifle in her direction.

"I believe we've done this before," she said.

"We have," Kurt replied, standing up. "And we're going to keep doing it until we get it right."

She studied him for a moment. He looked out of place with all the armor. Less handsome, less unique. As if he'd read her mind, he pulled off the hood.

"How on earth did you get in here?" she asked. "We have cameras, guards, motion sensors."

"Nothing's foolproof," Kurt said.

That much was certain. "You can't expect to get out alive," she said. "We're ready for you. We've been waiting for you to make a move."

His eyebrows went up. "Really?" he said. "Because it doesn't look that way to me. Your men at the front gate are half asleep. The gang in the bunkhouse are celebrating like it's Bastille Day. And we've already found the hostages while taking out two of your guards. All without the slightest peep from the rest of you."

"There are at least fifty men here loyal to my brothers and me. You're overwhelmingly outnumbered."

"For now," he said smugly.

She pursed her lips. So there were reinforcements coming. And coming soon. Her brother was sitting around foolishly thinking they were not in danger yet. Her feelings were torn. Silently she cursed him for his arrogance even as she wished she could warn him.

"If you've already won, then what do you want from me?" she asked. "Answers perhaps? Are you still trying to figure out what happened to you on the *Ethernet*?"

He smiled at her. It was a grin both endearing and proud. "Too late for that," he said. "I know what happened. Enough of it anyway. It all came back once they debugged me in Korea."

She shifted her weight. "Then you know if it wasn't for me, you'd have been killed and buried at sea in the hull of that yacht just like all the others we encountered."

"Considering that you caused the danger in the first place, that doesn't really carry a lot of weight with me. On the other hand," he added, "I do have a newfound appreciation for the importance of remembering the past accurately, thanks to you. That being the case, I thought I'd return the favor."

"What are you talking about?" she asked, growing tired of the conversation.

He studied her with those ice-blue eyes, taking her in, measuring her. Finally, he unzipped a diagonal pocket on the right sight of his vest and pulled from it a folded sheet of paper. He placed it down on the small stand between the chairs, smoothed it flat, and then pulled away.

"Take a look" was all he said.

She hesitated and then stepped cautiously forward, reaching for the paper like someone might reach for a dangerous animal, keeping as much distance between her body and the printed sheet as possible.

She tilted the page to catch the light and gave the image a quick once-over. "What is this supposed to be?"

"It's a family," he said. "Believe it or not, it's your family. Your *real* family."

She looked up at him suspiciously. "What are you talking about?"

She noticed he was watching her with a sort of detached, almost professorial look.

"The Brèvards aren't your family, Calista, the people in the photograph are. The woman's name is Abigail. She was your mother. Her friends called her Abby. The man's name is Stewart, he was your father. The two boys are Nathan and Zack—or I should say, they were *named* Nathan and Zack."

For reasons she couldn't pinpoint, she began to feel sick. "You expect me to believe this?"

"Look at the woman. Look at her face. You two could be twins."

She wasn't blind, she saw the likeness. It was nonsense. "You think you can trick me?"

He didn't blink. "It's not a trick. Your mother was a telecommunications expert, your father worked on satellite guidance. They were both very intelligent people, brilliant in their understandings of math and science. Just like you, I'm guessing. They had a good life in suburban England. Unfortunately, the Brèvard family came along, took them from the world, and made them disappear, the same way you kidnapped Sienna and her children. They were bartered for and used for what they knew the same *exact* way you and Sebastian and the rest of this sick family have used the people you're holding hostage."

She was shaking her head, filled with rage, a kind of

rage she was having a hard time controlling. It was unlike her—she was cold, emotionless. Why should this make her so angry? she wondered. Of course he would lie. Of course he would try something to confuse her. But why, if he and his friends were all but assured of victory in their own minds, would he bother?

She felt an urge to charge him, to put her hands around his throat and choke the life out of him if she could. Even if he shot her in response, at least she wouldn't have to listen to any more of this.

She lunged for him. "You're a liar," she screamed.

She slammed one fist into his chest, where it uselessly struck the body armor, and reached for his face with her other hand, intent on clawing out his eyes. But he was too quick and too strong. He caught her arm and stopped it. He spun her around and folded her arms across her chest, holding her from behind.

"I'm not lying," he said. "I'm not trying to hurt you. But you should know the truth."

"I don't want to know!"

"Believe me, you do," he said. "Because these people are better than the Brèvards. These people loved life, they didn't abuse and destroy it, and you're one of them."

She continued to thrash and tried to slam and elbow him, but it was no use.

"I know what kind of hell it is to wonder what's real and what isn't," he said quietly. "I know what you're going through right now. I lived it for months, but you've had it worse, you've lived it all your life. I can only imagine what it's done to you."

"It's done nothing," she insisted, trying desperately to kick him and pull free.

He turned her around and looked into her eyes. "Your father was killed trying to escape his captors," he said. "He was gunned down in broad daylight by a man who was never found. He'd been gagged and beaten. He'd been tortured."

"Stop it!"

"Your mother and brothers fared worse. They'd found a lifeboat on a ship half buried in the sand, but they didn't have enough water. They died from dehydration, drifting on the ocean a hundred miles from here."

She froze. "What did you say?"

"They died at sea," he repeated, "on a lifeboat half gutted with rot. We're pretty certain they found it on an old ship that was buried in the river several miles from here."

An image flashed in her mind, it struck like a bolt of lightning. A brief glimpse of the rivets on the dark metal plating, the rushing river, the sediment being scoured away. "A ship," she whispered. "An old iron ship?"

A second bolt of lightning struck. It was night. There was only a sliver of moonlight to see with. A woman had her by the wrist, leading her toward the hill. Two boys were dragging a small wooden boat from a cave they'd excavated in the sand.

"It's a lie," she protested.

"It's the truth," he said. "*Your* truth."

She'd ceased struggling now, her mind adrift. He continued to hold her tight, perhaps because he couldn't trust her. But as her legs began to shake, she felt he was holding her up, keeping her from buckling right then and there.

The memories continued to come. Men chasing them. A gunshot ripped through one of the containers. The water was spilling out. Disaster.

"There's not enough water," Calista spoke aloud.

More gunshots. The woman fell.

"They shot her," Calista said to no one.

"She was wounded," Kurt replied softly. "But it was superficial."

"She fell down the hill."

In her mind, Calista heard the woman shout.

"Olivia!"

Calista felt only fear—terrible, swirling fear.

"Mum!" one of the boys had yelled.

"Olivia, hurry!"

More gunshots sounded and the woman turned and ran.

Calista just stood there on the hill, while down below, her mother and brothers pushed the small boat out into the water. She saw them climb on board and paddle into the darkness, moving swiftly with the current. She felt the men rush by her, watched as they scrambled down the bank, and listened as they fired again and again into the dark.

But she never flinched. She just stood there and stared until eventually the shooting ceased and one of the men came up to her and took her hand.

"I let them go without me," she said to Kurt.

She was sobbing, dropping to the ground. Kurt eased her down gently.

"There wasn't enough water," he told her. "Not enough for three. Certainly not enough for four."

She was sobbing and shaking and then suddenly angry again. "You have no right! No right to . . ."

The insanity of what she was saying cut her off before she'd finished.

"The Brèvard family stole your life," he said. "Maybe they realized how sharp you already were. Maybe they knew they could mold you into one of them. Maybe they planned to kill you and just never got around to it. But, whatever their reasons, they stole your life. They stole the lives of your family and we think many others. And if you let them, they'll steal the lives of Sienna and her children and everyone else they're holding in that oversize Quonset hut halfway down the hill."

She noticed he kept saying "Sebastian" or the "Brèvard family," but she knew her part in it. For a second she wanted to scream out, to yell at him, "This is who I am," to claim it and own it and tell him to go to hell, but the desire faded. And tears returned uncontrollably.

Why shouldn't her name and memories be false? Everything else around her was a lie.

As she cried, Kurt moved to a spot in front of her and gently wiped the tears from her face.

"Help me get to Sienna before the Marines arrive," he said. "Sebastian is going to lose tonight. But I don't want him using her as a shield or killing her in a fit of spite when he realizes it's over for him."

She looked up at him. There was kindness and determination in that face. The white knight, she thought. He really was.

"It's not over for him," she said.

"It will be soon."

"No, you don't understand," she replied. "You may be early, but he knew a response would be coming. He's got some nasty surprises waiting for your friends. And he's got a plan of escape locked and loaded."

"He couldn't know we would be coming."

"Not you, but he knew someone would be," she said. "He's waiting for it. While *our* men are fighting with your forces, he'll blow this place to kingdom come. The hacking you're seeing now will end and he'll disappear—we'll disappear—and the whole world will assume we're dead."

"So history *does* repeat itself," Kurt said. "We have to stop him. And we have to stop whatever he has planned. Will you help me or not?"

She looked at him through the tears.

"I'll trust you," he said.

"Why would you?"

"Call it instinct," he said, offering her a hand.

She hesitated. Her true desire was to remain there on the floor, to lie there until the fires came and consumed her. A fate she'd never been more certain she deserved.

"A wise man once told me, 'We are who we decide to be,'" he said. "You have a choice. You can be Calista

Brèvard or you can reclaim your humanity as Olivia Banister."

The names seemed to fire something in her, but it wasn't what he might have expected. Olivia was a frightened child, Calista was unafraid. Calista was a survivor, an instrument of power. And now, she thought, an instrument of retribution. She took Kurt's hand and stood.

"No," she said, "this is who I am. I'll help you find Sienna. But don't get between me and Sebastian. Because I'm going to kill him for what he and his family have done. If you try to stop me, I'll kill you too."

"Your choice," Kurt said. "Either way, let's move. We don't have much time."

CHAPTER 53

With Calista leading the way, the two of them strode the halls. Though Kurt had professed trust in her, he wasn't about to give her a weapon. He just needed her to get him past the goons who would be guarding the control room. Or at least close enough so he could eliminate them.

"This way," she said, turning down the hallway on the right.

At that moment an alarm began to scream.

Kurt held still, wondering if she'd triggered something.

"It wasn't me," she said, apparently guessing his thoughts.

The sound of automatic gunfire outside the building reverberated through the hall followed by the unmistakable sound of helicopters passing overhead. The Marines had arrived and not unnoticed. The sound of a rocket screaming through the air was followed by an explosion and a flash of light through the windows at the far end of the hall.

"We need to hurry," Kurt said. He and Calista began to run. They were almost to the end when one of Sebastian's men came running the opposite way. "Calista," he shouted. "We're being attacked. No one is answering at the pen and . . ."

Just then he saw Kurt and quickly guessed that he was part of the assault. He swung a submachine gun around and fired.

Kurt saw it coming, pushed Calista out of the way, and dove to the polished floor. As shells ripped into the plaster behind him, he aimed the rifle and squeezed the trigger almost simultaneously. The railgun spat a swarm of lethal iron projectiles that ripped into the man, taking him off his feet and knocking him over. He landed on his back, but the muscles in his hand must have contracted in a spasm because the submachine gun continued to fire, spraying a line of bullets along the wall and up into the ceiling, shattering two of the mirrors and blasting apart a suit of armor.

"So much for the element of surprise," Kurt said. He got up, helped Calista to her feet once again, and took off down the hall.

AT THAT VERY MOMENT, Lt. Brooks and the members of the Force Recon platoon were thinking the exact same thing. They'd come in from the coast, flying along the deck, blacked-out and watching for any sign they'd been detected or painted by the sweep of a radar beam.

All signs pointed to a clean entry. And then they'd crossed the wall of the sprawling compound and slowed to a hover so the strike teams could begin a fast rappel to the ground. But even as the ropes went out, they'd begun to take direct fire, not from any human targets on the ground but from remotely operated weapons.

From at least three spots in the garden, twin .50 caliber machine guns had risen from small maintenance sheds. They were tracking and turning and firing on the helicopters. One of the Black Hawks was already smoking and pulling away when Brooks gave the order to the rest of them.

"Pull back," he shouted. "Take evasive action."

The pilot turned the craft away from the fire and began to move out, but the horrible rattling sound of shells ripping through the fuselage told Brooks it was too late. Shrapnel and bits of the cabin were blasted about like confetti. Blood splattered on the wall of the fuselage as at least one man took a hit.

At the same time, the helicopter lurched to the side, and Brooks saw that the pilot had also been wounded. They were spinning and going down.

The copilot took control and tried to right the craft, but they hit the ground with a crunch. The Black Hawk rolled over on its side, forcing the enormous rotor blades into the ground and shattering them into a thousand pieces.

"Go! Go! Go!" Brooks shouted, pushing one man out

through the door and then grabbing the wounded pilot and scrambling to safety.

The Black Hawk's crew and the twelve Marines were clear of the helicopter when it exploded. Three men were injured, as well as the pilot, and a mission that was supposed to be a walk in the park had suddenly turned into a desperate fight.

The men took cover near a rock wall and set up a defensive perimeter. Brooks saw the other Black Hawks fleeing to safety. It looked as if they would all clear the danger zone when a missile launched from another dilapidated shed.

The fiery tail of the rocket was easy to track—it raced south after the helicopter and illuminated it in a ball of flame.

"Damn!" Brooks cursed. "We've been set up."

By now men were streaming from the barracks, and small arms fire was whistling past overhead.

Brooks grabbed the radio and called out, "Dragon leader to Dragon team. Stay clear of the fire zone. I repeat, stay clear of the fire zone. Compound is more heavily defended than anticipated. Missiles and heavy-caliber weapons."

"Dragon Three clear," a call came back.

"Dragon Four also clear."

That meant Black Hawk Two had taken the missile. Brooks had no way of determining if anyone had survived the explosion.

Brooks pressed the talk switch. "Dragon Five, what's your position?"

Dragon Five was the spare helicopter brought in primarily to haul the hostages out, but it also carried two Navy medics.

"We're still at point alpha. Do you need us?"

"Negative," Brooks said. "Remain there until I contact you."

"We're not going to leave you down there, Lieutenant."

"You will if I order you to," Brooks replied. "Stay clear until I tell you otherwise."

Putting the radio down, Brooks looked around at his men. Three of them were injured. That left nine, plus the copilot, who had to do more than fly at this point.

"Jones," Brooks called to one of the men. "Get your squad to the south. Make sure no one flanks us."

"Yes, sir."

"Dalton, Garcia, you're with me. We've got to find those guns and that missile battery and take 'em out."

"Yes, sir," the men replied in unison.

Under a covering fire, the three men moved out, racing fifty yards to the north and then scampering up the wall onto the next terrace.

As the unexpected battle raged all around the compound, Joe remained with the hostages. He could tell by the din of the explosions and the volume of gunfire that something had gone wrong.

"Everyone get on the floor," he said. "Flip those tables over and pile up those mattresses."

Almost on cue, gunfire ripped through the top of the

building. Joe hit the deck along with everyone else. Prayers could be heard in three different languages. The sound of children whimpering needed no translation.

"I thought we were leaving?" someone asked.

"So did I," Joe muttered.

Wondering what had gone wrong, Joe crawled to the door and pushed it open a crack. Flames lit up the sky at the bottom of the hill.

He heard the sounds of the helicopters maneuvering in the distance and the report of the heavy machine guns. Over the headset, he heard Brooks calling out that they'd been shot down and warning the others away. Across the terrace he saw two separate groups of men rushing down the hill and firing wildly. Between these men and the men from the barracks, the Marines from the downed helicopter would soon be badly outnumbered.

Joe knew his help was needed, but if he left the hut the hostages would be utterly alone and defenseless.

He studied the action a moment longer. It was all going on down the hill from where they were, with the sounds of another battle raging at the main house. But to his right, out to the south, all was quiet.

"Time to go," he said. "Don't want to miss the bus."

He began waving them up to the door, pointing to the right, where it was dark and quiet. "There's a wall about seventy yards away. Get to it, climb over it, and keep going. Don't stop until you're at least a thousand yards from here and you've found some kind of shelter. A ditch, some bushes, a stand of those weird trees, anything that can hide you."

He handed Montresor the green flare. "If you see any helicopters overhead, light this and hold it up. They'll know you're the hostages and not enemy combatants."

As Montresor and the others gathered around the door, Joe took another look outside.

"What about my mom?" Tanner Westgate asked.

"Kurt will find her," Joe said. "You can count on that."

The little faces streaked with tears clutched at Joe's heart. When each of the young children was holding hands with an adult, Joe snuck forward, made sure the path was clear, and then waved them out.

He led them about halfway, and when he was certain they were clear of the firefight he pointed toward the wall.

"Go," he said, urging them forward, "get over that wall and don't look back."

As the prisoners scrambled into the darkness, Joe turned back toward the sounds of engagement. Gazing down the hill, he could see the firefight in all its nighttime iridescent glory. From the tracer fire it was clear that Lt. Brooks and his men were getting shot to pieces from three sides as thirty or forty of Brèvard's men slowly closed in around them.

Joe began to move forward. "Unbelievable," he whispered. "All this time I've been waiting to call in the cavalry and it turns out *I am the cavalry.*"

With that thought in mind, he pressed forward, unsure of what, if anything, he might achieve.

CHAPTER 54

As the chaos outside grew, Kurt and Calista found themselves in a running battle with the rest of Brèvard's men. They'd made it down one hall, with Kurt laying down a suppressing fire to keep those behind them at bay, only to run smack into a second group coming the other way.

Now, halfway to the control room, they were caught in cross fire, with shots coming at them from both ends of the hall.

"Get behind me," Kurt said to Calista as he returned fire.

"You should have given me a gun," she said.

"I had my reasons," Kurt said.

"How do those reasons sound now?"

"Not as good as they did back then," he admitted.

With little cover beyond an old wooden credenza, Kurt had to keep up a steady rate of fire to keep their enemies back. A blue digital counter on the top of the gun told him the status of his ammo. It hit zero rather quickly and he changed clips.

Realizing they had to get out of this battle before he used up the second clip, he began shooting out the lights one by one until the central section of the hall was bathed in shadows. In response, their attackers hit the main switch and doused the rest of the hall in darkness, which only helped his plan.

Kurt retreated along the wall, found a door, and kicked it open.

"Get inside," he said.

Calista did as ordered as more bullets skipped off the marble floor. Hoping to trick the two groups into shooting each other, Kurt fired a half dozen shots along one length of the hall and then loosed a few more back the other way.

As soon as he'd finished, he stepped backward and shut the door. As it closed, he heard volleys being fired from both sides. For a little while at least they would have trouble distinguishing between their own shots and Kurt's, but he knew all he'd done was buy him and Calista some time.

As Kurt plotted their next move, Calista was busy shoving a large couch up against the door and wedging the arm under the handle.

"Not a bad idea," he said.

"How long do you think we have?" she asked, pulling a dresser against the couch.

"They'll figure out pretty quickly that I'm no longer

firing at them," he said. "But it'll take a minute or two before they get up the courage to rush down the hall."

"And then what?"

Before Kurt could answer, the scream of a rocket sounded outside the building. As Kurt turned, he saw the white flare of another missile ripping its way into the night.

"Sebastian," Calista said. "Always another trick up his sleeve. Those are Acosta's. He was the arms dealer."

Kurt made a quick but grim assessment. "We have to stop this. Or none of us will leave here alive."

"We have to get to the control room," she said. "It's all operated from there."

They would never make it by charging down the hall, not even with the railgun blazing and the Kevlar armor to protect the most vital parts of Kurt's body. There had to be another way.

"What else is on this floor?" he asked.

"Nothing," she said, "just more rooms like this. As if we were going to hold court someday."

An idea came to him. "It just might work," he said to himself.

He moved up to the wall, felt along it, and then began to punch holes in the plasterboard with his fist. It was fairly standard, a wood-and-drywall construction. He found the studs and then stepped back and with measured precision pointed the railgun at a section of wall, blasting a vertical line of eight shots from top to bottom.

"What are you doing?" she asked.

"I prefer to stay in adjoining rooms," he said. With a

run of several steps, he crashed into the perforated section of the wall, smashing through it with his shoulder and plowing into the space next door.

Calista followed. And, in quick succession, they had done the same to the next three rooms.

Had he been using a standard rifle, Kurt might have expected the teams of men outside to hear him, but the railgun made no sound. The only noise was the projectiles flying through the plaster, a sound that reminded Kurt of an overzealous librarian energetically using a three-hole punch.

"This is the last room," Calista said.

Kurt checked the railgun. The counter on the top told him he had ten shells left. *Ten shells.* Just in case, he unzipped the diagonal pocket across his chest that held the old Colt revolver.

Hoping there would be no more resistance, he moved to the door, pulled it open a crack, and looked back down the hall. Their enemies had converged on the door to the room he and Calista had entered and were trying to break it down.

"Get ready," he said.

As the men down the hall blasted their way through the barricade she'd built and forced their way into the room, Kurt pulled his own door wide and dashed quietly across the hall and onto the stairwell. Calista was right behind him.

"Two levels up," she said.

Kurt raced up the flight, moving so quickly that he was skipping stairs.

As he neared the final turn, a trio of men came rushing down in the other direction. Kurt had no choice. He pulled the trigger. The iron shells went right through the first man and into the second, cutting them both down. They fell backward, knocking the third man to the floor, who opened fire with his Uzi submachine gun.

Several shells hit Kurt's chest plate, knocking him backward. He was fairly certain that at least one shell hit Calista because she screamed and tumbled down the stairs.

Lying on his back, Kurt hit the lower trigger and sent the prongs of the Taser blasting into the man's neck. He snapped into a prone position as the electricity surged through his body and he began to shake.

Kurt held the trigger and kept the electricity flowing as he got to his feet, ran forward, and kicked the man in the face like he was trying to punt a football out of the stadium. The man's head snapped back and he lay still.

With the situation in hand, Kurt grabbed the Uzi and dropped back to where Calista had fallen.

"You've been hit."

"My leg," she said.

Kurt pulled her up onto the landing. She'd taken a bullet to the thigh. It was bleeding, but not enough to suggest it had hit an artery. He took off her belt and wrapped it around her leg as a tourniquet.

"I think it's broken," she said. She tried to stand, but even with his help she couldn't put any weight on it.

"Just go," she said. "They'll be coming up here soon enough. You'll need me to watch your back."

Kurt hesitated and then handed her the Uzi. He figured she'd earned it at this point.

"Don't let him live," she said. "He has no right."

Without answering, Kurt propped her up against the wall, where she'd have some cover and a good angle to fire at anyone who came her way.

"Don't go anywhere," he said. "I'll be back for you."

"That's what they all say," she replied.

He turned and raced up the stairs, finally arriving at the upper landing. A solid-steel door blocked him. It was bolted shut.

Kurt checked his ammo. Seven shells left. He hoped it would be enough.

Stepping back, he opened fire on the lock. The iron projectiles tore it apart like armor-piercing rounds. The door burst open under the onslaught and Kurt rushed in.

He saw two guards, took one of them out, and then dove for cover as the other one started firing.

Scrambling across the floor as the man unleashed a hail of shells, Kurt rolled and fired back. The lethal shot blasted through one of Sebastian's computers and killed the last of Sebastian's bodyguards instantly.

Kurt stood and looked for Sienna. He spotted her at the back of the room. Sebastian had her up against his body and was holding a nickel-plated automatic to her temple.

CHAPTER 55

From where he stood, Joe had the advantage of elevation and could both see and hear the battle raging on the compound's bottom two terraces. Over the headset he heard Lt. Brooks directing his men, probing for a weakness and being pushed back. Across the dark lawns he could see the burning helicopter and red streams of tracer fire converging on the area around it from three directions.

He pressed the talk switch on his headset. "Dragon leader, this is Zavala," he said. "You're being surrounded. Suggest you abandon position and move down the hill."

PRESSED UP AGAINST the rock wall for cover, Lt. Brooks heard the call and sat dumbfounded for a second. None of his men were named Zavala. Then it dawned on him. One of the oceanographers went by that name.

"Zavala, we cannot pull back, we have five men wounded, two critical. There's no cover lower down. If we don't hold this wall, we're dead."

A burst of static gave way to the smooth-sounding voice of the oceanographer. *I'll swing around and try to relieve the pressure on your right flank.*

That would certainly help. But there were too many of Brèvard's men there for one man to take on even if he took them by surprise.

"Negative," Brooks said. "You'd be facing twenty hostiles. If you really want to help, take out those fifty-caliber guns and that missile site. Our only chance is to get the rest of the men on the ground, but they can't get within a mile of us as long as those things are active."

A delay that seemed like forever made Brooks fear Zavala had been taken out, but then his voice came through loud and clear. *I'll see what I can do.*

Brooks fired over the top of the wall and ducked as some incoming shells blasted chunks out of the top of it.

Lance Corporal William Dalton scrambled over and reinforced the position. "What's the word, Lieutenant?"

"Help might be on the way," Brooks replied, "though we're never going to live it down if we get saved by a marine biologist."

"At least the word *marine* is in the title," Dalton replied.

"Good point," Brooks said, snapping off a shot and ducking once again. "Good point."

*   *   *

MOVING IN A CROUCH, Joe made his way toward what he assumed was the missile site. But he came across the twin .50 caliber machine guns first.

He saw them track left to right, as if looking for the helicopters in the distance. Putting the railgun to his shoulder, he blasted apart the pivoting tripod mechanism they were mounted on. Hydraulic fluid spewed everywhere and the guns froze in place.

"One fifty-caliber weapon down," he said.

"Good," Lt. Brooks replied. *"See if you can get that missile launcher."*

"I can't see it," Joe said.

"Higher up," Brooks said. *"My guess would be the center of that hedge maze."*

Joe looked around. He could see the wall of hedges, but he had no way to reach the entrance. And considering the complexity of the maze, he doubted he could make it quickly to the center.

The rattling sound of the second .50 caliber weapon got Joe's attention and he had another idea.

Zeroing in on the sound, he cut through an ornamental garden filled with strange flowering bushes. On the far side he saw the second machine-gun emplacement. He raced toward it, but instead of tracking one of the helicopters in the distant sky, the guns whirled around toward him and the barrels began to depress.

Joe figured he'd run out of coolant and was now giving off a heat signature, but he was committed and continued his charge.

With Joe clinging to the base of the tripod, the clamoring stopped but the guns continued swinging from side to side, hopelessly trying to find a position from which to fire at him. It was no use, Joe was in too close and safely beneath their maximum angle of depression.

With a nod to whoever designed the system, Joe considered his options. Instead of destroying the mechanism that aimed and fired the guns, he began taking it apart.

Both machine guns began hammering away, tearing up the ground behind Joe, but he was beneath their maximum angle of depression. He crawled forward and made it to the tripod. Instead of destroying the mechanism that spun and aimed the weapons, he eased up next to it and began ripping out wires.

Eventually, the weapons stopped rotating.

Putting the railgun down, Joe pulled out his knife and began stripping the wires. Soon enough, he had a half dozen wires stripped to the copper.

"Zavala?" the radio cackled.

"I'm working on it," Joe said.

"Whatever you're going to do, you'd better make it quick."

Trying out different combinations of wires by pressing them together, Joe got the platform to turn in a herky-jerky motion until it was pointed back up at the center of the hedge maze.

Next he managed to elevate the guns. Now he just needed them to fire. He looked toward the trigger assembly. The weapons themselves were standard M2 .50

caliber machine guns. Nothing exotic, but the triggers were covered by a metal housing.

Using the back of the railgun as a club, Joe broke the housing free and got access to the triggers. A simple hydraulic clamp had been set up to pull the triggers remotely. Joe didn't have time to fiddle with that, so he put his hands around the trigger mechanism and squeezed.

Both weapons began to spit lead. Every fourth shell was a tracer and from those Joe could see his aim was a little high. He forced the barrels down a fraction and began to fire again. This time the shells found the mark, tearing into the missile battery and shredding it. One missile exploded, another launched and flew outward before quickly nosing over and thudding into the pastureland beyond the walls.

Joe was still firing when he heard Brooks calling the other helicopters. *"This is Dragon leader, the LZ is clear. Repeat, the LZ is clear."*

"Dragon Three inbound," came the first call.

"Dragon Four inbound."

With help on the way, Joe dropped back to the ground, picked up the railgun, and waited for the Marines to arrive.

CHAPTER 56

In the control room on the top floor of the main house a standoff ensued. Kurt had raised the deadly railgun and zeroed in on Sebastian Brèvard's head, but Sebastian had pulled himself behind Sienna and cocked the hammer on the shiny automatic that was pressed against her temple.

Considering the accuracy of his weapon, Kurt was certain he could kill Sebastian with a single shot, but the nerves of the body have strange ways of reacting to the death of the mind. If Kurt shot him, Sebastian might go limp instantaneously, or his hand might just as easily twitch, pulling the hair trigger of the pistol and killing Sienna.

The fact that Kurt had only one shell left in the railgun was also a concern.

"Kurt," Sienna cried, "I'm so sorry. This is all my fault."

He looked Sienna in the eye, willing her to be calm. "It's going to be all right," he promised. "He's going to let you go."

"Am I?" Sebastian said. "So that you can kill me? I don't think so."

"I'm not interested in killing you," Kurt insisted. "There are plenty of others lined up for that task. If Acosta doesn't get you, the North Koreans will—or even Than Rang, if he ever gets out of prison. Dead or alive, you're irrelevant to me at this point. Your plans are ruined. Whatever scheme you've been hatching here is going up in flames as we speak."

"Is that so?" Sebastian replied, his eyebrows arched in an exaggerated look of surprise. "Because—aside from your early arrival—things are going exactly as I've intended."

Kurt stared, not interested in a banal conversation with the man, but he was willing to have one if it led Sebastian to make a mistake.

"You expect me to believe this is all part of some master plan?"

"Come, now," Sebastian continued. "Surely you've realized that we could have killed you on Westgate's yacht. The discovery of the bodies on the wreck should have told you that. Have you even asked yourself why you were spared?"

Kurt had been considering that question for a while. "You were trying to keep the kidnapping a secret," he said. "You wanted me to tell the world that Sienna drowned. That way, there would be no investigation."

"Then why did we send you pictures of Sienna in Iran?" Sebastian asked. "Why lead you to the realization that she was alive after all?"

Kurt couldn't guess. In fact, he didn't believe a word of it. But he was running out of time. The battle outside appeared to be going badly, and the sound of gunfire on the landing told him Calista was trying to hold the line.

"Cat got your tongue?" Sebastian asked. "Then I'll tell you. We needed you to get the ball rolling. To begin the process of reevaluation among your smug leaders. To plant a seed of doubt."

"It doesn't matter what you had in mind," Kurt said, "it's over. You may have been ahead of us at the start, but we've been onto you since Korea. Our people are shutting down the vulnerable networks at this very moment. When the world opens up for business in the morning, Phalanx will be gone. It's being ripped out of every system it was ever installed on."

A broad smile crept over Sebastian's face. There was no falsity to it. Nor did he appear to be smiling in the face of defeat. Indeed, it looked to Kurt as if he'd just delivered Sebastian some glorious news.

"Of course they are," Sebastian said. "Which is exactly what I've been waiting for."

"You're lying," Kurt said.

"Am I?" Sebastian replied. "Ask your lovely friend here if Phalanx has been compromised."

Kurt refused to play along, so Sebastian turned his attention to Sienna.

"Tell him!"

"He's telling the truth," she said. "It's still secure. Because of the way its artificial intelligence protocols work, Phalanx can't be hacked. Not even by me."

Kurt narrowed his gaze. Tears were streaming down Sienna's face. "Then why go through all this?"

Sebastian answered. "Because I've spent three years perfecting the greatest criminal act of all time," he boasted, "and the sudden appearance of Phalanx nearly ruined it for me. Now, thanks to you, the Westgates, and an abundance of caution, your leaders are removing it for me."

Kurt saw it now. "And replacing it with the old systems," he said. "Systems you already know how to hack."

Sebastian looked like a man who thought himself a genius or even a god. His machines and his men were winning the battle outside, and the best minds in the security business had delivered to him the one thing he couldn't get for himself. They'd taken down the impenetrable wall of Phalanx and replaced it with what must have been a veritable tunnel that led right to whatever he was after.

"You're going to rob the world's banks," Kurt said, remembering what Montresor had worked on.

"Nothing so crass as theft," Sebastian replied. "I'm an artist. My crime will have much more style."

"What crime?" Kurt demanded. "What are you after?"

"It's the Fed," Sienna cried out. "He's planted viruses in the Federal Reserve banks."

"Shut up," Sebastian shouted as he tried to keep her from talking by compressing her windpipe with his forearm.

The act caused Kurt to move and almost fire, but Sebastian moved as well, effectively keeping her between them.

"The Fed?" Kurt repeated. "You can't rob the Fed. That's even more foolish than robbing a regular bank."

"If I was going to burglarize it," Sebastian replied, his words laced with pride and venom.

Kurt decided to prod him. Maybe, just maybe, Sebastian's ego was like those of many criminals, secretly eager for the world to know how brilliant they were. Certainly, he wouldn't be the first to boast about and claim his crime.

"If you're not going to rob the Fed, then what are you after? I assume you're not going to make a deposit."

"Actually," Sebastian said, "in a way I am."

Kurt held silent.

"Do you have any idea how the Fed creates money?" Sebastian asked.

"Printing press," Kurt said, thinking of the Brèvard's family history.

"To a minor extent," Sebastian acknowledged. "But they have more efficient ways, the most useful of which is the redemption of bonds. When they decide that investors or bondholders deserve to be repaid, they simply go to a computer, type in some numbers, and dollars magically appear in the bondholders' accounts as their notes are canceled."

Sebastian grinned. "I'm not going to rob the Fed," he insisted. "I'm going to use their own programs to create a series of bonds out of thin air and simultaneously create dollars to satisfy the redemption of those bonds. There will be no money missing. No losses to explain or trace. The balance sheet of the Fed will stand exactly as it does now. One side equaling the other. Liabilities equaling reserves. We're not stealing money. We're creating it."

"Of course," Kurt said. It made sense. "You're a counterfeiter. Like your ancestors. Just slightly more modern."

"So you know about them?"

"The Klaar River Gang," Kurt said.

Sebastian reacted to the name but not with shame. He seemed almost proud to admit it. "My great-grandfather was a brilliant man," he said. "The notes he created were perfect. They couldn't be differentiated from the real thing. Not until time affected the dyes. So he had to disappear. And he did. Even with the world looking for him, he disappeared without a trace."

"By murdering over two hundred people on the *Waratah*?" Kurt replied. "You're not artists. You're thugs and killers."

"I see you've put the puzzle together," Sebastian acknowledged as if he were complimenting Kurt. "All the more reason for me to leave."

"You can't honestly think you're going to pull this off," Kurt said. "There are checks and balances in the system, auditors and watchdogs."

Sebastian dragged Sienna up a step. "Are you that naïve? There are literally billions of transactions every day. Trillions of dollars change hands in a month's time. Do you think it's all tallied up by hordes of accountants with green visors above their eyes, toiling away in the government's back office somewhere? Computer programs do those checks and audits you spoke of. And guess who controls those programs now? I do. The data they spit out will satisfy the few humans that even bother to look past the top and bottom lines, I can assure you of that."

Sebastian dragged Sienna up another step.

"You can't know that for certain," Kurt said.

"I'm fairly confident at this point," Sebastian said. "And should your government eventually catch on, they will find that hundreds of billions of dollars have been created and disbursed to thousands of companies and straw men of my creation. They'll discover half the trail evaporates and the other half leads to political election funds in America and other spots around the world. They'll find billions have been routed through China, Iran, North Korea. And they'll be faced with a terrible dilemma: admit the truth and shake the world's confidence in the mighty dollar, in all likelihood crashing the international financial system, or let it go, fix the hole in the wall quietly, and chalk it up to experience."

Kurt had to admit that Sebastian was probably right. "They might not announce it to the world, but they *will* hunt you down."

"They will think I'm dead," Sebastian said, dragging Sienna up the final step and pulling her toward an alcove in the far reaches of the room.

Kurt could see another steel security door hinged to the alcove wall. He could not allow Sebastian to drag

Sienna through it. His posture stiffened. "Take another step and I'll kill you," he said, "regardless of what else happens."

Sebastian studied Kurt from behind Sienna. By now he'd tucked in so close that only his right eye could see past her to Kurt and his menacing glare. And yet even with that limited view, he had no doubt that Austin would fire. He'd lost this woman too many times already. He seemed unwilling to lose her again.

It left Sebastian only one choice. With Sienna held tight against him, he reached across her body and pulled a tiny remote unit from his pocket.

To Kurt it looked a lot like the one Calista had used in the tunnel beneath the DMZ. "If you're planning on zapping me, you're a little late, I've been deloused."

"It's not for you," Sebastian said. "It's for her."

With that, Sebastian whispered to Sienna, "I'll make you a deal. The same deal I've been making you all along. Your life or the lives of your children. Which will it be?"

He pressed a key on the glasslike screen of the remote and a fireball erupted in the center of the courtyard. It was so immense it shattered the windows behind Kurt and blasted splinters of glass across the room.

Kurt stood his ground as the shards pelted him.

"That was the armory," Sebastian gloated to Sienna. "If you resist any further, or if he tries to stop me, I will obliterate the prisoners in their quarters and your children will burn."

A blind play if ever there was one, Kurt thought. Neither one of them knew if the prisoners were in the hut. It was entirely possible that they were staying put and taking cover there, as the battle raged outside. It was also possible that Joe had led them away.

"Let me go," Sienna cried to Kurt, her eyes filled with tears.

"He'll kill you," Kurt replied. "He'll kill them either way."

"Please!" she begged.

At that moment a figure crawled through the main door, a pitiful figure, slithering on the ground. "Brother," it cried out. "Dear brother."

Calista's appearance was just enough of a surprise to distract Sebastian. He began to glance her way before catching himself. The pistol in his hand came away from Sienna's head for an instant and, in that blink of an eye, Kurt squeezed the trigger and fired.

The iron projectile from the railgun hit the nickel-plated handgun at a speed of two thousand feet per second, impacting it just ahead of the breach.

The blow shattered the pistol as its hammer fell and struck the bullet in the chamber. The gunpowder in the 9mm cartridge ignited and the lead shell began its journey forward. But the frame of the pistol had been mangled by Kurt's shot and instead of being exhausted out through the mouth of the barrel, the bullet blew the weapon apart.

At the moment of the explosion it was already out of Sebastian's hand, having been torn free and hurled halfway to the rear of the alcove. The impact broke Sebastian's wrist, and shrapnel from the exploding gun flew in all directions, cutting his face and neck like claws of some enraged animal.

In a blind fury, Sebastian flung Sienna toward Kurt, grabbed the door, and tried to swing it shut.

Kurt was already tossing the railgun aside and reaching into the open pocket of his armored vest for the Colt. He pushed Sienna out of the way and drew the revolver like a gunfighter in the Old West, extending it toward Sebastian, cocking the hammer, and pulling the trigger in one swift motion.

The booming report of the old .45 caliber shell echoed across the room as fire erupted from the barrel and a cloud of smoke burst from either side of the cylinder.

The heavy shell grazed the slamming steel door and caught Sebastian just to the right of his center of mass. He was thrown backward as if he'd been kicked by a horse. He slammed against the back of the alcove and fell on his side as the door banged shut, cutting him off from Kurt's view.

Kurt rushed forward and tried the handle. The door had latched but wasn't locked. He swung it open, ready to fire again, but realized instantly that he didn't need to. Sebastian lay dead against the wall.

The remote dropped from Sebastian's grasp and Kurt relaxed for an instant only to see on the small screen what looked like a second hand sweeping in a red arc toward the twelve o'clock position.

"Run," Kurt shouted, dashing to Sienna's side and pulling her up to her feet.

The explosions began in the distance. First, the prisoners' quarters, then the barracks, and then the two helicopters in the hangar.

Kurt had helped Sienna up and now did the same for Calista.

He turned for the door, but it was too late. A series of explosions shook the main house, blasting one section after another and heading toward them like a rumbling freight train.

Realizing there was no other way out, Kurt shoved Sienna toward the shattered windows and the veranda beyond.

"Jump!" he shouted.

Sienna leapt without question and Kurt propelled himself and Calista over the ledge half a second later. As he fell through the air, he felt the explosions closing in. Sections of the mansion to their right and left were blown apart simultaneously. The control room followed an instant later, erupting in a fiery detonation just as Kurt, Sienna, and Calista crashed into the deep end of Sebastian's Olympic-sized swimming pool.

Kurt felt his legs crunch into the bottom of the twelve-foot-deep pool and looked up. Seen through the kaleidoscopic lens of the swirling water, the distorted tongues of flame were almost beautiful.

A hailstorm of debris followed, including splatterings of napalm that burned on the surface of the water, and chunks of the stone from the house that crashed down around them like meteors.

Kurt grabbed Sienna to prevent her from surfacing as a second wave of fire streaked above them and retreated.

He could have remained down there for another minute or so, but Calista was struggling to pull free. He doubted she'd been ready for the dive. He gripped her tight and pushed off the bottom, angling away from the house and breaking the surface as the last smattering of fragments dropped from the heavens.

Treading water and helping Calista keep her head above the surface, Kurt turned in a slow circle and saw that half the world was on fire. The top floors of the mansion had been blown off, while the lower floors were consumed in flames. Waves of heat assaulted him, tempered only by the coolness of the water.

"That way," Kurt said, pointing toward the far end of the pool.

Sienna began to swim, and Kurt rolled over onto his back, dragging Calista in a rescue swimmer's stroke. When it became shallow enough to put his feet down, he did, and from there they waded to the wall.

As they climbed out, Kurt heard the sound of people approaching. He cocked the old pistol and readied himself for one more fight, but a friendly shout stopped him from firing.

"Easy there, cowboy," Joe Zavala said as he emerged from the dark.

As Kurt lowered the pistol, several Marines came into view, moving in behind Joe.

"Kurt, this is Lieutenant Brooks," Joe said. "Lieutenant Brooks, I present Kurt Austin."

Brooks flashed a grin at Kurt and then seemed to recognize Calista. He raised his weapon.

"It's okay," Kurt said, holding out a hand.

"But she's one of them," Brooks insisted.

"No," Kurt said. "As it turns out, she's not one of them after all."

Brooks made a quick decision. He lowered his weapon and clicked his radio. "Get the SARC up here," he said, referring to the Navy medic, two of whom had landed in Dragon Five. "We've got another wounded player."

Even before the medic arrived, Brooks dropped down beside Calista and began working on her wounds.

"What about my children?" Sienna asked. "And the others?"

"Safe and sound," Joe said. "I sent them for ice cream as soon as the battle got under way."

Brooks chimed in. "They made it over the wall and met up with a couple of the guys from Dragon Three."

"Where are they now?"

"Dragon Four swooped in and picked them up," Brooks said. "They're already on their way back to the *Bataan*."

Hearing that, Sienna's whole posture softened in a wave of relief. Her chest heaved, and she began to cry again. But this time they were tears of joy.

Kurt smiled. "So I'm guessing we won?"

"We did," Joe said. "While you were taking a midnight

dip with two beautiful women, the rest of us were working hard to turn the tide of battle."

"Glad to hear it," Kurt said. "And how are the 'rest of us' going to get out of here? We seem to be a little short on helicopters."

"Dragon Three will max out and take the wounded," Brooks said. "The rest of us will head for the coast. Madagascar has a pretty limited military—and we seem to be miles from anywhere important—but I don't want to run into any well-meaning members of the neighborhood watch."

Kurt nodded. "Are we walking?"

"No," Brooks said. "My men have rescued a bunch of horses from the stables on the lower terrace. We'll be riding."

At that, Calista looked up. "I'll ride," she said.

Brooks shook his head. "You're in no shape to ride, ma'am. You'll go on the helicopter."

She stiffened her back and pulled free from his grasp. "I said I'll ride. Besides, you'll need someone to show you the way."

"I think we can find the ocean on our own," Brooks insisted.

"Trust me," Kurt said, "there's no point arguing with her."

Brooks shrugged. "Suit yourself."

A few minutes later, the group arrived at the stables. The last of the Black Hawks sat in the pasture close by.

Sienna hugged Kurt tightly. "I owe you everything,"

she whispered in his ear. "My life, my family. How can I ever repay you?"

"Just go live," Kurt said. "And tell your husband I'm sorry for slugging him in the jaw."

She gazed at him with a look of confusion.

"Long story," he said. "Knowing what he's been through, I'm hoping he won't even remember it."

She nodded, began to cry again, and smiled through the tears. She hugged him tightly once more and then went aboard the helicopter.

As the helicopter powered up and lifted off, Kurt found his way into the stables. Calista was already on her horse, and the others were mounting up.

Kurt climbed on a sturdy-looking animal and took the reins.

"Look at me," Joe said, "I really *am* the cavalry. Now I'm even riding a horse."

Only Kurt laughed. No one else got the joke.

They rode from the stables single file, traveled down the main path and out onto the open plain with the Brèvard palace and Sebastian's mad dreams burning to ashes on the hill behind them.

Kurt noticed that Calista never looked back. Instead, she led them to a path she'd worn into the soil over the years.

Only now did she realize why she'd always returned to that strange hill where the ship had been buried. Only now did she remember her real brothers talking about a lifeboat. And then Sebastian as a young man with Egan and Laurent, working down there to cover what her mother and brothers had excavated.

Two hours later, they came out onto the shore, where a wide beach met slow-rolling surf. There, Lt. Brooks ordered the group to a halt, made a radio call, and lit a low-light beacon.

After a short wait, a pair of high-speed collapsible boats came racing in from the dark, manned by crews of two in camouflage and face paint. They entered the shallows and coasted to a stop just the other side of the low breakers.

"Someone call for a water taxi?" one of the camouflaged men asked.

With the Marines watching the shore in both directions, Kurt helped Calista down from her horse. She was pale and cold. She rubbed the blaze on the horse's nose and whispered something about running free. The horse took off, galloping down the shore, and Calista all but collapsed. Kurt picked her up, cradling her in his arms and carrying her into the surf as she wrapped her hands around his neck and held on.

"I should have left from here twenty-seven years ago," she whispered.

"Better late than never," Kurt said.

He carried her to the nearest boat and lowered her gently into it. He climbed in after her, and Joe followed suit, as the Marines took spots in the second boat. Moments later, they were cutting through the surf and racing out to sea.

Only Calista was surprised when a great black shape

rose up through the water and allowed the boats to slide up onto its back.

A group of sailors helped them out of the boats and directed them to a deck hatch. Calista was taken to the infirmary while the ship's commander shook hands with Kurt and Joe.

"Welcome aboard the USS *Ohio*," he said. "I hear you guys work for Dirk Pitt at Jim Sandecker's old outfit, NUMA."

They nodded in unison.

"Both men asked me to give you their regards," the commander said. "Plan on briefing them tomorrow morning. Which is in an hour and forty minutes, by the way."

"Just our luck," Kurt said.

"At least you spent three days snoozing in Korea," Joe said. "Imagine how I feel."

Kurt laughed. "I'll do the briefing," he said, "but I need to get a secure message through before we submerge. Would that be possible?"

"Sure," the commander replied. "What do you want it to say?"

"It's complicated," Kurt began. "Basically, I need someone to declare a bank holiday tomorrow. And maybe for the rest of the week. Just in case."

CHAPTER 57

In the last hours of that night the SS *Waratah* finally returned home. Some had wanted to delay her arrival until morning, but Paul would have none of it. He thought the venerable old ship had been away long enough.

Nudged forward by the *Sedgewick*, she came into the harbor virtually alone. But as she approached the dock, Paul noticed a sight he would remember for the rest of his life. It seemed as if half of Durban had come out, and thousands stood quietly in the dark with candles in their hands. They lined both sides of the inlet and the dock.

He saw no camera flashes, and there were no dignitaries waiting to give speeches. All that would come later. For tonight, the people of South Africa were welcoming this ship home.

The *Waratah* bumped the dock and was tied up. A

high-ranking officer of the South African Navy came aboard and Paul relinquished command of the ship. From that moment on, he thought only of finding Gamay and wrapping his arms around her.

True to her word, she was waiting for him at the bottom of the gangway. They embraced and began walking the dock. Paul had never in his life seen so many cards, flowers, and wreaths.

He stopped beside a picture that looked familiar to him. In the black-and-white portrait he saw a burly man with a handlebar mustache. His name was written below, as was his position, fireman, on board the *Waratah*, assigned to the aft boiler.

Paul still didn't believe in ghosts, but he wondered if they might exist after all.

Hand in hand, he and Gamay walked the rest of the dock without saying a single word.

CHAPTER 58

The details of Kurt's message explained what he knew about Brèvard's scheme. And when the President and the chairman of the Fed were informed, a three-day moratorium on all Fed activity was declared.

Meanwhile, Montresor, Sienna Westgate, and the other hackers willingly explained what they'd done, and been forced to do, revealing the viruses, blinds, and trapdoors they'd planted one by one until all the various dangers were uncovered and neutralized.

After twelve hours on board the *Ohio*, Kurt, Joe, and Calista were transferred to a ship bound for Durban. At the same time, Lt. Brooks and the other Marines were picked up and flown back to the *Bataan* after promising never to make fun of oceanographers again.

Upon their approach into the Durban harbor, Kurt and Joe marveled at the sight of the *Waratah*, back home after all these years. Untold thousands of bouquets lined the dock in front of her, and a proper cleaning and restoration was already under way. Plans were being made to turn part of the ship into a museum and the rest into a floating memorial to the two hundred eleven passengers and crew who vanished over a century ago.

A journal discovered in the sick bay gave some closure to the mystery. Though, sadly, the descendants had to live with the knowledge that those who weren't killed in the original hijacking were abandoned in lifeboats to perish at sea in the subsequent storm. A memorial service with full honors was being planned.

As they bumped the dock, Kurt looked around for friendly faces. "I thought Paul and Gamay were going to be here," he mentioned to Joe.

"I got a message from them," Joe said. "They're on a double date with Duke and Elena. Something about going to a shooting gallery to prove, once and for all, who saved the *Waratah*."

Kurt shrugged. The message made no sense to him.

Though Paul and Gamay weren't there to greet them, someone else was. An attractive woman in a white dress that contrasted nicely with her cinnamon-colored tan. She stood on the pier below, waving and shouting up to Joe.

"Didn't know you had friends in these parts," Kurt said, though Joe seemed to have a friend in every port.

"She's the reporter who did the story on how I rescued you from the maw of the angry sea," Joe explained. "We hit it off while you were recuperating."

"Well, if anyone's earned some R & R around here, it's you. See you back in D.C."

Joe nodded, sauntered down the gangway, and left with the young woman.

As others made their way off the ship, Kurt turned to Calista. She'd begun to recover from her injuries but looked more drawn than ever.

"What's going to happen to me?" she asked. "Am I going to prison?"

Kurt took a deep breath. "A lot of people have questions for you," he admitted. "The FBI, Interpol, Scotland Yard. But there are significant extenuating circumstances in your case. Beyond that, you helped us when it counted, and you've already provided useful information about the other conspirators."

She perked up a little bit and looked down at her legs. A cast covered the lower half of her left leg while a tracking bracelet on her right ankle reminded her that she wasn't free. The South African police and the British consulate intended to keep track of her until they decided her fate. She'd been told someone would be with her at all times and, indeed, a member of the Durban police force was waiting at the bottom of the gangway.

It certainly didn't look like she was going to have a lot of freedom anytime soon. She turned back to Kurt. "Will you come visit me in the klink? I'm sure I'll be in solitary most of the time."

He laughed. "Absolutely," he promised. "I'll bring you a cake with a file in it."

She raised an eyebrow.

"It's the least I could do," he added. "As far as I'm concerned, you're part of the pack now."

She looked at him strangely. "'Part of the pack'?"

He didn't bother trying to explain. "When you get some downtime, read Kipling's *The Jungle Book*. It'll make more sense after that."

She nodded and turned back to the pier, watching as a group of people filed out through the doors of the passenger embarkation building and stood together, waiting. The group seemed to be three generations. A couple with gray hair, three people in their thirties or forties, and several children.

"I don't know if I can do this," she said.

"These people are your family," Kurt said, "your *real* family. They've flown all the way from England to meet you."

"What are they going to think of me?" she asked. "What am I going to tell them? I've done terrible things."

"They're going to see you as the prodigal daughter," Kurt said. "They're going to find in you the reward for the hope they kept alive all these years. They're going to tell you stories about your mother and father. To be honest, if it's anything like my family reunions, you'll be lucky to get a word in edgewise."

She appreciated what he was saying, but the fear was overwhelming. "I can't," she said, shaking her head.

"Calista can't," Kurt replied, "but Olivia can. Remember how you set your horse free? Set Calista free too. It's time to let her go."

She took a deep breath, obviously trying to steel herself

against the waves of emotion. She turned toward him and changed the subject. "You really should have kissed me," she said. "Back on Acosta's yacht. It would have saved us a whole lot of trouble."

Kurt laughed deeply and a smile came to his face, giving him dimples and wrinkling the sun-kissed skin around his eyes. "I highly doubt a kiss from me is going to change anyone's life."

"Would have been nice to find out," she said.

He continued to smile and then slowly leaned toward her. Sliding his hand across her cheek and cupping her face, he pulled her gently toward him and their lips met softly in a lingering kiss.

When they parted, she was smiling broadly. "I don't know," she said. "That was pretty good."

Kurt laughed again. "Go see your family," he said. "They've been waiting for thirty years."

She nodded, looked at him one last time, and then was helped down the gangway by a ship's officer. The constable from the Durban police force met them and led her toward the family she'd never known.

TWENTY-SIX HOURS LATER, Kurt was passing through customs in the main terminal at Washington's Dulles International Airport. He'd lost all track of time, but it was dark outside. And considering how deserted the terminal was, it had to be late at night or very early in the morning. In fact, the only people he saw were members of the cleaning crew.

Kurt moved slowly toward baggage claim, pausing when he saw a gathering of airport police near one of the security doors. Outside on the tarmac, several vehicles with flashing red and blue lights were parked in a circle around a private jet that sat with its door open and its stairs down.

Curiosity gave way to surprise when he recognized David Forrester being escorted into the terminal by two agents in windbreakers with FBI written on the backs.

"Well, I'll be damned," Kurt said.

At the sound of Kurt's voice the agents and the prisoner looked up.

"Excuse me, sir, you'll have to step back," said one of the agents.

"It's all right," another voice interjected.

Kurt didn't recognize the speaker, but the man obviously knew him. He introduced himself. "Trent MacDonald out of Langley."

Kurt recognized the name, recalling that MacDonald was the first person at the CIA to share any information regarding Sienna's possible survival.

They shook hands. "Thanks for your help," Kurt said. "Caught yourself quite a fish, by the look of things."

"Not as big as the one you bagged," MacDonald admitted, "but we're happy. We passed the information your friend gave us to the FBI. Fortunately, they were able to grab Forrester before he took off for a country with no extradition treaty."

One more point in Calista's favor, Kurt thought. "So what part did he play in all of this?"

"Forrester was Brèvard's inside man," MacDonald explained. "All the financial maneuvering ran through him. He used his contacts to plant the computer viruses at the Federal Reserve, compromising the main system and the accounting protocols. He also set up a network of shell corporations that would have made it virtually impossible to track the money once it was moved."

Kurt wasn't surprised.

"And if that's not enough, he's been controlling Westgate," MacDonald added, "with an implant in Westgate's brain, making sure he didn't remember too much too soon."

That put a new light on the confrontation at the Smithsonian. "I knew this guy was a snake from the moment I met him," Kurt said.

"First impressions," MacDonald said.

Kurt nodded and looked past Forrester out the window, where he could see FBI agents clearing the plane, looking for evidence. As they worked, the first sign of daylight appeared, and the high clouds were brushed with the slightest hint of pink. Apparently, it was morning after all.

Kurt looked back at Forrester, who glared back at him without a trace of remorse. "Might want to enjoy the sunrise," Kurt said coldly. "You're not going to see many more where you're going."

A twitch ran across Forrester's cheek, but that was his only response. It was enough.

Kurt turned back to Trent MacDonald, shook hands once again, and then continued on his way.

He left the terminal and stood at the curb, wondering just how long he'd have to wait for the shuttle to long-term parking. Before he could hazard a guess, he spotted a familiar-looking black Jeep coming his way. His Jeep. It pulled up and stopped right in front of him.

As the driver's door opened, Anna Ericsson's pretty face, flaxen blond hair, and beaming smile popped up over the roof.

"Did you take up auto theft while I was gone?" Kurt asked.

She laughed. "With all your memory problems, I thought you might have a hard time finding your car in the parking lot when you got back."

Kurt pretended to be hurt, but he honestly couldn't remember driving to the airport two weeks earlier. "You might be onto something," he said, and then added, "Sorry for how I behaved. I wasn't exactly myself."

"I realize that," she said. "I crossed a line too. Any interest in starting over?"

"Nothing would make me happier," he said.

She jumped down, came around the Jeep, and offered her hand. "Hi," she said as if meeting him for the first time. "I'm Anna Ericsson. I'm a psychiatrist. And I'm not allowed to date my patients."

He shook her hand. "Kurt Austin. Fortunately, I no longer need a shrink." He opened the passenger door for her and asked, "Mind if I drive?"

She settled into the passenger's seat as Kurt made his way to the driver's side and got behind the wheel.

"Where to?" he asked.

"Somewhere we can look out at the river," she said coyly.

He shut the door, put the Jeep in gear, and pulled away from the curb, smiling. "I know just the place," he said. "And the best part is, we'll be the only guests."

New York Times Bestselling Author

CLIVE CUSSLER

The Dirk Pitt® Novels

clive-cussler-books.com
penguin.com

Penguin
Random
House
BERKLEY

M40AS0914